Angelique had no idea how desperately Devon wanted to take her into his arms. His whole body responded to the desire and his hand gently touched the side of her face.

"You're so very beautiful, Angelique," he whispered. She did not move, but stood with her lips slightly parted and her eyes locked with his. The warmth of his gaze left her speechless and her cheeks blushed in response. Slowly, his hand slipped to the nape of her neck and caressed her softly. Still, she could not break away from his eyes. She heard him whisper, "Angel," as he bent and touched her lips with his.

Suddenly, Angelique pulled away and the shock of it flowed through his body. He dropped his hand quickly as though he had been burnt.

"Angelique, I'm . . . sorry. I didn't mean to do that. It's just that you are so beautiful."

Angelique blinked as if she were coming out of a fog. Her body felt limp and weak because she hadn't wanted him to stop. She wanted again the strong feel of his arms and the hard pressure of his mouth against hers—but instead, all she could do was to run away . . .

FICTION FOR TODAY'S WOMAN

EMBRACES   (666, $2.50)
by Sharon Wagner
Dr. Shelby Cole was an expert in the field of medicine and a novice
at love. She wasn't willing to give up her career to get married—
until she grew to want and need the child she was carrying.

MIRRORS   (690, $2.75)
by Barbara Krasnoff
The compelling story of a woman seeking changes in life and love,
and of her desperate struggle to give those changes impact—in the
midst of tragedy.

THE LAST CARESS   (722, $2.50)
by Dianna Booher
Since the tragic news that her teenaged daughter might die, Erin's
husband had become distant, isolated. Was this simply his way of
handling his grief, or was there more to it? If she was losing her
child, would she lose her husband as well?

VISIONS   (695, $2.95)
by Martin A. Grove
Caught up in the prime time world of power and lust, Jason and
Gillian fought desperately for the top position at Parliament
Television. Jason fought to keep it—Gillian, to take it away!

LONGINGS   (706, $2.50)
by Sylvia W. Greene
Andrea was adored by her husband throughout their seven years of
childless marriage. Now that she was finally pregnant, a haze of
suspicion shrouded what should have been the happiest time of
their lives.

*Available wherever paperbacks are sold, or order direct from the
Publisher. Send cover price plus 50¢ per copy for mailing and
handling to Zebra Books, 21 East 40th Street, New York, N.Y.
10016. DO NOT SEND CASH!*

RAPTURE'S ANGEL

BY SYLVIE F. SOMMERFIELD

ZEBRA BOOKS

KENSINGTON PUBLISHING CORP.

DEDICATED TO

AUNT VIRGINIA AND UNCLE NORMAN PEARL—
FOR ALL THE GOOD YEARS

ZEBRA BOOKS

are published by

KENSINGTON PUBLISHING CORP.
21 East 40th Street
New York, N.Y. 10016

Chapter 1

The moon was golden orange and hung over the horizon like a Buddha. A few white clouds passed rapidly through the dark, misty gray sky. The breeze had dropped to a whisper, and the small ship that lay at anchor rolled with a small creaking sound. The only other sound was the soft lapping of the water against the hull as it moved with the gentle pitch of the ocean.

Few on the ship were asleep tonight. Some unseeable thing prickled the senses of the men and hung in the air. The sailor on watch hunched his shoulders uncomfortably and cursed mildly to himself, which drew a soft chuckle from the man who stood with him. The first man cast a quick look at his companion and muttered softly. "Can feel it in my bones. Nothin' good can come about on a night like this. We shouldn't be layin' at anchor here. We should get out of here and head for home, where we belong."

"Stow that talk," admonished his mate quietly. He had also been too unnerved to sleep, and had decided that a little friendly conversation might help ease his unrest. "If Mr. McMichaels or Cap hears you mumbling that kind of thing, you might find yourself with a lot of trouble on your hands."

The other man shrugged, and his eyebrows drew together in a deep frown. "Aye, Davy, but you got to admit somethin's wrong tonight. Can't you feel it in the air?" He hunched his shoulders again and glanced quickly behind him, almost as if he expected to see someone or something there.

"Aye, man," Davy whispered, "but what?"

"I'm thinkin' it's somethin' to do with the pair we took aboard at the last port. Her pregnant and so sick and scared lookin', and did you see him? So proud lookin' but somethin' about his eyes. Kinda like he was scared too. There's somethin' wrong with those two."

"Cap would never get us into anything outside the law man. He loves his ship too much, and he takes good care of us, to boot. It's maybe just the calm tonight. I ain' never seen the water so black and quiet."

"Maybe," his mate muttered. "But I still say somethin's happenin' we don't know anything about somethin' bad, and I think the trouble's lyin' below deck That lady ain't left the cabin since we took them aboard Only Cap goin' in and out. Quiet," he cautioned. "Here comes Mr. McMichaels. See what I mean? He's supposed to be asleep. I bet he feels it, too."

The two men watched the first mate of the ship walk toward them. McMichaels had been first mate for over five years. He was not a large man, but he gave the impression of strength. His dark eyes were calm and he moved slowly with the easy, rolling gait of the seaman. The men respected him and never hesitated in following his orders. His first love was his ship, and he was completely loyal to his captain.

"Evenin', Mr. Halt."

"Evenin', Sir."

"Everything well, Mr. Halt?"

"Aye, Sir."

"Why aren't you asleep, Mr. Morgan? Don't you have

next watch?"

"Aye, Sir, but . . ."

"But what, Mr. Morgan?"

"I just couldn't seem to get to sleep, Sir. I'll be ready to stand next watch when me time comes." He hesitated. "Sir, don't you feel somethin' . . . odd on board tonight? Kinda like there's somethin' strange that's not quite right?"

"Nonsense, Mr Morgan. Everything's quiet. Go get some rest, we'll be calling you for watch soon," assured the first mate.

"I think I'll just pace about a bit, Sir," he said stubbornly. "Just can't put my finger on what's wrong, but it's here, I can feel it."

"Mr. Morgan . . ."

"Aye, Sir." Davy moved slowly away, but he was still mumbling under his breath.

"And you, Mr. Halt?" McMichaels asked quietly.

"I don't know, Sir, but I feel it, too. It's kinda like . . . like . . ." He shrugged. "Sir? Who are those two people we took aboard at last port, and why all the secrecy? It kinda makes the men uncomfortable to have a woman aboard, anyway, but all this secrecy makes it worse."

"I don't know, Mr. Halt," he answered sternly. "I don't question Captain Cortland in his actions. I think it would be better for you and all the men to put those people out of your minds. They're the captain's business. Whatever the reason, you know Captain Cortland would not do anything to jeopardize either his men or his ship."

"Aye, Sir."

"Good night, Mr. Halt."

"Good night, Sir," Halt replied.

The first mate clasped his hands behind his back and walked slowly down the deck.

"All the same, Sir," Halt thought, watching him, "there's somethin' mighty queer happening aboard this ship tonight."

McMichaels walked slowly down the deck. He watched the gray-black clouds skitter in front of the moon, as if she too wanted to hide her face.

He also wondered who the two passengers were who had boarded the ship at the last port. They had come aboard at the last moment, mere seconds before they sailed. Quickly and, McMichaels thought, rather stealthily.

The man was a handsome Spanish fellow, about thirty. His brown eyes had glowed with compassion for the woman who accompanied him. She was obviously due to deliver her child at any time, but McMichaels, whose wife had given him four healthy sons, knew almost instantly that the woman was very ill.

They had been taken to the captain's cabin, and none of the crew had seen the woman again. He didn't know why, but he felt a deep pity for the woman. She was young, about twenty. Her silver colored hair had been coiled at her neck and her large, deep purple-blue eyes had been warm and friendly.

"Who are they?" he wondered, then he pushed the thoughts from his mind. He had too much respect and love for his captain to question his actions. Captain Cortland was a good man and a good captain; he felt sure that nothing would be done to affect either his men or his ship.

The ship's bell sent its soft melodic chime across the

dark water. It was very late, but time meant nothing to the pale-faced man who sat beside the still form on the ship's bunk. His face was drawn and exhausted. With eyes dulled by pain, he looked at the girl on the bunk. His eyes misted and his hands clenched together in front of him.

"Anna," he whispered. "I'm very sorry, Anna. I'm so sorry."

There was no sound from the still form. Anna was long past hearing his broken apology. The last few hours before her death, she had labored in silent agony to bear the small child who lay bundled on the cushions of the captain's chair.

"Miguel," she had whispered, as the life silently flowed from her body. "The baby . . . name her Angelique . . . take . . . take care of her."

"Anna," he sobbed, "don't leave me, *Querida*. I cannot go on without you."

She raised her hand to gently touch his tear-stained face. A soft smile touched the corners of her lips. "Miguel, we have loved. It is more than most people have. Now we must protect the fruit of our love. Please, Miguel. He must not find her."

"I will make sure she is safe, little one," he said as he took her hand in his and kissed the fingers gently.

She sighed. "I love you, Miguel, always remember, I love you." Slowly, her eyes closed and the hand in his became limp and cool.

"Anna," he whispered again, the tears falling unheeded down his face. "I should not let you go alone, my love. I cannot face this world without you. I shall see to Angelique's safety, then . . ."

He folded her hands gently across her breasts, then

rose. Straightening his shoulders, he wiped his tears away, then turned and left the room and made his way to the cabin where Captain Cortland waited word about Anna's condition.

He knocked on the captain's door. A deep, clear voice called for him to enter. He did, closing the door quietly behind him and leaning against it as though all the strength had suddenly drained from his body. The captain's back had been toward the door and when he heard no sound from behind him, he turned to face his visitor.

Captain Cortland was a man of about thirty-five years. His age had to be estimated by those who knew him, for he had the type of face that could have been twenty-five or fifty. His hair was thick and deep brown, matching the amber color of his eyes. Thick, heavy brows over fine intelligent eyes that crinkled perpetually from gazing into the sun. His skin was tan from long days at sea. He was tall, standing six feet, muscular, yet slender, for work was one thing he was used to.

"A quiet night, my friend," he said. "Come sit and share a glass with me." He motioned to a comfortable chair that sat opposite his desk.

Miguel made no attempt to move. "She is dead," he said quietly.

Sorrow filled the captain's eyes. "When?"

"Less than an hour ago."

"And the child?"

"Alive and well. Sleeping now."

"We must protect her, Don Miguel. If he gets his hands on her, he will have succeeded."

"He will never get her!" he cried vehemently. "Never!"

10

"Sit down, Don Miguel. We must discuss what we can do."

Don Miguel lowered himself into the chair as though the life had gone from his body also. Captain Cortland was a man who had seen a great deal of life and its pain; still, his heart was saddened by this young man's misery. He understood his deep grief. Don Miguel had loved his wife so deeply and planned their escape so well, that now he could not grasp the fact that he had lost her. The captain's voice was gentle, but firm. "Miguel, on the island of San Moro, high up in the hills, is the little village of Toloquay. It has a small convent. The order is the Sisters of Mercy . . ."

"A convent," Miguel repeated.

"What better place to hide her? I know the mother superior. She is a wonderful woman, compassionate and understanding. She would keep the secret well until the child is of age to claim her heritage."

Don Miguel's hands covered his face and his shoulders slumped forward. He stayed this way for some time until Captain Cortland again interrupted him.

"You know they will either catch up with us, or we will have to put into port for provisions. You must decide now, my friend. Either you hide her there or you take her with you."

Don Miguel raised his face from his hands, his eyes red-rimmed. "I promised Anna before she died that I would protect Angelique, and I shall do so. You know if I take her with me it is to condemn her to possible death. No, she must go to the convent. Can you get her there in secrecy?"

"Yes, Miguel. I promise you she will be kept safe, and when the time comes, and when she is of age, I shall tell her the story and you will again be reunited."

"If I live," Miguel said softly. He rose from the chair and held out his hand. "I have complete faith in you, my friend. I leave my daughter in your care. Put me ashore tonight, then leave as soon as possible. I . . . I will see to the burial of my wife. I will not contact you again until I know it is safe for you and my daughter. Vaya con dios, mi amigo."

"Take care of yourself, Miguel. See that he does not find you. One day this will be past and you and your child can be together."

Don Miguel left the captain's cabin and went back to his own. There, he gently wrapped the body of his beloved Anna in a blanket. One final time, he bent and kissed the now cold lips. Then, from about his neck he removed a thin gold chain from which hung a medal with a strange crest on the back. On the flat gold of the medal was a crescent moon, and in the arc of the moon were three stars made of diamonds. He pryed one of the diamonds loose and put it in his pocket. On the medal, he scratched, "A.M." Then, with gentle hands, he put the chain about his daughter's neck and tucked it inside the blanket, against her skin. He lifted her and held her against him.

"I love you, my child, and if the God is willing, we will meet again someday. I hope then you will be able to forgive me for leaving you. You are in the best of hands that I can place you. Go with God, my darling." He kissed her then placed her back in the bed and waited. Soon a knock came to the door. He opened it to Captain Cortland.

"The boat is ready, Miguel," he said softly.

Miguel nodded. "I am ready." He went back to the bed

and lifted the body of his wife in his arms and carried her out.

Devon Carlisle had been cabin boy aboard the *Wayfarer* for two years. He was ten, but very large for his age. The men on board the *Wayfarer* had long since accepted him as adopted son of Captain Cortland. Devon gave promise of being very tall. Already, his shoulders had begun to fill out. He had dark, raven black hair, and the most startling gray-blue eyes. Against the deep tan of his skin, they were like glittering flashes of light. He had large hands and feet, and was at the age when boys are awkward and sensitive.

He worshipped Captain Cortland almost single-mindedly. Captain Cortland had been the only person to stand between him and a cold hard fate in an orphanage, one which the captain knew too well. Devon had lived alone with his mother in the most meager conditions until she had met the captain. He had given his help to the lonely woman until her death.

Devon knew how lonely his mother had been after his father had abandoned her with no way to care for her small son. He had been grateful for the smile in her eyes and the laughter on her lips for the few years they were together. After she was gone, the captain had taken him on as cabin boy, but treated him more like a son. Devon would have died and gladly gone to hell for this man.

He stood before the captain's door now, wondering at the late night summons, but anxious to do anything the captain would ask. He rapped lightly and was ordered to come in. Inside, he stood silent, alert and waiting for the captain to speak.

"Dev, I've a job for you."

"Yes, Sir."

"I need you to do something for me and keep it a secret—tell no one, no one!"

"Yes, Sir."

"No questions, Dev."

"No, Sir." He half smiled at the captain. "Whatever you want me to do, Sir, I'll do. No questions."

With a slight smile on his face the captain clapped him gently on the shoulder.

"Thank you, boy, I knew I could count on you. Come with me, then."

Captain Cortland led the way to the rail. In the water below sat one of the long boats. In it was the passenger who had come aboard. He held in his arms the lifeless form of the woman who had accompanied him. Dev looked at the captain in surprise, but said nothing. He awaited his orders.

"Dev, you're to row them ashore and leave them. Return to the ship immediately. Do you understand?"

"Just leave them, Sir?" Dev questioned, watching the captain's eyes.

"Just leave them, Dev. Then come back to my cabin. I have another job for you."

"Yes, Sir," he replied, and scrambled over the side and dropped lightly into the boat.

Captain Cortland watched the boat move toward shore. "Go with God, Don Miguel. I hope you find peace and safety until we meet again, my friend."

When they had disappeared from sight, he turned and went back to his cabin.

Devon rowed in silence. The man sitting opposite him seemed to be deep in thought. He held the body of the beautiful woman close to him. Devon did not know any of

14

the reasons for what was happening, but he did not care to question this silent man with the pain-filled eyes. If Cap wanted him to know, he would tell him.

When the waves lifted and carred the small boat against the sand, he jumped into the water and pulled it ashore.

The man lifted the woman's body and stepped out of the boat. He turned to Devon. "Thank you for your help, my son. Return now to your captain with my eternal gratitude."

Devon was silent as the man turned and walked away from him. The night swallowed him up and soon even the sound of his footsteps faded away.

When Devon had rowed back to the *Wayfarer*, he returned to Captain Cortland's cabin.

"Sit down, Dev. There are a few things I must tell you."

Devon sat down and waited patiently for the captain to begin to speak.

"Dev, I'm going to tell you tonight what I think is necessary for you to know. By the time you know the rest of the story, the *Wayfarer* will be yours, and it will be up to you to make the decisions." He told him about the birth of the infant, and that they would be taking her to the convent. He warned him again of the importance of keeping this secret and never to tell a soul what he had seen or done this night.

They weighed anchor and, to the relief of all on board, moved slowly away from the cove in which they had spent the night.

Two days later, they again dropped anchor on a small island. Devon and Captain Cortland rowed ashore.

15

Between them in a small basket lay the child, Angelique.

Devon walked beside the captain in silence as he carried the child through the small village and up toward the convent that sat against the green side of the mountain. They passed the church along the way, and suddenly, as though in welcome, the church bells began to toll.

At the gates of the convent, he and the captain waited for permission to enter. A sister, dressed in black with a white bordered veil motioned them inside and led them to the mother superior's office. She knocked lightly on the door, then a soft voice from inside bade them enter.

The room contained very little furniture, yet gave the impression of comfort and warmth. The ceiling and walls must have been white at one time, but continual washing, and the passage of many years had given them a soft ivory glow. There was a small fireplace above which hung a huge wooden crucifix, majestically beautiful. The tiles of the floor glowed with the rich, warm shine of care.

Devon was most amazed and impressed by the woman who stood behind the desk. She was the tallest woman he had ever seen, and very slender. Her black habit gave the impression that she was even taller. Her face was lined and weathered. It was impossible for him to tell how old she was, but she gave him the feeling that she was quite old. Her eyes were a deep golden brown and Devon thought that, outside of his mother, he had never seen such beautiful eyes in his life. They smiled and seemed to hold out a welcoming hand to him, although she had not moved an inch since they stepped into the room.

"Welcome, Captain Cortland," she said softly, and her voice reminded Devon of the bells of the church they had just passed. He had the immediate feeling that they were as one, this woman and the church.

"Reverend Mother," Captain Cortland answered. He smiled at her and Devon knew that these two had known each other a long, long time.

"It is good to see you again."

"Thank you. This is my step-son, Devon Carlisle." He motioned toward Devon. The golden eyes turned toward him.

"Hello, Devon."

"Hello, Reverend Mother," he said in a cracked whisper, his eyes wide with awe.

She turned her attention back toward the captain.

"Robert, what can I do for you?"

He chuckled. "Must I always be asking favors of you?"

Her laughter joined his. "And when have you not, Robert?"

"I think Devon is quite hungry," he said. She took his hint without the blink of an eye and rang a small bell that sat on her desk. On silent feet, the younger sister who had led them in reappeared.

"Yes, Mother?"

"Take this young man to the kitchen and see if it's possible to arrange a meal for him."

The last thing Devon wanted to do was to leave the room. He wanted to hear what was said between these two old friends, but one look in the golden brown eyes and the protest was frozen on his lips. He turned obediently and followed the sister from the room.

"Sit down, Robert, and tell me the story."

Robert chuckled again. "I've brought the story with me."

"I see. The child. I imagine you intend to leave her with us as you were left."

17

"I do, and I hope you will give her the kindness and affection you once gave a little orphan boy washed up on your shores."

"You'll get nothing," she said with a touch of humor, "until you've told me exactly why you're bringing the child here and what you know about her background."

"Not knowing someone's background has never stopped you from being charitable before."

"That's because I've never had the chance to find out, but I'm sure you know a story and I would very much like to hear it."

He smiled again, and nodded to her. Again, she rang the little bell and another silent-footed sister appeared.

"Sister, take the child to the nursery and see if . . . ?" She looked toward Robert.

"Angelique."

"See if Angelique is hungry. She will be staying with us."

The sister took the baby from Robert's arms. He watched her as she silently left the room.

"Now, the story, Robert." She smiled. "I have a feeling this is quite interesting."

"First, I need a promise from you."

"A promise? Just what kind of a promise?"

"The child is not to know this story until she comes of age. Then I shall come back and tell her of her parents and take her back to let her claim her inheritance."

"As you wish."

Robert leaned back in his chair and began the story. There was no interruption as he spoke, no questions asked, yet the gold brown eyes left his until some time later he concluded the story and became silent.

"How very terrible," she said softly. "How it must

18

have grieved him to leave his daughter after so recently losing his wife."

"He knew it was necessary to protect the child. If it were found out that the daughter of Miguel Montalban and Anna D'Santiago is here, they would waste no time in coming for her. At that moment her life would be worth nothing."

"Rest assured, Robert. We will care for the child until you come for her. No word of her presence will leave the island."

"I knew I could depend on you. Now, I must return to my ship."

"This boy you call your step-son. How much does he know?"

"Dev can be trusted completely, but still I have not told him everything. In due time, I expect him to take over the *Wayfarer* as captain. Then I shall tell him all the truth."

She nodded and they both arose. They walked together to the kitchen where Dev was just finishing the remains of an extremely large meal.

"Are you ready, Dev?"

He jumped to his feet. "Yes, Sir."

"Come along then. The wind's with us, and we've got a lot of distance to make up for."

Devon made a hasty bow toward the mother superior and moved to the captain's side.

"Good-bye, Robert. I don't expect I shall hear from you again soon. God bless you."

"Thank you," Robert replied. There was a gentle tone to his voice that caused Dev to look up at him in surprise. Then, putting his hand on Dev's shoulder, he turned and left the kitchen.

Robert was quiet on the walk back to the dock, and Dev did not interrupt his thoughts. He knew at this moment that Cap would not welcome questions.

Once back on the ship, Dev went about his duties. In a few days, the child and the island were a fading memory. In a few weeks, they had completely been put out of his mind.

Chapter 2

Under the watchful eye of Captain Cortland, Dev grew strong in body and in spirit. Within a few weeks of their visit to the convent, the *Wayfarer* sailed into home port. Coming home was always greeted with enthusiasm by Dev. The first few years of his life had been spent in close acquaintance with hunger, cold and fear. Now, under Cap's care, home was a warm, love-filled place. The gentle hand of discipline was there in the form of Cap and his housekeeper, Mattie.

Cap and Dev gathered their belongings together and prepared to leave for home. Walking slowly along the dock, they were hailed often from the crews of other ships.

"I see the *Dolphin*'s in port," Cap remarked. "Looks like you and Andy will be terrorizing the town for the next couple of weeks."

Dev was pleased, for Andrew Ryan, cabin boy of the *Dolphin* was his very closest friend. Andy had met Captain Cortland under almost the same circumstances as Dev, and to put him on a straighter path, Cap had placed him as cabin boy on the ship that brought him to port often enough for Andy and Dev to build a friendship and for Andy to remain under Cap's personal care.

They stopped at the bottom of the *Dolphin*'s gangplank and asked about Andy. One of the men turned and shouted and within a few minutes, Andy's head appeared over the rail. Andy was a boy of devilish good humor. He was almost the same height as Dev, yet much slenderer. His shock of bright red hair, and his laughing green eyes had the ability to draw answering smiles and also, to his pleasure, allowed him to get away with quite a bit more mischief than Dev could.

"Good afternoon, Captain Cortland, Sir," he shouted down.

"Are your duties finished aboard, Andy?" Cap asked.

"Yes, Sir. We've been in port since last evening tide."

"Then, I'll expect you at the table for supper?"

"Yes, Sir."

Cap turned to Dev. "I expect you to be home in plenty of time to get yourself scrubbed up for supper. Now you know how upset Mattie gets if you come to the table late, or not in condition to be present at the table. I don't expect Mattie to have any reason to be upset with any of us this trip, understand?"

"Yes, Sir," Dev answered. Cap clapped him on the shoulder, then walked on toward home.

"Hey, Dev! Wait, I'll be right down," Andy shouted, then his head disappeared. In a few minutes, he was running down the gangplank. The two boys walked along the docks together.

"Where you been this trip?" Andy asked.

"Spain and back," Dev answered. "Where you been?"

"Oh, we had all kinds of trouble this trip. Had to make port a couple of times. Once with a broken mast when we hit a squall. Capt'n finally had to turn back."

They walked along in comradely silence for a while.

"Let's go down to the cove for a swim," Andy offered.

"Good idea," Dev agreed.

*   *   *

They made their way along the docks and soon were well away from the crowds. The small cove in which they swam had been a place they had often shared many times in their friendship. After swimming until they were exhausted, they lay on the small grassy knoll that overlooked the beach and talked.

"I can't wait until I'm a few years older," Andy said.

"Older, why?"

"I'd like to get off that ship. Maybe if I asked, Cap would find room for me aboard the *Wayfarer*."

"You know you have to serve as cabin boy at least two more years."

"I know, but when I'm old enough, I'll be off that ship. The Captain, he ain't like Cap. He's kind of . . . I don't know what. He's got something wrong with him. He makes my skin crawl whenever I'm anywhere near him."

Dev was about to question Andy further when a shout from about sixty feet down the beach drew their attention. A slender young girl of about eleven stood shading her eyes with her hand and watching them. Since Dev and Andy had been sunning themselves in the altogether, there was a mad scramble for their clothes as the girl made her way toward them.

"Who is that, Dev?" Andy snapped.

"Polly Dillon, she lives down over the hill from Cap. She was visiting with Mattie the last time I was home." Dev grinned. "She's kind of attached herself to me like a big brother. I've got a feeling she's going to turn into a pest."

"Well, you entertain your pest; I'm goin' home. Maybe if I'm lucky, Mattie baked some of those special cookies of hers and I could snitch a couple before supper. I'm starved. See you at home."

Dev waved and watched Andy walk away, then turned to look at the girl who was making her way up the knoll to his side.

"Dev," she panted when she reached him. "I saw your ship come around the point. I'm glad you're home. How long are you going to be here this trip?"

"I don't know, Polly, I'm not the captain of the ship, you know. The cabin boy just doesn't get told about the captain's plans."

"You're cabin boy, now!" she said positively. "But you'll be her captain someday."

"You're so sure of that," he laughed teasingly, but inside he was pleased with her wide-eyed flattery. It was obvious by the way she looked at him that she believed in him completely. It made him stand a little taller and talk with just a little more authority.

"Of course, I'm sure. Why, my mama and papa said they expect you'll be doing well some day."

"What are you doin' down here anyway, Polly?"

"I told you, I saw your ship come around the point and I wanted to see you."

"I've got to get back now, Polly. I don't want Cap and Mattie mad at me. C'mon, I'll walk you home."

"All right," she laughed and she bounced beside him as he walked back toward town.

Polly's house was on Dev's route home. They were nearing her house when Polly's feet began to drag. Following her eyes he could see her mother standing by the front gate waiting for them. Dev had never really liked Mrs. Dillon, and although he was always as polite as he could be, still he did his best to stay away from her.

"Polly Dillon!" her mother shouted in a shrill angry voice. "Polly, you get yourself home. Who are you with?

I'll teach you to go running off after boys all the time! I'll warm your bottom!" Her voice faded as they drew nearer and she saw who it was Polly was walking with. Polly was red with embarrassment and her eyes were filled with tears.

"Oh," Mrs. Dillon said, her voice changing to a smooth sweet tone. "It's young Carlisle. How are you, my boy?"

"I'm fine, Mrs. Dillon. Polly was coming home and we met. I just decided to walk her home."

"That's very gentlemanly of you," she replied.

Dev did not understand, and did not care for the way her calculating gaze examined him, and he hated the way she had hurt and embarrassed Polly in front of him.

"If you'll excuse me, Ma'm, I've got to get home. Mattie and Cap will be waiting supper for me."

"Of course," she replied. Dev moved away without looking at Polly again. He knew she was close to crying and he did not want to make it any worse for her. After he had gone a few feet, he took a quick look over his shoulder in time to see Mrs. Dillon grab Polly roughly by her two long braids and thrust her toward the door. He could hear Polly's stiffled cry of pain and he felt a surge of anger and pity. When he arrived home, Andy was seated on the front porch steps nibbling on a cookie. When Dev approached, he drew another from inside his shirt and handed it to Dev.

"Better wash up quick. Supper smells great and I don't want to have to sit around waitin'."

Dev nodded and went inside. There he found Cap seated in the small living room. He was about to speak when Mattie appeared in the kitchen door. With a quick smile, he went to her. Next to his mother, who had died

25

the year before, Mattie was the one woman in his life for whom he felt a deep and abiding affection. She had nursed him through the deep sorrow of his mother's loss in a way only a woman could have with sympathy and understanding.

"Hello, Mattie," he smiled.

"Dev, child, I'm glad you're home," she said as she drew him close into her arms for a warm hug. "It is good to have all three of my men home at the same time for a change."

Supper in Cap's home was a comfortable, laughing affair. After a prayer of thanks, which began all their meals, Mattie urged them to talk and tell her of all their experiences since their last trip home.

They were home for over two weeks, both Andy and Dev thoroughly enjoying the pampering that Mattie gave them. Most of the days were spent swimming in the ocean, or wandering the fields and the town. Dev did not see too much of Polly, who seemed to shrivel with embarrassment each time their eyes met.

Their days at home finally came to an end. The *Dolphin*, with Andy aboard, was the first to leave port. It was only a week later that Cap announced that he had a full cargo and the *Wayfarer* would be sailing on the morning tide. This trip was a long and uneventful one. It saw only the arrival of Dev's fourteenth birthday and the happy occasion when he was promoted from cabin boy to carpenter's mate. It was not a tremendous advance for him, but he was jubilant, for to him it meant he had taken the first step toward his life-long dream—to captain his own ship.

The following two years were a repetition of the past. By the time Dev was sixteen, he had taken his next step

26

up the ladder. It was a voyage that he would remember the rest of his life. For the first time, Dev was initiated into the more pleasant side of life.

They had reached a port along the coast of Ireland. They were to be there only one night. It was then that some of his mates decided that Dev should be raised from the ranks of boy . . . to man. Taking him ashore and making the rounds of the local taverns, they bought drinks until Dev's head began to swim. He was seated at the table with four other men. Despite his years, Dev had grown tall and muscular. His dark hair and light blue eyes and quick smile soon drew the attention of a pretty barmaid.

"She's got her eye on you, boy," one of his friends teased. Dev was just drunk enough to develop a bravado he would never have had sober. He smiled at the girl and before too long, she was leaning over their table, depositing their drinks and giving Dev a bigger view of the female anatomy than he'd ever seen before. He was embarrassed, yet fascinated, not only with the sight but with the strange effect it was having on him. He had no idea when his friends had faded away, but in the wee hours of the morning he found himself, hand in hand with the pretty girl, walking in the direction of her home. Once there, he discovered to his delight that she lived alone.

"Come in," she whispered. Her head was on his shoulder and his arm about her waist. They stepped inside the dark room, and as he pushed the door shut and turned around he found a soft warm woman in his arms and an eager mouth searching for his. It was the first girl he had kissed and she knew it immediately. It took no urging for her to get him to her bed, but once there, he

27

really didn't know exactly what to do. He was to be grateful to this girl the rest of his life, for he began his eager fumbling in a heavy handed way, following only the demand of his heated body.

"No, darlin'," she whispered in his ear. "You've got to be slow and easy. It's much more fun when we're both enjoyin' it."

They removed their clothes and lay on the bed together. He could feel the softness of her skin as she guided his hands gently over her. Her hands were busy, too. Touching, drenching him in fire wherever her fingers found him. Her kisses drove him wild with desire and after a while, she drew him to her and for the first time in his life he felt the keen edge of passion. He wanted to shout with the beautiful ecstasy when his body joined with hers and he heard her moan in pleasure.

Although he was extremely ill the following day, and annoyed by the secretive smiles of his shipmates, he remembered in exact detail every bit of the pleasure he had found the night before. He vowed it was one pleasure he was going to enjoy as often as possible.

Slowly, and with a great deal of hard work on Dev's part, he began to rise in position on the ship. Not once did the captain reward him with anything he did not earn; in fact, Cap was harder on Dev than he was on the rest of his men. At eighteen, he stood two inches taller than the Captain's six feet and outweighed him by twenty pounds.

Many ports and many girls added to Dev's experience. But never, on all his leaves at home, did he attempt to touch Polly. Maybe it was still a small drop of pity, but Dev began to feel that Polly was something very special in his life.

Polly was pretty in a little girl kind of way. Her eyes were a deep amber brown and her hair hovered somewhere between light brown and gold. She had a little ridge of freckles that ran across her pert upturned nose. Her face was heart-shaped and her mouth wide and sensual: A sensuality that Dev firmly overlooked.

On the trips when Dev and Andy happened to reach port at the same time, they developed their friendship into a strong, lasting relationship. They shared a bond of brothers under Cap and Mattie's roof. Away from the house, they shared more: Their drinks, their escapades, and sometimes, their girls.

Dev's charming little boy looks developed into an extremely handsome man. Conquests were easy for him, and he enjoyed the favors of women wherever he found them, but he shied away from any lasting relationships.

It was spring of 1779 and Dev had reached his twenty-sixth birthday. The *Wayfarer* was three days away from home port. Dev had been summoned to Cap's cabin and stood outside the door and knocked gently.

"Come in."

Dev closed the door behind him and faced Captain Cortland. The years had been good to Cap, although there was a fine sprinkling of white in his hair and tiny lines at the corners of his eyes, he still smiled easily and often at this much-beloved adopted son.

"You wanted to see me, Sir?"

"Yes, Dev. Come in and sit. I have to talk to you."

Dev sat in the chair opposite Cap's desk and waited patiently.

"Dev, I'm promoting you. After we make port and the *Wayfarer* sails again, you will be her second mate."

Dev's delighted smile could not be hidden.

29

"Thank you, Cap. I'm grateful for the opportunity."

"Don't thank me. You earned it, boy. The men respect you. You've gotten not one step because you are my son. I want you to know. I'm very proud of you."

"I'll certainly do the best job I can, Cap," Dev replied. "And what you said just isn't so. If it hadn't been for you, I'd still be a dock rat stealing for my food. No matter what you say, I'll always be grateful for what you've done for me. I guess making it worth while is the only way I can repay you, now."

"Stubborn cus, aren't you," Cap smiled.

"Yes, Sir. I guess it rubs off." Dev chuckled. "Both me and Andy seem to take after the old master and, I suspect, Andy is just as grateful to you as I am."

"We haven't seen Andy for almost five years. I miss that boy. I wish he'd get home more often."

"Cap, you know Andy's workin' for his own ship one day. No matter what he does or where he travels, his heart's here, we both know that. I wouldn't be surprised if he sails home one day, captain of his own vessel."

"I suppose you're right. Now suppose we get back to work. I don't want my second mate shirking his duties the first day he's promoted."

"Yes, Sir."

Dev rose to his feet and left the cabin. He closed the door behind him and was half way up the ladder before he gave vent to an exuberant shout of joy.

Dev expected another pleasant few days leave at home, then a return to his ship with the exulted title of second mate.

"Second mate," he said to himself, rolling the words gently in his mind. He remembered far back to his cabin boy days and felt a sense of well-being and contentment steal over him. His life was well planned and happy. He knew exactly where he was going and what he wanted. Everything was going almost exactly as he had planned and worked for all those years. Now the ultimate goal was in sight. He felt assured he would one day realize his one great love and ambition, making his way to be Captain of the *Wayfarer*.

He stood now at the rail of the ship and looked out over the white-capped waves. His body swayed with the rise and fall of the ship. They were on their way home from a long voyage. He would be glad to see home again, he thought, with a smile. He was hungry for some of Mattie's good home cooking, and the charms of a certain young lady whetted another appetite. He had passed his twenty-sixth birthday during this trip, and he looked forward to the fuss Mattie would make over him when they did get home.

Mattie had been Captain Cortland's housekeeper for as long as Dev could remember. Their little house had always been warm and filled with laughter and a great deal of love.

It was only a short time before the look-out shouted, "Land Ho!" and the dark line of the horizon slowly enlarged until he could make out the port. His eyes searched out the white frame house that sat halfway up the hill on the other side of town. He grinned broadly, his white even teeth flashing in his tanned face. Home! Home! There was no place in the world that could make him feel this good. They were supposed to be in port for more than a month this time, and he was delighted.

"Maybe," he thought, "just maybe, if Mattie approved, I might propose marriage to Polly Dillon." It was time he settled down, and with the possibilities of being first mate on the next voyage, it was time he looked for a wife and home of his own.

The docking finished, Dev waited impatiently for Cap to finish his business. Then, together, they walked as they always did, through the town and up the hill to their own special port of heaven.

The town of Bedloe was very small. It had one main street, and two streets that crossed it. There were several shops and one church. They walked through town slowly, waving to a friend now and then, or stopping to talk to someone. Then the street began to rise, and they were walking uphill. Soon, they were at the front gate. Cap pushed it open and they walked toward the front porch. It was always a secret wager between them whether they could reach the front door before Mattie was there to meet them. So far, they had never succeeded, and it was no different this time. The front door was thrown open and Mattie bounced out to greet them.

Bouncy was a good word to describe Matilda Fletcher's greetings. Matilda, lovingly called Mattie by both Captain Cortland and Dev, was round. Everything about her was round, from her pink apple cheeks to her voluminous body. She grabbed Dev in her arms and squeezed him to her. Wrapping both his arms about her, he lifted her and whirled her about. Then, setting her back on her feet, accepted with pleasure the many kisses she placed on his cheeks.

"Mattie!" he laughed. "Do you want to smother me?"

"Oh, Devon, my boy. I'm so glad you're home!"

"How about me?" asked Cap.

"Of course, I'm happy to see you, but Dev had his birthday without my cake, and I'm going to make up for

32

the neglect he's suffered at your hands. Now, come, come, Dev. Take a hot bath, I've drawn the water and laid out all your things, and when you're done, come down. I've made your favorite meal and one of my special cakes. Now, hurry!'' She pushed him toward the stairs.

It was less than an hour before he was back down, hastily dressed, his hair still wet from washing. He stood over the table and inhaled deeply, closing his eyes in pleasure.

"Oh, Mattie, that smells marvelous. I've missed you very, very much."

"Missed my cookin', you mean, you skalawag," she retorted with a sniff.

"Mattie," he said with a twinkle in his eyes. "You know you're the only woman in my life."

"Yes, me and another little lady we both know."

"I don't know what you're talkin' about Mattie."

"Polly."

"Polly?" He pursed his lips and looked as though he couldn't remember who she was speaking about. "Polly, who?"

"Don't you Polly who me, Dev Carlisle," she laughed. "The young lady's been here almost every day since word came that your ship was spotted. I'd say the lady had more than a passin' interest, wouldn't you?"

He reached out a hand to sample some food from one of the dishes, and she promptly slapped it.

"I always taught you. We wait until Cap comes to the table. Haven't I pounded manners in your hard head yet?"

He laughed again. It was good to be home. He leaned against the doorway and folded his arms across his chest and watched Mattie putter from the kitchen to the dining room.

"Well, Mattie, what do you think?" he asked softly.

She pretended to be quite busy. "What do I think about what?"

He grinned. "What do you think about me marryin' Polly Dillon?"

She almost dropped the dish she was carrying. *"Marry!"* she said as though shocked.

"Yes, marry."

Slowly, she put the dish on the table and turned to leave the room. Dev was surprised, so he pushed himself away from the door and followed her. She did not look at him, but found several things to occupy her hands, until finally he went to her and took her shoulders in his hands.

"Mattie?"

"Now, Dev. You know you'll do whatever you set your mind to do. You've never asked me for permission to do anything before."

"I'm not asking for your permission, love," he said gently. "I'm asking for your opinion. And your blessings."

"Oh, Dev," she said. "You know I love you like my own son, and I would never say anything to hurt you, but . . ."

"But, what?"

She looked at him and her eyes were wide and honest. "She's not the woman for you, Dev. She's not. Somewhere there's the one for you, but if you want my honest opinion, it's not Polly Dillon. If you want my advice, you'll wait. Wait for the right one."

"And how am I supposed to know the right one?"

"You'll know, son," she smiled again. "You'll know."

Chapter 3

Cap finally came downstairs and they sat down to supper. Dev was famished. He waited patiently while grace was said, but after that he dug in enthusiastically. By the time he finished dessert, he had slowed and after the last mouthful of cake, he pushed his chair back from the table and with a completely relaxed smile, complimented Mattie.

"Mattie, my love, I shall never marry anyone. No other woman in the world can cook like that. I guess you'll have me under foot for a long long time."

"I agree, Mattie," Cap said. "You've outdone yourself this time. I don't think I can move."

"Oh, thank you," Mattie smiled, her apple cheeks turning pinker. To cover up her embarrassment, she looked sternly at Cap. "Someone has to take care of this boy. I swear from how thin he's gettin you never feed him on board that ship."

Cap and Dev exchanged glances of amusement.

"Well, I think I'm going out for a while," Dev said as nonchalantly as he could, but he caught the glance that shot between Cap and Mattie who smiled innocently at him.

"Good," she grinned. "You run over and see Polly, I'm sure she's waiting and watchin' for you."

He chuckled. "You know too much, Mattie. Mind your own business." He could hear her laughter as he pulled the door shut behind him and shrugged into his jacket.

He walked slowly with his hands in his pockets, thinking over Mattie's words. There was no doubt in his mind that Mattie loved him completely, and that she would never have offered any advice if he had not pressured her into it. He also knew that Mattie liked Polly, and he wondered why she was against them getting married. He tried to sort out his feelings about Polly.

He approached her house which was just at the foot of the hill on the edge of town, less than a mile from Cap's. The door was open, and Polly came out quickly, pulling it closed behind her.

"Dev," she smiled, and in a moment, she was in his arms. She felt delightfully feminine in his arms and he held her tightly, enjoying the sweet, clean smell of her hair. Then he kissed her thoroughly and hungrily. It had been a long time since Dev had held a woman in his arms.

She stepped back, out of his arms for a moment and looked up at him with a slight pout to her soft red lips. "Dev, you beast. You've been home for hours and you've just now come around to calling on me."

"Now, Polly," he laughed, "you know how Mattie is about havin' her suppers interrupted. You know I came just as soon as I could." His eyes smiled into hers and he pulled her back into his arms and again sought her lips. This time, there was no resistance at all from her.

"Come on," he whispered. "Take a walk with me along the shore."

She let him take her hand in his and lead her away from the house. A short time later, they walked along the beach together. He had his arm about her waist and they walked slowly and in silence. Only the soft sound of the surf touching the beach could be heard.

36

"Papa said he heard you'd probably be first mate on *Wayfarer* when she sails again, if McMichaels retires. Is that true, Dev?"

"I hope so, Polly. If Cap thinks I can handle the job, he'll give it to me."

"Oh, Cap knows you're the best man on the *Wayfarer*, Dev, and besides, he's lookin' forward to you bein' captain one day."

Dev smiled. He felt proud of the way Cap felt toward him and just a little pleased that she and everyone else thought he'd be captain soon.

"Just think, Dev! Captain of your own ship. Isn't that wonderful? And maybe you wouldn't have to sail too often. You could just stay here and run the business."

"Business? What business?"

"Why," she said softly, "Devon Carlisle and Sons, Shipping."

He stopped and looked down at her. Her eyes were serious now, and the smile had faded.

"Devon Carlisle and Sons," he repeated. "It does sound nice, doesn't it?"

"It's nothing more than you deserve, Dev," she replied softly. "Papa says you're going to be rich one day, and I don't doubt it a bit."

"Well," he laughed. "I don't know about some day, but I'm certainly not a rich man right now. In fact, I don't really have much of anything to offer."

"Oh, Dev," she said, "you've a lot more than money to offer. I think you're . . . well, you're a wonderful person. I care a great deal about what happens to you."

"You do?"

"Why, Dev, you know we've been close. Even when we were children and you chased me around the beach

37

threatening to drown me."

He looked at her intently, and a quiet little voice deep in his mind told him the truth. Yes, he wanted her, as a man wants a woman. But, he realized he did not love Polly with the depth he had been searching for. Unspoken words remained so, and suddenly marriage seemed to be a huge step he was not prepared for. He was sorry for both of them, and the next gesture he made started out to be one of affection but not a proclamation of love. He put both hands on her shoulders, but had not planned on what happened next.

She seemed not to move, but he was not sure whether she stepped into his arms or he took that one step toward her. He only knew that her warm mouth was only inches from his, parted and waiting expectantly for his kiss. He touched her lips with his and closed his arms about her, pulling her tightly against him. He could feel her soft, rounded curves pressing against his chest. Her lips parted under his and she held herself against him, her body moving gently. Things now seemed beyond him to control. His hungry body demanded release and he gave up any idea of refusing what it desired. Her hands carressed his shoulders and her fingers twined in his hair as they both slowly dropped to the sand in the shadows of the rocks. Under his seeking hands, her clothes seemed to vanish and soon, he held her silken body next to his. His body ached to possess her immediately, but Dev had had enough women to know that it was much better when both of them enjoyed it. His hands and mouth roused her to passion, and her soft sighs of pleasure urged him on.

Her body gleamed like pale gold in the moonlight, the shadows touching curves and hollows, places that soon felt the warmth of his lips. He heard the soft words of love that escaped her as she urged him to deeper and deeper passion. She was wanton in his arms, and he let himself fall into the fire of her passion. He could think of nothing but the soft velvety skin under his hands and the way her body searched for his in a wild abandon. Then, they merged completely, moving in one rhythm, playing out the eternal dance of love.

They held each other in silence as they both began the slow spiral downward from the heights. It was several moments before either of them could speak. Then Dev rolled onto his stomach beside her and looked down into her eyes.

What could he tell her? What they had shared had no depth of love. The silence was uncomfortable.

Polly sensed how Dev felt, but she closed her mind to those feelings. With time, she could make him love her. Polly's life was a misery because her parents, silent, firm people, had put great demands on her, yet gave her little in return. Polly had sought love in many places. Now, since they realized that Dev was going to be a man of substance one day, they continually urged her to coax him into marriage.

"Polly," Dev began gently. "I didn't mean for anything like this to happen. I have to tell you . . ."

"Don't Dev, not now. I don't want to hear any regrets. Give us time, Dev, give us time."

"Time, Polly?"

"You've always meant so much to me, Dev. I've tried so many times to tell you how I felt. Give us time. You can learn to love, Dev."

Polly told Dev aloud the words she was telling herself in silence. To please her parents, she, too, would learn to love. She hoped that maybe their encounter had left her carrying his child. It would solve the problem.

They talked for a while, but no matter how Polly tried to seduce him again, he refused.

Several hours later, he took her home and kissed her good night. He walked back toward home, his hands in his pockets and his head down in deep thought. He remembered the words Mattie had said to him. "You'll know, son, you'll know." Polly had been his girl since they were children. Then another thought burst on him. "If Polly had never had another beau, then why hadn't she been a virgin?" He stopped for a moment, stunned by this realization, then he walked on a little faster. A short time later, he arrived home. Quietly, he opened the front door, trying to not waken anyone. The fire in the hearth had burned down to red embers. He removed his shoes and walked toward the stairs, then he heard the rustle of movement in the big chair by the fire. He grinned to himself. Mattie had waited up for him like he was a little boy, and now she would pretend she had fallen asleep in the chair and just wakened.

"Mattie," he said softly, "is that you?"

"Oh, Dev," she said sleepily. "I'm afraid I fell asleep. I'll just take myself up to bed now." She rose from the chair and he almost laughed to see how slowly she walked, waiting for him to say something. When she got to his side, she realized that, not only was he not offering any explanation, but he was, if she read the twinkle in his eye properly, laughing at her. Her eyes glittered in response.

"You nasty boy," she laughed. "You're not going to tell me a thing, are you?"

"Mattie," he smiled, "I'll tell you anything I think you should know."

"But not what I want to know."

"What is it you want to know, love?" he asked innocently.

"Devon Carlisle, did you propose to Polly tonight?"

He let her wait for a few minutes. Then as he saw her impatience begin to build, he said quietly. "No, Mattie, I didn't." He was surprised to see relief in her eyes. Then he added, "Not tonight, or any other night, love."

"Dev," she began, then stopped. She put her hand on his arm. "I guess I have to say the truth. I'm glad, son."

"Why, Mattie?"

"Like I told you before, Dev, I don't think she's the one for you, that's all."

He realized he was going to get nothing more in the way of an explanation of her feelings. Whatever Mattie knew about Polly, she intended to keep to herself.

"Well, stop you worryin' about me, love. I've no intention of gettin' married this trip. Maybe not for a long time."

He put his arm about her shoulders and they walked up the stairs together.

"Now, I think it's time for you to get some sleep. I'm sure Cap will have us up and busy first thing in the morning. *Wayfarer* needs some repairs. It should keep us busy for a few weeks."

They stopped by her door, and he kissed her.

"Good night, Mattie. And thanks."

"Thanks for what?"

"Oh, for a lot of things. For the way you've always been around when I need you, for always having my interests at heart, for being someone I can talk to, and most of all . . ." He paused then laughed. "For being my guardian angel."

41

She watched him walk across the hall to his room, and close the door behind him. She breathed a sigh of relief. He was not going to marry Polly. There was no way she could tell him that she knew of several affairs Polly had had since he had been gone, or that Polly's parents wanted her to marry Dev because they realized he was going to be a man of position. Polly was wild and only restrained by her parents' firm hand, but once out of her parents' sight her wildness had full reign. Dev, she knew, was a boy who loved deeply, and he would be badly hurt by the wrong woman.

She went to bed and slept well. The next morning, she was up with the dawn preparing a hearty breakfast, and soon, she heard both Dev and Cap coming down the stairs.

"We've got to turn her up for a good scraping this time, Dev. Her hull's covered with barnacles," the captain was saying as they came down.

"Yes, Sir. We'll take good care of her, Cap. I think she needs some new canvas too. The mainsail's been repaired as many times as she can be."

Mattie was kissed good morning, and both men sat down to eat. She was content to bustle about the table and listen to their talk. It was good to have them home again.

Breakfast over, they both took their coats from the peg behind the door and left.

The days fell into a pattern for the next few weeks as they worked from early morning to suppertime on the *Wayfarer*. Occasionally, they would come home at midday, but most often, Mattie brought a basket of lunch to the dock.

She was just leaving the house one afternoon when she was met by Polly at the front gate.

"Mattie, can I walk to the dock with you?"

"Of course," Mattie replied, but she knew there was something on Polly's mind.

"Mattie," she said hesitantly. "Dev's been to call on me only three times since he got home."

"They've been awful busy, Polly. Refitting the ship is a lot of hard work."

Polly nodded half-heartedly, then after a long silence, said, "Mattie, is there someone else in Dev's life now?"

"As far as I know," Mattie said, "there's no other woman in his life if that's what you mean."

"Mattie, I . . . I love Dev. Why is he suddenly ignoring me?"

Mattie stopped and looked at the girl. She liked Polly, but she knew her too well. Polly dropped her eyes away first. She knew at that moment that Mattie understood her completely, and she also knew that any chance she had had to marry Dev was irrevocably gone. Her eyes filled with tears.

"I . . . I knew," she said in a trembling voice. "I'm going away to visit my aunt and uncle. I won't be back before Dev leaves again." She looked again into Mattie's eyes. "But, no matter what else you think, or what you know, Mattie, I do love Dev. That's why I'm going. I know now he doesn't love me and I can't stay here, I just can't."

Mattie felt sympathy for the girl and she watched with sad eyes as Polly turned and ran from her. Dev would be upset for a while when he found her gone, but he would get over it soon. It was best this way, she thought. Then she continued to the dock.

Dev saw her coming and shouted hello. Stripped to the waist, he was a magnificent golden brown Adonis. His body was muscular, yet gracefully lithe.

"Mattie, I'm glad to see you. I'm starving."

"When aren't you? Where's Cap?"

"He got some kind of message a while ago and went off to see about it," he said as he reached and took the basket deftly from her. "You don't want me to die of starvation before he gets back, do you?"

Mattie gave a little click of her tongue. "You! Starve to death! Never! You eat like a horse."

Dev cleared a place for them and she sat down with a sigh. It brought his attention from the basket to her face.

"Mattie, love," he said softly, "you don't have to walk down here with lunch. I can come and get it. Are you all right?"

"I'm all right, Dev," she said quietly. Then she looked intently at him. "I saw Polly on the way down."

"Oh?"

"She's going away for a while, Dev."

"Away? Where?"

"To visit her aunt and uncle."

Dev looked at Mattie, and she knew that he was accepting this with no problem.

"Maybe it's better this way, Mattie," he replied. "I just couldn't say what she wanted to hear and it's certainly no good for us to go on the way we are. It's not fair to her, either. I hope she finds what she wants and is happy."

Mattie nodded and they sat quietly for a while. She was about to say something when Cap joined them. Both of them could see he was worried about something.

"Dev, if we work hard, how soon do you think we can

get the *Wayfarer* on the water?"

Dev and Mattie exchanged looks. "She still needs a lot of work Cap, about two weeks, I'd say."

"No, Dev. We've got to get her out now, today."

"Today? That's impossible!" Dev said.

"Impossible or no, we've got to do it. Stop all repairs and get her ready to sail by tonight's tide."

"But, Cap . . ."

"Dev, do you think you could get her ready then?" It was not a question.

Dev looked at Cap, then said quietly, "She'll be ready to take the evening tide, Cap. You can count on it."

"Good." He began to turn away, then stopped and said, "I'll explain to you after we sail, Dev."

"I wonder what's wrong," Mattie said softly when Cap had gone.

"Well, whatever it is, it's important and he needs the *Wayfarer* now, so I'd better get to work."

Mattie watched as he shouted orders and the men began to move about rapidly. She had a feeling that this would be no ordinary business voyage.

Chapter 4

Angelique sat on a small white bench in the garden of the convent, under the shade of the trees and listened. The chapel bells were ringing, their melodious chimes carrying up the hill. "Oh, the lovely sound of it," she thought. "I'm so happy today, I could burst." Everything looked bright and shiny. She was seventeen, and since it was a festival day in the village she had been given permission by the reverend mother to go to the festivities.

Even in the dark black dress of the convent, Angelique was a strikingly beautiful woman. Her face was oval and her complexion pink and smooth. Her eyes were wide-set and deep violet blue. In startling contrast, her hair was the color of spun silver. It had amazed the sisters when she was a child. They thought as she grew older it would darken, but it did not. It hung below her waist in two thick braids. She was a very tiny woman, but even her severe clothes could not hide the soft rounded curves of her body.

The convent and the sisters were the only home and family she had ever known. Until today, she had never even left the convent grounds. She had questioned the sisters hundreds of times over the years, but none of them seemed to know anything of her origins. They had told her the same story over and over again, succumbing to her questions. They told of the tall ship that had put her into the harbor seventeen years before. No one knew where it came from or where it had gone. It unloaded no cargo and it left nothing but a small baby girl at the convent of the Sisters of Mercy . . . Angelique. The captain had spent some time with the mother superior before he left but nothing was ever told to any of the others. Angelique was sure the mother superior knew everything about her background, and had questioned so often and to no avail that she finally became exhausted with the efforts and let the matter die. The mother superior would smile her beautiful smile and the amber eyes would be gentle. She would pat her hand and say, "You are God's gift to us, my child, and we love you dearly. Be content here, my little one."

But she had not been entirely content. She had dreams about being a great lady and going to balls and parties. She would laugh and have such great fun in her dreams. She could feel the difference between herself and the others at the convent.

Then, last year, Maria had come from the village to join the order. Maria was a small, beautiful, affectionate girl who seemed to love the world and everyone in it. They had been immediately drawn to one another and in the year that Maria had served as novice, they had become like sisters. Maria was as dark as Angelique was fair and it often amused the sisters to see them together. They were often referred to as Day and Night. Maria's eyes were brown and her hair deep black. She had deep golden tan skin.

It was Maria's understanding and constant affection that made Angelique decide to take her vows and join the order with her. Even so, there were times in the past year when she would get the feeling that they would never

47

share this life together. Vague feelings of unrest would capture her during prayers, and late at night. She would go to the mother with regrets on her lips and be forgiven again and again for her restless lack of attention.

Today, for the first time in seventeen years, she would go to the village, and with Maria. Her heart was bubbling with joy.

Tonight was festival!

The murmur of quiet voices brought her attention around to see the mother superior and Maria walking in her direction. They were moving too slowly for Angelique's excitement. She literally bounced from the bench and ran toward them. She made a quick genuflection to the mother superior.

"Good morning, Reverend Mother."

"Good morning, Angelique," she smiled. "Very impatient as usual, my daughter."

"Oh! But it's festival, Mother, and I may go to the village for the first time. Oh, Mother, I want to see everything!"

"Patience, my child. You will have your festival."

"Angelique," Maria said. "I take my vows next week when Monsignor comes to bless the chapel."

"I'm happy for you, Maria," Angelique said sincerely. "Maybe I may be able to take my vows next year."

"Oh, I hope so!" sighed Maria. "It will be wonderful when you and I can work together to serve God."

"May we go now, Reverend Mother?"

"Of course. Maria, Angelique, go and enjoy your day."

They walked away slowly, too slowly for Angelique. She wanted to grasp Maria by the arm and fly down the hill.

The convent sat on the mountainside, its white beauty

standing out like a beacon to the villagers. The small church sat halfway between the village and the convent. The path that ran from the convent to the village had been cobbled many many years before with stone hewn from the mountain. It had been worn smooth by the feet of the sisters in their constant journeys to the church and the village on their errands of mercy.

The tapping of their feet and the swish of their skirts against the stone were the only sounds in the still morning air. As they neared the village, the excited bustle of activity reached them. The village had been decorated for fiesta with every flower that could be gathered from the mountain. Brilliant hues of bright red, yellow, purple and green assaulted Angelique's senses as they came to the edge of town.

"Oh, Maria," she breathed happily. "I didn't know there was so much beauty to see."

Maria turned to Angelique, and said suddenly, "When Mother called you to her yesterday, did she finally tell you why you were never allowed to go any further than the church?"

"No," Angelique replied. "There must be something so dreadful about me and my past that they can't even tell me."

"Oh, Angelique, nonsense. What could possibly be so bad? Mother must have done it for your benefit. We will understand when she is ready to tell us. You really have no patience at all," she laughed.

"Well! I don't care now. Today is festival and next week you take your vows. Maybe next year I can take mine."

"Maybe. If you keep your mind on your prayers instead of letting it flit like a butterfly," Maria laughed, "you would have been prepared by now and we could have taken our vows together."

"I know," Angelique smiled. "I try, but it just seems to jump beyond my control. Mother has been very patient with me. Come, Maria. Let's hurry. I don't want to miss anything."

Maria stood still for a few minutes looking at the village, then her gaze lifted to look out to sea. "Look, Angelique, away on the horizon. A ship!"

"It's so far away. Do any ever stop here?"

"The last time was about two months ago. It put in for about two hours. It's funny now you mention it. The captain walked into the village and spoke to some of the people, then they left. I've not seen another since, except the one that drops off our medical supplies."

Shading her eyes with her hand, Maria watched the ship for some time. Suddenly she shivered as though she were cold, and turned to look at Angelique. Her eyes were fear filled.

"Angelique, I've a bad feeling," she said quietly. "Let's go back!"

"Maria," Angelique cried, "not now! Please. Don't spoil my only day. Please, Maria. Just for a few hours. We'll come back early if you want. Oh, please, Maria," she pleaded.

Maria seemed to shake off her fear. She smiled. "Of course, I forgot. Besides, it was a silly notion. Come, let me show you the village." They began to walk rapidly toward the square.

All the houses in the village were made the same. Small, one-story stone houses painted brilliant white. The roofs were thatched with rafters made of small logs. Today, flowers adorned every house and hung in

50

garlands across the stone-paved streets. Happy laughter of children running about the square and a small group of musicians on a platform in the center created a holiday atmosphere.

Stalls had been set up around the square and people from all over the island were trading and selling their wares. Pieces of jewelry made from gold mined out of the mountain. Pearls from the lagoon on the opposite side of the island, furniture and fabric made with great skill and months of laborious work. There were also vegetables, fruit, and rich pastries in abundance. All were being hawked loudly and happily from every stall along the square. Angelique and Maria went from stall to stall, examining and exclaiming over every article they touched. Angelique fondled the few coins she had in her pocket and watched for something special. Finally, with an exclamation of delight, she held up a beautiful rosary made of tiny pearls with a fine slender gold cross on the end.

"Look, Maria, my gift to you. I've been looking so long for just the right thing."

"It's lovely," Maria answered. "I shall cherish it as long as I live. I'll pray every night for you." She leaned over and timidly kissed Angelique on the cheek.

The two friends spent the midday hour lunching under the trees at the edge of town with friends of Maria's. The young people shared their lunches happily with the two girls from the convent. They were as delighted with Angelique as she was with them.

"Why have we not seen you before, Sister?" one girl asked shyly.

"Oh, I'm not a sister . . . yet," replied Angelique. "I was an orphan and the sisters took me in."

"But why haven't we seen you?" repeated another. "You are so pretty, we would all remember you very easily."

"I . . . I have not been given permission until today," she answered quietly.

"Come," Maria interrupted. "There are many things to do and so little time."

Angelique cast her a grateful look and rose quickly, brushing the dust from her skirt.

Evening found them happily clapping their hands to the music and watching the dancers.

"Oh, Maria," Angelique said. "I don't remember ever being so happy." She turned to face Maria, who was looking off in the direction of the sea. Following her gaze, Angelique could see that the ship that had been on the horizon that morning was standing at anchor not far from the shore. Several longboats were headed in their direction.

"Angelique," Maria said quickly, "let's start back to the convent." Her solemn eyes and firm tone alarmed Angelique, and she agreed without hesitation. They turned and started across the village and the path toward home. It was then that the first guns from the ship opened fire.

As the shells began to land among the merrymakers, panic broke out. People began to run in all directions. Roofs of homes were suddenly ablaze from the shelling.

"Pirates!" someone shouted, rushing past the two girls. "Run! Run!"

Angelique stood frozen to the ground. Maria grasped her hand and began to run as fast as she could. They were gasping for air and trembling with fear when they reached the path that led to the convent and sanctuary.

"I must stop for a minute, Maria," Angelique gasped holding her hand to her heaving breasts. "Please, I cannot breathe."

"If they catch us here . . . they must not, Angelique, come now, we must hide!"

They had got as far as the church when Maria gasped, "We'll never make it! We must hide here."

The outer wall of the church had several small alcoves in the sides in which stood statues of the saints. Pushing Angelique behind one, Maria looked at her steadily and said very firmly, "Angelique, do not come out for any reason until I come back for you. We'll be all right." She softened her voice slightly, for she could see Angelique's terror mounting. "I will hide in the other alcove. They will pass us by." With these words, she pushed Angelique deep into the black shadows behind the statue. The next alcove was about twenty-five feet away. She ran toward it. She never reached it.

Under their captain's orders, the convent was not to be touched, but he had said nothing about the church. The pirates had decided to sack it first. They broke from the trees at the same time Maria turned to run. She had covered no more than a few feet when they caught up with her. In the darkness, they could not see her habit, but it probably would not have meant anything to them even in the light.

Watching with horror filled eyes, Angelique was completely powerless to move.

Two of the men made a grab for Maria, but she managed somehow to elude them. Veering from her first direction she ran for the convent. Two more men ran out to cut her off. A few steps before she reached the shelter of the trees they caught her. They dragged her screaming and kicking back toward the others. Maria fought with every ounce of strength she had but it was useless against the strength of four men. They tore at her clothes, impatient to get them off. In the process, they had to strike her several times to control her. The brutality of the attack played out in front of Angelique made her head swim, and she prayed for unconsciousness.

Maria was resisting no longer. Her face, neck and parts of her body were bloody and bruised. She seemed like a lifeless child. They released her and let her sag to the ground. The first man, a large brutal looking man, loosened his trousers and fell upon the girl. Angelique gagged with the agony of the girl who was her friend. She watched as the man forced his way into Maria's body. His thrusting body, and the animal grunts of pleasure nauseated Angelique, and the hot tears fell unheeded down her cheeks.

When the man rolled away from Maria, Angelique thought the horror was over, and they would leave her and maybe she could get to her in time to save her—but she was wrong. The next man fell upon her, then the next, and the next. In the midst of the nightmare Angelique began to believe it would never end. They tore at Maria's body like wild animals. Handled her brutally, using her over and over in an abandon of wild passion inflamed by Maria's cries, then moans and finally, quietness.

After what Angelique thought was an eternity, the four men readjusted their clothes and left, going out through the shadows of the trees, and away from Angelique's hiding place. For a while Angelique was too paralyzed with fear to move. She could feel the blood pounding in her head, and she sagged to her knees almost in a faint. She could feel the soundless screaming deep inside her and she put both her hands over her mouth to hold it back.

Maria had hidden her well, but not well enough to keep her from seeing. Maria's body lay still and white against the ground. The pale moonlight picked up the bloody and bruised patches on her body. She was still, like a small doll that had been broken and thrown away. The words she had been hearing in her mind still pounded through Angelique's brain . . .

"Oh, my God! Please don't let them find me. Don't let them do that to me. Please. Please. Please," she moaned over and over to herself. Her legs would no longer hold her weight, and she sank slowly to the ground. She curled herself in a small tight ball, squeezing herself as tightly as possible as though she could make herself so small no one would ever find her again.

She didn't know how long she lay there before she became aware of the stillness. Slowly, she stirred to her knees and crawled toward Maria's unmoving body. She lifted Maria's head to her lap and looked down at the eyes, still terror-filled in death. A slow moaning escaped her as she held the body of her friend against her and rocked back and forth in her grief. The voice in her mind kept repeating over and over. "It's my fault. It's my fault. It's my fault."

They found her the next morning in the same position. Holding the body of Maria in her arms and crying, "It's my fault."

She was in such a state of shock that it took the efforts of two men to pry her hands loose. When they were carrying away the body of her friend, she began again the soft, moaning sound. It was so eerie that it frightened

55

the men.

When she was taken back to the convent, she was put into bed where she lay like a frozen statue. The mother superior sat by her side for hours, but Angelique's mind could not be reached.

The mother superior said softly to the sister who stood behind her, "We have a message to send, Sister Cecile. I hope I can find someone to help this child out of her darkness." She gave the message to the sister who departed, then she turned back to Angelique, who was murmuring something softly. She bent her head to listen closely. The words were barely audible.

"It's my fault. It's my fault. It's my fault."

Chapter 5

The *Wayfarer* was still a little sluggish. It had been several days now, and Cap had made no effort to tell Dev what their sudden sailing was about. Dev made no motion to ask, but he did notice that Cap was very preoccupied. It took everything Dev had not to ask what the problem was. He watched Cap closely and took over as much as he could to give Cap enough time to think over his plans.

Now he stood outside the captain's quarters and raised his hand to knock.

"Come in."

He went in and closed the door behind him. He stood in silence waiting for Cap to speak. This was the first time Dev had ever seen the captain in this state. He was almost ill from worry. His hands trembled as he put away some papers he had been reading. It shocked Dev, for he had thought of Captain Cortland as invincible.

"You wanted to see me, Cap?" he asked gently.

"See you?" Cap asked as though his mind was far away. "Oh, yes, Dev, I did. Are you free for a while? Do you have time? I have to tell you something before we reach our destination."

"Our destination. Just what is our destination, Cap?"

"The island of San Moro."

"San Moro! What in heaven's name are we going there for? It's nothing but a small village with a church and a con . . . a convent," he added slowly, his mind going back to their last visit to the island.

"Yes, Dev. The convent. I know you remember our last trip there."

"Yes, we took a baby to the sisters. But Cap, what does that baby have to do with us now?"

"A very great deal, Dev," Cap said, his voice agitated. "I've got to get back there to repair the damage that might have been done."

"Cap," Dev began again, "maybe you ought to start at the beginning and tell me everything."

Cap sighed deeply. "Yes, I have to tell you everything." He rose slowly from his chair and paced back and forth in deep thought. Dev did not interrupt him, but sat patiently waiting for Cap to begin.

"I guess I have to start back twenty years ago. Twenty years, back in a time of dread and fear in Spain, back to days when people lived in dread of the Inquisition. You have never been in direct contact with it, Dev, but I know you have been to Spain often enough to know about it. And I know you have seen some of its results."

Dev nodded, but remained silent waiting for Cap to continue.

"I was a young sea captain then, with my first command. Our trips took us to Spain where I met and became friends with Miguel Montalban. Though I was never entertained in the lush court of King Ferdinand VI, I was close enough to Miguel to hear from him all the fascinating stories of intrigue that were rampant there. Miguel told me of the hatred that existed between the Montalban family and the Ortega family, but before I get to that I must tell you what was happening in Spain so that you will understand the foul current that birthed a hatred that caused such destruction.

"The Spanish church was wealthy and extremely powerful, mostly because the people were so intensely religious. Pope Sixtus IV passed a decree instituting the Inquisition in 1480. It had grown in power as a wielder of fear. Medina Del Campo established the Holy Office in Castile as a Royal Instrument to strengthen the power of the crown—a power that became more and more abused, more and more used as an iron fist to control the wealth and power in Spain. They had everything in their power from the Inquisition General down to paid servants. Nothing was strong enough to stop them. There was no account taken for the privileges of nobility. If the inquisitors wanted to reach out and touch someone, nothing, not even their nearness to the throne, stopped them.

"Ferdinand was a good king, a king who had the interests of his people at heart. He was the one who confirmed the commercial privileges between Spain and England. There began to spread an enlightenment under him and he even tried his best to modify the power of the Inquisition. But in that one thing he failed; it was too powerful. Now that you understand its power let me tell you of some who used it.

"In the office of the Inquisition General was a man named Rodrigo DeSalva. Directly under him was a man of such evil, such a black soul, that I can hardly describe him to you. His name was DeVarga. Esteban Ortega worked as DeVarga's right hand. There were few that could hold back the hand of the Inquisition. One family close to the throne were the D'Santiago's. There was always a subtle and consistent battle going on just under the surface between DeVarga and the D'Santiagos. Into this came the Montalbans. I do not know exactly how, but they shared a relationship with the Antonio Larente family, who were distant cousins of the D'Santiagos.

"I still do not understand, mostly because of Miguel's vague explanations, why there developed a deep burning hatred between the Montalban family and the Ortegas. What, in the distant past caused it I do not know. I only know that Esteban and Ortega hated each other with a deep and burning passion.

"I do not believe that DeVarga would really have tried to destroy the D'Santiagos so ultimately if Miguel and Esteban had not both met and fallen in love with Anna D'Santiago. The final disaster came when Anna chose to marry Miguel Montalban. Esteban was in a black and violent fury. He could not, would not, let the wealth or the power—yes and the court influence—slip through their fingers.

"The minds of DeVarga and Ortega came together in a plot and the hand of the Inquisition came down and destroyed the D'Santiago family—Anna's father Ramon, her mother Constancia, and her younger sister, Inez. The night they came for them, Anna and Miguel were away. The three of them were taken.

"The next day a very subtly worded letter came for Anna from Don Esteban. He would do his best, it said, to get her parents and her younger sister set free if Anna would agree to an arrangement between them. Miguel tried every way he knew to get information about the D'Santiagos but it was as if the world had been closed to him. There was an aura of silent terror in the air. When a family as influential as the D'Santiagos could be touched, then who was safe?

"Anna became desperate. She was filled with fear when she could get no word about her family, whether they were alive or dead. So, finally, she went to Don Esteban and told him she would agree to marry him if her parents were set free. He agreed, insisting that the wedding had to take place before their freedom could be accomplished. Again she agreed. After weeks of watching and worrying she was too frantic to do anything else. How was she to know that at that moment her family were already dead?

"Angelique was born on my ship that fateful night, and her mother died giving her life. I think at that moment Miguel felt that he too had reached the end of his life. All the wealth—both his family's and Anna's—was gone. He was an outcast from his own country, afraid to return. He had no other friend in the world except me and, unknown to him, you. The night she died, Anna put a gold chain about Angelique's neck that had been in the D'Santiago family for generations. With that and the papers Miguel left with me, I could prove Angelique's identity to the world if the time ever came that their name was cleared.

"Miguel was desolate at the tragedy of his double loss, but he had no choice. He had to find some place to hide until the searching ceased or until he was cleared and free. That night, he took his wife's body ashore on a small island only he and I knew. There he buried her. Since then I have gone back and placed a stone to mark the grave of a very courageous lady who died too young. I know, without having seen him, that Miguel has returned also.

"I do not know if I can find the words to tell you of the merciless beast that took the lives of Anna's parents and her fifteen-year-old sister. All I can tell you is what we found out much later. They began by torturing the child. The child, Dev. They subjected her to a torture no man could bear. She died under the strain. Then they turned to the mother, who had already been subjected to watching her daughter tortured to death. In front of Ramon, they proceeded to inflict unmentionable atrocities upon Constancia. Combined with the emotional shock, the physical pain made Constancia surrender her life.

"When her father tried, in his unconsollable rage, to attack their persecutors, he was killed. Then the one miracle happened. I don't even know how, but Miguel found out just before the wedding what happened to her family. He took Anna out from under Don Esteban's nose and ran with her. For over a year, Don Esteban hounded their trail. There was no place they could go that was safe, and they did not want to bring disaster to their friends.

"Somehow they survived that year, but then Anna found that she was going to bear a child. It was impossible now, Miguel knew, for them to be able to remain in hiding. Anna was delicate and he knew she would need a midwife's care when the time came. He decided to try to find a way to leave Spain completely. Although all the harbors were watched closely by Esteban's men, Miguel had one last desperate opportunity. He needed a captain and a ship he could trust.

"I was in the harbor at Cadiz when Miguel and Anna came to me. She was heavy with child, ill, and there was no place for them to go. I took them on board when she gave birth to a child, Angelique. Miguel's plans were destroyed by the hand of fate that decreed Angelique would come into the world a month before she was expected. We expected to be docked at a more sympathetic country when Anna's time came. I took

Anna's child to the convent and placed her with a woman of unsurpassable compassion and generosity. Her convent doors have always been open for the poor, the homeless and the needy. What else could I do? I hid her in the only place I thought to be safe. I hid her at the convent in which I spent my childhood. I . . . I really thought it would be the best place."

Dev nodded his head. "Surely, she is safe at the convent."

"I thought so, Dev, until I got this message before we sailed." He handed a letter to Dev, who read it slowly, his face turning white.

"My God, Cap," he said. "Was it Don Esteban's men who attacked the island?"

"No, it was not. You can see by the letter the condition the girl is in. But somehow, Ortega has learned of it and now knows where the child has been. He is on his way now. I hope and pray we reach the island first."

Dev nodded again and left the room. Cap could hear his shouted orders above the sound of the ocean, and soon, he could feel the quicker rise and fall of the ship. He prayed that they would be in time.

Within two more days, the island was sighted. When they dropped anchor in the harbor, there was no other ship in sight, but they could not tell if one had already come and gone. Dropping the long boat over, they quickly rowed ashore and made their way as quickly as possible to the convent. Once they were shown to the mother superior's office, they were relieved by her assurance that Don Esteban had not got there ahead of them.

"How is she?" Cap asked.

Dev stood silently at his side. He remembered so

clearly those deep compassionate amber eyes. They were filled now with pity as the mother superior replied.

"Not much different from when I wrote to you. She is trying to escape from the reality of her friend's death. For some reason, she seems to blame herself. When we talk to her, it's as though she does not hear, then suddenly she will turn to one of us and repeat over and over. 'It's my fault, it's my fault.' It is heartbreaking, Captain. She needs someone strong to help her now. She could stay here, and I'm sure that in time we could reach her, but as you know, I discovered Don Esteban is on his way here now. You and I both know what will happen to her if he gets his hands on her, especially in the condition she is in at the moment. We—" She was about to add something when a knock sounded on the door. "I must advise you before she comes in. Don't act shocked at the way she acts. Make no motions to touch her. She seems to be terrified of being touched. Just speak softly."

The mother superior's eyes were moist with unshed tears. "Captain Cortland, I hope you can help her, but whatever you do, keep her out of his reach. She is fragile. In hands like his, she would be crushed." Then she raised her voice and called, "Come in."

Both Cap and Dev stood up and faced the door when it opened. They were both shocked, but in different ways, by what they saw. Her large, violet eyes seemed to dominate her face and were filled with shadows. Her silver hair hung loose about her slender body. Just looking into her eyes brought a surge of anger up in Dev that left him shaken and weak.

"She's the most beautiful woman I've ever seen," he thought. "And she is like a little broken bird." He wanted to go to her, to assure her that nothing would ever hurt

64

her again.

"Angelique, this is Captain Cortland, a very dear friend of mine, and his son, Devon. You are to go with them now, and they will help you," the mother superior said softly.

For a time, Dev did not think the girl had heard her. Then she spoke, her voice soft and weary. "Yes, Reverend Mother."

"Child, it is necessary for your safety, that you leave us for a time. If God is willing, we will see you again. I hope you will let my friends help you."

"Yes, Reverend Mother," came the soft reply.

"Angelique, go with the captain and his son. They will take you to a place of safety. If you can, write to us."

"Yes, Reverend Mother." Again the soft, expressionless reply.

"Come, my child." The captain turned toward her and reached out his hand.

"Don't," the Mother Superior said quickly.

The captain's hand hesitated a few inches from Angelique's arm. Her large violet eyes were turned to him and fear filled them. She began to tremble and large tears ran down her cheeks. She looked at him as though begging for something, then whispered, "It's my fault, it's my fault."

"Oh, child," the mother superior whispered almost to herself. She said to Angelique, "Go Angelique. They cannot stay here any longer."

Angelique nodded and followed Cap from the room. It was plain for Dev to see that the mother superior would liked to have kissed her good-bye. Instead, she said softly, "God bless you, my daughter."

She turned again, and once more Dev was overpowered by the compassion in those penetrating eyes.

"She has not cried since they took Maria's body away. All the fear and horror are deep inside. Someday, somehow, you must open that door or I am afraid we will never have her back again. Do you understand, my son?"

"How, Reverend Mother? Tell me how and I'll do anything," he replied.

"I don't know. Maybe when the right moment comes you will recognize it. I pray so. Take good care of her. Life has not treated her well. Help her find a way out of that dark place into the light."

"Believe me, Mother, I will do anything in my power to help her."

They left the convent with the girl walking between them, her eyes focused on the ground. As they neared the church, her steps hastened. Dev could see every nerve and muscle of her body quivering with anguish.

They rowed out to the ship, the captain insisting they hurry, for Don Esteban's ship could arrive at any moment. Getting her settled in the captain's cabin took a considerable amount of maneuvering. Cap explained to the crew that she was very ill and was to be left completely alone. Dev and Cap shared two stiff drinks together before they could get their frustrated rage under control.

"Dev, we've got to try our best to help her. I owe that much to her father. Somehow, we've got to reach her."

"We'll try, Cap, we'll try. But I think this is something that is beyond us. I think it would take an act of God to erase the memory of what she's been through."

Dev arranged a kind of routine for them to follow. He thought that if they did everything routinely, she would develop a dependence and be a little more secure in his presence.

Each morning, at six, he knocked on her door. She was always up and always answered immediately. He began to believe she never slept. He would bring her a breakfast tray and stay until she ate it. The first day, he had made the mistake of leaving it, only to return and find it untouched. From then on, he ordered her to eat and sat across from her until she did. After a while, he tried conversation. He would chat aimlessly on any subject he could think of, from ships to sea gulls, but nothing elicited a response. When she had finished her food, he would tell her to put on her cloak and they would walk around the deck a few times. Often, they would go to the captain's quarters, and he and Cap would talk of as many things as they could think of. By the time they left Cap, Dev could see the same kind of frustrated grief in the older man's eyes as he was feeling.

Sometimes, she would sit on the deck on a coil of rope, covered with his jacket. It was several days before he even realized that although she did not answer him, she had begun to listen. Watching her, Dev would feel again that terrible surge of helpless anger at the man responsible for her condition. The deep pity and affection he was beginning to feel for her would sometimes cause such heaviness in his breast that he could not speak. They would sit together for hours, sometimes even he would not speak the whole time. Again there were times when her eyes would moisten with unshed tears as she fondled the tiny pearl rosary that was always with her.

At such times, he could feel the pain which emanated from her like warmth from a fire, and he would feel his helplessness mount until he could stand it no more. He would jump to his feet and go get Cap to sit with her while he would attack some piece of work or other to exhaust himself.

Today she seemed to be in a lucid moment. She clasped the rope of tiny pearls tightly in one hand, but she was not twisting and pulling at it as she usually did.

"Someday," thought Dev, "I'll take those from her hands. Maybe I'll even be able to make her smile." He chuckled ironically to himself. "What makes you think, Devon Carlisle, that you can cure her when for six months the people she loved and lived with couldn't reach her?"

He chatted on and on, speaking softly as though he were talking to someone else. He was never really quite sure she even heard him.

During the following two weeks, he told her his whole life story, beginning with his illegitimate birth to being signed on as cabin boy of the *Wayfarer*. He told her of his mother and how happy his home had been with Cap and his mother before her death. He told her of the gifts Cap had brought back from all over the world on his travels and how their house was filled with astonishing things. Day after day, they sat on the deck while he talked and talked. He began to panic when he realized he was running out of life to talk about.

He had never wanted anything more desperately in his life then to strike a spark and watch her eyes light with response.

He lay on his bunk that night with his hands behind his head, unable to sleep. In his mind's eyes lingered a pair of haunted violet eyes. Why couldn't he reach her? Why did something so vile have to happen to someone as lovely as she? Dev had always been an honest man, honest with others and honest with himself. He was drawn to this girl out of more than pity. He wanted to touch her, to hear her laugh, even to hear her cry. There was no use denying his feelings to himself.

He chuckled when he remembered the words Mattie had told him about Polly. "She's not the woman for you."

"How will I know this . . . right one?" he had laughed at her.

"You'll know, Dev," she had replied. "You'll know."

Mattie was right. He could not deny the feelings this tiny person aroused in him. He could almost feel the way she would be in his arms. With determination, he made plans for the next day. It was now or never. He had to reach out and touch her. He was going to try a more direct approach. If he caused her any damage, he would catch hell from Cap, but he had to take the chance. Tomorrow, he would put his plan into action. He smiled in satisfaction and, turning on his side, fell into a deep contented sleep.

Chapter 6

It was only two days since they had taken Angelique away, but already the mother superior missed her. Maybe she had been wrong. Maybe Don Esteban did not know where she was, for so much time had passed since Robert had left her with them. She thought of Robert and his son, Dev. She had looked into him. He was a good, strong man. Just what Angelique needed. If only God would see fit to open her mind and heart to him.

A knock sounded on the door and she looked up in surprise. "Come in," she called.

Sister Cecile came into the room quietly. "Mother, you told us to inform you if another ship was sighted."

"And one has been?"

"Yes, Mother."

"How far away?"

"It should be here by this evening."

"Thank you, Sister Cecile, you may go."

She waited until the door was closed, then walked to the window. A tiny speck on the horizon verified her fears. Don Esteban was on his way. Thank God, she thought, that none of the sisters except herself knew who had Angelique and where they were bound. She thought for some time, then a half smile formed on her lips and the faint hint of wicked humor sparkled in her eyes. She rang again for Sister Cecile.

"Yes, Mother?"

70

"After evening prayers, Sister Cecile, you will lock the front gate of the convent according to the rules. If someone rings for entrance, you will inform them that the gates cannot be opened until morning."

"But, Mother, the new arrivals will . . ." she began, but the words faded away as the mother superior turned to look at her.

"We must at all times abide by the rules, Sister," she said softly. "And I believe they specifically state that the gates be locked after evening vespers and not opened again until sunrise."

"Yes, Mother," came the softly whispered reply. As she turned away, she could have sworn she heard the mother superior chuckle.

The mother superior went on with her day's work. Several hours later, the bells rang time for evening prayers. She went with the rest of the sisters to the chapel. When the prayers were over, she saw Sister Cecile walking toward the front gates to lock them. She returned to her office to await patiently the confrontation she knew was coming.

In the darkness, the faces of the men who disembarked from the ship could not be seen clearly. But people stayed out of their way. From the purposeful way they walked toward the convent, it was obvious they would brook no interference. They walked past the small church and on up to the convent gate, which they found firmly locked. The gates of the convent were huge oak doors several inches thick, which could withstand assaults far greater than three men. In the center of the gate was a small door, big enough for one person to look in or out. One of the men lifted his fist and pounded against it. Within minutes, it opened, and the frightened face of Sister

Cecile peered out.

"Yes?" she said.

"Open the gates," came the reply.

"I'm sorry, Sir. The gates of the convent are closed for the night."

"Sister," the man grated through clenched teeth, "open these gates immediately."

"I cannot, Sir."

"And why can you not?"

"Reverend Mother has ordered them closed for the night."

"Don't be foolish. Open these gates at once."

"I would have to ask mother's permission first."

"Then," he said in a deeply aggravated voice, "I suggest you do so immediately."

"Don Esteban," one of the men said softly, "do you think we have arrived ahead of them?"

The taller of the men spoke, his voice smooth and soft.

"I believe we might have. I see no signs of any other ships. If not, and they have beaten us, the sisters will know where she has gone. I will have her before this night is over."

Sister Cecile arrived and knocked timidly at the mother superior's office.

"Come in."

"Mother, there are three men at the gate demanding that we open them at once."

"Did you tell them they were locked for the night?"

"Yes, Mother, but they still demand to have them opened."

"Then, Sister Cecile," she said calmly as she moved from behind the desk, "we must convince them that their demands are not important here."

Slowly and with great dignity, Mother Superior walked through the halls, down the steps and out through the door to the front gate, with a frightened Sister Cecile beside her. She stopped in front of the gate and opened the small door.

"Yes, gentlemen. May I help you?"

"You are the mother superior?"

"Yes, I am."

"Open the gates. We have business to discuss with you."

"I'm sorry gentlemen, that is impossible," she replied, unperturbed. "The rules of our order are that the gates are locked after evening prayers and not opened again until sunrise."

The taller man again came to the door, his voice smooth and gentle. She immediately knew to whom she was speaking.

"Reverend Mother, I am Don Esteban Ortega. I suggest for everyone's benefit that you open these doors and let us in. We have only to ask you a few questions."

"Good evening, Don Esteban. You seem a gentleman, so I am sure that you will understand if I tell you that the rules of the convent cannot be broken for anyone—anyone."

He looked at her first in amazement, then in deepening anger. "Do you know who I am?"

"You have told me, Sir, and I repeat that the doors cannot be opened after vespers for anyone. Come back at sunrise and I will be happy to discuss whatever it is you wish at that time."

"I am the representative of Don Carlos DeVarga. Does the name mean nothing to you?" he asked, his voice now deceptively soft.

"DeVarga!" she thought. The man responsible for the deaths of so many innocent people!

"Don Esteban, the rules of the convent were made by Holy Mother Church, including Don Carlos DeVarga. They will not be broken by me or anyone else in this convent without a special order from the bishop. Now, I suggest you sleep tonight, and in the morning I will be very happy to speak to you. Until then, I bid you good night."

She closed the small door, and for a moment she leaned against it weakly. She had got Angelique another eight hours' lead. Straightening, she motioned Sister Cecile to follow and went back inside.

She could not sleep the rest of the night, but tried to form in her mind what she would say to them in the morning. When she had everything clear, she knelt in front of the huge wooden crucifix and prayed in silence.

The sun was barely over the horizon when Sister Cecile came to her chambers and announced that Don Esteban Ortega wished to speak with her. She stood behind her desk, tall and calm.

"Show him in, Sister, please."

She watched the door as it was pushed open and Don Esteban stepped inside, closing it after him.

"Good morning, Don Esteban," she smiled.

He walked toward her desk slowly, his eyes holding hers. She had never seen a more handsome man in her lifetime, or a more deadly one. He was tall and slender, and gave the impression of strength and power. He was olive-skinned and had hazel eyes that showed not the least glimmer of human compassion. The broad smile flashed against his deep skin and he said in the soft, smooth voice that she was decidedly wary of.

"Good morning, Reverend Mother. It is a pleasure to meet you, finally. It is a lovely day," he added.

"Yes, it is usually quite beautiful here."

"I still prefer Spain," he began. "The charm, the . . ."

"Don Esteban, excuse me, but I must be about my daily work. We have much to do here and I cannot spend my time with light conversation."

"Yes. And we do have something of importance to discuss. You have a young girl here, about eighteen. She goes by the name of Angelique Montalban. I would like to see her immediately. She is to return to Spain with me on my ship today."

"I am afraid you are misinformed, Don Esteban." She smiled. "There is no one in this convent by that name."

"I am never misinformed," he replied quietly, his eyes holding hers in a cold stare. "If she is not here now, then she has just left here. I want to know who took her— Robert Cortland or her father?"

She was taken by surprise. "Her father—but I thought . . ."

"You thought her father was dead. So it was Captain Cortland who brought her to you? It was also Captain Cortland who took her away, was it not? How long ago did they leave, and what is their destination?" he demanded.

"Don Esteban . . ."

"Reverend Mother," he interrupted, "understand me well." He leaned over the desk. She was stunned by the fierceness of his eyes and the coldness in his voice. "You will tell me who has taken her and where before I leave here, for mark my words—if you do not, the villagers and your sisters will suffer the consequences."

"They are not responsible," she said. "They did not know how or why she came here."

"I do not care if they knew or not. If you do not tell me today what I want to know, I will destroy the village and everyone in it. Then I will obliterate your church and your convent."

"What kind of a man are you?"

"The kind of man who gets what he wants, and I want Angelique."

She knew he meant every word he said. For the first time in all the years of her life, she was prepared to tell a direct lie. But, she realized, she must not make it easy or he would be suspicious of the information.

"Don Esteban, can I do nothing to dissuade you from this terrible path you are on?"

"Reverend Mother, I am tired of playing with words. You have information which I need, and I want it now. If I do not know their destination by the time I leave this room, I promise you that by nightfall, there will be no one left on this island."

She sighed deeply and turned away from him, to the window. She let her shoulders slump and her head bent forward slightly. In a cracked, broken voice, she said softly, "Captain Cortland has friends in France. He has taken the child there, where he feels she will be safe."

"And how long ago did they leave here?"

"Just a few minutes before your arrival," she lied.

"Good, then we still have a good chance of overtaking them." Then he added almost to himself, "I should have realized long ago that Miguel must have fled to Cortland. They were such good friends."

"Robert Cortland is a good man," she said. "He is a man of compassion and gentleness. Did you expect he would turn his back on a friend when he was needed?"

He slowly walked to her side. She looked up into his

face and saw as she had before the complete lack of human feeling. His eyes were cold, and his lips twisted into a sardonic smile. "His compassion and gentleness are going to cost him dearly for interferring in my affairs. But I shall find a special way of repaying Robert Cortland."

"You are of the devil," she whispered.

He laughed and shrugged his shoulders eloquently. "I will catch up with them eventually, but it will be easier if I know their precise destination in France."

"I do not know their precise destination," she said quietly.

"Is their secret worth the lives of everyone in your village?"

"You would have the deaths of innocent people on your soul, Don Esteban," she pleaded quietly. "In the name of God, let that child go in peace. She has been through a terrible ordeal. Her mother died at her birth. If her father is alive—and I do not believe he is or he would have come for her—he has also paid the price by sacrificing his daughter all these years. What good can it possibly do you now to make a girl who is innocent suffer for some imagined wrong?"

"I do not need your pleading on their behalf," he replied coldly. "I want the exact location where I can find her. I already know who is protecting her. He also will regret the day he decided to go against me and help them escape." He stared at her again. "All right. I believe you. You do not know their port in France. No matter. You have told me enough. I shall find them."

"If I did not see you for what you are, Don Esteban, I would feel sorry for you," she said slowly, returning his stare.

His eyes turned colder and harder and his smile faded. "Send your pity to those who will need it more than I. Their days are numbered, for nobody takes from me what is mine!"

She smiled a half smile, "Not even God?" she said in a gentle voice.

He looked at her with a black scowl, then turned abruptly and walked from the room, slamming the door behind him.

Moments later, she turned back to her window and watched as the sails of Don Esteban's ship unfurled and the ship eased out of the harbor. She hoped and prayed that her maneuver had given Angelique enough time to make good her escape, and she hoped she had not been wrong about Devon Carlisle's strength. She felt in the days to come he was going to need it, for a black-hearted enemy had just turned his face in his direction.

Chapter 7

Angelique sat on a blanket on the deck of the *Wayfarer*. Her bright silver hair glimmered in the early morning sun, little tendrils of it whipped about her face as she lifted it to catch the breeze. Her eyes were calm, but remote.

Dev sat beside her. They had just come up on deck a few minutes before. He had spread the blanket and she had sat down quietly and obediently as always, accepting what she was told without question. Dev was determined that, somehow, he was going to do something about the situation. He was tense and felt an unfamiliar and uncomfortable tightening in his throat.

He had lain awake until late into the night, reasoning to himself that if shock had put Angelique in this condition, then maybe another kind of shock would bring her out of it. At least, he hoped he was right, for it was what he was about to do.

He leaned forward and took one of her hands in his, then, looking directly into her eyes, he smiled and said, "The day is beautiful, isn't it, Angelique?" The tiny hand quivered in his and she tried to pull it free but he refused to let go. Tiny beads of perspiration appeared on her brow and her whole body trembled as she tried to pull free of him.

"No, Angelique, don't run away," he said gently. "Look at the sky, it's so blue. And look at the white clouds. Listen to the sea, Angelique. Don't run away, please. Look at me, Angelique, I'll help you. I'm strong enough for two of us. Let me share my strength with you. I'll help you. Please, Angelique, hear me, listen to me."

A soft murmuring moan came from her as she shrank from him in terror. Large tears filled her eyes. He held her eyes with his, feeling that if he let her go even for a moment, he would never get her back again. He was drowning in the violet pools of her eyes, but he dare not release her for a moment.

They sat for several minutes, locked together in silent combat. She tried again to pull free, but he stubbornly held on. Tears glistened on her cheeks and her lips trembled as she spoke the first words he had heard from her in two weeks.

"Oh, God," she said in a strangled whisper, "don't hurt me, please."

"I won't hurt you," he said as gently as he could, but his heart was thudding in painful delight at her response. "I won't hurt you, let me help you." He pulled her close to him, gently surrounding her with his arms. Her head dropped to his chest and he could feel her heart beating frantically as a captured bird.

"Angel, Angel," he murmured against her hair.

Sobs racked her slender body. She shook so violently with her crying he had to tighten his arms about her, lest she collapse.

He held her for some time until her sobs quieted and the tension began to leave her body. She lifted her eyes to meet his, and for the first time since he had seen her, there was a spark of life in their depths. Then, another, more violent sensation came to him, and it shocked him. He did not want to let her go, he wanted to hold her in his arms, to kiss her—*My God!* he thought, *this is all she needs to push her back into that hell we've been trying to drag her out of.*

He looked down again into her eyes and smiled. "Cap and I want to help you, Angelique. You're safe here and you need never be frightened again. Cap was a good friend of your father's and after you've rested, we can go to his cabin, and he will tell you all about your parents."

"My parents," she whispered, and the small glow in the eyes grew. "The captain knew my parents! Oh, how I've prayed that somewhere, somehow, I'd find them . . ."

They stood, and were only inches apart. Slowly, all the shadows faded from her face. Her lips parted in a small smile, and her eyes seemed to glow as though a light were behind them. Dev was so stunned by the beauty of her face, he stood in absolute silence, trying with every ounce of strength he had not to bend down and kiss the soft corners of her lips.

"We . . . we'd better go down and see Cap. You have no idea how worried he's been since we brought you aboard."

She nodded, then slipped her arm through his as they began to walk toward the captain's cabin. A fiery shock ran through him at her touch and at that moment, he was reminded of Mattie's words. "You'll know, son. You'll know." He looked down on the bright head of the girl walking next to him, and without doubt or reservation, he knew.

"But," he thought glumly to himself, "there's nothing I can do about it." One touch might bring back the whole nightmare she'd been through.

They went to the captain's cabin. Captain Cortland had

his back to the door as they entered. He turned to them. When he saw Angelique, the familiar pain came into his eyes. Dev smiled. He was going to give him the greatest surprise of his life.

"Captain Cortland," he said formally, "may I introduce Miss Angelique Montalban? Angelique, this is Captain Cortland, one of your father's dearest friends."

Dev smiled in pleasure as he watched the expression on Cap's face as Angelique smiled at him.

"Good morning, Captain Cortland. I am so very pleased to meet you. I want to thank you for saving my life, not once, but twice."

"Angelique!" the captain replied with a delighted smile. "Oh, it is so good to have you finally with us."

"It is good to be here."

For a few minutes, the captain could only look at her and smile, uncertain of what to say or do.

"Captain, Devon tells me you know my parents well. Could you tell me of them? I have wanted to know all my life where I came from, where I belong."

"Of course, child. Nothing in the world would give me greater pleasure. Sit down, and I will tell you the whole story."

Dev watched Angelique's face as Cap unravelled for her the mystery of her past, and why her parents had been in flight when she was born. Dev wanted to reach out and touch her when her eyes filled with tears as he talked about her mother's death. Then he told her of how they had smuggled her into hiding before her whereabouts were known. He told her of her father's deep love for her mother and for her.

"He would gladly have sacrificed his life for you, my child. As things were, the best he could do was to see to your safety. That he left in my hands. Before he left, he put about your neck a gold chain with a medallion on the end."

Angelique smiled as she pulled from the high neck of her dress the golden chain.

"That is the crest of the Montalban family. It and the papers I have secreted away are your legitimate claim to the Montalban and D'Santiago fortunes. You are a very wealthy girl. There is only one thing that stands between you and your inheritance. If you go back to claim it, Don Esteban, your father's enemy, will have you where he wants you, and consequently, he will have your father also, for I firmly believe, he is still alive."

"Oh, do you think so?" she cried. "That would be reward enough. We do not need the Montalban fortune if only I could find my father and be with him."

"It would not surprise me at all to find that he has been keeping track of you all these years. Somehow, I feel that he knows what has happened. If you come to our home and stay with us, he will be able to contact you safely."

"Do you think that is possible?"

"We must have faith and," he said, "a great deal of patience."

"I have spent my whole life locked away from him, not knowing if I should ever see him at all. I have yearned all those years to find someone who knew of my parents and my heritage. I will be patient enough now that I have you to answer a lot of my questions. I would not want my parents' sacrifices to be in vain. I am content to stay with you until he feels it safe to contact me. I will only pray that it is soon for I should so love to meet him, to know him and . . . and to love him."

"And you shall in time, I'm sure. For now we will take

you home with us. I do not know of any way to reach your father. We agreed it was safer for him that way. Time is something we need now. Time for your father to contact us."

The beginning of excitement was in her eyes. "There are so many things I do not know, so much I have never seen. Oh!" she cried. "I would love to see everything, the whole world, all that I've never seen before."

"Angelique," Dev said, "when we get home, you will see some of the beautiful things you've missed. We could sail up the coast. Let me be the first to show you some of the things you've missed."

Angelique walked to Dev's side and put her hand on his arm. She had never known men, so she did not know what effect her touch had on him. He stood still, but his eyes could not seem to draw themselves away from hers. "That would be so wonderful, Dev. But—but I have no clothes except the ones I'm wearing now. If you would help me—I don't know what the styles are. You could tell me what to wear, and . . ." She laughed. "I'm sorry, I'm chattering away. It was always one of my problems. Mother Superior could never get me to keep still long enough to study my prayers."

He smiled, so deeply engrossed in her vibrant enthusiasm that he didn't even notice how closely Cap was watching him. "Angelique, we'll dress you like . . . like the angel you're named for."

She laughed, and the sound was beautiful to his ears. He was lost, and he knew it. Caught between his feelings for her and the fear of what the knowledge of that feeling could do to her. He swore to himself, he would never say a word to her unless he knew she was completely cured.

"For now, enjoy the rest of the voyage. In a few more

days, we'll be home," Cap said.

"Yes, and I imagine Mattie will be only too happy to take you under her wing and help you along," Dev laughed.

"Mattie? Who's Mattie?"

"She's Cap's housekeeper, my foster mother and probably the very best friend either of us has ever had. You'll love her, and I know she'll love you."

"Oh, this is all so wonderful I can't believe it's happening to me."

"You deserve everything life can give you now, for all the past years you were cheated of the life you could have had. We'll do our best, child," Cap said, "to help to start over. I'm sure you'll be happy, and someday, in the near future, you can be reunited with your father. Until that day, we will do our best for you."

"Why don't we start right now?" said Dev. "Let me give you a guided tour about the *Wayfarer*."

She nodded and smiled. Cap watched them as they left his cabin. Both of them would have been astonished if they had seen the glitter in his eyes as they left. An idea had occurred to him, and he was enjoying the thought immensely.

Dev and Angelique walked together about the ship while he introduced her to some of the crew. She was shy, but smiled and spoke quietly to each. As her shyness began to fade, one question after another tumbled from her lips, until Dev threw up his hands and laughed.

"Angelique, don't you ever run out of questions?"

"Oh, I've just begun, Devon Carlisle. By the time my father finds us, you'll be happy to get rid of me."

"Rid of you?" His smile faded as he stood and looked down into her deep violet eyes. "I'll never be glad to get rid of you."

She was stilled, unable to recognize the feelings that made her suddenly warm and trembling.

"Come on, Angelique, let me walk you to your cabin. You can get some rest. Then get ready to have a big dinner with Cap and me." He made himself take her by the arm and guide her toward her cabin, where he left her just as rapidly as he could.

He thought he had himself completely under control by the time he went back to get her for dinner. Their meal with Cap was pleasant and filled with Angelique's delightful laughter as Cap and Dev filled her with amusing stories of places they had been and things they had done. But by the time he rose to escort her back to her cabin, he knew that if he had to spend any length of time alone with her, all his good intentions would be swept away. He was going to spend the next four days, before they reached home, as busily as possible.

Cap rose from his seat and escorted them to the door to say good night.

"Dev, when you've taken Angelique to her cabin, would you come back here? I've some things to discuss with you."

"Sure, Cap."

He walked her to her door, and left her so abruptly that she was a little surprised. He went back to Cap's cabin and went in without knocking. "What is it, Cap? Is there something about Angelique? Did you find . . ." he started anxiously.

"Whoa, boy," laughed Cap. "Settle down."

Dev sighed, "What is it, Cap?"

"Dev," Cap began slowly, "I've been doing a lot of thinking, and one thing bothers me very much. If, by chance, Esteban does find us, we *can* protect Angelique, unless . . ."

"Unless what?"

"Unless he comes at us through the law."

"Through the law?"

"Angelique has no legal right to be in England."

"What . . . what can we do?"

"Well," Cap said slowly, "she could get married to an Englishman."

Dev stared at him, as if he could not understand what he was saying. "Married!"

"Yes. If she were married to an Englishman, he couldn't touch her legally."

Dev began to smile. "You're crazy, Cap. She hasn't . . ." The smile faded. He looked at Cap as the idea finally came through to him. "I suppose you have someone in mind as the groom for this wedding?"

"Yes," Cap said. "You, my boy."

Chapter 8

He was so stunned for a while, he just sat and stared at Cap. His mind raced, looking for excuses.

"Cap, it's impossible. You know the condition we found her in. Just to suggest something like that to her might be enough to . . . No, no. It's impossible."

"Listen to me for a moment. I don't mean this should be a real marriage, but a marriage in name only. Until her father can come for her. After that, there could be a quiet divorce, and you both could go on with your lives."

It wasn't bad enough, Dev thought, that Angelique was to live in the same house with him, but to live there as his wife. But he realized that Cap was probably right. "Have you thought of what Angelique might think? She's had no reason to develop any kind of trust in men. She might think I intend to take advantage of the situation."

"If you agree, I intend to discuss it with her tomorrow. But I think you'll find her a sensible girl. She'll see the advantage in this marriage."

Dev stood up and paced. He could feel Cap's eyes studying him intently. His thoughts were torn, he wanted to refuse, to shout at Cap, "What do you want from me!" But he kept silent. He turned again to look at Cap. "I don't think she'll agree to it," he said. "But if she does, then it's all right with me."

"Good! Good!" Cap replied. "First thing in the morning, we'll talk to her. If it's acceptable to her, we can have the wedding now, while we're at sea."

Dev nodded, and without another word to Cap, he left the cabin and went up on deck, his mind in deep thought. He'd have to find a way, when they got home, to keep himself as busy as possible, and as far away from Angelique as possible. She was now a woman of great wealth, a woman of the nobility. She was too far above him for him to even think of having her. No. No matter how he felt about her, he would never interfere with the bright future she would have when she was reunited with her father. Still, no matter what arguments he made against it, he could not deny that he wanted her. He thought of Polly, and of the other women he'd had, and chuckled mirthlessly to himself. All the women he had taken and never been touched by—and now the one woman he really wanted, he couldn't have.

Sleep was almost impossible. He tossed and turned all night.

Cap sat at his desk for some time after Dev had gone, his mind drifting back to Miguel Montalban. "I hope you understand old friend, what I'm about to do. Dev is a good, strong man, and he can give Angelique the best life has to offer. I know how he feels about her, and I'm almost sure she feels the same. She just doesn't understand it yet. I've taken the first step, and I hope fate does the rest."

The next morning, Dev and Cap stood outside her door and knocked. She opened the door and smiled at them both in welcome. "Good morning. My, you two look glum this morning. Is there something wrong?"

"Angelique, we have to talk to you. It's important," Cap answered. "May we come in?"

"Of course," she replied and stepped aside, regarding

their faces as they came in. Cap smiled at her, but Dev's face was serious, and for the first time his eyes refused to meet hers. He stood quietly while Cap turned to Angelique.

"Can we sit down?"

She motioned to seats for both of them, then sat on the bunk and watched them expectantly.

"Angelique," Cap began. "Don Esteban, your father's enemy, is on our scent. We have no way of knowing if he will reach us before we can reunite you with your father. If he does, he might exercise legal means to take you away from us. It would not be for long, but long enough to bring your father to him."

"What else can we do?" she asked. "It seemed that you have taken every precaution you can to protect me."

"There is a way we can tie his hands legally, as well."

"And that is?"

"You could marry."

"Marry!"

"Yes. If you were married to a citizen of our country, he would have no legal means to reach you. We can protect you every other way."

"And just who would I marry?" She knew what the captain would answer, and she only wondered why, if he was agreeable to the situation, Dev's face would look so white and withdrawn and why his eyes continued to avoid hers. Was he against this? Was the captain forcing him to comply with his wishes? She wanted to know the answers to these questions more than anything else.

"You could marry Dev," the Captain said. "It would be a marriage in name only, and when your safety is assured, it could be annulled."

"Dev?" she said, turning to him. His eyes lifted and

met hers. "How do you feel about this?"

"I'm sure it's the best thing for your protection," he answered quietly. "You know I'd do anything in my power to help you, Angelique. And you have my word of honor, that I would never . . . well, never. I mean, you'd be perfectly safe with me."

She watched Dev's face as he spoke. There was no doubt in her mind that these men were probably the best friends she would ever have.

"Well, Angelique?" Cap asked.

She turned back and looked at him, then smiled. "I have all the faith in the world in you, Captain Cortland. I trust you and Dev completely. I will do whatever you think is best."

Cap smiled in return. "Your father once said almost the same words to me many years ago. I was grateful for his trust then and I feel the same for his daughter. Rest assured, your faith is not unfounded. We will do everything that's in our power to keep Don Esteban at bay. Isn't that right, Dev?"

Dev had not realized that he had been holding his breath in anticipation of Angelique's answer and had slowly expelled it when he heard her agree. She was to be his wife. And he would have to spend God knows how many unbearable days and nights in her company without being able to touch her or tell her how he felt about her. Which was more unbearable, having her near where he could see her, or having her gone?

He knew without a doubt that he wanted to have her nearby no matter what the circumstances were. "You're absolutely right, Cap. There's no way he can reach you now, at least not after . . . after we're married."

"Then, if it is agreeable to you, Dev, it is agreeable

with me."

It was only an hour before they stood side by side in front of Cap with Mr. McMichaels and Davy Halt as witnesses and listened as Cap read the wedding vows. Both Davy and McMichaels were rather surprised at this solemn wedding, where the bride wore black instead of white. They signed the papers Cap presented to them and left. There was a silence after they had gone. None of the three seemed to be able to say anything.

"I'll see you back to your cabin, Angelique," Dev offered at last.

"Thank you," she replied quietly and rose to leave. Then she looked back at Cap and smiled again holding out her hand to him. "Maybe someday there will be another way to reward you for the kindness you've shown me and for your loyalty to my father. Until that day, accept my thanks and gratitude."

They walked slowly down the length of the deck in silence. Each was caught up in private thoughts. It whould have amazed each of them to know that the thoughts of the other were almost identical to their own.

They reached Angelique's cabin and Dev stopped. She turned to him.

"Dev, I want you to know just how grateful I am for what you're doing for me. I know that this will interfere with your life. You must have someone . . . someone who means a great deal to you." She said the words quietly, and waited for his reply.

"No. There's no one special," he said. "And I'm glad to be able to help you." He looked down into her upturned face. "Angelique, don't worry about anything. This will be over soon, and you will be able to live the kind of life you were meant to live."

"The kind of life I was meant to live," she mused. "What kind of life is that, really, I wonder?"

"Oh, there'll be castles and balls, and beautiful clothes. Kings and queens and dukes and counts to meet . . ."

"I don't know if I would be very happy in a castle or meeting a count . . ." Her eyes were thoughtful, her tone filled with something close to doubt.

He wanted at that moment to say the thing he really felt: *Stay married to me, Angelique, let me show you the world. Let me try to make you happy.* But instead, he released her shoulders and stepped back from her. "Well, who can judge the future? You might find you enjoy it immensely. At least, I hope so," he lied.

"Thank you, Dev," she said. Then before he could say anything else she stood on tiptoe and kissed him. Leaving him in frozen silence, she turned and went inside and closed the door behind her.

He stood and looked at her door for one stunned moment, the feel of her soft lips still warm on his.

"This is not going to work," he muttered hopelessly. "I'm not going to be able to live in the same house with her. It's too much to ask of any man."

He turned back and walked determinedly toward Cap's cabin. But when he arrived, he could not knock. Cap depended on him. How foolish it would look if he went in and told him he was afraid. Afraid of a tiny wisp of a girl whose head came no higher than his shoulder. How could he tell Cap that he would go out of his mind living in the same house with her? No, he couldn't. He lowered his hand and turned away.

For the next two days, Dev drove himself and his men,

who looked at him with surprise. Dev had always been easy to ship under—considerate of his men, and not one to push them unless it was an emergency. Now he seemed driven. He stayed away from Cap and Angelique as much as he could, trying to sort out some kind of plan in his mind to handle the days and nights when they were home. It would be in a short while now, and for the first time in his life, he was dreading the sight of the familiar coastline.

Cap and Angelique stood at the rail. They had come to join Dev when the shoreline was sighted, but to Angelique's dismay, he had suddenly found several jobs that called for his undivided attention and had left them abruptly.

Cap stood beside her now and pointed out the white house against the side of the hill.

She was thrilled with her first sight of a town of any size and even more curious now about the home Dev and Cap lived in.

No matter what other excuses Dev had had since the wedding, there was no excuse he could use not to accompany Cap and Angelique home. They walked together, the men shortening their steps to match Angelique's. They were stopped often, and Dev quietly introduced his wife to friends. His hand was shaken, and his back patted until he was gritting his teeth with the effort to keep smiling.

Angelique could sense his tension. The only thing she could conceive to be the cause was that he had, indeed, been forced into the marriage and regretted it. She promised herself to tell him at the first opportunity that he was free, that he need not be tied to her if he didn't want to be.

They walked up the hill and stopped in front of the white picket fence that bordered the house.

Dev was so accustomed to the comfortable beauty of his home, he did not realize how it would look to Angelique. On either side of the stone walk that led to the door, flowers bloomed in profusion. Angelique stood still and gazed quietly at the loveliness of the white house sitting among the flowers.

"Oh, Dev," she whispered, "how lucky you are to have lived in a place like this. I've never been in a house before."

Cap reached out and unlatched the gate and let it swing inward. Still, Angelique did not move, but stood gazing at the picture before her. Then the door opened and Mattie came out. Her smile of welcome changed to one of question as she looked closely at the newcomer who accompanied Dev and Cap.

Dev leaned down and said softly, "Come, let me introduce you to my favorite lady."

Angelique reached out and slipped her hand in his as they walked toward Mattie.

"Mattie, love," Dev said, "I want you to meet Angelique Montalban Carlisle. My wife."

Chapter 9

It was the first time in his life that Dev saw Mattie struck completely speechless.

"Angelique, this is Mattie."

Angelique held out her hand and smiled warmly. "Hello, Mattie. I'm so pleased to meet you. Dev has told me so much about you, I feel I know you already."

Mattie finally found her voice. "You are Dev's wife?" she repeated, as if she were not sure she had heard him right. Now, both Dev and Cap laughed. Mattie took Angelique's hand in hers and looked into the wide violet eyes. Slowly a smile appeared on her face and her eyes recaptured their old twinkle. "Welcome home, Mrs. Devon Carlisle," she said. Then she turned to Cap and Dev. "And what do you mean, keeping this poor child standing outside when she must be tired and hungry? Shame on you, Dev! Is that the best I've taught you? Come, child, let me get you a hot bath and a good supper. Then we can talk."

She put her arm around Angelique's shoulder, and the two women walked into the house, leaving the men watching after them in surprise. Dev had never seen this kind of reaction from Mattie toward any girl he'd ever brought around. They exchanged glances, then Dev shrugged and they walked into the house.

Supper was a pleasant affair. Mattie had received help from Angelique and was surprised at the training she'd had under the care of the sisters. They chatted together, and Mattie's quick mind put together some of the pieces of the puzzle.

It was late, but the four of them sat talking for some time after the meal was over. It was beginning to get rather uncomfortable for Angelique, who did not know what the sleeping arrangements were to be; and for Dev who really did not know how to bring up the subject in Mattie's presence.

Cap, with a paternal smile, put an end to all the problems. "Mattie, why don't you show Angelique to the guest room? I'm sure she's tired and would like to get some sleep."

Now, for the second time in the past few hours, Mattie's eyes registered uncomprehending surprise as they moved from Cap to Angelique, who blushed furiously, and then to Dev, who studiously ignored them.

She rose slowly to her feet and finally answered. "Come, child, I'll show you the the . . . guest room."

Angelique followed her silently. When they were gone, Dev grinned at Cap. "Mattie will never forgive you for this, Cap."

Cap laughed in reply. "Why don't you go get some sleep, too, boy? And I suggest you do so before Mattie gets back down here."

Mattie helped Angelique prepare for bed. She gave her one of her own nightgowns, then took down her hair and brushed it. She stood behind her as she brushed and spoke gently.

"You've lovely hair, child, such an unusual color."

"Yes, it is a strange color. It's always been so."

"You've not known Dev very long, have you?"

"No."

"Is he good to you?"

"Oh, both Cap and Dev have been very kind."

"Kind, is it?" Mattie said softly. "Well, you'd best get in bed. I'm sure you're tired. Good night."

"Good night, Mattie." When Mattie left, closing the door behind her, Angelique snuggled down under the covers. Being in such a comfortable home was a completely new experience, and she wondered if all homes were filled with the love and comfort that this one seemed to be.

"Nothing," she thought as sleep overtook her, "could do any harm here."

Mattie came down the stairs. Her eyes fastened on Cap immediately, and her curiosity could not be concealed by the firm way she approached him.

"All right, Cap. Out with the story."

"Story, Mattie? What story?"

"Don't 'what story' me, Cap Cortland. You aren't moving out of this room until I know all about that pretty child upstairs. And this marriage that isn't a marriage."

"Sit down, Mattie. I'll tell you everything that's happened."

She sat down and did not take her eyes from him as he began to speak.

He told her about Angelique's parents and how Angelique came to be left in his charge. Her eyes filled with sympathetic tears. He was delighted, for he had every intention of employing Mattie's well-placed sympathy and her love for Dev in the near future. He went on with the story of how the pirates had overrun the island, and the death of Maria. He told her of the condition they had found Angelique in and how only Dev's care and constant attention had brought her out of it.

She smiled in pride at Dev. "Dev could always charm the birds from the trees."

"Well, that's the whole story, Mattie."

"The whole story? Not by a lot, it isn't. What about this marriage?"

"Oh, that!"

"'Oh, that,' he says, like it's nothing at all. If those two love each other and are married, why are they sleeping apart?"

"It's not like it seems, Mattie." Cap began again. Then he told her how Don Esteban's men were on their trail, and to keep Angelique from being taken from them legally, he had suggested a marriage temporarily between the two."

"Oh," Mattie said softly. "Poor Dev. But, Cap, he seems so, so . . . different. I think . . ." she began, then her eyes met Cap's and for the first time she noticed the deep, amused twinkle in his. "Why," she laughed, "you old matchmaker! And I thought I was bad."

Cap chuckled, then his face became serious again. "Mattie, I know Dev like I know my own ship. He's in love with her, but he's afraid. If you had seen the condition she was in, you would understand his feelings. He's afraid he'll push her over the edge again, or worse. I think he's afraid it might look to her as though he's taking advantage of the situation to get himself a wealthy wife."

"Dev's not that kind of boy!" she said defensively.

"We know that, Mattie, and I believe Angelique does, too. It's Dev who doesn't seem to realize it."

"Well, why don't you tell him so?"

"Now, Mattie, we both know Dev better than that. He's got to come to these things on his own. You know he won't take kindly to anyone interferring in his private affair. Of course . . ." he began, then paused. "Of course, if we didn't let him know we were interferring, it might be different."

"We," she said, but her eyes mirrored the gleam she saw in Cap's.

"I can't do it alone, Mattie. But those two belong together. I thought maybe you'd have a few ideas."

"Cap, you surprise me. You're really very sly."

They laughed together and Mattie leaned forward and put her hand on Cap's arm. "What do you want me to do?"

"I leave that in your very capable hands, Mattie. You've certainly had more experience along those lines than I have."

"Well, you just see that you stay in port a little longer than usual this time."

"Don't worry. I'm going to make sure *Wayfarer* doesn't leave port for as long as necessary. I gave orders for her to be turned up and scraped today. That should make her unable to sail for at least a month. After that," he shrugged expressively, "who knows what other repairs she'll need?"

Mattie's eyes held a mischievous contemplative look. "Now all I need is an excuse to have a party," she said, almost to herself.

"Well, maybe I can supply that, too," Cap grinned.

"What?"

"After this voyage, McMichaels retired. I'm going to promote Dev to first mate. Is that excuse enough?"

"It certainly is," she said, and rose to her feet. "I'm going to bed, Cap, and I suggest you do the same." She laughed lightly, "We're going to need all our wits about us in the next few weeks."

He heard Mattie chuckle to herself as she went up the stairs, and for a moment he almost felt sorry for Dev. "You don't stand a chance, boy," he said quietly.

Angelique and Mattie were already in the kitchen when Cap came down in the morning to the smell of breakfast cooking and the sound of chatter and laughter. He sat down at the table. Before long, Dev joined them.

"Mornin', Cap."

"Mornin', son."

"We going to check on a new cargo this morning, Cap?"

"No, not this morning," Cap said. "I've had the *Wayfarer* turned up for scraping. She's in need of a lot of work if we want her seaworthy."

He pretended not to notice the stillness that had fallen over Dev's face, or the intent look in his eyes. "And how long is she going to be tied up?"

"'Bout a month, I'd say, maybe more. Depends on what condition we find her equipment in."

Dev's face was a mask of studied control. "But we just made a lot of repairs. I thought she was in fine shape."

"She ran a little sluggish for my taste. Best we finish all repairs while we can."

Dev had been hoping desperately that they would be sailing before he said or did something he knew he'd regret. Now Cap had just put an abrupt end to that idea. He was about to say something else when Mattie and Angelique came from the kitchen and put their plates in front of them.

"Eat hearty, Dev," Mattie said. "Since you won't be sailing for a while, I've got a lot of things around here

101

that need doin'."

Dev looked from Mattie to Cap. Except that they avoided his eyes, their faces were portraits of innocence. "How did you know we weren't sailing for a while, Mattie?"

"Cap told me last night before we went to bed."

"What is it you want me to do?" He was watching her closely.

"Well," she began, "since I've got so much to do today, you can start by taking Angelique into town for some supplies. Oh, and by the way, you might stop at Mrs. McCracken's and have her measure Angelique up for some dresses. The only thing this child has to wear is that black dress. Do you want our neighbors and friends to think you mistreat your wife?"

"Me? I . . . well, I've a lot of things to do, too, Mattie," he said weakly. "Besides, that's a woman's job."

"Dev," Mattie said gently, "that's a *husband's* job." She rose quickly before Dev could answer again and went into the kitchen for the coffee.

Dev could think of no reasonable excuse for not accompanying Angelique; and Cap was no help, for he told him very firmly there were no jobs for him on the *Wayfarer* at the moment. Feeling thoroughly trapped, Dev asked Angelique if she could be ready to leave right away.

"I'm ready right now," she smiled.

He rose slowly from his chair and with one last hard glance at Cap and some truly wicked thoughts about Mattie, he left with Angelique.

They started down the hill. Dev walked in silence, his mind searching for possible ways to find something to occupy his days for the next few weeks. He didn't realize that his thoughts had fueled his stride until Angelique gasped breathlessly, "Dev, I can't keep up with you if you continue to walk this fast."

"Oh, I'm sorry, Angelique." He slowed his steps to match hers. They walked along slowly for a few more minutes before she spoke again.

"Dev?"

"Um-hum?"

"Are you angry with me?"

He stopped short and looked down at her in surprise. "Angry? With you? Why should I be angry with *you?*"

"I . . . I thought maybe you had changed your mind. I wouldn't want you to be forced . . ."

Now he scowled and, more sharply than he meant to, said, "I don't get forced to do anything I don't want to do, Angelique. What gave you the idea I was being forced into something?"

Her voice dropped to a whisper. "You . . ." she gulped, "you just seemed so cold and angry. I thought it was at me."

She was trembling with fear and on the verge of crying. "I'm sorry, Angelique. It's not you I'm angry at, it's just . . . well, sometimes things don't seem to work out the way you plan them."

"I don't understand what you're talking about."

"I know." He laughed shortly, then took her arm and began to guide her down the other side of the hill toward town. "Believe me, Angelique, I can't tell you right now exactly why I was angry. I'm sorry if it distressed you. Forgive me."

He began to point out and name all the places they passed. Several times, they stopped at shops to pick up items from Mattie's list and chat with shopkeepers.

Angelique was beginning to relax when they neared the residence of the dressmaker.

"I agree with Mattie. You should certainly wear some other color than black," Dev said as he reached out toward the door of the shop. Before he could touch the knob, the door was opened from inside and they were looking into the shocked face of Polly Dillon.

"Dev!"

Angelique looked from Polly to Dev and knew immediately that there was a current between these two. At the moment, she did not, in her own innocence, know what it was. But Polly was about to enlighten her.

Chapter 10

Polly smiled warmly at Dev, but the smile for Angelique stopped at her lips. She had heard the rumor that Captain Cortland had brought a woman home with them, and she had been as curious as every other person in town. Someone had told her that the woman was Dev's wife, but she refused to believe this.

"Good morning, Dev. Won't you introduce me to your . . . friend?"

Angelique felt the tug of another emotion she had not felt before. She was suddenly finding herself unreasonably angry with a complete stranger, and, worse yet, she felt another, stronger emotion she could not define. She did not recognize the swift pang of jealousy for what it was. It was a new and alien experience for her, but she unthinkingly responded to it in the way of all people since the beginning of time. She linked her arm through Dev's and smiled at the girl in the doorway. "Good morning. I'm Angelique Carlisle, Dev's wife."

Polly could not stifle her gasp. Her face turned pale. Angelique could feel the tension in Dev's arm as Polly's eyes turned to his.

"You didn't tell me you planned to marry so soon, Dev," she said coolly.

Dev was not sure what to do or say. But he found that he thoroughly enjoyed the way Angelique clung to his arm and had stated the fact firmly, "as though" he thought, "as though she enjoyed the idea of being my wife."

"Polly," Dev began, "I really haven't had time to tell anyone anything. We've only just got home."

Polly's eyes were taking in Angelique, not missing anything. "She looks like a child playing at being a nun," she said icily, as though Angelique were not present. "Really, Dev, this young innocent should be back in her convent."

Dev looked at Angelique, at the black fury that rose up in her eyes. He could feel it in the trembling of her body. He knew he had to do something before Angelique exploded. He wanted to laugh and pull Angelique into his arms, for he knew, if she did not, that she was violently jealous of Polly. He also knew that jealousy did not come without affection. He slipped his arm about Angelique's waist and pulled her against him.

"Looks are sometimes deceiving, Polly," he said softly, his eyes holding hers and warning her to silence.

Polly looked, for one quick moment, as if she had been struck.

Dev turned to Angelique and pressed a swift kiss on the top of her head, keeping her angry body tight against his. "Come, darling, we've got to get you measured up for some new clothes, or Mattie will be angry with both of us. Would you excuse us, Polly? You know how Mattie is if her orders aren't carried out exactly."

Polly stepped aside, and, with a last angry glance at Angelique, she walked away.

Angelique was sputtering. "How dare she!" she choked. "That . . . that . . ." She could not go on. Her fury combined with her innocence left her almost wordless.

"Cat, I believe, is the word."

"I wouldn't insult a cat," she stormed.

Dev's heart bounded with delight as he urged Angelique inside the store and calmed her as best he could, but she was still barely under control when the dressmaker came out to help them.

"Good morning, Dev," she smiled, her friendly eyes moved to Angelique. "And this is your new bride we've heard so much about. Welcome to Bedloe."

"Angelique," Dev smiled, "this is Mrs. McCracken."

"Good morning," Angelique said, her voice still trembling from this new emotion.

"We've come to get Angelique some clothes made. I'm afraid she only has what you see right now, so she'll need everything."

"Very well. Will you come with me?"

Angelique nodded. Dev looked at Mrs. McCracken. "You're to spare no expense. I want her to have everything she needs. Oh, and make her a party gown also." He turned to Angelique. "I'll do the rest of Mattie's errands and come back and pick you up in about an hour."

Angelique smiled a weak smile and watched him leave the room. He would have been delighted if he had known her thoughts at the time.

Mrs. McCracken took her into a back room and briskly asked her to remove her dress. She did so, and stood patiently while she was measured and re-measured.

"You have a lovely figure, child. Although," she added as she cast her eye over Angelique, "no one could really call you a child with that body. The black dress you wore was quite deceiving."

"It's the only dress I have," Angelique said softly, but

her mind's eye was remembering the pale green dress that the girl, Polly, was wearing. "It was no wonder Dev looked at her. She was very pretty and the dress had made her look so . . . so very womanly," she thought.

Mrs. McCracken put her finger against her cheek and contemplated Angelique. "I think," she said as her experienced eye took in Angelique's distressed expression, "that I may have something here. With a little alteration, you might be able to wear it today." She was rewarded by an excited flash of Angelique's smile.

"Oh, do you think? Really?"

"Let me go and see." She smiled at the girl's enthusiasm. "Dev has picked himself a lovely wife," she thought. Secretly she was glad it had not been Polly Dillon, for she knew Polly as very few others in the town did.

Angelique looked at herself in the long mirror after Mrs. McCracken had gone. At the convent, she had been told that it was vain to look at one's self, and so she had not done so. Now she looked critically, comparing herself to Polly. She was much smaller, her waist tiny, and her breasts were only half the size of Polly's. She thought of Dev, and the way he had looked at the girl in that first startled moment. "As though," she thought miserably, "as though, he knew what she looked like without her clothes." Why did she want Dev to look at her that way? It was something she could not comprehend. Tears formed in her eyes as she blindly reached for answers to questions she didn't even know.

Mrs. McCracken reappeared. Over her arm she carried the dress. Quickly ordering Angelique to lift her arms, she slipped it over her head and stepped around her to fasten the hooks.

Angelique looked into the mirror again and gasped in surprise. The dress was deep orchid, very simple, with a small white ruffled collar about her throat. The sleeves were long and fitted to her slender arms. It hugged the upper part of her body and accentuated her softly rounded curves. At her slender waist the dress flowed out in a full skirt that reached the top of her boots. The color accented the deep violet blue of her eyes and made them seem to glow.

"It . . . it's so beautiful," she whispered. "I've never seen anything so beautiful in my life!"

Mrs. McCracken laughed. "It's you that's beautiful, child. I think Dev will be very pleased with this."

"Do you really?" Angelique asked anxiously. "Do you really think he'll like me in this?"

"*Like* you!" Mrs. McCracken smiled, "I'm sure he loves you the way he looks at you. And why shouldn't he? You've not been married very long, and if he's only seen you in that black dress . . . well, he's got a most pleasant surprise when he returns."

"I hope he's pleased," Angelique said almost to herself. Mrs. McCracken watched Angelique in the mirror. "There's more to this than meets the eye," she thought. She had known Dev all his life, and had liked him. Even as a small boy, he had been considerate and polite. Now she wondered why his young bride was so worried about him liking her in a pretty dress. It was as though she were not yet married to him and wanted his admiration and approval. A million questions formed in her mind, and she was about to begin asking some when Dev's voice came from the front of the shop.

"Mrs. McCracken? Angelique? Where are you?"

Angelique opened her mouth to answer, but Mrs.

McCracken motioned her to keep silent. Then turned her around so that she faced the door. The surrounding mirrors reflected her image.

"We're back here, Dev. Come on back," Mrs. McCracken called.

Angelique stood in agonized suspense as she heard the sound of his approaching footsteps. Her violet eyes watched the doorway and she remained motionless, unable to breathe as he drew aside the curtains and his eyes fell on her.

He stood frozen, his hand still holding aside the drape. "Angelique," he breathed softly. "You're lovely." His eyes devoured her.

Mrs. McCracken slipped quietly from the room, unknown to either of the two young people who could, at that moment, see only each other.

Slowly, Dev walked to her and she lifted her questioning eyes to his. "Do you like it, Dev?"

She had no idea how desperately he wanted to take her into his arms. His whole body responded to the desire and try as he did, he could not resist reaching out to touch her. His hand gently touched the side of her face.

"You're so very beautiful, Angelique," he whispered. She did not move, but stood with her lips slightly parted and her eyes locked with his. The blue-gray of his eyes deepened until they were almost the color of slate. The warmth of his gaze left her speechless and her cheeks blushed in response. Slowly, his hand slipped to the nape of her neck and caressed her gently. Still, she could not break away from his eyes. Slowly, he began to pull her toward him. She heard him softly whisper, "Angel," as he bent and touched her lips with his.

It was like a bolt of lightning had suddenly struck him.

The shock of it flowed through his body. He dropped his hand quickly from her neck as though he had been burnt, and stepped away from her.

It happened so suddenly that she stood silently, her eyes half opened and her lips parted.

"Angelique, I'm . . . I'm sorry. I didn't mean to do that. It's just . . . you are so beautiful."

Angelique blinked as if she were coming out of a fog. Her body felt limp and weak. She hadn't wanted him to stop. She wanted again the strong feel of his arms and the hard pressure of his mouth against hers. She looked with surprise into his deep gray-blue eyes, then she uttered a small cry and quickly stepped around him and was past him before he could stop her.

Dev cursed silently to himself and stood alone, getting his wayward body under control.

When he came back out, Angelique and Mrs. Mc-Cracken were discussing fabrics and colors for her new dresses. Angelique refused to meet his eyes and kept a rapid flow of conversation with Mrs. McCracken while he waited in a miserable silence. She could not meet his eyes—he might see the unashamed longing in hers. She was absolutely sure she had never felt more miserable in her life.

When Angelique could think of no more questions, she said a reluctant good-bye to Mrs. McCracken, and she and Dev walked slowly and in painful silence all the way home.

Mattie was in the parlor. She smiled at the two of them and started to say something, then closed her mouth as Angelique moved past her and ran up the stairs. She turned to Dev and was surprised at the unhappy look on his face as he watched the stairway. She laughed to

111

herself, but gave no outward appearance of her delight as Dev walked slowly into the parlor and sat down dejectedly in a chair.

"Well," she thought happily. "I do believe my two lovelies have discovered each other." Then she said firmly, "Dev, what's the matter with Angelique?"

Dev rose from his chair, ignoring her question. "Where's Cap?"

"Down at the docks," she said to his broad back as he headed toward the door. "I said, what is the matter with Angelique?"

"How the . . . how should I know?" he snapped as he closed the door none too gently behind him.

She almost shouted from delight with the way things were beginning to go. Dev had never been cross with her in his whole life. It only proved how distraught he was. She knew exactly how he'd been upset.

Mattie made her way upstairs and stopped outside Angelique's door. She could hear the faint sound of her crying through the closed door. She opened the door and walked across the room and sat on the edge of the bed. She patted Angelique gently on the shoulder.

"There, there, child. Nothing can be so bad that you can't tell me. That's what family is for. Now, come along, sit up and wipe away those tears and tell me what is wrong."

Angelique sat up and wiped her tear-stained face. Then she began to sob out the whole story. Mattie's face darkened a little when Polly's name was mentioned, but she did not say anything until Angelique finished. "This poor innocent child," she thought, "should have had a mother or an older sister to explain her feelings to her. Then she would not feel so terribly."

112

"Oh, Mattie, what am I going to do? She's so pretty, and Dev . . . well, I know he hates being married to me when he wants her. How can I stand it, Mattie?"

"Angelique, look at me," Mattie said quietly.

She lifted her tear-filled eyes to Mattie.

"You said Dev kissed you?"

"Yes, Mattie, but it was just because the dress was so pretty that I reminded him of . . . of her."

"Angelique, Dev would not have kissed you if he didn't want to. If he had wanted to kiss Polly, he would have done that, too."

"Do you really think so, Mattie?"

"I know so. Angelique?"

"Yes, Mattie?"

"Are you in love with Dev?"

Slowly, Angelique nodded her head. "Mattie, what am I going to do? I've got him in a marriage he hates. I know he feels trapped. He was so angry all the way home that he wasn't free to go after . . . her."

Mattie took Angelique in her arms and hid her smile against her hair as she said softly, "Don't worry, child. Take my advice. Things have a way of working out the way you'd least expect them."

Chapter 11

Dev walked toward the dock in morose silence. He needed Cap's advice badly. He wanted to explain to him in case Angelique was really upset at his behavior. When he arrived at the dock, the *Wayfarer* was aswarm with workers. They were doing a complete overhaul on the ship. He was told that Cap was not around, but should be back soon.

Dev removed his shirt and threw himself into the most strenuous work he could find. When Cap returned, he spotted Dev immediately, for he was hanging alongside the ship in a rope chair scraping away intently on the hull of the *Wayfarer*.

"Dev," he called.

Dev turned his head and looked down at Cap with a broad grin on his sweat-covered face.

"Hello, Cap," he shouted. "I'll be right down." He grasped the rope above him and effortlessly drew himself up and climbed over the rail. Within a few minutes, he was down the gangplank at Cap's side. "Afternoon, Cap. She's beginnin' to look pretty good, isn't she?" Then his voice became quieter as he looked at Cap intently. "Why, I'll bet there's not another week's work to finish her up."

Cap glanced once in Dev's direction, then shifted his eyes back to the ship. His voice became strong and commanding. "I believe, Mr. Carlisle, that I'm captain of the *Wayfarer* and in charge of such decisions."

"Yes, Sir, but . . ."

"And I believe, Mr. Carlisle, I've cared for the welfare of the *Wayfarer* for more years then you've been living."

"Yes, Sir," Dev said quietly. "I guess you have, Sir."

"And," Cap continued, his eyes never leaving the ship, "since you're only her first mate, you still take your orders from me. At least," he smiled as he turned to look at Dev, "until you're her captain."

Dev stared at him in astonishment. "First mate!"

"That's right, son," Cap said. "I've been all morning seeing to your papers. When the *Wayfarer* sails again, she'll have a new first mate. McMichaels retired this trip, and I figure you've earned it, boy."

"Cap, you'll never regret it. I'll give her everything I've got. I'll be the hardest working first mate that the *Wayfarer* ever had."

"I didn't doubt that for a minute or you'd never have gotten the job. Quite a raise in pay, too, son. Why," Cap said nonchalantly, "you'd probably have enough money this trip to even settle down and start building a family."

"You trying to get rid of me, Cap?" Dev laughed.

"I ain't gettin any younger, boy. I'd kind of like to bounce a couple of grandchildren on my knee before I die."

"Cap, you'll live to be a hundred, and probably bounce my children's children on your knees."

"Not if you keep dilly-dallying around like you do. A new girl every port we hit. Can't you find what you're lookin' for, son?"

"Cap, I want to talk to you about that. There's something I think you should know. Maybe after I tell you, you'll be ready to put *Wayfarer* back on the water."

"What's so serious, Dev?"

"You . . . you think Angelique's father is still alive?"

"I'm certain of it. I believe he has been at work to gain the support of certain influential men before he finally faces Don Esteban and claims his fortune and his daughter."

Dev looked thoughtfully up at the ship for a few moments, then: "Angelique has never seen anything of life. If her father comes for her, he can offer her a world no ordinary man could touch," he said, as if to himself. "I guess she has a right to know all those things." He shook his head. "What I'm trying to say, Cap, is that Angelique never had anything to compare things with. She thinks life here is beautiful, but don't you think she needs to try the other life just to be sure of what she really wants?"

"You're in love with the girl, aren't you, son?" Cap asked gently.

"Yes, Cap, I am. I love her enough that I don't want to cheat her out of anything she could have."

Cap gave a little exasperated click of his tongue. "I never raised you to be stupid, Dev, but sometimes you try my patience, you really do. Just what do you think you'd be cheating her out of?"

"It's not simply her father's fortune. It's her place in the Spanish court. That is what she would lose—her position."

"What if she doesn't want it?"

"How could she ever be sure? How could *I* ever be sure? Don't you see? She has the right to choose for herself."

"Then why don't you show her the best of your world?" Cap asked. "Why don't you ask her really to be your wife and show her just what your world has

116

to offer?"

"What about the condition we found her in? I'd never want to see her that way again."

"Dev, I figure she was more hurt and upset by the death of her friend than anything that was done to her. She's got over that pretty well, thanks to you. She knows your strength, and you've become very important to her. What if . . ." he paused for a moment. "What if you had to choose between the life you have now, and a life in the royal court? Which would you take?"

Dev laughed again. "Now that's no choice, Cap. I'd not exchange what I have for the entire house of Hanover!"

"And maybe," Cap smiled, "just maybe Angelique feels the same way. Take your time. Win her over. Let her know how much you and all of us love her. Then when the time comes, she can make her choice. And if I know people, I believe she's wise enough to choose love over the coldness and petty jealousies that rule the Spanish court."

"What about her father? After all this time, don't you think he has some rights, too?"

"Of course. He has the right to know her, to love her. But she has the right to a life that makes her happy. She is not responsible for what exists between Don Esteban and her father. It is not right that she should continue to pay the price for it. Seventeen years of living out of contact with the rest of the world is enough. So find out if it is you she wants, and if it is, take her, fight for her, and keep her no matter what anyone else thinks or wants."

Dev stood watching the *Wayfarer* without really seeing it. His mind was searching inside himself for the truth. Cap did not interrupt his thoughts, but hoped he would make the right decision, not only for himself, but for Angelique as well. Finally, as though he had come to a decision, Dev straightened his shoulders and turned a steady-eyed, determined face toward Cap.

"Well, I guess it's time to go home for supper. I've got a lot of wasted time to make up for," he added with a grin.

Cap smiled and clapped him on the shoulder and they headed for home.

Angelique and Mattie were working in the kitchen preparing supper when they heard the front door close and the voices of Cap and Dev as they entered. One pair of footsteps could be heard going up the stairs. Mattie cast a surreptitious look at Angelique but her face was unreadable as she went about her work.

Dev came to the kitchen door. A small smile played on his lips and he folded his arms across his chest and leaned against the door frame.

"Good evening," he said quietly. "Something smells very good."

"Supper will be ready shortly," Mattie replied. But Dev's eyes were on Angelique, who was concentrating on readjusting all the dishes and flatware on the table as though the task was of the utmost importance.

It took Mattie only a few seconds to understand the current that flowed between them. She untied her apron and said, "Would you mind stirring the stew one more time, Angelique? I've just remembered something I have to do."

Before Angelique could protest, she moved past Dev and was gone from the kitchen. Quickly, Angelique picked up the spoon, and, turning her back to Dev, began the unnecessary stirring. She could feel his gaze. He reached around her and firmly took the spoon from her hand.

118

"Angelique, I have to talk to you."

"I ... I have to help Mattie get supper." She took a step away from him as if she could not bear to be so close to him. "What is it you have to say?"

"Well, first I'd like to apologize to you for this afternoon, Angelique. I acted like a bore and I'm really very sorry for it."

"Oh, that's all right, Dev," she said, struggling to make her tone light.

"No, it isn't all right. After supper, will you go for a walk with me along the beach? I'd like to explain everything to you. Please," he added very gently.

She looked up into his intent eyes and once again felt the magnetic pull. It was one step that separated the two and she trembled with the desire to take that step and feel the gentleness of his touch as she had that afternoon at the dressmaker's. But she didn't, for another more painful feeling intruded itself. He was, in all likelihood, going to tell her of his feelings for Polly. "I ... I don't know if I can," she stammered, her mind searching for some reason not to go. "Mattie will probably need me."

He stepped closer, and his nearness, the clean smell of him, and the strength of his large frame left her weak and trembling. She lifted her eyes to his and watched them darken with something she did not understand, but could feel like a live thing. Gently, he lifted her hands and held them. His eyes never left hers for a moment. "Is it too much to ask for a few moments of your time?"

"No, Dev. Of course, I'll go with you."

He smiled, "Well, then come and feed me, woman. I'm starved." He stepped away from her, and she would never knew how empty his arms felt when he did. For the first time, he felt as if this was completely right. Why should he let the one thing he ever so desperately wanted go to another without a fight to hold her? He was determined from that moment to try his best to win her love.

Supper was a happy affair. Angelique's heart sang at the thought that at least she would be with Dev for the rest of the evening instead of watching his broad back as he left to go to the arms of Polly. Cap sent her off in delightful giggles as he and Mattie joined ranks against Dev and told her some of the stories of his boyhood. Dev grinned and pretended mild anger, but Angelique could see the brilliant glow of affection in his eyes as he watched the two.

"How I wish he would look at me like that," she thought.

Finally, dinner was finished and Angelique helped Mattie clean the table and wash the dishes. When the women came back into the parlor, Dev rose to his feet.

"If you and Cap don't mind, Mattie," he smiled, "I'm taking Angelique out for a walk. We'll be back soon. It's time she sees just how pretty it is along the beach."

He went to the coat hook behind the door and brought Angelique her shawl and draped it gently about her shoulders. Then, taking her elbow, he guided her toward the door and closed it gently behind them.

For a few minutes, neither Cap nor Mattie said anything. Then Mattie smiled at Cap. "I see Dev has finally made up his mind. It's about time. For a while there, I thought that boy was blind."

Chapter 12

They walked along the beach slowly and in silence. Angelique was so sure that he was going to tell her about himself and Polly, she was afraid of the moment he would start speaking.

The night was warm, but the cool breeze, or maybe her fear, made Angelique pull her shawl more tightly about her.

"It's a beautiful evening," Dev said.

"Yes. I've never seen such a huge golden moon before, and there must be billions of stars."

Again silence fell. Ahead of them was a grassy slope with a narrow path that ran down to another stretch of long white sandy beach on the other side. Dev reached out and took Angelique's hand to help her up the path, but when they reached the other side, he did not release it.

Angelique's nerves were stretched taut. If he was going to tell her this terrible news she wanted to hear it now and not prolong the agony any longer. It was more than she could bear. She stopped suddenly, and Dev looked down at her in surprise. Angelique stood with her back toward the moon. Her face was a dark shadow.

"What's wrong Angelique?"

"Dev, you said there was something important you had to tell me. Tell me, now, I . . . I need to know now."

"All right," he said determindedly. "It's something I

should have told you a long time ago. I've put it off because I was afraid. I didn't want anything I said or did to upset or hurt you."

Oh God, thought Angelique, *make it quick. Give me enough strength not to let him know how badly this hurts.*

"I want you to know," Dev continued, "that I've thought this over for a long, long time. I don't really know, even in my own mind, whether it's right or wrong. I just know I can't go on living so close to you the way we've been without letting you know how I feel."

Although he could not see her face, he was close enough to feel the tension in her body and the trembling in the hand he continued to hold.

"I love you, Angelique. I've loved you and wanted you almost from the beginning. I want you to be my wife, really be my wife. I'll do everything in my power to make you happy, to make you forget the past. We could be happy here, Angelique. There's . . ."

He continued to talk, but all Angelique could hear above the thundering of her heart were the words, "I love you. I've always loved you." Hot tears of relief fell and she became dizzy with the brilliant burst of happiness that crowded every other thought from her. Her body began to tremble now with the urgent need to feel the strength of his arms about her, to be held close to him and feel the security and peace she had longed for. Suddenly, she realized that Dev had stopped talking and was looking at her in misery and alarm.

"Angelique," he pleaded, "don't cry. I'm sorry if my words were so strong for your ears! I—I should not have . . ."

She lifted her hand and stopped his words with her fingers on his lips. "Say them again, Dev," she whispered. "Say, 'I love you.'"

For a moment he was silent. Then slowly he took her shoulders and turned her so that the bright moonlight fell on her face. Tears were on her cheeks, but her eyes were aglow and she had a smile on her lips. He gave a low laugh and pulled her toward him. "I love you, Angelique. I think I've loved you since that day at the convent when I first saw your lovely face."

"Oh, it's so hard to believe this is really true," she whispered. "Dev, when you asked me to go with you tonight, that you had something to tell me . . . well, I thought . . . I thought you had seen how foolishly I fell in love with you and you were going to tell me that it could not be, that you loved someone else and I must not think of you that way."

"Someone *else?*"

"Polly," she answered.

"Polly!" he said in amazement. "Now, whatever gave you an idea like that?"

"Today at the dressmaker's, when you left me so quickly, I thought you were going after her. I thought . . . well, I thought . . ."

With one hand he tipped up her chin so he could see her eyes.

"We've been working at cross purposes for too long. I think it's about time I convinced you that I love you, and only you."

His lips sought her willing mouth in a gentle kiss that tipped her world and sent it spinning. When her lips parted under his Dev felt the shattering impact of her innocent love, and lost control. This tiny little wisp of a woman had done to him what no other woman had ever done before. She had reached into his heart and found a quiet, lonely place that had been empty, and now filled it to overflowing. His arm tightened about her and the hand that held her chin slipped to the back of her head and held her firmly against him.

He thought he wanted to drown in her. The sweetness of her body sent a burst of flaming desire through him that consumed him and he knew he would never give her up. He was lost to everything but the feel of her soft warm body in his arms. He felt her arms creep about his neck as she clung to him and held herself tightly against him.

He lifted his lips from hers. For one moment, he held her tightly, then, slipping his hands to her shoulders, he moved her a little away from him so he could see her face clearly. It was bathed in the silver moonlight, her eyes were half closed, and her lips parted in breathless anticipation.

She reached up and put both hands to his face, pulling him toward her. A soft murmur escaped from her as though she could not bear for them to be even this far apart.

"Angel . . . Angel," he said softly. "Will you be my wife and let me love you, for I need you so very desperately."

"Dev," she whispered, "you are what I have waited for all my life, the one God intended me to find. From the depths of my soul, Dev, I love you."

He turned his lips against the palm that rested on his cheek and kissed it, then slowly he pulled her to him again, his eyes holding hers. His mouth found hers again and this time he did not try to control the warm magic of her that surrounded him.

Angelique clung to him, for she suddenly felt as if all her bones had melted. Her world consisted now of nothing but the strength of the arms that held her and the lips that took away her breath and her heart.

He wanted to possess her, to possess her now. But deep within himself, he knew that he wouldn't take her now. What he felt for Angel kept him from pulling her down beside him on the sand and removing the offending dress that stood between his body and hers. But he knew he'd best do something soon, for his body refused to respond to his logic as it burned with the desire to join with hers.

As if by agreement, they moved a step away from each other—Angelique, because she was frightened of the unknown; and Dev, because he wanted to gain some control over his wayward body. Dev almost laughed to himself. With any other woman there would have been no hesitation, no second thought. What had this child-woman done to him? With her gentleness and her sweet purity, she controlled the raging fire that burned in him.

"Dev, may I ask you one favor?"

"You could ask for the moon, Angel, and I'd do my best to get it for you."

"I . . . I would like to be married to you again."

He looked at her, surprised. "I don't understand, Angel. We're as tightly married as we can be."

"I would like to be married by a priest if you do not object. If you do not want to, I will understand," she said hesitantly.

He chuckled as he put his arms about her and kissed her gently on the top of her head. He held her to him and gently rubbed his cheek against her silken hair.

"Angel, if a priest can make you happy, then a priest it shall be. Why don't we make it a proper wedding and have a big celebration? That would make Mattie happy."

"Dev," she said, delighted at the thought, "it would be

my first party. That is such a wonderful idea."

Dev's face became serious. She had had nothing in her life of fun and gaiety. He felt again the sharp nudge of conscience that these things could be an every-day part of her life with her father, much more than Dev could ever offer her. She slid her hand in his, and he pushed aside every thought of giving her up. She was his, and she was going to stay his no matter what happened. He would face the problem of her father when it arose. "I think we'd better go back and tell Mattie and Cap." He laughed. "Where Mattie is going to find a priest is beyond me. But to get us married to suit you, she'll accomplish it."

He put his arm around her shoulders, and she lay her head against him. They slowly made their way home, stopping now and then to share a whispering touch of lips.

When they reached the door, Dev stopped and looked down at Angel's questioning face. She saw the wicked glitter in his eyes and her lips curled in a responding smile. "What are you thinking? Having some fun with them?"

He nodded. "When we go in, act as if there is nothing out of the ordinary that has happened. Mattie and Cap will be beside themselves with curiosity."

She giggled, then nodded. When they both had straightened their faces, Dev opened the door and they walked inside.

No matter how they tried to control themselves, both Mattie and Cap looked at them with expectant faces. With great effort on her part, Angelique kept her face blank and unreadable. She was fascinated by the performance Dev put on as he leisurely strolled across the room and dropped down in a chair and stretched his

126

long legs out in front of him.

"Mattie, love," he said, "is there anymore of that pie left over from supper? I'm starved."

Mattie's mouth fell open. "Pie?" she said at last.

"Pie," he answered.

Slowly, their little prank came to Mattie. She rose from her chair and advanced toward Dev. Step by deliberate step, she walked toward him.

Dev gave a laugh and leapt from the chair before Mattie could pounce on him. He moved quickly behind Angelique, and with the thread of deep laughter in his voice he said, "Now, now, Mattie. You needn't get violent. All I did was ask for another piece of pie."

Angelique was laughing uncontrollably, and Dev gave her shoulders a slight squeeze.

Mattie waggled her finger at Dev. "You young scalawag! Don't you play your tricks on me. I want to know. Do I have a daughter-in-law or don't I?"

"No, you don't. At least not yet!" Dev replied.

Mattie looked from Angelique's face to Dev's in complete surprise. "I don't?"

"Not until you find a priest."

"A priest?" Mattie said. "A Roman priest?"

"A Roman priest," he nodded.

"But this is England! Where am I going to find a Roman priest in England?"

"Angel wants to be married by a Catholic priest, and if that's all it takes to make her happy, then she'll have it."

"I'll find a Roman," Mattie said with determination. Then she smiled and held out her arms to Angelique, who stepped to her. She hugged Angelique close to her ample breasts. "I'm so happy for you, children," Mattie choked, then began to cry softly. Dev came to her side

127

and put his arms about her shoulders. Holding the edge of her apron, Mattie wiped her eyes and smiled up at Dev. "We'll have to plan a party," she said, her excitement bubbling to the surface. "A big celebration so that I can show the whole town what a beautiful bride my Dev has." She collected herself and turned to Angelique. "Well, come along, Angelique. We'll begin planning your wedding." She took hold of Angelique's arm and pulled her toward the kitchen while Dev and Cap regarded their departure.

"Congratulations, son. You have picked yourself a lovely bride."

Dev gave Cap's closed face a close scrutiny. "I'm not too sure yet that I've done any of the picking at all."

Cap's eyes twinkled and Dev's smiled in response. If Cap and Mattie did have anything to do with bringing Angel to him, he was grateful.

"Tell me," Cap began as he sat back down in his chair, "did you discuss Angelique's father, and what might happen if he comes for her?"

Dev sat slowly back down in the chair, the laughter gone from his face now, and his brows drawn together. "No. No, Cap, I didn't."

"Then what's going to happen if he does return?"

"Cap, I'm going to take your advice. I'm going to try to show Angel the best of my world. If her father does return . . . well, he can share her love, but he can't have her, for I'll do everything in my power to keep her. He'll have to fight the biggest battle of his life if he decides to try to take her away from me."

"Well, there is always the possibility that her father will never return. But if he does, friend or no friend, he will have to face a united front here. Neither Mattie nor I

128

would let Angelique go without a fight."

"You know him well, Cap. Just what do you think he might do?"

"Dev, it's been almost eighteen years since I've seen Miguel. At the time I knew him best, I would say that he would be happy for Angelique, and would probably want to stay here and enjoy both a daughter and a son. But that was the man I knew years ago. How many things could have happened to him since then, how he could have changed into another person, I do not know at all."

They were interrupted when Mattie and Angelique came into the room. Angel came to Dev's side. "My goodness, Dev, I think Mattie plans on inviting every one in town to the party."

"Most certainly do. Everyone in this town is our friend. Dev, tomorrow, you can take us to town, we've a lot of things to do. In the meantime," she smiled, "I think it's time we all get some sleep. Come along, Angel. I'll help you with your hair."

Angel and Mattie started upstairs. Suddenly, Angel stopped and turned to look down at Dev. She turned and came back down to him. "I love you, Dev," she whispered.

Then she was gone from his side, up the steps before he could say a word. Dev stood still for a moment, then said quietly, "Good night, Cap." He moved up the stairs as though he had already forgotten Cap was there.

Cap watched him go with a faint smile turning up the corners of his lips. He went to his favorite chair and sat down. He reached for his pipe and slowly filled it from the jar of aromatic tobacco that sat on the table next to his chair. His mind drifted back to Dev's mother and the happiness they had shared during the short life she lived.

He knew only too well the way Dev felt now. To give love, and to have love given freely and happily in return was probably the best thing that could happen to anyone.

Life in this small house had sometimes been very lonely for him. It was probably why he did not retire, but sailed on each trip of the *Wayfarer*. Maybe, he thought pleasantly, if Angelique and Dev had children he would give over the captaincy to Dev and retire to the enjoyment of new young life in his home.

He knew that Dev was an intelligent, strong young man and would not be sailing the seas for long. Not with his heart here at home. But he knew that Dev had the strength and ambition to build a shipping empire here. Something to pass down to his sons and the generations that followed them.

Cap was grateful at that moment for the working of the hand of fate that had led him to Dev's mother in her deepest hour of despair. He remembered clearly the first time he had seen Dev crouched behind the large crates that were being unloaded from his ship. From his vantage point he could look directly down on the young boy who was intently watching the unloading. Cap couldn't understand his motionless, expectant watching. Then his question was answered as a crate slipped from the hands of the men carrying it and crashed to the deck. The side of the crate cracked, and several oranges tumbled out and rolled across the dock.

Quick as a wink the boy dashed out and snatched up several oranges, shoving them inside his shirt. If he hadn't been greedy, and been content with the three he already had, he would have gotten completely away. But in the process of trying for the fourth, the heavy hand of one of the sailors fell on him and he was dragged, fighting every inch of the way, and deposited in front of Cap, who was doing his best to contain his amusement at the boy's anger.

Dev planted his feet firmly on the deck and glared, unafraid, up at the captain.

"What's your name, boy?"

The stubborn chin tilted even higher, but the boy remained silent.

"How old are you?"

"Eight."

"You're big for your age. What are you doing hanging around the docks stealing at your age? Where are your parents? They should be keeping a closer eye on you."

Again, the glittering sparkle of anger appeared in the bright blue eyes.

"I wasn't stealing."

"What do you call what you were doing?"

Cap actually laughed as the boy answered belligerently, "Salvaging, Sir."

Cap looked down into the blue eyes which returned his stare without fear, and with a deep glow of pride.

"Well . . . salvaging, were you? Just how do you go about claiming salvage on a cargo that's not lost?"

"The law says, Sir, anything that's lost from its original crating and shipping can be considered salvage. I've a right to it."

Now Cap was really surprised, that an eight year old knew the laws of salvage.

"Mr. Halt," Cap called.

"Yes, Sir."

"Take over, I'll only be gone a short while."

"Yes, Sir."

"Come along, boy," Cap said to Dev.

"Wh . . . where are we going?"

"We're taking you home to your parents. We'll see what they have to say about your . . . salvaging."

Now Dev's face turned white and he was as close to tears as he could get, yet he controlled his trembling lips and would not let Cap see them.

"There's only my mother, Sir. She's sick. You don't have to go with me, Sir. This is the first time I've ever done anything like this . . ." Dev's voice cracked with panic. "I swear, Sir, I'll never come near your ship again. Honest Captain, let me go, I'll never do it again."

Despite Dev's continual protests, Cap literally dragged him to his home. The house Dev led him to was small, containing, Cap thought, at the most four rooms. It was in extremely bad shape, a hovel in one of the shabbiest parts of town. Cap realized that although the boy was proud and unafraid, this type of living could ruin him.

Dev's eyes lifted to him and the proud defiant look returned.

"This is where I live, Sir. If you'd like to come in you could meet my mother."

"Then let's go in."

"Captain, Sir?"

"Yes?"

"Would you . . . I mean . . . could you not tell my mother I was stealing, Sir? She would be ashamed of me."

The boy's eyes were pleading with him and Cap again wondered at the boy who would steal, then worry whether or not his mother would be ashamed of him.

Dev led the way and they stepped inside the door. A voice called from the kitchen. "Dev? Child is that you?"

"Yes, Ma'm," Dev called. He removed his hat from his

tousled head and stood at attention. It was so very obvious that he had been well raised that Cap's curiosity was again aroused. He waited expectantly to meet the boy's mother. "Dev you . . . Oh," she said, startled that Dev was not alone.

Emma St. Joseph had at one time been a very beautiful woman. Cap could see at first glance the lines of worry and strain on her face. He knew also that she must have been a gentle-born woman. She was slender, almost thin. Cap knew immediately that Dev must have been stealing the fruit for her. She had the weary look of someone who had been ill for a long time, yet refused to submit to it. He glanced down at the boy and read again the silent look of pleading on his face.

"Good afternoon, Ma'm. Your boy here says you would be happy to receive some oranges we are trying to dispose of. They've broken from their crates and are impossible to sell. We have to find a way to get rid of them before they rot on the docks."

A quick glance at Dev told the Captain just how grateful the boy was.

When Cap returned that day to his ship he took with him a bright-eyed, expectant Dev who had been promised the chance to board the *Wayfarer* and look about. Cap sent not only a crate of the oranges, but several packages of food he had stopped to buy.

Cap was a man of thirty-six, and had been given his command of the *Wayfarer* only a few years before. He had traveled to all corners of the world, and had never found it difficult to attract many of the fairer sex. That was probably why he was a little surprised at the magnetic drawing he felt toward Emma. There was no doubt that she was pretty, but he had seen many who were prettier.

133

He put the search for reasons aside as he admitted to himself that something about Emma reached out to a spot in him no other had ever touched.

The next four months he spent in port were mostly spent in Emma's house. He watched the gentle and loving way she treated Dev and was rewarded by the unrestrained and complete love Dev felt for her. He knew without doubt, that he too was falling deeply in love with her, but she seemed to be frightened of any relationship. It was just a few days before he was due to sail that he arranged to keep Dev busy aboard ship and went to see Emma. He was determined to discuss several things with her. One was the future of her son, and one was her future. He pushed open the rusty gate and walked up the broken walk to the door. He rapped and waited. He heard the bustle of movement inside. After a few minutes Emma opened the door. No matter how often he conjured up the memory of how she looked, each time he saw her she seemed to look lovelier. Her skin had a pearly translucent glow, but there were dark shadows under her eyes and he noticed not only how very thin she was, but the fact that her hands trembled nervously.

"Good afternoon, Robert," she smiled, but her eyes went beyond him, looking for her son. "Dev isn't with you?"

"No, Emma, I wanted to talk with you alone," he began, and again he saw the fleeting look of fear cross her face. "Mostly about Dev."

She seemed relieved. "Come in, Robert." She led him toward their nearly empty sitting room. "Can I make you some tea?"

"Yes, thank you," he replied. He sat on one of the two chairs in the room. Although Emma kept the house spotlessly clean, there was nothing in this room, and he guessed in the others, beyond the bare necessities. He thought of his own warm and quite comfortable home and knew at that moment he was going to ask her to share it with him. To have a wife as lovely as she, and a son as strong and good as Dev was becoming, seemed to him most important now.

She came back carrying the tray with the tea pot and two cups. He watched her closely. The quality in her was obvious. She handed him his cup, then sat back in her chair watching him expectantly.

"Robert, has Devon gotten himself into some kind of mischief?"

He laughed. "You know better than that, Emma. Dev's a good boy. He's going to grow into a fine young man, one you can be proud of."

She looked relieved, and a small smile appeared.

"I know I have you to thank for helping him. You'll never know how grateful I am, Robert. Dev worships you. All he seems to be able to talk of now is being captain of his own ship someday. You've given him a goal in life."

"What would you say Emma, to me taking Dev as cabin boy aboard the *Wayfarer?* He needs the company of men now and the crew of the *Wayfarer* are probably the best you can find on the sea."

He was surprised at her reaction. Her eyes filled with tears, and she rose quickly from her chair and turned her back to him, trying to control her tears. Her whole body quivered like a slender reed caught in a heavy storm. He went to her side and, gently turning her toward him, put both his arms about her and held her against him. She dissolved into heavy sobs, and he let her cry.

When she finally had herself under control he lifted

her chin and looked into her eyes. Very gently he kissed her tear-moistened lips.

"There's more to this than my offering Dev a berth on my ship," he said gently. "You have known for a long while how I feel about you, Emma. Let us have honesty between us. I want you to marry me and come to my home to live, you and Dev. I can make a good life for you and your son and . . . I do love you, Emma, very deeply."

"Yes, Robert. We must have honesty. Sit down, and let me tell you a story. If you still want me when I have finished, then I will be happy to marry you."

He sat back down in his chair and she sat opposite him, composing herself. Clasping both hands together in her lap to control the trembling she began to speak.

"I was born Emma St. Joseph. My family was very wealthy, and I was the only child. Everything was given to me, and much was expected in return. My family has a very proud heritage; yet I'm afraid I have not done much to carry on that tradition. I met Dev's father, Andrew Carlisle, when I was nineteen. I fell deeply in love with him.

"His family seemed well off. I had no idea they were destitute, and were looking for a wealthy bride to bring money to their family. When my family found out the truth they refused permission for us to marry. I believed," she said, her voice dropping to a pain-filled whisper, "I believed him when he said he loved me. My parents told him if we married they would disown me. Then I found I was pregnant. When he found out he . . . he simply disappeared. I hated my parents, more, I imagine for showing me the truth than any other reason. I ran away. Dev was born here. I used what money I could get by selling some jewelry I had brought with me."

"Emma, for God's sake, why shouldn't I want you because one man was foolish enough to let you go?"

"There's more, Robert."

"What more?"

She looked at him directly now, watching his eyes as she spoke the final words. "Something has happened to me. I imagine it is the emotional strain and the combination of Dev's birth. I have only a few years left to live. I have been worried about a place for Dev when I'm gone. My heart is slowly giving up the battle. Now that Dev's future is secure I will find the first peace I've known in ten years."

Robert was stricken at the pain in her words. "How long have you known this?"

"Since Dev was born. The doctors did not expect me to live through that. I . . . I really think I've done so only to see that Dev gets some kind of start in life. He is a good boy and he deserves a chance."

Robert went to her then. Bending down, he took her hands in his and drew her to her feet.

"Emma, come home with me. Be my wife. Let me take Dev as a son. I swear I shall see that he has the best I can offer. Let me try to give you something you deserve also, at least let me share this time with you."

"Robert, you need not have pity for me. God has given me a son and some time with him. I am grateful. I don't want you to sacrifice your life to me or to my problems."

"The only thing I am sorry for is that we did not find each other sooner, Emma. What I feel for you is love, not pity. Don't throw it away. Come with me. Come with me now."

Her eyes held his as though she were trying to read his

very soul. She saw the clear, honest gaze and she knew Robert was the first person in long years to reach out to her with gentle, sincere love.

"I will Robert, if you wish," she said softly.

Slowly, Robert drew her to him and kissed her, holding her in the protection of his strong arms. Emma relaxed against him and felt the safety he offered her and her son enclose her.

They were married the next day, much to Dev's delight. Not only to have his revered captain as a father, but to know that he would sail with him on their next voyage made him almost ecstatic with joy.

Emma and Dev moved into the home with a new housekeeper Robert had hired named Mattie.

The love that developed between Robert and Emma was a slow, gentle thing. More beautiful because they knew they had so little time together.

Each voyage made Dev happier, but made Robert worry more and more that one day they would come home and find Emma gone. Then, when Dev was twelve, the tragedy struck. Dev was prostrate with grief and if Mattie and Robert had not been there to support him he would have been lost. Dev and Robert were a consolation to each other for both of them knew and understood the love each of them had felt for Emma St. Joseph.

Now, Robert's eyes misted with tears at the beautiful and grief-filled memories. He sat back in his chair with a deep sigh and held a loving conversation with the woman he had loved so deeply for such a short time.

"Emma, I've done my best for the boy. You would be very proud of him." He gave a half laugh. "Emma, it was the one thing in his young life that always worried him.

Now, he's found a woman as gentle and sweet as you were. You would like her, Emma, I'm sure. She's a lovely child. Watch over them, Emma, as I will to the best of my ability. I hope we have grandchildren soon to fill this house again with the laughter and the happiness it knew when you were here." He leaned his head back against the chair and gave free rein to the beautiful memories.

Chapter 13

In the light of several candles, the dark robed figure bent over the desk. She wrote slowly, stopping now and then to read over what she had written. Finally, she signed her name on the bottom and lay down her quill. As she sat back in the huge chair to relax, the candles sent dark shadows across her face. Her black robe whispering in the quiet room, she rose slowly and went to the window. Pushing it open, she leaned her head against the cool stone of the window frame and looked out to sea. As far as she could see, it was calm. The bright moonlight cut a path across the water. There was only one ship, and it was rolling gently back and forth at anchor in the small harbor. The captain waited in his cabin patiently for the message she had lying on her desk.

It had been months since Dev had taken Angelique away from the convent. She would not have sent any message for fear of it being followed, but news she had just received that morning was of such importance that it was necessary to pass it on to them. After she had received the news, she prayed for an answer: Should she take a chance to send a message or not. As if in answer to her prayers, the ship now lying at anchor had arrived—a ship and captain she could trust.

She thought back over the past two days. The message that had come to her had been sent from a dear friend in Spain. It was a joy-filled message, for it told her that Don

Carlos DeVarga was dead, and even greater news had accompanied that. The charges against Miguel Montalban had been brought forward by his friends in the presence of a more merciful judge. Miguel had been absolved of the crime of heresy and all his property including that of his wife Anna, had been reinstated to him.

But that would not stop Don Esteban. "No," she said, half aloud. "No, it will not stop him. That man is of the devil and nothing short of Miguel and Angelique's death will stop him."

She sighed deeply and returned to the desk. There she folded the message and sealed it with black wax and the imprint of the ring she wore on the middle finger of her right hand. When Robert saw this, he would know not only that the message was from her, but that it was of the utmost importance.

She lifted the small bell that sat on the corner of her desk and rang it lightly. The door opened, and Sister Cecile came in on her always silent feet. "Yes, Mother?"

"Would you send a message down to the dock to ask Captain Ryan if he could come here to me for a short visit?"

"Yes, Mother."

She waited patiently, thinking of Captain Ryan, another protege of Captain Cortland. He was not much older than Dev, approximately thirty, and a very handsome man. Tall and slender, he had a thatch of thick red hair and a moustache to match. His eyes were always filled with laughter and a hunger of adventure. Yet, no matter how reckless he was, Captain Cortland trusted him, and she knew she could trust him also.

An hour later, there was a light rap on her door, and

Sister Cecile reappeared.

"Captain Ryan is here, Reverend Mother."

"Thank you, Sister. Would you show him in, please?"
The door opened a few moments later, and Captain Ryan
came in. He stepped forward slowly, and she watched him
approach. The crystal green eyes never left hers as he
came to a stop in front of her desk.

"You wanted to see me?"

"Yes, Captain. Won't you please sit down?"

She noticed with a glimmer of amusement, that he was
not silent in defiance of her robes, but he was wary of her
request.

"I see you have not found it easy in your lifetime to
trust anyone, Captain," she said quickly.

He chuckled and his white teeth flashed in a quick
smile. "The last person I trusted, Sister, was my mother,
and she's been dead these twenty years. God rest her
soul."

"Maybe if I told you we have a mutual friend to whom
I have to send a message of great importance, you would
find the situation easier."

"A mutual friend?" Now he laughed aloud. "Us? I
doubt that. The kind of friends I have are certainly not
the same type you would have."

"Robert Cortland," she said softly.

"Robert Cortland! Captain Robert Cortland?"
She nodded.

"Captain of the *Wayfarer?*"
Again she nodded. "Robert and I, and his stepson,
Dev, have been friends for many years. Now can I
interest you in carrying a message to him?"

"For Robert Cortland, I'd walk the plank. And Dev—
why that son of a . . . I'm sorry, Sister. Dev and I haven't

shared a drink in years. I'd enjoy crossin' their bow again. Give me your message, Sister, and tell me whereabouts I can find them, and I'll guarantee they'll get it."

She picked the paper up from the desk and handed it to him, watching as he slid it inside his shirt.

"I wish you Godspeed and fair winds, Captain Ryan. The message you carry means a great deal to Captain Cortland. And even more to his son."

"Thank you, Sister. You can rest assured, I'll see to it's safe delivery."

"There is one more thing, Captain."

"Yes?"

"You may be followed by someone who intends Robert harm."

"Me? Followed? Not on your life, Sister. The *Sea Hawk* can outsail anything on the ocean. If I see a strange sail, she'll see the heels of the *Hawk*."

She smiled at his joyful arrogance.

"Good luck, Captain Ryan."

"Lady luck has been a close friend of mine for many years, Sister. We sleep well together." He stopped and became silent, realizing what he had said.

She laughed delightedly and wished the embarrassed captain farewell.

Andrew Ryan could still hear her laughter as he closed the door behind him. He left the convent and walked back to the harbor. As he stepped aboard the *Sea Hawk* he began to shout orders to his men, and soon the white sails unfurled and the *Hawk* eased from the harbor and headed toward the shores of England.

Andrew stood at the wheel. He enjoyed the feel of the wind at his back and the almost imperceptible lift of the ship as she left the quiet waters of the harbor and touched the mighty currents of the open sea.

His first mate came to stand at his side, but made no move to take the wheel or to say anything to interrupt his captain's deep concentration. "With the *Hawk*," he thought, "the captain was as in love as if she were a woman."

Once free of the harbor and under full sail, Andrew smiled. "Keep a close eye for another sail, Mr. Briggs. A day and a night watch. If there's any sign, I want to know immediately."

"Aye, Sir."

Briggs would never have questioned any request. He knew from many past experiences that Captain Ryan was the best and most dependable friend he would ever have.

They had been on their way for almost three days and Ryan was at the wheel with the late afternoon sun behind them when the lookout shouted. "Sail ho!"

"Where away?"

"Off the starboard bow, Sir."

Ryan snapped his fingers and Briggs handed him the telescope he carried. Putting it to his eye, he spotted the ship and cursed mildly under his breath.

"She's a Spanish galleon, Briggs. All sails on. She must want to catch up with us pretty quick." He turned around and Briggs saw, as he had seen so often before, the glint of the devil's laughter light Ryan's eyes.

"Show her the *Hawk*'s heels, Briggs. We'll see if she has enough speed to catch us on the open sea.

Andrew Ryan and his crew were phenomenal sailors who respected the *Hawk*'s abilities. When Briggs waited for orders, they were snapped precisely.

"Put up all sails, Briggs. I want everything on

including your shirt. There's no galleon on the water that can run down the *Hawk*."

Andy stood on the quarter deck, his strong hands holding the wheel, one eye on the horizon where the first tinge of evening clouds hovered. He guided the *Hawk* expertly while he cast an occasional look back over his shoulder, at the ship that followed, and up to the straining, creeking mast that held the wind-filled sails. The ship vibrated and quivered under the force of the wind, until some of the men were afraid the mast might crack.

Andrew could feel the strong flow of the currents underfoot, and guided the *Hawk* expertly with them. It was an ability he had always had, and was the difference between him and others that sailed the sea. It was as if he and the mighty ocean were one. He would have been quite pleased if he could have heard the captain of the ship that followed as he cursed furiously when his ship listed heavily in an'effort to keep his vessel from being swamped in the high waves. It was only the beginning of the captain's frustration as Andy and the *Hawk* continued to dance just out of reach ahead of them, with the distance between them slowly widening. He watched Andy's full white sails seem to capture every ounce of breeze, and knew without doubt he had met a man who was his superior on the sea. Andy seemed to sense every change of breeze and swung the *Hawk* so that not one breath of them was wasted.

A sudden shift of wind took the pursuing galleon on the starboard side, and flattened several sails, throwing her off the crest of the wind. For just a few moments she wallowed in a deep trough between two high waves. It was only a matter of minutes before the captain's swift orders

145

had her again on Andy's trail, but they were minutes that put considerably more distance between the two ships.

Andy was grateful for nightfall, for the galleon continued to dog his heels. Not close enough to overtake him, but close enough to keep him in sight. Andy was also grateful that the night was filled with rapidly skittering black clouds, that a storm was brewing near. It did not take him long to map out a course that would head them directly into it. The clouds blotted out the moon and made the night as black and concealing as he could hope for. He swung the *Hawk* off the course she was on, one he hoped the following galleon would retain, and headed into the wind-ruffled sea which heralded the beginnings of the storm.

The men watched for words to hoist down the sails before the wind could rip them to pieces, but Andy gave no sign until the *Hawk* was pitching deeply in the troughs and in danger of overturning. When the order was given sailors scrambled aloft and the sails were furled and tied firmly to the spars. The men smiled with relief, first at losing the galleon, and with the ease with which the *Hawk* righted herself and rode out the storm.

During the storm Andy changed their course several times, and when the first rays of sun came over the horizon the Spanish galleon was nowhere in sight. Andy smiled in satisfaction and held the wheel as gently and caressingly as he would a woman. He imagined he was as grateful to his ship for a good night's performance as he would have been to any woman.

Briggs approached, and Andy laughed when he reported that all was well with the *Hawk*.

"Break out the bottle, Briggs," he laughed. "The men deserve a drink for that little race. After that set a straight

146

course for England. We've a message to deliver to an old friend. I've a feeling he has a story to tell us that ought to be very interesting. Messages from nuns, chased by a Spanish galleon . . . Yes, Briggs, this sounds very, very interesting, indeed."

Don Esteban slammed his hand down on the desk. His face filled with fury as he was told that the *Sea Hawk* had escaped them.

"How could they have escaped you? We were right behind them? What did they do, sprout wings and fly?"

"I would say that the *Sea Hawk* was warned that she might be followed. What other reason could she have had to fly at the first sight of us? We had no time to get near enough to make the race a contest. No. She was watching for us."

"You astound me, Captain. Now, maybe you have the answer not only to where they are, but where they are going."

The captain of the *Dona Anna* had no liking for Don Esteban. He smiled grimly, angry with Don Esteban's insults.

"Perhaps, Don Esteban, just perhaps I might be able to do that."

For the first time since he had hired the service of Captain Ortega and the *Dona Anna*, Don Esteban controlled his temper and his tongue and looked at the captain with full attention. "You know where they might be going?"

"I've an idea."

"Well, where?"

"England."

Don Esteban gave a low guttural growl and moved from

147

behind the desk to pace the cabin slowly. "Captain, I also know their destination might be England," he said slowly and precisely. "I know, too, that the people I am seeking might be in England. What I do not know is *where* in England they might be. Can you enlighten me to their exact destination, Captain? If so, the news would be most welcome."

"Yes, Don Esteban, I think I can tell you exactly where the *Sea Hawk* is headed. Her port must be Bedloe. And I would stake my life that the people you are looking for are also there."

"Why do you believe this?"

"I know nothing of your Captain Cortland or any of the others you seek. But Captain Ryan I am familiar with. I know that in the past he sailed quite often to Bedloe."

"You have known this all along and never mentioned anything to me?"

"This is the first I've known that Captain Ryan was connected to your search."

"Then let us make as much speed as possible now," Don Esteban said.

The captain replied, "I have taken the liberty of setting the ship on the fastest course to Bedloe."

"Good, good." Don Esteban smiled and sat slowly back down in his chair. "I do hope you are right, Captain. I have waited a long time for this."

The captain was uneasy in the presence of the burning hatred which Don Esteban exuded, and he made a hasty retreat.

After the door to the cabin clicked shut, Don Esteban opened the drawer of his desk and withdrew a folded piece of paper from his desk. Slowly, he unfolded it and reread words he already knew by heart.

"DeVarga," he muttered. "You picked a very inopportune time to die, my friend. But it makes no difference. Now that I am this close to Miguel's daughter, and to Miguel himself, I shall not give up." He rose from the chair and walked to the window and looked out over the white-capped waves with unseeing eyes. "I will have him in my grasp soon and he shall pay and pay dearly for every moment that I have searched for him. If you have her, Captain Cortland, you too, will know the wrath of Don Esteban. She will belong to me, and through her, I will soon come face to face with her father. No one will stand in my way without being destroyed. Do you realize, Miguel, wherever you are, that you have brought death and destruction to all who have given you aid?"

They had traveled as fast as the galleon could move under full sail, but it was almost two weeks before they sighted the coast of England. Don Esteban gave the orders to drop anchor in a small, hidden cove. From there, a longboat was sent out to check the harbor at Bedloe, to see if either the *Wayfarer* or the *Sea Hawk* were docked. Don Esteban waited now impatiently for word to come, and finally it did: Both the *Wayfarer* and the *Sea Hawk* were anchored in the same harbor.

"Then I was right," he chuckled. "That nun did make the mistake of sending him a message. I knew if I waited long enough, she would be foolish enough to contact him."

He had gathered three or four men about him. "What do you want us to do now?" one of them questioned him.

"I want you to go into Bedloe, and, without being observed, find out all you can about Captain Cortland and his family. I want to know every move they make and every person to whom they speak. Is this understood?" They nodded, and in a few minutes, they were gone.

A feeling of euphoria hovered over the Cortland home since Dev and Angelique had announced the plans for their re-marriage. Mattie was in a dither over arrangements and plans. Both Angelique and Dev had got caught up in her whirlwind enthusiasm, and it was several nights after they had made their announcement that Dev at last had found an opportunity to be alone with Angelique again.

They strolled among the flowers in Mattie's back garden. The night was so quiet that they could hear clearly the whisper of the waves breaking against the sandy shore.

Angelique looked up at Dev. His eyes were lost in some private dream while she admired him—his manly frame towered over her. The top of her head came only to his shoulder. She regarded his eyes, so startling blue against his tan skin, and the thick unruly black hair that curled against his collar; the quick way he smiled at her—it turned her heart over within her and caused the warm rush of blood to her cheeks. Then, the sudden desire to be held in the hard circle of his arms, to feel his lips touch hers with gentleness and love.

Several small white benches had been strategically placed about the garden for sitting and contemplating its loveliness from different spots. Drawing her with him, Dev found the most secluded bench, under a tree in the furthest corner from the house. She sighed contentedly and lay her head against his chest. She closed her eyes and allowed herself the luxury of feeling the strength of his arm about her and the hardness of his body against

150

hers. She heard the steady throb of his heart.

"Dev," she whispered. "I love you so."

Dev reached down and slid one hand about her slender throat to the back of her head. He gently caressed her with a slow, soft movement of his fingers. He heard her sigh contentedly as she lay against him. Then he gently shifted his position so that she was lying in the circle of his left arm. He looked down into her up-turned face. Her eyes overflowed with love. He cupped her face in his hand and slowly lowered his lips to hers, touching them very gently once, twice, and again, then raised his lips reluctantly from hers. He knew if he did not, in another moment the dam of his love for her would burst. But he had not taken into account the new stirrings he was awakening in Angelique. Her body had answered the hunger in Dev's lips. She slipped both arms about his neck and brought his head down and lifted her parted lips to his. He gave a low groan as he pulled her tightly against him until she could hardly breathe, yet she did not want him to release her even for a minute. Her lips were warm and moist, and he kissed her expertly and thoroughly until he felt her body tremble and move against his. As if they had a will of their own, his hands explored the soft curves of her body. Deftly, he opened the clasps on the front of her dress and slid his hand inside her bodice. She gasped as his hand gently cupped her soft breast. His mouth moved to her cheeks, her ears, and then down the curve of her throat and to her tender nipple.

Some part of his mind screamed for him to stop, and, with an agonizing effort, he pulled himself slowly away and silently reclasped her dress. Then she looked at him, her eyes were wide with confusion.

He pulled her against him and held her gently. "I love

you, Angel, and I sure hope Mattie's plans for our wedding are completed soon." He chuckled. "This is too much even for a man with my noble temperament." He cupped her face in both his hands and kissed her forehead, her closed eyes, each cheek, then her mouth, very gently. "Come, let's go inside and pin Mattie down to just how long I have to put up with this beautiful agony."

They walked slowly back to the house. Inside, they found Cap, enthroned in his favorite chair and puffing his pipe in contentment.

"Where's Mattie, Cap?"

"Don't know, son, she went out about an hour ago. Said she'd be back shortly."

As if in answer to Dev's question, the door opened and Mattie came in. Behind her was a short, rather round gentleman, with apple cheeks and laughing eyes. He stepped into the light of the room.

"Dev, Angel, Cap, I'd like to introduce you to Father Sheehan. Father, this is my family, and this is the young couple who would like your blessing on their marriage."

Both Dev and Cap contained their smiles as they acknowledged the introduction, but they exchanged quick glances of amusement at Mattie's ability to find a Roman priest in a part of the country where the nearest Catholic church was forty miles away. Angel's eyes sparkled with delight.

"Oh, Father, I'm so very happy to see you. It has been months since I've been to confession. I would so like to receive absolution before my marriage."

"Of course, my child," Father Sheehan smiled, then turned back to Mattie. "When is the wedding to be?"

"From what I've understood of your faith, Father,

the announcement—"

"The banns," Father Sheehan said.

"Yes, banns. Well, they have to be announced for three Sundays in a row. Is that right?"

"Yes, quite right."

"Then," Mattie beamed in pleasure, "the wedding can be performed next week. I've had the banns published two Sundays ago and this Sunday makes the third."

All three members stared at Mattie, astonished once again. She arched an eyebrow and returned their stares. "I have friends in the next shire," she said with imperial aplomb. "Catholic friends." Then she turned to Father Sheehan, her tone changing to its usual motherliness. "Now, Father, is there anything else we'll have to see to?"

"Well, I understand the young man is not a Catholic."

"That's right," Dev answered. "Is it necessary that I be?"

"No," Father Sheehan answered, "but I must have a signed pledge from the young bride that she promises to raise her children in her faith."

Angel turned to Dev. "Oh, Dev," she said, "do you . . ."

Dev smiled. "Do I mind? No, Angel, I don't mind. We'll overcome any kind of barriers we must. Sign your paper, go to confession, and then make me the happiest man in the world."

With a small cry of pleasure, Angel threw her arms about Dev and kissed him, then in sudden embarrassment at the presence of the priest, she dropped her arms and turned pink.

"Don't be embarrassed at being happy, child." Father Sheehan grinned. "It is a state our good Lord would like

153

to see us all in."

Cap offered Father Sheehan a glass of wine which he was quick to accept. Soon they were all comfortable and chatting about the wedding.

During most of the next week, everyone was busy with the preparations. They were to be married in Cap's parlor. Mattie cleaned the house with Angel's help until it sparkled. Then she spent days baking and sewing. What Dev and Cap managed was mostly to stay out of their way.

Then, two days before the wedding day, everything was ready. Now came the hardest time of all. For two days, none of them had a thing to do. Angel was nervous; Mattie was excited; Cap was pleasantly exuberant. And Dev was miserable enduring the final, slowly passing time.

That morning he went down to the docks to make the final preparations for their wedding trip. He said a quick good-bye to everyone, but still did not get away without a list of last-minute things that Mattie swore she was in dire need of.

He was halfway down the hill when he saw the ship enter the harbor. Shading his eyes with his hand, he watched it move closer and closer to shore. Then, suddenly, his eyes registered recognition and he smiled and quickened his steps. On the wharf, he watched the ship ease gracefully to a berth, then walked to the edge of the gangplank as it touched the dock.

"Ahoy board the *Sea Hawk*," he shouted.

A deckhand came and looked over the rail. "Can I help you?"

"Captain Ryan still command the *Hawk?*"

"Yes, Sir."

"Would you tell him an old friend would like permission to come aboard?"

"Yes, Sir!" the man replied, then disappeared.

It was only a few minutes before Andrew's head appeared. He saw Dev and a bright smile covered his face. "Dev, you bastard, wait there. I'll be right down."

Dev grinned. Andy hadn't changed in all the years he'd known him.

He reached out and grasped Andy's extended hand as he stepped on to the dock. "What the hell are you doing here, and at just the right time, too."

"Right time?" Andy questioned.

"You can stand as my best man at my wedding day after tomorrow."

Andy's face was a study in disbelief. "You!" he said. "Dev Carlisle gettin' married? I don't believe it!"

"Quite true, old friend, and since you're here, I'm glad she's marrying me before she gets to know you too well."

"Well, this little story is gettin' more interestin' day by day."

"Little story? What does that mean?"

"Where's the nearest tavern?" Andy laughed as he clapped Dev on the shoulder. "I've a few things to tell you, and you've a lot to tell me."

They walked to the tavern, sat down and ordered drinks before either of them spoke again.

"Now," said Dev, "just what did you mean 'this little story'?"

Andy explained about the message he carried to Cap, and told him of his race with the Spanish galleon. Then he sat back in his chair and his eyes twinkled with excitement. "Now, my friend," he said, "you put the pieces together for me and tell me what's goin' on around here."

155

Dev chuckled, then motioned to the barmaid and ordered another drink for each of them. He waited until they were served and the buxom young girl, who had drawn attention, had gone. It was a surprise to Andy that Dev hadn't worked for the barmaid's attention. In the past, a playful contest would have ensued between the two friends to see which one would be favored for the night. His curiosity about Dev's bride was sparked by this new behavior.

Dev leaned forward and put his elbows on the table and started explaining in a low voice about Don Esteban Ortega and Miguel Montalban, and the political struggles of eighteen years before.

"But how is this all connected with a nun hundreds of miles away, a convent, Cap Cortland, and you?"

"You'll understand if you just keep quiet and let me finish. I'll answer all the questions you have."

"Okay," Andy laughed. "Go on, go on. I'll not say anything until you're finished."

Dev told of how he and Cap had taken Angelique to the convent years before, and that Don Esteban finally found where Miguel Montalban's daughter was living. The story of the pirate attack on the island and the resulting condition of Angelique brought a lift to Andy's eyebrows as he heard the anger in Dev's voice.

Andy's lips twitched in a half smile as he listened to his old friend describe Angel. "You believe her father is still alive?" he asked after Dev had finished.

"I just don't know, Andy. All I know is that Angel has agreed to marry me. From there on, I know nothing, except that I will protect her, no matter what I have to do."

"Umm, this girl sounds beautiful. When do I meet her?"

"If I had my way," Dev grinned, "you wouldn't meet her until the day of the wedding. But," he sighed with exaggeration, "I must take you home now so you can deliver that message to Cap. And," he added harshly, "whatever is in it is of more than frivolous interest to me, too."

They rose, paid for their drinks, and left the tavern. Walking up the hill toward home, Andy and Dev gave each other comradely pictures of the things they had been doing in the years since they had last seen each other. Mattie was the first to greet them as Dev opened the door.

"Andrew Ryan," she squealed, "where have you been all this time, young man? We missed you."

Andy hugged Mattie and kissed her soundly. "You look as pretty as ever, Mattie. And I missed you, too. Where's Cap?"

"Right here, Andy, my boy." Cap's voice came from the stairway. Andy looked up, and respect and pleasure shone in his face as he extended his hand to Cap.

"Welcome home," Cap smiled as he gripped Andy's hand firmly.

"Thank you, Cap," Andy replied. He felt again the warmth of this house which he always felt when he returned to the only home he'd ever known. "Dev tells me he's gettin' married. I'm anxious to meet the lady who finally landed him."

"She'll be right down," Cap replied. "And she is a lovely young lady, a blessing to all of us."

Almost immediately, they heard a door close and the

157

sound of Angelique's light footsteps. She descended the stairs, her silver hair, twisted in a knot on top of her head and soft curls about her face, catching the stray beams of sunlight. Andy stared at her, like a man transfixed.

She blushed prettily, her cheeks turning pink at the intensity of his look. She went to Dev who slid a possessive arm about her waist.

"Andy, this is my fiancee, Angelique Montalban. Angel, this is the best friend I've ever had in my life, Andrew Ryan."

Angel extended her hand with a bright smile that gave Andy the sensation that someone had just struck him in the pit of his stomach.

"How do you do, Mr. Ryan. I'm pleased to meet you. I hope we can be friends also," Angelique said softly.

Andy took her small hand in his and answered with words he didn't even hear. Then he followed them all into the parlor where they urged him to sit and have a glass of port with them before he returned to the ship. After a polite interval, Mattie and Angelique excused themselves. When they had gone, Dev said, "Andy has a message from the Reverend Mother for you, Cap."

Andy took the message from his shirt and handed it to Cap.

Chapter 14

Slowly, Cap broke the seal, and while Dev and Andy watched with expectant faces, he read the letter. His face showed no sign of his thoughts as he read, and both of them patiently waited for him to tell them the news. Finally, he looked up from the paper.

"Dev, DeVarga is dead."

"DeVarga. Who is DeVarga?" Andy asked.

"The man who passed sentence on Angelique's father. The man who is indirectly responsible for her mother's death—and the man who was the puppet judge for Don Esteban."

"Then . . ." Dev began.

"Then, Miguel is absolved and all his wealth can be restored to him. It probably already has been."

Dev was frozen into stillness. "Then he'll come for Angelique if he knows about this."

Cap regarded him soberly. "We have always known of this possibility, Dev. But beyond that, there are other considerations Miguel will make—if, that is, he is still alive. He knows that he still has to be extremely cautious. Don Esteban will not forsake his revenge because DeVarga is dead. His vindictive heart will not let him rest until he comes face to face with Miguel or his daughter or both." He turned to Andy. "You said a Spanish galleon followed you from the island?"

"Not exactly, Cap. A Spanish galleon *tried* to follow

me. You know me and the *Hawk* better than that. The sister warned me about the ship, so I kept an eye out for him. At the first sight of his sails, my lady and I gave him a lesson in sailing the seas. He did not follow me to this port."

"Good, but we've got to keep our eyes open and be prepared for anything. We can hope and pray Angelique's father finds out about this soon. Then he will know that Angelique is either at the convent or with me. I feel safe in saying that if he is alive, it will not be long before Miguel makes an appearance here."

Dev rose from his seat and walked to the window. He stood there looking out, but without seeing. He could feel that something bad was going to happen. And in the back of his mind hovered the nagging thought that Angelique's father could convince her that she should take her place in the Spanish court. Cap came and stood behind him.

"Have more faith, Dev," he said quietly. "Miguel is not an unreasonable man. If he had not wanted his daughter to have a happy life, he would not have left her with me in the first place. He is a good, honest man, and when he sees the love you have for each other, he will not try to interfere. Indeed, I hope he will decide to live here among us the rest of his life."

Dev turned and smiled weakly at Cap. "Perhaps you're right. Let's put other things aside and celebrate. Between Andy's arrival and my wedding, we've reason to be happy."

Cap clapped him on the shoulder and suggested that they retire to the same tavern from whence Andy and Dev had just come. "We'll lift a few glasses, just us men," he said. And the three of them left for the tavern.

There, among the laughter and good memories and good friends, they all three became rather tipsy.

Making their way home on rubbery legs just after dark, they used one another to lean on. Half stumbling up the front porch steps, they were met at the door by a stern-faced Mattie. It took all Angelique could do to suppress her laughter when she saw the condition they were in. "Angel, my love," Dev grinned rather foolishly as he tried to put his arms about her and kiss her.

That brought a smile to Mattie's lips. "Let's get these three to a bed, Angelique," she said as she maneuvered Cap through the door and up the stairs.

"Ummm," Dev murmured as his arm caught Angelique unsteadily about the waist and drew her against him. "Bed sounds perfect to me. Come with me," he whispered, and his kisses covered her throat and bare shoulders.

Andy staggered after Cap and Mattie, but Angelique could not maneuver Dev's huge frame. His arms tightened about her and his lips sought hers.

"I love you, Angel," he said, his arms crushing her against him. She looked up into his eyes. "Don't leave me, Angel, don't go away."

"I won't, Dev. I'll never leave you. You need not have any worries about that. Soon I'll be your wife, to live with you always, to share the rest of your life, to have your children." She spoke pertly, then smiled.

His lips found hers in a kiss so filled with the fire of his need that she ceased fighting him and put both her arms about his waist.

"Come and stay with me tonight, Angel."

She thought it best to humor him; she smiled and

agreed. He grinned and pulled her toward the door. She let him pull her along as he stumbled up the steps and into his bedroom. "Sit down on the bed, Dev. I'll be with you in a moment," she said softly.

He sat on the edge of the bed, then slowly leaned back against the pillows. Within minutes, he was asleep. Angelique removed his shoes, but she had not the strength to move him, so she covered him with a blanket and left the room.

Going to her room, she undressed and slipped into bed. Remembering his state, she collapsed against the pillows laughing. Before she fell asleep, she decided to have a little fun at his expense the following day.

Just after the first light of dawn, Angel awoke and dressed. Going downstairs to the kitchen, she found Mattie already there, sitting at the table sipping a cup of fresh hot tea.

"Aren't you preparing breakfast?" Angelique asked.

"I don't suspect there will be much call for breakfast this morning," Mattie laughed. "Nor, if I've got my men figured right, will there be much call for lunch, either."

Angelique giggled. "Oh, Mattie, they all must feel quite miserable this morning." Her laughter was contagious and soon they were seated together laughing over their tea. They were still there when the slow methodical thump of heavy footsteps descended the stairs, one painful step at a time. Angelique leaned across the table and whispered conspiringly to Mattie. "Mattie, would you do me a favor?"

"Of course."

She explained quickly. "All you have to do is to act as though you're very suspicious of what went on last night.

162

You might even give him a few angry looks. I'm just going to tease him a little Mattie. And, perhaps, teach him a little lesson."

"All right," Mattie laughed. "I'll go along with your little game, but Dev's not the only one who needs some comeuppance after last night. Cap should have known better, too. And at his age! My word!" She winked as the kitchen door opened and Cap stepped slowly into the room. His complexion bore a light greenish cast. His eyes were red and he moved slowly as if every inch of him was in agony.

"Good morning, Cap," Mattie chirped brightly. Cap sat down, leaned his elbows on the table, and held his head between his hands. "Must you make such confounded noise, woman?" he moaned.

"But, Cap," Mattie argued in a loud, cheerful voice, "it's a bright, beautiful day, and I'm going to cook you a nice big breakfast. Eggs and ham, with lots of bread and creamy butter, and . . ."

Her voice ended in a trill of laughter at Cap's hastily retreating form. They followed him out to the parlor where he was soon joined by a silent Andy, whose color attested to his condition. Clearly it was not one of his better days. Before long, he and Cap left the house and slowly walked down toward the harbor. There, on board ship, both would get themselves back into working condition before they returned to the house.

"Now," Mattie said gleefully, "we'll attend to Master Devon when he awakens."

Dev was already awake, although he was wishing he was not. His head thudded painfully and his mouth tasted vile, but what was bothering him most was the suspicion that he'd done more last night than get drunk. He remembered well his arms about Angelique and the soft feel of her lips against him. He even remembered the warmth of her voice telling him she would join him in just a moment—but, damn, if he could remember one more thing.

Very slowly, he sat on the edge of the bed, then rose to his feet and went to the wash basin. There, he splashed cool water on his face and rinsed the wicked taste from his mouth and put on his clothes.

Downstairs, he could hear Mattie and Angelique in the kitchen. He went to the door and pushed it open. Both women turned their faces toward him, but it was Angelique's eyes he sought. She looked at him for a moment, then her cheeks turned fiery red and she turned her head away.

"In one foolish moment," he thought miserably, "I undid my beautiful bride."

"Good morning, Dev," Mattie said, stone-faced.

"Mornin', Mattie," he said thickly. "Angel, may I speak with you alone?"

"Oh, Dev," she said, regret in her voice, "I have to run an important errand for Mattie. Perhaps later."

Dev looked from Mattie to Angel. How could he ask her in front of Mattie if he'd tumbled her into his bed last night?

"All right," he agreed reluctantly. "Will you be back soon?"

"Well, not for some time. I've a number of stops to make."

Mattie turned her back on the two of them and pretended involvement in work so she could hide the smile on her face.

"Where's Andy and Cap?"

"Gone down to the harbor," Mattie replied dryly. "I imagine they'd like me to believe they had pressin' work to be done there, but I bet if you went down now, you'd find them both in their cabins resting up from last night."

"I'd best go down too," Dev answered. Neither Angelique nor Mattie stirred from their work. "Cap might need me," he added feebly.

"Oh, I'm sure he will," Mattie replied flatly.

Dev turned and left the kitchen. After closing the front door behind him, he stood squinting in the bright sunlight for a few moments. "Why should I walk down there in this heat when it would be easier just to go back to bed for a while?" he reasoned. He went back into the house and was just about to start up the stairs when the sound of laughter echoed from the kitchen. He stepped quietly to the kitchen door, listening.

"He surely did look miserable," Mattie was saying. "Serves him right. I always warned that boy that drinkin' would get him into trouble. What really did happen last night?"

Angel giggled. "Oh, Dev was very affectionate, but he collapsed on the bed before he could do anything except kiss me a few times. I must admit he had the intention for more, but he was in no condition."

They both burst into gales of laughter.

"The little minx," Dev thought. Then, a wicked grin spread over his face. He turned and crept as silently as he could to his room, closing the door softly behind him. He went to the window and watched the front gate. Within an hour, he was rewarded for his patience when he saw Mattie, market basket in hand, open the front gate and walk toward town. Slowly and silently, he crept down the stairs. He heard her humming softly to herself in the kitchen. The humming was a bright happy song which made Dev even more determined to repay her teasing.

He cracked open the kitchen door. Her back was to him as she stood over the table, her hands busy and all her attention on what she was doing. Very slowly, he pushed open the door and closed it behind him. Moving silently, he came up behind her until he was only two or three steps away. Then he said in a soft, suggestive voice. "Good morning, love."

She whirled about, shock written on her face. She managed to recover enough to cry, "Dev! What are you doing here? I thought . . ."

"You thought I went with Andy and Cap. Well, I wanted you to think that. It got Mattie out of the house and left us alone for at least two hours." He grinned, and the grin was decidedly evil. "After last night, I was sure you would want Mattie gone as much as I do." He reached for her, and she backed up against the table. Dev's arms came about her and pulled her close to him. Both her hands pressed futilely against his chest, and she looked up into his eyes and read more intent than—had she known—really existed. How could she convince him now that nothing had really happened last night. If she let him kiss her again as he had the night before, she would be lost, for she knew there was no resistance in her to Dev's love. She wanted him as badly as he did her.

"Dev, what you think—it isn't . . ."

His mouth stopped her with a searching kiss that left her gasping and trembling in his arms.

"Dev," she gasped, trying to wriggle free of the arms that confined her, but that only helped to inflame them both.

166

Holding her with one arm, he loosened the pins from her hair and let it fall around her shoulders in a bright, silver cascade. Running his hands through her heavy mane, he held the back of her head firmly and slowly lowered his lips again to hers. His mouth touched hers gently, and she whimpered softly and suddenly stopped struggling and slid her arms about his waist. Her lips parted gently under his, and he could feel every line of her body molded to his as she surrendered. His arms tightened possessively about her. He realized that what had started out in his mind as a joke was rapidly getting out of his control. He raised his head and looked down at her. Her violet eyes were half closed and her moist, red lips were parted in passion. Her slender body trembled against him, but she was no longer trying to escape. Now, she clung to him.

The decision was quick and final. He would deny himself no longer. He wanted her and he knew she wanted him. Slowly, he relaxed his arm and with both hands, he cupped her small face and lifted it to his, then explored it with his seeking tongue. She answered with shy trembling response of her own tongue, tasting his hard masculine mouth.

Expert hands sought the clasps of her bodice, and in seconds had them open. With very gentle hands, he slid the dress off her shoulders, then the straps of her chemise. His hands touched the warmth of her velvety skin. Cupping her breasts in both hands, he lowered his head and caressed the pink nipple with his tongue in light circular motions, feeling them rise and harden in his mouth. Her hands pulled him even closer to her, and the hot fire surged through his blood as his body demanded hers.

He raised his head to look down on her sweet face. "Angel, it's too late to turn back. I want you now," he moaned. "We'll be married tomorrow, but I can't wait 'til then." His arms held her close and his lips traced the soft column of her throat.

"And I need you, Dev," she whispered. "I love you, and I want you. What is the difference in a day?"

He smiled and kissed her again and again. Then with a quick laugh, he bent and lifted her up in his arms. She echoed his joyful laughter and wrapped her arms about his neck and kissed his face and neck as he carried her to his room. He put her down and closed and locked the door behind them.

Then he turned to face her. The bright sunlight from the window made a golden halo about her body and sent silver sparks from her hair. He reached out with both hands and gently eased the dress from over her hips to fall in an unheeded mass at her feet. He gazed at her beauty, ripe, petite, perfect. "Angel, you're the most beautiful woman I've ever seen in my life."

She lifted her arms to him. He removed his clothes more rapidly than he had ever done before, then came to her and gently took her hips in his hands. Slowly, he drew her against him, savering the thrill that coursed through him when her soft, velvety flesh touched him. The perfume of her, the feel of her, the taste of her overcame his senses. He kissed her leisurely and thoroughly, letting his hands drift over her smooth soft skin until he could barely stand it any longer. If he had followed his urges then, he would have brought her to the bed and taken her immediately, for he was almost overcome with the desire to be within her, to be a part of her. But he knew this first time would be difficult for her and he wanted it to be as much a pleasure for her as it would be for him.

Gently, he carried her to the bed. Lying beside her, he continued to kiss and touch her, his hands seeking every soft curve, every secret place that was his Angel. One hand slipped between her silken thighs and, controlling himself, he gently pushed her legs apart while his fingers found and caressed the virgin womanhood. Her hips arched upward at his ministrations and she clasped his withdrawing hand and held it to the small mound of moist silver hairs.

He rose to his knees over her and his mouth came down on hers and caught her lips at the same moment his throbbing manhood entered her. He felt the thin membrane of her maidenhood break at his first thrust, and heard her muffled cry against his lips. He lay inside her, not moving until her body ceased its violent trembling. Then he slid his hands under her and lifted her against him as he began slow, rhythmical thrusts.

Angel was answering him move for move. She clung to him, her silken legs wrapped 'round his shoulders. He allowed his passion free reign now, feeling the fire of it flood over him. It consumed him as, slowly, she matched his rhythmic movements. They moved like one person. Soft, sighed words of love passed between them, though neither realized what they were saying. Of all the women in Dev's life, none of them had touched his soul as the gentle creature he held in his arms. He wanted to stay deep within her forever. He held himself, until he felt her shudder in release, and only then did he join her in a blazing completion.

For a few moments, they lay exhausted, wrapped tightly in each other's arms. Slowly, he rolled to his side and pulled her close to him.

He rose on one elbow and looked down into her eyes. The love he saw there warmed him and he smiled. Beads of perspiration lay on her brow among damp locks of her hair. He lifted one hand and gently brushed them away. "Angel, Angel," he murmured as he touched her lips with a feather light kiss.

Her fingers ran through his hair. "I love you, Dev. I shall love you forever."

"Once I offered you a choice, Angel," he said. "Life with me or in the Spanish court. Now, I take back that offer. I have made you mine and I'll not let anyone take you from me."

"Dev," she smiled. "I have never felt so complete. Now, we are together and we shall stay so. I want no choices in life, Dev, I want you and only you." With one small hand, she touched the side of his face and let her fingers drift slowly down his cheek as if she wanted to imprint on her heart the memory of something sweet and beloved. He turned his lips into her palm and kissed it gently, then let his kisses roam to her wrist, the soft flesh of her arms, the rounded white curve of her shoulder, the long slender column of her throat, then up to the soft, parted lips that waited impatiently for him.

This time, there was no holding back for either of them. They had tasted the beauty of their love and now they both wanted to drink deeply of it.

After over another hour, they lay still on the big bed, both silent, both reluctant to let go the joy they had just discovered. It was Dev who reluctantly rose from the bed first. Angel watched him as he picked up their hastily discarded clothes and walked back toward the bed. She watched his muscular body as he moved gracefully about the room.

Their eyes met across the room and a half smile tugged at the corners of his lips. Slowly, he walked back to the bed.

"My love," he said softly. "If you don't want Mattie to find you here in my bed, you'd best get up and get dressed, for she should be back soon." She laughed, then gathered up her clothes and slipped from the bed.

She dressed, then, leaning forward, drew her long hair over her shoulder and braided it. When she finished, he stood up and went to her.

"Now, how about breakfast?"

She smiled, and they walked to the door. Before he opened it, he slid his arm about her and kissed her quickly.

"Angel?"

"Yes, Dev."

"Tonight . . . will you come to me, tonight?"

She looked up into the tender blue gaze. "Dev, I would have come even if you hadn't asked me."

Chapter 15

The faraway cry of sea gulls brought Angelique awake just before dawn the next day. She did not know how she had got back in her own room. The last thing she remembered of the night before was lying curled close against Dev's warmth and resting her head against his broad chest.

She had fallen asleep so, and no matter how badly Dev had wanted to keep her with him, he knew Mattie would be coming to waken her early the next morning. Gently, not to disturb her sleep, he lifted her in his arms and carried her to her room. He kissed her gently, and smiled as he heard her murmur his name. Then he left the room, closing the door silently behind him, and went back to a bed that felt decidedly lonely.

Now, Angelique lay back against the pillows, stretching and smiling contentedly. Today was her wedding day and after this day she would never have to leave Dev's side again. Getting up quickly, she went to the closet. Reaching in, she drew forth the wedding dress that Mattie had sewn so lovingly for her. The ivory lace gleamed in the early morning light. Walking to her mirror, she held the dress up in front of her and tried to imagine what Dev would see.

Mattie had chosen the ivory lace for her because it enhanced the deep purple of her eyes and the startling silver hair. Using her own eye, she had created a dress of rare beauty. The neckline was high about her throat and the sleeves cut to a narrow peak at each wrist. The bodice was tight and fitted to Angel's rounded breasts and tiny waist; the skirt flared out in yards and yards of lace over ivory satin.

A light rap on the door interrupted her reverie and Mattie came in.

"You're up early, child," she smiled.

"I'm so excited, Mattie." Angel ran to Mattie and hugged and kissed her enthusiastically. "The gown is the loveliest thing I've ever seen in my life and I thank you, dear Mattie."

"Oh, child," Mattie replied, happy tears forming in her eyes, "it was a pleasure. You've made my Dev so happy. And you've brought a great deal to Cap and me. Youth and beauty and the rare privilege of sharing the happiness you and Dev have found." She patted Angel's head. "Come, it's time for a hot bath, then I'll do your hair for you and help you into your gown. By that time, Cap will be knocking impatiently on your door."

A huge wooden tub was carried in by two young girls Angel did not even recognize.

"They are the daughters of one of my friends," Mattie explained. "They offered their services to us today."

Angel turned to the two shy young girls. Each was about fourteen and watching her with timid, yet excited, eyes. "Thank you. It was kind of you to offer your help."

"You're welcome, Ma'm," one replied.

"Now, scat, girls, and carry up that water before it gets cold. We don't want our pretty bride shivering her way to the altar now, do we?"

They giggled and left the room quickly. Each returned with two large buckets of hot water and poured it into the tub. Mattie produced an ewer of scented oils, and Angelique climbed into the tub and allowed the heat of the water to relax her.

When she had finished her bath, Mattie rubbed her briskly with a soft towel; then she sat on a bench in front of her mirror while Mattie brushed her hair until it sparkled like silver in a bright sun. Pulling it back from her face, yet letting a few wispy curls frame her face, Mattie coiled the hair in a thick heavy rope and wound it about her head. Then she went to the door and opened it. Reaching out, she picked up a basket and carried it in. Inside was a large bouquet of deep purple wildflowers tied with an ivory ribbon. Alongside it were as many more loose flowers of the same color. Mattie handed the bouquet to Angel.

"Dev was up long before dawn and picked these for you to carry today. Said to tell you they remind him of your eyes."

"Oh, Mattie," Angel said, "how lovely they are."

Mattie took the loose flowers from the basket and, one by one, nestled them in Angel's hair. Angel slipped into her underclothing then stood in front of the mirror, again prepared to don the wedding dress. Mattie dropped it over her head and adjusted it.

Mattie was speechless as they stood together looking at the combination of the lovely dress and Angel's extraordinary beauty.

A knock sounded, and Mattie went to answer the door. She opened the door to find Cap outside.

"Most of the guests have arrived, Mattie. The priest is ready, and as for Dev, if we don't bring him his bride soon, I wouldn't put it past him to dash up here and drag her down."

174

"Come in for a moment, Cap. Angel is just about ready."

Cap came in and stopped still in his tracks. Then he went to Angel's side and took both her hands in his. "You are so very lovely, my dear." He touched her cheek with his lips.

"Thank you, Cap," Angel whispered.

He smiled and turned to Mattie. "You'd best go on down and see if Dev is still standing." He turned to Angel and offered her his arm as he said softly, "I'll bring our daughter down."

Mattie and Cap had arranged the small altar directly across the room from the bottom of the steps. Chairs were facing it on either side of a two-foot-wide aisle. The entire village seemed to be crowded in the room, some standing, others turning in their chairs to behold the bride.

Dev stood watching the stairway with Andy at his side. Both men were spellbound at the ivory and purple vision that descended on Cap's arm and walked slowly toward them.

"You lucky man," whispered Andy. "If I had a woman like that, I'd find me a hideaway and never come out."

Dev nodded, his eyes holding Angel's as she walked toward him. Cap stopped and placed Angel's hand in Dev's and they both turned together. Shoulder to shoulder, they knelt before the priest.

Angel watched Dev's face as he repeated the priest's words. "How strong and handsome he is," she thought. Warmth flooded through her as she remembered his gentle love during the night.

The celebration party was held in the garden.

Dev and Angel chatted with their guests with happy smiles, thanking them for all their good wishes given. It was just as they were parting from Mrs. McCracken and thanking her for her blessings that they came face to face with Polly. For a moment, they all stared at each other. Then Polly smiled—a bright smile, but one that did not extend to her eyes. "May I wish you the best, Mrs. Carlisle." She spoke the words to Angel, but her eyes were on Dev.

"Thank you," Angelique managed, but her hand tightened on Dev's arm and he squeezed it against him.

"And if it's proper to kiss the bride, it should also be proper to kiss the groom, shouldn't it?" she laughed.

Before either of them knew what was happening, Polly had stepped close to Dev and was putting her hands on the sides of his head. She drew his head down and kissed him in a way that was nothing if not seductive.

When she stepped back from a flabbergasted Dev, she looked at Angelique, disdain curling her lips.

She had misjudged Angelique for the last time. Angelique smiled a deliciously amused smile and said just loud enough for the other guests nearby to hear, "A gentleman should always be allowed to kiss all his past follies good-bye."

Both Andy and Cap exchanged looks of silent laughter. Polly's face flushed as though she had been slapped, and she remained frozen, her narrowed eyes peering at Angel's serene face. Anger filled her face as the force of the words came through to her. She raised her hand to strike Angel, but before her hand could descend, her wrist was held by a hand like iron and her gaze swung up to Dev's angry face.

"Say or do whatever you will to me, Polly, but know

this—whatever you received here, you asked for. Angelique is innocent of your world. Don't ever try to harm her in any way or you shall find my anger more than you can tolerate." His voice was a whisper—only Polly heard the words, but their sentiment was obvious from the bright anger that flooded his face.

With a stifled groan, Polly moved past them and ran from the room. Dev looked down into Angel's wide eyes, his face glowing with warm laughter as he slid his arm about her waist and drew her against him. "I didn't know I'd married such a strong tigress," he whispered.

Angel laughed up at him. "Where you are concerned, Dev, I'll tolerate no interference from another woman. I will never share you with anyone. Be warned."

"Consider the warning well taken, love. Why don't we slip away from all these people? There's a honeymoon I'm anxious to start on."

"Where are we going?"

"That's a surprise I've saved for you. Have you the patience to wait and see? I think you'll be pleased."

"I'll go and change and have my baggage brought down."

"I've already seen to that. You just change . . . and, Angel?"

"Yes?"

"Hurry up, will you?"

She nodded and left his side. He watched her climb the stairs. He didn't even know Andy was standing beside him until he heard his muffled laugh.

"That is a true lady you've married. And I hope, old boy, that you don't run across any more of your 'past follies.' If I were in your shoes, we'd have been gone by now."

Dev laughed. "Have you got everything on board for me?"

"I've seen to everything. The boat's at the dock ready and waiting, all your baggage is on board, and no one knows where you're goin' except Cap, Mattie, and me."

"Good. Now, why don't we have one farewell drink before I leave. It's the last one I intend to have tonight."

They were sharing a drink when Cap joined them and pulled Andy into a conversation to which Dev paid very little heed. His eyes continued to stray in the direction of the stairs.

It was almost an hour later when Angel came downstairs accompanied by Mattie. She had changed to a pale blue cotton dress of plain cut, fit for traveling. Her hair had been brushed out and tied back with a matching blue ribbon. Several people stopped her on her way toward Dev to speak to her and wish her well. Dev watched her, his eyes glowing with pride. She finally reached his side.

"Are you ready, love?"

"Yes, Dev. I'm ready, but I'm curious about all the secrecy. Can't you tell me now where we're going?"

"Impatient lady, do you want to spoil my surprise?"

"Very well, lord and master," she said, her eyes sparkling. "Your wish is my command."

"That's a most agreeable idea," Dev said. "You can say a quick good night to our family, that's all I'll allow. I want to be at our destination by nightfall. And we've some traveling to do to get there."

"But, Dev, how are we traveling?"

"Angel," he laughed, "will you quit your questions before I drag you away from here without being able to say any good-byes at all?"

Laughingly, Angel turned to Cap. "Cap, I want to thank you again for the lovely wedding." She rose on tiptoe and kissed Cap on both cheeks.

"And what about the best man? Doesn't he deserve a kiss, too?" Andy said.

"Of course," Angel replied. She went to him and put both hands on his shoulders. Andy was at least a foot taller than she. Since she could not reach him, she lifted her cheek for his kiss, and was shocked when his huge hands encircled her tiny waist and his lips caught hers in a most unbrotherly kiss. Surprised and completely unprepared, Angel felt her breath taken away. Andy was grateful that she didn't know the effect it had on him or she would have been frightened to death.

Since he had first seen her Andy had known that he'd tumbled head over heels in love with Angel. He had no intention of ever telling her so, for he valued Dev and Cap's friendship. But this kiss shook him to the core, and when he released her, her cheeks were pink and she was flustered.

Angel may not have known the effect she had on Andy, but Dev did. He had tasted the sweetness of her lips too often not to know just how Andy felt at the moment. Their eyes met over Angel's head. Both knew no words would ever be spoken on the matter, just as both knew exactly what the other felt.

Dev led Angel to Mattie, where they exchanged a tearful farewell, as though they would never see each other again. Getting through the crowd of people and their good wishes took another half an hour. They left the house and were driven to the harbor. There, tied to the dock was a sail boat with its sails furled and tied against the mast.

179

Dev stepped down into the boat and reached up for Angel, then lifted her effortlessly into the small craft. Dev had arranged a comfortably padded seat and cushions to make her as comfortable as possible.

Quickly and expertly, he detached the rope that held them to the dock and pushed the boat away. The sail was unfurled and Angel could feel the lift of the boat as the wind caught the sails and filled them.

They left the small harbor and headed the boat southward along the coastline. He hugged the shore and kept a close eye on the sail. One hand on the tiller, he guided the boat easily as it skipped lightly over the water.

Angel lay back among the pillows and watched him.

They sailed for more than an hour before she noticed that Dev was slowly edging the boat toward shore. Then, there suddenly loomed before them a huge wall of rock. At first, she was afraid. Then she saw that Dev was calm and intent on where they were headed. The wall had a huge V in the center, and they sailed through the split in the rock into the most beautiful blue-green lagoon she had ever seen. It seemed as if they were separated from the rest of the world. Angel looked back over the way they had come. The bright orange globe of the sun sat cradled in the V where they had entered, casting its glow directly across the water. The lagoon was peaceful and quiet, protected from the currents of the ocean by the rocks. It had a long white sandy beach which was surrounded by high green trees. Deep in the trees sat a small cabin. It was like walking from the ordinary world into paradise. Angel sat silent, amazed more and more at the man she had married.

They docked, and Dev jumped ashore, tying the boat up firmly, then he reached out for her and lifted her out beside him. They stood together, marvelling at the amazing beauty of this place.

He smiled and with his arm about her waist and her head resting against his shoulder, they walked toward the cottage ahead of them.

He let her enter before him, and she walked about and examined it as he lit several candles about the room.

There were two rooms in the cottage. A small fireplace with a long rather comfortable looking, but old, couch in front of it, and a table with four chairs were the furniture in one room. The bedroom had the largest bed she'd ever seen in her life. One large window faced the setting sun, and there was a huge oval braided rug on a rough hewn plank floor. The cabin was neat, clean and orderly. She knew without doubt that Dev had been there recently. The bedclothes were fresh and clean. She turned to face him.

"What a lovely place to spend a honeymoon. You are a most remarkable and wonderful husband, Dev Carlisle, and I do love you so very much."

His quick grin and the way his arms tightened about her were enough reward. Slowly, he bent his head and lightly touched her lips with his again and again and again. Light feather touches that sent her heart pounding and warmed her.

Her hands lifted to caress his face and to slide to the back of his head where she let them twine in his thick hair and hold his lips firmly against hers.

They parted, touched again, parted, and they both became lost in the fire of their love. Gently, he nibbled at her mouth tasting the sweet honey taste of her. He released her and stepped back. Their eyes held as he reached out and slowly unbuttoned the buttons of her dress; then her hands were there to help him and with a light whisper, it fell to the floor, followed by the soft fabric of her chemise.

She stood naked, and his eyes devoured her beauty. Everything about her was miniature perfection. Half light of the now dying sun turned her skin to pale gold. Her silver hair flowed about her like a bright halo and her eyes held his like a magnet. She revelled in what she saw in his face and stepped closer to him and began to unlace his shirt. He made no move to help her, but let his hands move gently over her shoulders and down the soft curve of her back to rest on her hips. She slid her hands under his shirt and pushed it back off his shoulders, and it joined her clothes on the floor.

They stood inches from each other, their bodies barely touching. Her round breasts grazed the mat of black hair on his chest. His hands rested again on the curve of her hips. Slowly, his head bent again to hers and her lips parted to receive him. Then, with a low murmur, he gathered her into his arms.

Time spun away and they lost all thought but each other. Movements unrestrained, the blazing fire of their love dominated everything. His hands found all the sensitive spots on her body and his lips followed their journey, drawing forth soft cries of pleasure from her as she writhed against him, her need overpowering her.

She wanted to feel him deep within her, but he waited to lift her even higher. He toughed her flat, taut belly with his lips and brought a low moan of pleasure from her. Then his mouth moved to search her thighs and the soft, damp hairs of her womanhood. Her passion out of control now, she cried out his name over and over until her lips were silenced by his as his body became one with hers. He moved into her deeply with sure even movements of his body and felt her rise to meet him, her arms and legs twined about his back.

She cried out her passion and he, his until the brilliant flash of their universe left them floating earthward in a slow spiral of contentment. Then, silently, they lay in the huge, soft bed and watched the moon rise until it had cast its light over them.

"Angel, have you ever gone for a swim at midnight?"

"I've never swum. I don't know how."

"Let's go down to the beach. I'll teach you."

She looked up at him, surprise in her eyes.

"Dev, I've nothing to swim in."

Dev laughed heartily and squeezed her in his arms until she could barely breathe. "You're wonderful, darling. Swimming is like making love, it's better without clothes. We're miles from any other human and, besides, I'd like to see you naked in the moonlight." He rose from the bed and pulled her up beside him. "Ready?"

She slid her hand into his. "Yes."

They walked from the cottage and crossed the strip of sand toward the water. The moon made a bright path across it, lighting the scene with pale light. Angel had never experienced anything so free and exhilarating. She looked shyly at Dev's tall hard body walking beside hers and felt a thrill of expectancy engulf her. What could she expect next from this handsome man who planned on opening so many doors for her?

The warm water washed about her ankles and suddenly, she was afraid.

"Don't be afraid, Angel. Trust me. I won't let anything hurt you."

Hand in hand, they walked out until the water was up to her breasts. Then he put his arm about her and moved her into deeper water. She clung to him as her feet were lifted free of the bottom. Suddenly, she felt weightless and free. She could see the flash of Dev's smile as he put her hands on his shoulders and floated backward, drawing her with him. She laughed in excitement. Then she realized that she was lying almost atop him and that his hands were drifting over her with abandon. He began to laugh softly.

"You're caught again, my love, in one of my most devious traps. You're at my mercy, woman. Will you give in freely or must I force you?"

She giggled. "I'm afraid, Sir," she said in mock horror, "that you have taken advantage of me again. I see I have no choice but to give in to your evil ways. You are rapidly leading me astray."

He laughed and, grasping her by the buttocks, pulled her against him, holding her afloat with his own body. Then, he was taken by surprise by Angel's sudden attack. She began to kiss him wildly and passionately. He was so shocked, he almost dropped her.

"Little tigress," he said softly, "you constantly surprise me. One moment, you're a sweet little child, and the next you're the most wanton woman!"

They laughed and played in the water like children until the nearness of her slippery naked body began having some definite effects on Dev.

"I believe I'd better dry you off and feed you, woman."

He swam with her until the water was shallow enough for her to stand in. They rose from the water and stood gazing at each other.

He took her shoulders and drew her close and

whispered against her hair, "I want to make love to you here and now on the warm sand with nothing over us but the stars."

She smiled and put her arms slowly about his waist, then lifted her face for his kiss. Slowly, they knelt together on the sand, then lay with the warm waves washing over them, and he poured all his love into her warm body and she took it to hold through eternity.

Chapter 16

Polly Dillon sat facing her mirror and examined her face. What, she wondered, made that half-child whom Dev married so attractive to him? Many men, even Dev, had told Polly that she was pretty. Pretty and womanly. She was no child, she had put away the girlish ways which, so her mother often said, men come ultimately to despise. Why, then, had Dev chosen a mere girl, ignorant of the world, over her?

Polly had dreamed of herself as Dev's wife. She knew that one day Dev would be a wealthy and influential man. Hadn't her father often told her what sort of future she could have as Dev's wife? She would have all the dresses she wanted and be able to travel to all the distant places she dreamed of, and she would have servants to care for her. These things she hungered for.

But she hungered for something more than that. Polly had been seduced by a young man of the town when she was fifteen. He had succeeded by offering to buy her a pretty gown she had seen in a store window. Unknown to Polly, the word had gone about that if one had the correct price, Polly's favors could be bought. Then she had tasted the passion of Dev's lovemaking and her heart had been lost to him. She hungered again for the feel of his hard body in her arms. She was so sure that she would have him, for he had been away so long that he knew nothing about her past, that she made eloquent plans for her future and even assured her parents that they would probably be married on Dev's next trip home.

Then he had come home with that "silver-haired witch," and all Polly's dreams had been shattered.

She turned away from the mirror. "I hate her. There must be some way to get rid of her." She paced the floor in mental anguish. Somewhere, she knew, they were lying together, locked in a passionate embrace as she longed to be.

She sat on the edge of her bed and promised herself that if she ever found the way to have revenge on Angelique Carlisle, and to get her out of Dev's life, she would not hesitate. "Dev was mine," she said softly to herself, "and somehow, some way, he'll be mine again."

Other curses were being uttered at that same moment, and just as fervently. Several miles from where Polly sat, a tall man paced the floor of a ship's small cabin. Two men sat side by side, uncomfortable in the presence of this elegant though frightening man.

Two weeks before, they had been sent by the captain of their ship to watch the family of Robert Cortland. Tonight, they reported back, in detail, every move the family had made, including the marriage of the captain's adopted son to a young woman the captain had brought home with him on his last voyage. No one in the town seemed to know where the young woman had come from, but all were of one mind about her beauty.

They watched the man's expressionless face as they told him that everyone in the town seemed to like the woman. "Of course, that don't mean the lady what started the fight at the weddin'," added one man.

"Fight?" questioned Don Esteban. "What kind of fight?"

"Well," laughed the other man, "to me it looked like

187

the boy was beddin' the other gal and she got right mad with him for marryin' someone else."

Don Esteban smiled, and both men exchanged quick glances. They did not like this man any better when he smiled, for the smile extended only to his mouth. His eyes remained cold and hard. They stood silently as Don Esteban formed a plan in his mind. Cold shudders ran up their spines when they heard his low, growling chuckle.

"A woman scorned," murmured Don Esteban. "Well, well, let us see if we can persuade the young woman toward a little revenge. The fury of hell, indeed!" He turned to the two and said in a clipped voice, "Find her, alone somewhere, and bring her to me. Make no mistakes, for I do not want anyone to know there is any connection between me and this woman. Do you understand?"

They both agreed quickly, most anxious to be away from this man who gave them both the feeling of something deadly. After they had gone, Don Esteban walked to the portal and seemed to look out, but his eyes were seeing something long past.

"Did you truly believe you would escape me, Anna? What you tried to cheat me of, I shall have from your daughter. It will bring Miguel to my side as easily as breathing. Once I have him, I promise, he will join you. Then, your lovely daughter and the D'Santiago fortune will both be mine. Oh yes, Anna," and his voice softened to almost a whisper, "she will pay the price for your treachery."

Both men spent the next days watching Polly's movements. It was on the fourth night that Polly made the mistake of walking to the beach alone.

She was confused and unhappy, caught up in her

188

unbidden thoughts about Dev and Angelique. She walked slowly down the white sand, retracing the path she and Dev had walked the one and only time they had made love.

When she reached the spot where they had lain, she sat upon the grass and looked out over the calm sea. Soft waves broke gently against the shore, and the moon sat contentedly on the horizon casting its pale white light in a wide path across it. She closed her eyes and felt the breeze brush lightly against her overheated skin. She wanted again to feel Dev's mouth, hard and seeking against hers. She sighed and lay back against the cool earth, letting her imagination bring the scene to life in her mind.

She did not hear the two men creep toward her from the shadows until it was too late and they were already upon her. Her screams were muffled by the huge hand clamped over her mouth, and it took them only a few seconds to tie her hands firmly behind her. They tied a gag over her mouth, and one of them, the largest, hoisted her over his shoulder. His hands pawed at her ample buttocks, reaching up under her skirts as he carried her toward the longboat they had hidden, and he laughed at her furious twisting to dislodge his seeking hands.

She felt herself lowered into the longboat, then both men climbed in and began to row. She could not see over the sides and began to cry in fear at where they could be taking her. It was almost two hours before she heard the longboat bump against something solid. She looked up at the outline of the huge ship that loomed above her. Her body was numb from lying in one position so long; her fingers were beyond feeling; and she felt she would never be able to walk again. Her mouth was aching from the tight gag about it, and her face was wet with tears.

The large man reached down and lifted her effortlessly to her feet, ignoring her moan of pain as her blood began to recirculate. Tossing her over his shoulder again, he climbed the ladder with her and walked across the deck to the companionway. He descended the ladder and walked to the door of a cabin and knocked.

"Come in."

He opened the door and went inside. "Here's the gal you wanted, Sir."

"Put her down in that chair and get out," came the reply.

"Yes, Sir," said he and dropped her unceremoniously in a chair. Polly had her first look at her captor. She examined him almost as closely as he was examining her. He was no one she had ever seen before.

Don Esteban stood in front of her, with his hands clasped behind his back. His eyes took in everything about her, and she began to tremble in fear at his intense gaze. It made her feel naked as though he had stripped away the dress that covered her.

"You will listen to me in silence," he demanded. "If you agree with my suggestions, I will untie you and we will talk. If not . . ." He shrugged and laughed. "I shall give you back to the men who brought you and forget you. Are you listening?"

She nodded violently, her eyes wide with fear at what the two men who brought her could do to her.

"Good. You are Polly Dillon?"

She nodded.

"You were once to wed a man named Devon Carlisle."

Again she nodded.

"Now he has married another."

She watched him, the line of his questions gathering her interest.

"I understand you were not too happy about this marriage?"

Her eyes flamed with anger and she nodded again.

He chuckled. "How would you like it if I were to erase Angelique Montalban from this world and leave Carlisle free to come to you?"

She did not need to nod again, he could tell her thoughts by the look in her eyes.

"Now, if I untie you, are you agreeable to my plans?"

One quick nod brought him to her side, and within minutes she was untied and the gag removed from her mouth.

"Who are you?" she asked.

"That knowledge is unnecessary to you. Who I am and what I want is none of your business. But we can help each other get what we want. I will remove Angelique Montalban from Devon Carlisle's life forever. You need only give me a little help, and soon the way will be clear for you to have what you want."

"Why do you want her?"

"If you continue to ask questions," he said angrily, "then we will cease talking and you can leave."

"No!" she said hastily. "I'll ask no more questions. I want Dev and I want that silver-haired witch out of his life forever!"

"Then I see we both have the same goal." Don Esteban smiled. "If you will sit down, I will pour you a glass of wine." He laughed lightly. "Then I shall explain what you are to do."

When Don Esteban had finished explaining his plan and rose from his chair, the light from the lantern cast a golden glow about the room. It played across his face as he leaned over the table, placing both hands on it. The shadows that fell across his face gave him a satanic look. His mouth broadened in an evil smile. Polly shrank back into her seat.

"Do not think to betray me. My punishment is swift and sure. Do you understand?" he said in a voice that was deceptively soft.

"I will not betray you," she whispered.

"Now, I will have someone row you home."

"Not the two that brought me," she pleaded.

"You don't appreciate their company?" he laughed. "I do not blame you. They are pigs. I have another man who can row you back. He is not very pretty to look at, but he is harmless. Come," he said.

She followed him to the door, and passed quickly through. The passageway was lit dimly and at first she did not see the dark misshapen form that detached itself from the shadows and started toward them. She looked toward Don Esteban, and he motioned her forward. Turning quickly, she came face to face with the person who was coming from the other end of the passageway. At that moment, the ship swayed slightly and the lantern light flooded over him. Polly screamed and backed toward Don Esteban.

"Don't be frightened. I told you Carlos is not very pretty to look at. But he is harmless."

Polly swallowed thickly and looked at Carlos again. His body was bent almost double by the rounded hump on his shoulder. His neck twisted upward, and he looked at her from under thick black brows. His hair, at one time black, was thickly sprinkled with silver. A black patch covered one eye and his lips were twisted grotesquely. As he moved closer, she could see that he dragged one leg behind him. His shoulders and arms seemed powerful, for they were layered with thick heavy muscle.

"I picked up Carlos about six months ago. It seems the local authorities near his home wanted to hang him for some misdeed or other. I don't particularly care what it was. He is useful to me and he is silent. You see, my dear, he can't talk. Can you, Carlos?"

Carlos smiled a twisted grin that made him look even more grotesque. Ugly guttural sounds came from his lips. Polly leaned toward Don Esteban.

"Carlos, I want you to row this young lady back to the harbor. Polly, you will come to the same spot where we found you at the agreed-upon time. By then, our loving couple should be back, and we can begin our plan."

Polly nodded and followed Carlos to the waiting longboat. She sat, amazed at his strength as he made the boat skim quickly over the water. When they reached the beach, he jumped out quickly to help her to the beach.

Fear lent wings to her feet as she ran from him. Partway up the beach, she turned. She could see that he was still standing by the boat, watching her. She turned and ran again, and this time she did not look back.

Carlos stood by the boat watching the girl's receding figure. His one eye gleamed in the bright moonlight. Then, slowly, he pushed the boat out into the current and jumped in and began to row back to the waiting ship. He tied the boat alongside the ship and laboriously climbed the ladder. Once on board, he made his way back to the captain's cabin. A light rap, a silent answer, and he opened the door and went inside.

"You delivered her safely?"

"Uh huh."

"Good. Now I have something I want you to do. You remember where you left her?" He waited for Carlos' affirmative nod. "You will go ashore, keep yourself out of people's way, for you would be quite easily remembered. I want to know when Carlisle and his wife return. If possible, find out where they have gone. Keep your eyes open. Meet this girl at the same rendezvous in two weeks. After the meeting, report back to me. Is that all understood?"

Several low guttural grunts served for an answer, and Carlos turned and left the cabin. He made his way back to the longboat and rowed himself ashore. Hiding the boat, he crept into the shadows of the rocks that lined the beach and disappeared as thoroughly as if the ground had swallowed him up.

The days passed slowly for Polly. She did as Don Esteban had instructed. The day after her abduction, she went to Cap's house. Apologizing for what she had done the day of the wedding, she begged Cap's forgiveness.

Cap felt sorry for her. He knew how she felt about Dev. Quickly, he forgave her and made her welcome again in his home.

He did, Mattie did not. She eyed Polly suspiciously, but did not let it show. Some instinctive feeling told her to beware, something was amiss. She could not put her finger on what it was, but she promised herself to keep an eye on Polly.

Although she watched her closely, Polly did nothing more to arouse her suspicions, and by the time Dev and Angel were due to return, even Mattie's guard was lowered.

Andy was another whose suspicions had been aroused. He was a man who had depended on his instincts for survival too long. He had watched Polly's face the day of the wedding, and he knew without a doubt that she hated Angel completely, hated her with a violent poison. Like Mattie, he kept his eyes open for any overt signs of trouble.

Of course, it did nothing to detract from Andy's charm and attraction to a pretty girl. He took Polly riding, sailing, and for picnics on the beach and tried his best to bed her. Neither of them realized that eyes watched every move they made, noted their weak spots, and stored methods of reaching them at the proper time.

Andy had been thinking, too, of Dev and Angel. He realized it would be impossible to stay here once they returned, knowing how he felt about Angel and, worse, knowing that Dev knew, too. He began to get his ship ready for sea. Cap recognized his preparations.

"Are you planning on leaving before Dev and Angel get back?"

Andy was silent for a time, then he turned and looked into Cap's steady gaze. There was sympathy there, and understanding.

"Cap, you and I know it's best I leave soon. There's no sense in asking for trouble, not trouble that can only hurt everybody and break up a good friendship. I'll be back one day. Maybe by that time, Angel will be fat and have six babes." He laughed, then his eyes became serious again. "But I doubt it," he added softly.

"You're right, Andy, it is best. And you might find another woman by then. One you can marry, who'll tame those wild ways of yours."

"Never gave it a thought, Cap," he laughed, his crystal

green eyes twinkling with merriment.

"How soon are you leaving?"

"Oh, I guess the *Hawk* will be ready to set sail in less than a week."

"Where will you be headed?"

"I don't know for sure. Away from here. Maybe I'll try those south sea islands I've read so much about. They tell me there's a lot of pretty girls down there."

"We'll miss you, Andy. I know that both Dev and Angel will be disappointed, but I see the wisdom of what you're doing."

"Thanks, Cap."

Preparations continued on the *Hawk,* and it was late at night when they were finished. He would leave on the morning tide. He regretted that he would not be able to see Dev and Angel for a long time. The night was going to be long. Sleep would not come. After trying in vain for hours, he rose, dressed, and walked the silent decks of his ship.

He stood at the rail and looked down on the deserted harbor and wharf and thought of how he was going to miss this place. The call of adventure had dimmed in his ears. Now, his heart called for a more gentle, quiet life.

He was about to turn and go back to his bunk when he heard a slight sound from the docks below. He gazed, narrow-eyed, but could see no signs of anyone. Again he turned away, but froze in his tracks as a quiet voice called out his name from the dock below.

"Captain Ryan?"

"Who's there?"

"A friend, Captain Ryan."

"Come out into the light, *friend,*" Andy said. "Let me see who I'm talking to."

196

"It is better that you do not, right now."

"Better? Better for whom?"

The soft voice chuckled lightly.

"Better for me. Listen closely. I have little time and what I have to say is important to you and your friends."

"What?"

"When Mr. Carlisle gets home with his bride, tell him to protect her well, for a sinister hand is reaching out for her. She is safe with him only as long as he is alert and watches carefully. Tell him not to trust all who call themselves friends."

"Who are you? Why don't you come aboard and tell me what's going on?"

"The time is not right, my friend. All I can do for now is to warn you, and have you carry my warning to the others."

"But, damn it, man, what am I warning them against?"

"Captain Cortland knows. I wait, and I watch. When the time is right, I will do more. For now, Captain Cortland must be told, 'Be warned, the time is near.'"

The voice faded away.

The rest of the night, it was useless to try to get any sleep. The new morning sun found Andy at Cap's door.

Cap's brows drew together in a heavy frown as he sat in quiet contemplation of what Andy told him.

"Dev and Angel are due to arrive home the day after tomorrow. I hate to upset them as soon as they get home. We'll keep this to ourselves for now, and I'll keep a close watch for trouble. I'll warn Dev if I think anything is wrong. Until then, I'll keep my own eyes open."

"Cap, if we just knew what to look out for."

"*We?*" Cap questioned.

"You don't think I'd leave now," Andy grinned. "Just

197

when everything is about to bust loose. A good Irishman never ran away from a fight in his life."

"Andy, for the next few days, why don't you run the *Hawk* up and down the coastline. There are hundreds of small coves and places for a ship to be anchored."

"A ship . . . like a Spanish galleon?"

Cap nodded.

"I'll sail first thing tomorrow. Would you like me to leave a couple of my men here just in case something does happen?"

"No. That would only warn him off and make him more careful about his future plans, and we might not get a warning about them. We know for sure that they won't move against us until Dev and Angel are back. By that time, you will have scouted the coastline. If our luck holds, we might ferret him out before he can get a chance to move against us."

"All right, Cap. I'll do whatever you think is right."

"Be alert, and be patient, Andy. We have two days left before Dev comes back. If we don't find them, it might mean he isn't close enough to cause any problems yet. If we do find him, we'll do our best to settle the problem once and for all."

Andy nodded and after they finished breakfast, he returned to his ship.

Cap walked to the window. He stood quietly looking out over the calm blue sea. Then he said softly, as if to himself, "Well, it's about time you got here, Miguel. We'll keep your daughter safe for you until you are ready. Go with God, Miguel Montalban."

Chapter 17

Andy eased his ship out of the harbor, its sails unfurling in the first gray light of dawn. He slowly paced the quarter deck, his mind on his quarry. He remembered childhood days along this coastline and he tried to place some of the coves and areas where a ship the size of the galleon could hide. Some places he eliminated from his mind as not having depth, and others were too obvious from the sea. This left only six or seven places that he knew of, and he wondered just how many places he did not know of. It was going to take some time, and he felt the tug of instinct again that told him time was limited.

He planned on sailing northward along the coast for at least a hundred miles, then turning about. He would retrace his path to try to find anything he might have missed on the way. Then he would sail southward for a hundred miles and repeat what he had done before.

He did most of his sleeping in the heat of the early afternoon so that he would be awake and alert at night when a spot might slip by them.

Each time his crew spotted a hidden harbor, he would send a longboat to examine it for any trace of a ship.

Two days later, he had covered the first hundred miles northward, and had retraced his path without any sign of a ship. He passed Bedloe and headed southward to inspect the next hundred miles. The further south he went, the more his premonition of trouble bothered him.

Four days later, he dropped anchor off a small cove whose entrance was almost completely hidden by a deep, narrow channel with giant trees on each side that grew out over the cove in an arch and clasped branches over the water. "How easy to push them aside and slip into the quiet of the cove, letting the branches cover their presence. The longboat was sent out, but before it could cover half the distance to shore, the branches trembled, then parted, and the Spanish galleon, under full sail, made for the open sea. Andy stood in surprise for only an instant, then came quickly to life.

He turned to Briggs. "Signal our longboat to go on to shore, then bring her about, Briggs. We'll overtake them and maybe find some answers to a lot of questions."

If Andy thought it was going to be a simple matter overtaking and boarding the mysterious ship, he was rudely awakened. The ship out-maneuvered and outran him for seven days. It sent him from laughing amusement to frustrated anger.

He knew it was a matter of time, for no matter how the galleon maneuvered, the *Hawk* was close behind him, and the distance slowly but inevitably closed.

He had to admit that the man guiding the Spanish vessel was one hell of a seaman.

As suddenly as it had begun, the race came to an abrupt end. The galleon slowed her speed. It was a blow to Andy's pride, this signal that he could not have caught her if the captain of the galleon had not wanted him to.

By the time he had a signal sent that he wanted to come aboard, and permission was granted, he was in a state of cold, hard fury.

When he stepped aboard, he was met by the captain himself, who stood with his hands clasped behind his back and watched Andy intently.

"I'm Captain Andrew Ryan of the *Sea Hawk*," Andy said in a clipped voice.

"And I, Sir, am Captain Emilio Martinez. May I welcome you aboard the *Santa Anna*." He smiled and bowed ever so slightly. "Would you join me in my cabin, Sir? I am sure we can talk much better over a drink and, ah, in private."

Andy nodded, and followed the captain to his cabin, where the door was closed firmly behind them. The captain motioned Andy to a seat and went to a side table. Picking up a decanter of wine, he poured two glasses, then came to Andy and handed one to him with a small half smile on his lips and a faint twinkle of amusement in his amber eyes.

"Why did you run when I signaled that I wanted to talk to you?" Andy asked.

The captain gave an eloquent shrug. "Why did you pursue me, Sir? I do not know you. Spain and England are at peace. And since piracy is very prevalent on the high seas today, you can see why I did not stop."

"I flew no black flag," Andy snapped. "You could see my colors clearly."

The captain chuckled. "Once I was almost taken by a pirate who flew no black flag. I must repeat, Sir, why did you pursue me?"

Andy watched the captain as he slowly sat behind his desk, folded his hands on the top and waited for Andy's reply.

He was shorter than Andy, with a square, sturdy build. His skin was a deep olive, and his dark hair was long and tied back. His amber eyes glowed under winged black brows and his thin mustache twitched with the amused curve of his full lips. He was definitely not what Andy had expected in an accomplice of Don Esteban's. Then Andy's wits caught up with his anger. He leaned back in his chair and chuckled, mostly at himself.

"You," he said softly, "led me away from the coastline on purpose."

The captain did not reply, but gazed at Andy. The smile had faded from both his lips and his eyes.

"Where is the man I seek, Captain?" he asked in the same cool voice. "Where is Don Esteban?"

Their eyes held across the desk, but it was Captain Martinez whose eyes fell away first. He flushed under Andy's steady gaze and abruptly stood up. His hand pounded the top of the desk in a solid thud.

"Don Esteban is not on this ship, has not been on this ship for over a month."

"Then he *was* with you, and you probably know more than anyone else where he is and what he is doing."

"I do not know, either where he is at the moment, or his plans. I had no idea of anything he had in mind when he hired my services."

"Then why did you run?"

"It was the last thing he hired me to do, and I am glad I need have nothing more to do with the man."

Andy contemplated the captain for a few moments, then he said, "He had no intention for us to ever meet, did he? I was not supposed to catch you. From what I have seen of your expertise, I believe it would have been impossible to catch you unless you wanted me to. Why did you make it possible?"

Captain Martinez sighed deeply and turned his back on Andy. He stood looking out over the sea. "I am a man of honor, I would like to believe. I have wanted done with

202

this business Don Esteban is about. There is something deep within me that tells me that what he is doing is wrong, is evil. I do not even know what it is about." He turned and faced Andy again. "I only know that he harbors a great hate, a hate that has driven him close to insanity. I do not know toward whom that hatred is directed, but I feel pity for them if he succeeds in whatever he plans."

"Why," Andy asked gently, "did you decide to stop and tell me all this?"

"Because in all good conscience, I could no longer be part of it, and I wanted to give you warning so your friends would be aware. Don Esteban must have known of my feelings, for he came to me more than a month ago and told me he no longer needed my services, that I was to do this one last thing and I would be free. I was to keep you away from the coast as long as possible. I fought with myself, but I could no longer stand the man and his vile temper. So . . ."

"So . . . we are here, and I know nothing more about Don Esteban, his plans, or his whereabouts than I did before."

"What is it you want me to say, Captain Ryan? I have told you all I know."

"No," Andy grinned. "You have told me all that you believe you know."

Captain Martinez sat back down in his chair, his eyes narrowed. "What are you trying to say, that I am lying to you. If I had not wanted to tell you anything, Señor Ryan," he added in a hard quiet voice, "believe me, you, or no other, would have caught me."

Andy chuckled. "I do not doubt that for a moment, Sir. And I do not believe for a moment that you are deliberately lying to me. I think that you just do not know that you have more information to give."

"Perhaps you will tell me what it is you believe I know?"

"All right," Andy replied. "Do you know who Don Esteban is?"

"Yes."

"How long have you known him or of him?"

"More than twenty years. A man with Don Esteban's power and reputation cannot remain unknown."

"But you know nothing of his situation?"

"That is correct."

"Did you know of a man named Miguel Montalban?"

"Miguel Montalban? The family name is very familiar, but . . . no." He said with a puzzled look on his face, "No, I know no Miguel Montalban."

"Then, tell me, do you know of a family named D'Santiago?"

"D'Santiago? Yes, of course! They were one of the wealthiest families in Spain. There was a terrible tragedy in the family. The church, the trials. And then the daughter ran off with a young man. I know that there were many rumors at the time. One of them was that she gave birth to a child, and they all died. I never listen to rumors with a believing ear, however."

"In this case, the rumor is true, as far as it goes."

"Well then. If there is a child of that union, it is a very wealthy child. The D'Santiagos died leaving all their wealth in trust for their child. The wealth it would inherit would be beyond a man's wildest dreams. But you said as far as it goes. Perhaps it would be better for us both and save a lot of time if you just began at the beginning and told me the entire story."

"I agree," Andy laughed. "And if I could persuade you to another glass of wine, I will do just that."

"But, of course, Señor. I am an inattentive host. But you must pardon me, it is my curiosity about the story you will tell me. You see, I knew Anna D'Santiago. She was one of the loveliest women I have ever met, the most beautiful purple-blue eyes and, you will not believe me, Sir, but she had the most angelic hair. It was like spun silver." He laughed an embarrassed chuckle. "I imagine you think I am a romantic fool."

"Oh, no, Captain. I have seen your vision myself and I agree, she is the loveliest woman I have ever met."

"You have met Anna D'Santiago! She is alive and you know where she is?"

"No. I have met the daughter of Anna D'Santiago and Miguel Montalban. She is as lovely as you say her mother was. Anna D'Santiago . . . is dead."

He watched the captain's face darken with pain and understood he must have known Anna much better than he admitted.

"You say you have met the daughter, then Anna and this . . . Miguel . . . they were married?"

"They were, and Captain Cortland has proof of this hidden away."

"What is her name?"

"Angelique D'Santiago Montalban."

"Angelique," the captain repeated softly. Then he looked closely again at Andy. "You say Anna is dead. What of her husband, this child's father? Where is he now?"

Andy sipped his wine, then set the glass gently on the edge of the table. Leaning back in his chair, he looked deep into the captain's amber eyes. Martinez returned his gaze honestly, and an unspoken trust was established between the two men. Andy sketched the story for the attentive Spaniard, whose unrequited love for the mother was the same as his for the daughter. Then he picked up his glass of wine and drank.

"And so," Captain Martinez said when he had finished telling of Angelique's marriage to Dev, "you are a conquest of the daughter, as I was of the mother."

Andy lifted his head in protest, but when their eyes met, he knew it was useless to deny it. "You are right. I love her. But I would do nothing to jeopardize her marriage or my friendship with her husband."

"You are a good man, Captain Ryan. One I should like to know better, one I should like to one day call friend. Come, let us have another drink and put our heads together. Maybe we can come up with some clue to the whereabouts of Don Esteban or at least some plan of helping your friends."

It was another three hours of deep conversation before Andy was escorted to the ship's rail. He was quiet while Briggs rowed him back to the *Sea Hawk*. Once aboard, Andy went straight to his cabin and closed the door behind him.

When Briggs brought him his supper later, he found him bent over his desk, pondering several maps.

"Put the tray over there, Briggs. I'll eat later," he said.

"Yes, Sir," Briggs replied. He moved slowly toward the table, but his eyes strayed to the maps Andy had on the desk.

"We changin' course, Sir?" he asked hopefully.

"No," came the terse reply.

"We goin' back home?"

"No."

"We just gonna sit here?"

This brought Andy's attention to him for the first time since he'd entered the cabin. He looked at Briggs' inquisitive blue eyes and laughed. "Briggs, I don't know at this moment where we're going, but I promise you, just as soon as I get this little puzzle worked out, you will be the first to know."

"Thank you, Sir," Briggs laughed. "I thought I was goin' to have to pull the story from you piece by piece. You ain't always been this closemouthed about what we were doin'. Now, all this mystery about that other ship has sure got my curiosity up."

"I don't doubt that a bit, knowing your curiosity," Andy replied dryly.

"Well, you got to admit, Sir, things ain't been the same since you walked up the hill to that convent. Whatever happened up there sure made some changes in our way of life."

"Yes, I'll certainly admit to that, Briggs. Right now, I've got to figure out a way to help Dev and Captain Cortland out of a bad situation."

"Does that problem have anything to do with that other ship we just overtook? You took a lot longer than just a polite visit."

"You're a very observant man, Briggs."

"I been observin' you since you was knee-high to a puppy. There ain't no way you can keep a secret from me very long. I know for sure something about this whole mess had got you tied in knots. The best thing we could do is fill our sails with a strong sea breeze and leave this place once and for all. I got a feeling this whole mess is going to cost us a lot more than it's worth. I don't want the price to be you and the *Hawk*."

"I imagine you're right, Briggs," Andy replied, "but I can't walk away from the debt I owe Captain Cortland. I can't turn my back on a friend like Dev, and I can't . . ." He stopped himself. "Briggs," he said sharply, "have the men prepare to put on every ounce of speed we can get. I want all sails up. Within the hour, I'll give you a destination."

"Yes, Sir," Briggs answered. He knew from Andy's tone and the cool sharp snap of his order that he meant business. When Andy was in this mood, Briggs never questioned him. He left immediately. Andy sat down at his desk again and pulled toward him the map he had been looking at when Briggs had entered. He marked several places. Then he stood up and folded it and took it to a small chest in the corner of his cabin.

No one was more amazed than Briggs when Andy set his course. He wanted to question Andy more, but the set of his shoulders and the glint in his eyes told him otherwise.

Briggs had sailed with Andrew Ryan for many years, even when Andy had been an ordinary seaman. They had been together on the *Eastern Star* when the incident occurred which had drawn them together in lasting friendship. The captain of that vessel—"Damn his soul," thought Briggs—harbored an unreasonable hatred toward Andy. Briggs did not discover the cause of this vile feeling until after he and Andy had become fast friends.

Andy had been a handsome young man; some called him "Pretty Boy." Briggs had noticed that the captain, before his hatred of Andy, had been attentive to the boy. Too attentive, to the mind of ordinary folk. Then came the voyage when Briggs had taken ill with the beginnings of scurvy. Andy was tending his watch, and when he was not on deck during his or Briggs' hours, he was down belowdecks, tending to Briggs in his illness.

Briggs would never forget the evening when the foul captain came belowdecks to ask why he wasn't on his watch. "You've been shirking your duty," the womanishly fat captain had whined.

"No, Sir," Briggs protested, struggling to a sitting position. "Truth is, I been under the weather, Sir. In a day or two . . ."

"You seem well enough now, Briggs," the captain said. "I'll expect you on deck at next watch."

"I'll take his duty, Sir," Andy interrupted from his bunk.

The captain waddled about and stared down at the young redhead. "And who are you, sailor?"

"Ryan, Sir. I've been taking his duty these past days, and—"

The captain was gazing intently at Ryan, a menacing gleam in his watery eyes. "Ah, I see. And you look like a strong lad, too."

He moved to Andy's bunk and reached out a hand and squeezed his biceps. "Indeed, you *are* quite strong," he said in a thick voice. "We shall have to discuss this, Mr. Ryan. I don't know if I should let you take his watch or not."

"But, Sir . . ."

"Come, come, Mr. Ryan," he laughed. "The situation can be discussed further in my cabin. You will accompany me there now and we shall see just what— ah—*arrangements* can be made."

Andy cast one look at Briggs over his shoulder and followed the captain out the door.

Briggs did not see Andy again for almost a week, and when he did, Andy was tied to the mast and the first mate was whipping him.

It was the first day that Briggs could maneuver about unaided, and he had come on deck because he heard the commotion there. He stood frozen as the whip cracked against Andy's bloody back for the last time. Andy was unconscious by then, his body limp against the mast, held only by the ropes that bound him.

"Goddamn it," Briggs whispered to a sailor who stood near him. "What's the boy done to deserve that kind of treatment?"

"I'd not say it's what the boy *has* done. I'd say it's what the boy *refused* to do."

"But he's never disobeyed an order!"

"Briggs, don't you know the captain wanted to bed the boy? Kid put up one hell of a fight. Finally ended it all by smashin' him in the face. I think this is only the beginning of what Andy's goin' to get until he comes around."

Briggs looked up at the quarterdeck where the captain stood. His pale eyes glowed with pleasure as he watched Andy's body being taken down and carried away. Briggs knew then that the sailor was right. The captain would brutalize the boy until he surrendered. He knew that would destroy Andy's pride and eventually kill him.

He made plans then. Stealing food and water, he stored them in one of the longboats. Then, when Andy was well enough, he got him into the longboat and they pushed away from the ship. He remembered Andy's feverish energy as he helped him row.

He had been with Andy since then.

Briggs thought back over all this and smiled. It did not

matter where Andy wanted to go or what he wanted to do. Daniel Briggs would be with him. He pursed his lips and began to whistle an off-tune melody.

Andy heard the echoes of the whistle in his cabin and chuckled to himself. Good old Briggs. The one person he could always count on.

Chapter 18

Angelique blinked and tried to listen for whatever it was that had wakened her. Dev lay beside her, breathing evenly in a deep sleep. The room was still dark and she lay still until her eyes became accustomed to it.

She rose from the bed slowly, not to waken Dev. Walking to the open window, she looked out, then understood what it was that brought her awake. Heavy black clouds passed rapidly over the face of the moon, and the low rumble of thunder could be heard in the distance. Heavy waves rushed toward the shore in advance of a wind that was stirring the ocean to a boil. The trees around the cottage and those that ran along the edge of the beach were bent almost double by the force of the wind.

She folded her arms on the window frame and rested her chin against them and smiled to herself. She felt so safe, from the storms of nature, from the storms of life. "How grateful I am," she thought, "that God has given me the love of so many wonderful people."

Tomorrow she and her husband would go home, and she regretted it. She did not want the wonderful days and nights she had spent here, alone with Dev, ever to come to an end. They had been days filled with laughter and happiness. Dev had taught her to fish, then to clean and cook her catch. After that, when they went fishing, she made sure she did not bait her hook; therefore, she caught nothing. It was several days before Dev realized what she was doing. He had promptly tossed her overboard.

He had taught her to swim well, but when she was tossed in, she swam down deep, then quietly came up on the other side of the boat. Dev, who had been watching for her to surface, had become alarmed, then frightened. He dove into the water and searched for her. In the meantime, she pulled herself aboard and waited for him to surface. He came up after an interminal time, gasping for air and with a look of terror on his face. She hadn't realized the effect her little prank would have on him.

That night, Dev had built a fire on the beach and cooked their meal, then they sat together on the warm sand and watched the sun set. The dark, azure ocean was bordered by ribbons of red satin as the sun settled for the night. Then, suddenly, bright diamond stars glittered in the cloudless sky.

They had made love there on the warm sand with a tenderness that caused Angel to cry at the beauty they shared. Then they had strolled the beach together and returned to their small cottage.

She was so involved in her thoughts that she did not hear Dev awaken and stir in the bed to watch her. She was outlined against a window brightened with flashes of lightning. The blanket she had wrapped about her had loosened, and she held it together between her breasts. Her pale skin glowed in the dim light, and her hair hung loose and free about her like silver mist. Slowly, he rose from the bed. She was so engrossed in her thoughts that she did not hear him approach until he was beside her. Then her lips parted to meet his. They stood at the window together.

"If it continues to storm like this, we won't be able to leave tomorrow. The sea will be too high for our small boat," he said.

She turned to face him, and the blanket dropped away as she twined her slender arms about his neck. "Are you so anxious to leave here?" she whispered.

He drew her against him. "Angel, I could stay here and be completely happy as long as I have you. I was thinking about you. Aren't you anxious to get back home?"

"Dev," she said, her eyes seeking his in the pale half light, "don't you know yet that I want only to be where you are, that I want only to share your life and your love, no matter where we are. Have I not convinced you yet that you are all I want?"

He lowered his head to touch her lips gently with his. The storm outside raged, but it went unheard by the lovers in the small cottage by the ocean, whose own raging passions engulfed them.

The next day, they were greeted affectionately by both Mattie and Cap when they arrived. After a huge meal—Mattie insisted upon it—Dev and Cap took a walk to the harbor and checked on the *Wayfarer*.

They walked in silence, and Cap grinned to himself in understanding of where Dev's wandering thoughts had taken him.

"Where's Andy, Cap?" Dev asked at length.

"Took off the day after you left, looking for the Spanish galleon."

"You two still looking after me like a mother hen after her chicks. I think we're safe now. Angelique's father—if he's alive—is safe from Don Esteban now, and Angel will be guarded with my life."

214

"Still, if we can find it, it's best we know where it is so we can keep an eye on it."

Dev laughed. He felt secure that the future was bright and he was enough protection for Angelique. "Have it your way, Cap. How long has Andy been gone?"

"Well, I'm surprised he isn't back by now. He was only going to roam up and down the coast—like you two did when you were boys, adventuring into all the little coves and outlets. If he finds her, we'll watch. If he doesn't, I'd feel a lot safer."

As they neared the harbor, Dev could see that there was a number of ships at anchor. Some of them, he'd never seen before, but none of them was Spanish.

They checked the *Wayfarer* over completely. Both were pleased with the condition she was in. She had been repainted and refitted with new canvas. Only the spot where her name had been needed attention. It was now blank, and awaiting the sign-painters from the village.

"We goin' to be sailing on an unnamed ship now, Cap?" Dev laughed.

"Well, in the two weeks that you and Angelique were gone, I made some decisions."

"Decisions?"

"Yes, I've begun to realize how good it is to be home all the time, and what with the grandchildren . . ."

"Aren't you rushing things a bit."

"I don't think so," Cap replied, his glittering eyes on Dev. "I expect I'll be a grandpa before too long."

"What are you driving at, Cap?"

"Well, I think the proper place for a grandpa is sitting at home in the shade of a tree and spoiling his grandchildren."

"Cap! You aren't going to sell the *Wayfarer*, are you? I

can't see myself serving under any other master but you."

"Don't worry about me, boy. I'm healthy as a horse."

"Then what kind of nonsense are you talking—selling the *Wayfarer*, staying at home? I don't understand what you're doing."

"Now, Dev," Cap replied with a laugh. "*You* said I was selling the *Wayfarer*. I didn't."

"Then, why . . . ?"

"Why don't you let me finish what I want to say before you begin asking questions?"

"I'm sorry, Cap. Go ahead."

"Well, I decided to wait for the new captain to come and name her." He grinned at Dev.

It was several moments before Dev understood.

"Cap!" he nearly cried. "How can I ever thank you? I hope I can make as good a captain for her as the one she is used to."

"If I weren't sure you'd be a fine captain, son, you would still be cabin boy. Consider it my wedding present to you and my new daughter. By the way, what are you going to name her?"

Dev grinned and turned to look at his ship. He knew instantly what he was going to name her, and as he turned to Cap, he realized that he did, too. They laughed together.

"I'm going home right now. Will you have the name printed on her? I want to show Angel right away."

"Aye, Captain," said Cap.

Dev paced himself so that it would take a good half an hour to get home, for he knew it would be impossible to keep this exciting news from Angelique once he was there. When he was at the front gate, he could contain himself no longer. He moved quickly up the walk and when he opened the door, he shouted for Angelique. Mattie appeared from the kitchen and stared at him in shock. Never had Dev ever come home like this. They both heard the rapid tap of Angel's feet as she left their room and ran down the stairs. Her face had turned completely white.

"Dev, what is it? What's wrong?" Mattie asked quickly.

"Nothing's *wrong*," he laughed. "I want you both to come to the harbor with me. I've a great surprise."

"Come along," Mattie laughed good-heartedly, and scurried Angelique out the door. "The carriage is hitched. We may as well see what the to-do is about."

Dev held his own against Angelique's questions all the way to the docks. He helped Mattie down, then Angel.

"Look!" he said as he pointed to the ship. There, on the side in bold letters, was her new name, *Lady Angel*.

"She's ours, Angel," he whispered against her hair. "Cap has given her to us as a wedding present. You are now married to Captain Devon Carlisle."

She turned to him, and they spoke wordlessly to one another. Then he took her in his arms and held her tightly against him. There was a lot of laughter and congratulations as the men came ashore, and soon it began to turn into a party. Cap had arranged for food and drink, and before too long, rousing music could be heard across the harbor. The captains and crews of the closely berthed ships had been invited.

The party extended long after the sun had disappeared and a huge yellow moon had taken its place. Angel danced until she was exhausted. She'd drunk a little too much wine for her own good. Her head was spinning and she giggled helplessly as an amused Dev helped her into the carriage and drove her home. Once there, she declared firmly that she could get out of the carriage herself; whereupon she stumbled and fell into Dev's arms.

"Oh, dear," she murmured against him as she lay her head on his shoulder, "I think I'm a little drunk." She could hear the laughter in Dev's voice as he replied that truly, she was.

"Angel," he said after he had carried her to bed, "you're going to hate yourself in the morning."

She pouted. "You don't love me anymore."

"Of course, I love you."

She nodded her head and lay back on the pillow, and instantly she was sound asleep. He stood above her and smiled at the picture she made. Then he took off his clothes and got into the bed. As soon as he was beside her, he heard her murmur something, and she turned about him as mistletoe does the oak.

A soft moaning sound brought Dev awake in the early hours of the morning. Angel was turned with her back to him and curled into a small tight ball. In the pale morning sunshine, he could see she was trembling.

"Angel, are you all right?"

A low groan was his answer.

"Angel?" He gently rolled her toward him. When he saw her face, it took all he could do to keep from laughing. Angel was suffering severely from a hangover. Her face had a faint green cast and her eyes were filled with tears of self pity. She held her arms crossed about her stomach.

"Oh, Dev," she moaned, "I'm dying. Some terrible illness has stricken me."

"That terrible illness, my wife," he laughed, "is the result of too much wine last night."

He rose from the bed and walked around to her side. She looked up at him with pleading eyes.

"Just be still, I'll go down to get you something to help relieve some of the pain in your head."

She nodded, her face a mask of helpless anguish. He went downstairs and in one glass he poured a substantial amount of brandy, then he brewed a strong pot of coffee and poured a cup. With both containers, he went back up the stairs. Going to the bed, he set both on the stand beside her, then helped a moaning, miserable Angel to a sitting position. He handed her the glass of brandy first.

"Drink it all, straight down. No stopping," he ordered, and while she tried valiantly to obey his command, he reached under the bed and slid out the chamber pot.

As she swallowed the last gulp of brandy, she gasped as the warm liquid struck her stomach. Dev reached out deftly and removed the glass, putting it on the stand just in time to grasp her trembling body and hold her head over the pot. Her stomach relieved itself violently, and she whimpered and moaned in misery. Tenderly, he wiped her mouth. Laying her back among the pillows, he handed her the coffee.

"Now, sip this. In a few minutes, you'll begin to feel better."

"Oh," she sighed. "I shall never, never do that again."

He sat on the edge of the bed and watched as she sipped the coffee. In a few moments, the pallor of her face told him she was reviving.

"I certainly hope not."

She looked at him, her eyes wide with horror. He kept his face straight with tremendous effort.

"Oh, Dev. What did I do last night?"

"Don't you remember?"

She shook her head, distress in her eyes.

"Well," he said seriously. "First, you told Davy Halt that he was the most charming man and the greatest sailor on the seas."

"Oh," she said softly.

"Then, you told Cap you intended to give him and Mattie all the grandchildren their house could hold."

Her face flushed bright pink. "I didn't, I didn't!"

"Yes, you did, and then when I brought you home, you begged me to come to bed with you. You said you wanted to make love all night, and that upset me no small league."

She cried out, "I'm sorry."

"Well, do you know why I was so upset?"

She gave a helpless shake of her head.

"Because you fainted before I could take advantage of your offer." He began to chuckle, then threw back his head and laughed heartily as she eyed him with surprise, then with growing knowledge that he was teasing her. Slowly, she placed the cup on the table, then reached behind her and grasped the edge of one of her pillows. With a thud, it landed in his face, bringing his laughter to an abrupt halt. He gave a muffled cry of surprise.

"Why, you little . . ." He gasped as he threw himself forward to grab her, but she slid quickly out the other side of the bed and he was rewarded with another armful of pillows and blankets. She stood on the far side of the bed and laughed at him as he rolled over on his back and watched her. The laughter died as he slowly rose from the bed and began to move toward her. She backed away, her hands out in front of her as if she could control him.

"Now, Dev," she cautioned, "you behave yourself. You deserved that for teasing me."

"Have you ever been spanked, you little imp?" he said as he made a grab for her.

But with a yelp, she put a chair between them. "Don't you dare!"

But the chair was a useless object of protection as he took hold of it in a firm grip and began to move it aside.

"Dev!" she squealed as she ran for the bed, but he was entirely too fast. He ran after her and gathered her up into his arms, and they fell into the bed together. She struggled and fought but his superior strength was too much for her tiny body. He held her back against him as he pulled the nightgown she wore up over her hips, and in a quick jerk, he brought it over her head and threw it aside on the floor. Holding her effortlessly with one arm, he caressed the round soft skin and chuckled.

"It would be a shame to damage my most valuable property," he whispered as both his arms came about her and drew her against him. His lips found hers, and he felt her body mold itself against his. Rose-tipped breasts pressed against his chest and her slender legs entwined in his, took his mind off any intentions he had had. He looked down into her deep purple pools of her eyes and smiled.

"Dev?"

"What, love?" he replied as he brushed his lips gently across her cheek and to the soft shoulder.

"Did I really do all those things?"

He chuckled as he kissed her quickly again. "Angel, you were your sweet wonderful self all evening. You sang, danced, and laughed and said nothing you should be ashamed of. The very best part of the evening was when you were trying to coax me into your bed."

"Well, now that I've found out what I wanted to know I guess we'd better go down for breakfast," Angel said with a wicked smile, her eyes aglow with mischief.

"You little devil," he laughed. His face pressed against the hollow of her throat. "If you think I'm going downstairs in this condition, you've got another think coming. Why, I'd shock Mattie out of ten years of her life."

He heard Angel's muffled giggle against his shoulder and looked up into her eyes to be rewarded by a look of passion that matched his.

"I love you, you silver-haired witch. You came from nowhere and turned my world upside down. Now I find I can't do without you, that my day has no light without you in it and the nights would be ones of misery if I could not feel you close."

Angel put both her hands against his cheeks, then slowly she slid them up to twine them in his hair and pull his mouth down to meet hers.

It was another two hours before they came down to breakfast. Mattie was alone in the kitchen and would have prepared their breakfast except Angel insisted she sit down and allow her to prepare Dev's breakfast herself.

"Where's Cap?"

"He ate early, then went to see about transferring the *Wayfarer*—I mean the *Lady Angel*—from his name to yours. He'll be back before dinner."

"Angel, why don't we take a walk along the beach this morning. It's a beautiful day," Dev offered, and Angel readily agreed.

After he ate, they left the house and walked in contented silence to the beach, where they strolled hand

222

in hand enjoying the warm salty taste of the sea breeze and each other.

Neither of them knew of the unblinking eye that watched them, or sensed the presence of the twisted form that had them under close surveillance. He made no sound, but his one eye was glued, not on the man, but the beautiful silver-haired girl whose laughter drifted to him and whose beauty he devoured.

"Dev, I have never been so happy in my whole life," Angel bubbled. "The world is the most beautiful of places."

Dev smiled and held her close to him. He did not say anything that might spoil her delight. But suddenly, he felt the urgent desire to cling to her as if some evil thing from somewhere was about to snatch her away.

Chapter 19

Dev hated to do it, but after two weeks of enjoying the leisure life at home, he had to prepare to take the *Lady Angel* out. With Cap's contacts, it took him no time to acquire a full cargo.

"I'll be gone only a little more than a month Angel, but I think this time will feel like years."

"It will to me, darling. I hate the thought of sleeping in that big lonely bed without you to keep me warm."

"I've two days left at home," he smiled. "What are we going to do with them?"

Dev and Angel were walking along the beach, hand in hand as they discussed their plans. Her eyes were caught by the ship that was making its way into port. Now she stopped, not answering his question, as she narrowed her eyes against the sunlight.

"Dev, isn't that the *Sea Hawk?*"

Dev turned to watch the ship approach, then nodded. "Yes, that's the *Hawk*. Looks like Andy has finally made it home. I was surprised that he left like that without saying good-bye. I wonder where he's been for the past five weeks?"

"Well," she replied lightly. "We'll never know until we ask him, will we? Let's go home before he disappears again."

They walked home and found Cap seated on the front porch.

"Cap, Andy's back," Dev said.

"Good, it's about time that scalawag showed up. I'd like to know just where he disappeared to."

Angel went into the house while Cap and Dev conversed on the porch, and found Mattie in the kitchen.

"Mattie, Andy's ship just entered the harbor, so we'd best set another plate for dinner."

"Good," Mattie replied. "I'm glad he's back. Cap has been fretting at the way he vanished."

Angel and Mattie were finishing the preparations for dinner when another familiar voice was added to the ones on the porch. Angel went to the door and stood and watched the three men in deep conversation. Their voices had lowered now so they would not carry into the house, and Angel began to wonder just what they were discussing that they didn't want her and Mattie to hear. Her natural curiosity got the best of her and she slowly opened the door and stepped out. Fragments of conversation came to her before her presence was discovered. The few words she heard alarmed her: "Don Esteban . . . galleon . . . Captain Martinez . . . maps . . . discovered . . ." The last sentence remained unfinished when Andy spotted Angel standing so still, listening intently.

"Angel," he laughed. "You know, you really are prettier than I remembered. I had to come back just to make sure."

"Where have you been, Andy? We've been home for over two weeks. We didn't expect you to leave before we got back."

"Oh, I just had a little unexpected business to take care of," he replied nonchalantly, dismissing it with an airy wave of his hand.

"Yes," she replied without answering his smile with one of her own. "Business that concerns Don Esteban, the Spanish galleon, someone named Captain Martinez and something about maps. I know this all concerns me and I won't be protected like a child. I've a right to know what you discovered."

Andy's smile faded to a guilty grin and he looked helplessly at Dev and Cap.

"You may as well come in, eat, and explain everything to Angel," Dev said. "She's right, she certainly has a right to know something that concerns her so deeply."

They ate a quick meal, then sat over coffee and discussed what Andy had been doing for the past few weeks.

Andy had committed to memory the maps and the list of names Captain Martinez had given him, then destroyed them. He had decided to try to check into a few things Martinez had told him by going directly to Averio. There he had contacted some of the names on the list and had been rewarded by a story he thought expedient for Dev and Cap to know, so he had returned as quickly as possible.

"And what is that story, Andy?" Angel questioned.

"Well, at the time of Miguel and Anna's trials, there were two factions in Madrid vying for power. One led by DeVarga and one by Emilio Perez. Don Esteban was DeVarga's right hand man, and the Montalbans were deeply involved with Perez. The D'Santiagos were wavering between óne faction and the other, but their influence and wealth were in great need by the DeVarga group. Don Esteban doesn't just hate Miguel for taking the woman he wanted, he hated Miguel for tipping the scales toward the Montalbans. I imagine the D'Santiagos felt she was safe because they were near the throne. They were to find out that to the Inquisition General and the men who followed, nothing was safe, nothing was sacred. Once suspicion was thrown upon a family, they were taken in for questioning. What happened behind those closed doors no one knew. But most people confessed before too long. There were witnesses, if you can call them that, brought forward to testify to the guilt of the victim. It was always the same. Usually the victim was found guilty and punished rather violently for his 'crimes against God.'

"DeVarga had the ear of the Inquisitor General, and since he had been after some way to reach the D'Santiagos it did not take Esteban long to show the way.

"Don Esteban used DeVarga's power to strike out Miguel. He had the D'Santiagos declared heretics. But now DeVarga has died and slowly the wheels of justice are turning the other way. Friends of Miguel are working day and night for his benefit. I believe he is constantly in touch with them. One day soon, they will succeed completely. Don Esteban would sell his soul to get Angelique in his power."

"What makes you think that?" Dev asked.

"Because I've talked with Miguel, or at least I think I have."

"You what?" Dev demanded.

Andy told him about the mysterious visitor he had had and what he had said.

"I believe it was Angel's father and that soon, very soon, he will be declared completely absolved of all crime, that the Perez group will be in control, and that he

227

will come out of hiding to meet his daughter," Andy said and watched with fascination as happiness lit Angel's eyes.

"Thank you, Andy," Angel replied softly.

"You're quite welcome," he grinned, enjoying the pleasure he had given her.

"All we have to do, Cap, is to keep Angel safe and out of Don Esteban's reach. If all goes well, Angel will be one of the wealthiest women in Spain and reunited with her father."

Dev remained quiet, his gaze intent on Angel's face as she listened to Andy's words. He could see the happiness there, and he suddenly became weak from the fear that all his nightmares might yet come true—that Angel's father would come like the night wind and steal away the thing he loved most in the world. He knew he was being unfair to Angel, but he found himself wishing Miguel Montalban would never reappear. He was brought out of his musing state when Andy asked him a question.

"What?"

"Angel tells me you're leaving."

"I don't know if I should. The *Lady Angel* has a full cargo, but . . ."

"*Lady Angel?*"

"Andy, you don't know all that's happened, since you've been gone," Angel laughed. "Cap has given the ship to Dev and Dev named it *Lady Angel.*" She turned a loving gaze on Dev who smiled at her. "I'm so proud and so grateful," she added softly, her gaze filled with the love she felt for her new husband. Andy looked away, for a deep jealousy almost overwhelmed him. No matter what, he loved Angel and he could not deny it to himself.

"You have to go now, Dev. You've a contract for this

cargo," Cap said. "Andy and I will take good care of Angel for the short time you will be gone. When you come back, you'll be able to stay home for a while. By that time, Miguel might be free and all this problem might be over."

"The reverend mother has not sent word of Miguel's complete freedom, has she?" Andy asked Cap.

"All we know is what she said in the message you brought, that DeVarga was dead and Miguel should be free of all that hangs over him. I'm sure he'll come to us as soon as he can. Knowing Miguel, I can safely say he wants to see his daughter as badly as she wants to see him." He smiled at Angel as he spoke, and she nodded.

The next two days moved entirely too swiftly for Dev. He denied the reason he was reluctant to leave, and blamed his feelings on the hovering shadow of Don Esteban. But he knew, deep in his heart, it was more Andy's presence in his home that upset him. He had seen Andy's irresistable charm work before. Then he cursed himself for having any doubts about Angel. He knew she loved him and never gave a thought to another man. The tables had been neatly turned on Dev, who had walked away from many entanglements, his heart intact. It was no longer intact. It belonged completely to Angel.

The day came when the white sails unfurled and he stood on the deck and watched Angel's tear-stained face as it slowly grew smaller and smaller, yet, he saw with a quick smile, that her tiny figure stayed on the dock until his ship vanished.

Cap helped Angel into the carriage and they started home.

"You're so quiet, Angel," Cap said, after they had traveled some distance in silence. "Don't worry about

229

Dev. He'll be back in a little less than thirty days. It's not a lifetime even though it feels like it."

"It's not just that, Cap. I know I'll miss him terribly, but I can wait patiently for his return. It's just that . . . I know he's worried to death about something and it hurts me that he doesn't feel he can tell me what it is."

Cap chuckled. "Maybe, my dear, he just doesn't know the name to put to it since he never felt it before."

"What is it, Cap?"

"Jealousy."

"Jealousy? Why, in heaven's name, should Dev be jealous. He knows there is no one in my life but him."

"When one is jealous, Angel, they're not judging rationally. He's too aware of Andy's charm for young women. He's also too aware of the life your father could offer you. Put the two together, and . . ." He shrugged, then his eyes turned to Angel and she could see the twinkle of mischief in his face. "The jealousy of Andy is good for Dev, keeps reminding him that if he doesn't care for and love you properly, someone else will, and the jealousy of your father can only be absolved with time. When and if he comes, and Dev discovers that you're still more willing to share his life than the court life in Spain." He patted her hand. "Don't worry about anything, Angel. Time has a way of solving problems."

She smiled and they let the conversation flow in other directions.

As the days rolled along, Angel became more aware of Andy's feelings toward her, just as she realized that Andy had no intention of saying a word to her. He was charming and entertaining company. He took her sailing and made the long days without Dev bearable. Angel was relaxed and contented with him and the easy comradeship they had.

It was almost two weeks later that a small incident occurred which took away some of Angel's protection when it was most needed. Andy had occupied the guest room at Mattie and Cap's home since his arrival. He spent quite a few sleepless nights there.

Cap and Mattie had planned to go to a small party to celebrate the retirement of McMichaels. It was to be held at the beach. A huge bonfire would be made and there would be an abundance of food and drink with music to brighten the later part of the evening. Andy and Angel were both invited. Angel was excited, but for some reason, Andy had some misgivings about going, but he did. The party was filled with laughter, the weather was perfect. The combination of free-flowing drink and a large full moon, a night sky crowded with stars, all succeeded in undoing Andy's good intentions where nothing else had.

He spent most of the evening trying to keep his eyes away from Angel, but found it a useless endeavor. After a while, he gave up and allowed himself the pleasure of enjoying her happy company.

It was some time later when he strolled alone down the beach and sat on one of the large rocks and watched the waves crash upon the sandy shore. "When Dev comes home," he promised himself, "I shall take the *Hawk* to the south seas for a while. A year or so might put an end to this constant desire for her." He made the promise to himself and knew, for the good of all, it was one promise he intended to keep.

He didn't hear her as she approached and stood a little away from him, watching him intently. She was upset by the deep frown lines between his eyes and the downward pull of his lips. She knew that she was part of the reason for his unhappiness, and it hurt her. She knew that Andy and Dev were the closest of friends and that Cap and Mattie considered him family. She didn't want to be the reason for the breakup of these relationships.

"Andy," she said quietly, and he turned to face her.

Andy could not make out her features in the dark, but he felt her questioning eyes intent on him. He knew he should laugh away the serious side of this situation, say something nonchalant, and get them both back to the crowd of people as quickly as possible, but no words would come. He rose and went to her. Standing a few inches away, he could smell her delicate scent, and he watched the pale moonlight glaze her hair like silver flame.

"Andy," she repeated gently, then she reached out and put her hand on his arm. She could feel the tremor in the hard muscle of his arm.

"Would you understand and believe that I know how you feel? But you and I, we love Dev, and we know it is impossible to do anything that might hurt him. There is and always will be a very special place in my heart for you, just as I hope there is a place in yours for me. You are very special to me. First, because you are Dev's friend, and, second, because I hope you are mine also."

"Damn it, Angel," he laughed, "if you had presented me any other argument, I'd have fought you. You completely unman me. You know without asking that you'll always have a special place in my life. I wonder if Dev knows what a lucky man he is to have your love. We are friends, Angel, and I hope we remain so. Always."

He slid a small gold ring from his little finger and took

her hand in his. Putting it on her finger, he said, "If ever, for any reason, you should need me, send this ring. You can send it to me by taking it to Randy McIver. He has a small house on the beach just past Rose Point. He'll see it gets to me, and I'll come no matter where I am."

"Thank you, Andy."

"Angel? Would it upset you if I kissed you? It would be hello and good-bye. For one time only, to remember."

She stepped closer until their bodies almost touched and he sensed her consent. He put both hands gently on her waist, and was surprised that his two hands could almost enclose it, then he drew her into his arms and his lips slowly lowered to hers. He wanted to savor it, to enjoy the sweetness of her for as long as possible. Her lips were warm and soft under his. Slowly, his arms enclosed her and he held her gently against him. He knew for her it was exactly what he had said it would be, a kiss good-bye for a dear friend. But for him . . . Andy surrendered to her his soul, and his love forever.

He let her go as gently as he had held her and he knew it was all there would ever be. "Come, Angel," he said gently, "let's go back and join the party."

They walked away together. The place where they had stood was silent for several minutes after they left. Then a small piece of the shadows surrounding the rocks seemed to separate.

The figure's face could not be seen clearly, but the bent, twisted figure moved quickly, and in a few minutes, it was gone.

Polly stood alone on another small stretch of beach and looked about her nervously. She waited unhappily for Carlos. She hated the ugly man, but he was her only

233

connection to Don Esteban and Don Esteban was her only way to get Dev back.

"Would that beast never come!" she muttered angrily to herself. She was suddenly startled as he seemed to appear from nowhere. "Oh, you frightened me! Can't you make a little noise instead of creeping up on people like you do?" she snapped. But Carlos eyed her with a glint of amusement as he motioned her to follow him. She went with him to a small boat he had pulled up on the sand in the shade of nearby rocks. When they were both aboard, he dropped the oars into the water and began to row.

It was less than an hour before they came alongside a huge ship. Polly looked up, then glanced at Carlos in surprise. "This is not the same ship. What are you up to, you ugly beast?"

Carlos' face became frozen in an ugly grimace and he motioned to her to climb the ladder. She was about to refuse when his eye fastened on hers. She shivered in fear. Then, without another word, she climbed the rope ladder to the deck of the ship. Carlos came after her, then moved ahead of her to the companionway and led her down to a cabin. He gave one rap on the door and was told to enter. He stood aside and let a surprised Polly go in ahead of him.

Don Esteban stood up from behind the desk and fixed her with his cold gaze as she walked toward him. "Miss Dillon. You have some news for me, I hope."

"Yes," she said in a small voice.

"And," he said impatiently.

"Dev Carlisle has been gone for two weeks. He got a contract to deliver a cargo. It will probably be two more weeks before he's back."

"And you'd like to see what I'm going to do to get rid of your competition?"

She flushed a little and bit her lip, then looked up at him, her eyes storming. "Yes! Do something to get rid of that witch. You're the one who said it was what you were going to do!"

He chuckled, but it was not with humor. "I intend to do something very soon now."

Carlos stood in the shadowy doorway. Don Esteban looked toward him.

"Is there anything new in the situation at the captain's home, Carlos?"

Carlos moved forward with his slow, twisted movement. When he was close, he made a few sounds deep in his throat and some gestures with his hands while shaking his head negatively.

"Then Captain Cortland, Mattie his housekeeper, and Angelique Montalban are there alone."

Carlos glanced quickly at Polly, then back to Don Esteban and shook his head affirmatively.

"Carlos, does the girl ever leave the house alone?"

Again the negative shake of his head.

"Have you watched her everyday? Do you know all her movements?"

Affirmative.

"Does she have a special friend in town for whom she might answer a distress signal?"

Negative.

"We have to find a way to get her away from that house alone."

"What good is that going to do me? Dev would just go after her," Polly said.

"Not if he received a letter, a very sad letter, that said

235

he must not look for her."

They laughed together while a silent Carlos looked from one to the other.

"Go back, continue to be a friend of the family. Be nice to the girl. Be careful so that the family will believe you when the time comes and she disappears." Don Esteban turned to Carlos. "Take her back and wait until she tells you it is time. Then bring word to me."

Carlos nodded and moved toward the door, Polly following. She went to the deck and climbed down the ladder into the boat. They rode back in silence. Polly was uncomfortable, for she felt an odd emotion emanate from the twisted man who sat opposite her. She watched him covertly; his eye never left her. She was happy when her feet touched the sand of the beach, and she ran, without looking back to see the man who stood and watched her go.

The next day, Polly called at Cap's house. Angel's open heart accepted her apologies easily, and before the week was over, Polly had taken the first step in removing what she thought was the only obstacle between herself and Dev. She and Angel went shopping together and discussed things close to the sentiments of young girls. The one and only female friend that Angel had ever had was Maria, and now she enjoyed Polly's company. It made her feel more at peace with Maria's memory.

Polly felt no guilt at her deception. She wanted Dev, and she was determined to have him.

Cap and Mattie were pleased with Angel's happiness, but neither of them could bring themselves to trust Polly completely.

A bright Sunday morning found Angel up almost before dawn. She began to prepare breakfast as a surprise for Mattie. Andy, who had decided to sleep on board the *Hawk* after the night of the party, was to come and pick them up for church services. She was surprised when she heard a soft rap on the kitchen door. She was even more surprised when she found Polly there.

"Is anyone else up yet?" Polly asked.

"No," Angel replied in a whisper. "Come in and have breakfast with us."

"Not right now, Angel. I just came to ask if you would like to go sailing with me after church."

"Oh, that sounds lovely. Would you like me to make up a picnic basket?"

"Oh, no. We won't be gone that long. Angel?"

"Yes?"

"Couldn't we do without Andy for just a few hours?"

"I don't know, Polly. Cap and Mattie might be angry with me."

Polly's eyes twinkled mischievously and she smiled. "Cap and Mattie don't need to know. By the time they found out that Andy wasn't with you, we would be back. Oh, do come, Angel, it would be such fun, just the two of us!"

"Well . . ." Angel began hesitantly.

"I promise, only a couple of hours and we'll be right back. Long before lunch. Oh, Angel, after Devon gets back, you won't have much time for me! Do come," she pleaded."

"All right, but we must be back before lunch."

"Oh, yes."

"I'll meet you on the beach after church."

"How will you get away from Mattie and Cap?"

"I'll let them believe I'm meeting Andy."

"Good. I'll see you." She laughed as she closed the

237

door behind her. "Good!" she thought again, "for by lunch time, you will be far away from here."

Mattie was pleasantly surprised that breakfast was ready. They ate and prepared to leave for church.

"Cap, where do you suppose Andy is?" Mattie asked. But before he could answer, a rap on the door drew their attention. They found Andy's cabin boy on their doorstep with the message that Andy could not come this morning, but that he would see them later. Angel was relieved, for she did not know how to get away from Andy's protecting eyes. She would let Cap and Mattie believe she was sailing with Andy and by the time Andy arrived, she would be home.

The church service was long and Mattie noticed the way Angel moved restlessly in her seat. When they arrived home, Angel changed clothes quickly, then, softly made the statement that she was going sailing.

"Oh, Andy's taking you for a sail," Mattie smiled. "That's good. It's good for you to get out in the sun and air."

"I'll be back soon, Mattie."

"Don't fret, child. Go and enjoy yourself. You're too young to be cooped up in the house on a Sunday. Andy's wise to see that."

Angel felt a moment of guilt about letting Mattie believe a lie, but it faded with the feeling of freedom she had. She ran down the beach and found Polly waiting for her with a small boat.

"Does anyone know?" Polly questioned as they pushed the boat into the water.

"Andy couldn't come to church, and Mattie and Cap think I've gone sailing with him. Polly, we've got to be back in two hours. I promised Mattie."

238

"Oh, don't worry, Angel," Polly replied. "In two hours our sail will be over."

Putting up the sail, they skimmed over the water, and Angel felt again the joy of sailing which Dev had taught her. She was so engrossed, she didn't notice how quiet Polly was, or that she was slowly edging the boat toward shore.

They entered a quiet little cove, and Angel did not become alarmed until she saw the tall ship anchored there. She turned to Polly, fear in her eyes. "Polly, we've got to turn about and get out of here. We don't know whose ship that is! It may be . . ."

"Don Esteban Ortega," Polly answered softly. Her eyes were no longer shielded, showing her open hatred. "It is his!"

"Polly, what are you doing?" Angel cried.

"Giving Don Esteban what he wants, and getting rid of you, you silver-haired witch." She glared at Angel. "Dev will now be mine as he should have been in the first place."

Angel was frightened, yet unbelieving of the hatred she saw in Polly's face. "Polly, in God's name, don't do this. Don Esteban will destroy so many people. Please, turn around before it is too late."

"And miss the chance of doing away with you? No, he can destroy you *and* your father for all I care. I want Dev, and I shall have him," she snarled.

Angel leapt toward Polly and tried to wrest the tiller from her hand, but Polly was prepared for that. She had laid a small club on the deck of the ship beside her. When Angel reached out for her, she lifted it and struck Angel a solid blow on the side of her head.

Angel stumbled forward and fell into a heap at Polly's

feet. Polly edged the boat against the sand, and two men pulled it ashore.

There were four men awaiting her. One was Carlos and the others were Don Esteban and two of his sailors. They walked with her to the side of the boat, and Don Esteban laughed a cold pleased laugh.

"Carlos, bring her along to my ship." He turned to Polly. "My thanks, my dear. I'll have the messages sent. You be there to console the broken-hearted bridegroom."

Polly smiled as she watched Angel being carried out of her life. Then she climbed into her boat and sailed for home.

Carlos carried Angel on board the *Avenger* and took her down to the captain's cabin where he lay her gently on his bed. Don Esteban followed. They both stood in silence and watched Angel regain consciousness. Slowly, she opened her eyes and looked at him blankly for a few minutes. Then, the knowledge of where she must be struck her. With a small cry, she sat up and looked with fear into the cold brown eyes of Don Esteban.

"Welcome, Angelique Montalban. I have looked forward to having you as my guest. Allow me to introduce myself," he said gently as he bowed toward her. "Don Esteban Ortega."

Angelique trembled with fear for a moment. Then she thought of her father, her family, her pride. Slowly she rose. Standing erect, she glared at Don Esteban and lifted her head proudly.

Chapter 20

Dev was pleased with himself. For his first voyage as captain he had made what had been a five-week trip into a little over three weeks, and a very rewarding trip it had been. He was coming home with enough money that he wouldn't have to worry for a while. He could hardly wait for the *Lady Angel* to dock, and he was the first one down the gangplank to hurry the unloading of the return cargo.

He noticed that Andy's ship was still in port, and he went to see if Andy was there. Andy was just about to leave. He had regretted that he could not escort Angel to church, but he promised himself he would make up for it by asking her to go sailing with him this afternoon. He knew he would rather have her alone, anyway, than to be with her in the company of all the people at church.

He had just closed the door of the companionway behind him and was walking across the deck to go ashore when he saw Dev climbing the gangplank. He didn't know at that moment whether he was happy to see Dev or not. It meant the end of his shared days with Angel.

"Andy!" Dev shouted with a grin, then he was beside him offering the hand of friendship.

Andy smiled slowly, then reached out and took it. "You really made that trip in record time, Dev."

"When you've got the best ship on the ocean and you're coming home to the most beautiful wife in the world, you would have broken some records, too."

"I imagine you're right."

"Where are you bound?"

"Up to Cap's. I was going to take Angel sailing today, but now that you're here . . ."

"Come with me. I've got a lot to tell you and I'm too anxious to get home to tell you here."

"All right."

They left the *Hawk* and walked home, Andy listening to Dev's excited explanation of his trip. His ears heard Dev's words, but his mind was planning his departure as soon as possible. They stepped into Cap's small house and heard conversation coming from the kitchen. Cap was seated at the table drinking coffee and Mattie was working over a half-made pie when they entered. Cap looked up and his face broke into a wide grin when he saw Dev. Mattie ran to Dev's side, and he hugged her to him. Then she looked questioningly at Andy.

"Andy, where's Angel? I should think she wouldn't bother changing her clothes now that Dev's home."

"What?" Andy asked, his eyes wide in surprise. Dev looked from one surprised face to the other, his excitement beginning to turn to fear.

"Mattie?"

"Andy," Mattie said in a stern voice, "you and Angel stop teasing. Dev's home and I'm sure he is in no mood for jokes."

Andy's face went from surprise to fright. "Mattie, where's Angel?" he demanded.

"Why are you asking me? She went sailing with you right after church. You should know where she is."

Dev's face turned pale. He and Andy exchanged questioning glances.

"Mattie," Andy said softly. "I haven't seen Angel all

day. She had no appointment to go sailing with me."

"Oh, God," Mattie whispered softly as she slowly sat down in her chair, her pleading eyes on Andy.

"When did you see her last?" Dev said stiffly. His paralyzed mind was still not accepting what his heart already told him was true.

"Just before lunch," Mattie whispered, then buried her face into her hands and began to cry.

Dev knelt in front of her. He pulled her hands gently away from her face. "Mattie, tell me, what did she say to you?"

"She said that she was going sailing. I was so sure it was Andy she was going with, I never questioned her. Oh, Dev, oh, my poor Angel. Where is she, what have I done?"

Slowly, Dev's gaze rose, first to Andy then to Cap. His thoughts were echoed in their faces. All three were sure of what had happened to Angel.

"Good afternoon, everyone!" came a bright voice from the doorway. "Dev, how wonderful to see you home. I'm sure Angel will be pleased when she returns." Polly stood smilng in the doorway, her eyes taking in the stunned look on all four faces.

"Returns!" Dev said quickly. "Polly, do you know where Angel is?"

"Why, I passed her today on the street and she told me she was going sailing. I thought, since she was *always with Andy*, that she was sailing with him. But since he's here, she must have gone alone."

Andy's narrowed eyes watched Polly closely. Something did not ring true to him. "Angel wouldn't have gone alone," he said gently.

"Well," Polly replied in a voice as soft as his and just a

little suggestive, "maybe she went with someone else."

"No!" Dev said firmly as he rose to his feet and looked at Polly. "She knew how dangerous it was for her to be caught alone. She must have gone with someone she trusted or . . . Polly, was anyone near her, could anyone have been threatening her? Did she seem to be afraid?"

"No, she seemed quite confident. She smiled at me and seemed to have no fear. She acted as though she knew exactly where she was going and why."

"Dev," Andy said quickly, "if it's only a matter of hours, we'll find her. We'll go to the docks and see if anyone left in a small boat today, and in which direction they went. It shouldn't take as long to track down a small sailboat. I know that none of the ships left the harbor today."

Dev nodded agreement and they prepared to leave.

"Dev," Polly called softly to him. He went back to her.

"Was there something else you remembered, Polly?" She shook her head and touched him gently on the arm.

"I'm sorry, Dev. Maybe if I'd have come sooner she might not have gone. We've become such good friends, Angel and I. I hope everything is all right. Please let me know what you find."

He patted her hand and Polly smiled to herself at the gentle way he touched her.

"Soon, Dev," she thought, "soon you will forget that child, and remember only that I love you."

Angel looked at the two men who were regarding her with completely separate reactions. Don Esteban, with a cold half smile on his face, looked at the prize he had long sought and now was so pleased to have captured. She could see the pleasure deep in his eyes and she was

244

astonished at her own anger. It flowed through her with glowing heat as she looked at the man who was responsible for her mother's death and the loss of her father.

"What do you want from me, Don Esteban? Have you not done enough evil to my family? Are not the deaths of my parents enough for you? What kind of a monster are you, that you cannot leave me in peace? You have taken enough from the Montalban family. When will your hatred be satisfied, your revenge complete?"

He walked to her side and it took all the courage Angel could find not to shrink from him. She refused to let him have the satisfaction of seeing how frightened she really was.

"Enough?" he said through clenched teeth, his eyes burning into hers. "When I have your father in my hands, when I can make him pay the price for what he has done to me, then perhaps it will be enough."

"My father is dead."

"You believe that?"

"How could a man who loved his child, not contact her, not see her for eighteen years. I believe my father loved me. That is why he saved me from you, and that is why I believe he is dead."

"Well, I do not. I will hold you for a while. If he is alive, he will know."

"And if he does not come for me?"

He smiled again and said softly, "Then you, my dear, will pay the penalty for what he has done."

"Dev will find me," she whispered. "He will not let this happen. He will search for me until he finds me. Then he will kill you."

"Oh, child," he said in a mocking voice. "You are so

naïve. *You* are going to write a *letter* to your loving husband. You are going to tell him that despite your marriage, you have found that you had the deep desire to see your *home*. You will tell him how your *father* found you at long last and *persuaded* you to go with him. You will tell him that your marriage was a *mistake* and that you desire now to be free. And after you have cast him aside, he will turn to another for comfort. Another who is quite ready to accept him."

"Polly?"

"Yes."

"Dev won't believe it. He knows I love him. He knows I would not hurt him."

"It is best you convince him of that. I should hate to have to force you. That could become very unpleasant for you."

Angel stood stiffly. Her eyes burned with unshed tears and she clasped her hands in front of her to keep them from trembling. Her chin lifted and she said defiantly, "I will not write your letter. Do with me as you will. I will not write it."

"Maybe you are not frightened enough, or hungry enough," he replied. "But, believe me, you will write it. Carlos, take her to the deepest, darkest cell in the hold. She is not to be fed until I say." He turned and looked at her now white face. "We shall see if you will not become obedient. When you have had a taste of hunger and of the evil crawling things that dwell there, you will be happy to write what I say."

Carlos took hold of her arm and almost dragged her to the door. He led her deeper and deeper into the ship. Holding his lantern aloft, he dragged her to a small room and pushed open the door. The smell of the small room

246

was enough to terrify her, and the soft sounds of things she could not name made her skin crawl. She wanted to cry out her fear, to agree to write the letter. But her deep love for Dev and her native Montalban pride would not let her.

Slowly, she moved to cross the threshold, when Carlos's hand stopped her. She looked down on the twisted form. His one eye regarded her intently and he patted her arm gently, then put a finger to his lips. Slowly, from under his shirt, he took a packet and pressed it into her hand. Quickly, he made gestures. First he pointed to the light, then to the packet.

"Candles? Flint?"

He nodded his head violently, then pointed to his stomach and to his mouth and the packet.

"Food," she said quietly.

His one eye glowed with satisfaction as he grinned at her. Then he made motions with his hand as though he was writing and pointed again at the packet.

"A message for me?"

Another affirmative shake, then slowly, but gently, he began to push her into the room. He waited to see if she could light the candle. When she succeeded, he went to the door, looked back at her once, then pulled the door shut. She could hear him lock it, then his dragging footsteps as he left. Then, suddenly, *she was alone!*

The hours slipped slowly by and Angel was grateful for the small candle and the tiny packet of food that had been left by that strange, twisted man. After a few hours, she felt the change in the motion of the ship and realized they had set sail. "Where?" she wondered. Would she be able to hold out against Don Esteban? She doubted it, for she did not think she would have the strength to stand up to what she knew his mind was capable of.

She clasped her hands together in front of her and began to pray. When she did, her eyes fell on the small golden ring Andy had given her. She could almost hear his words when she looked at it.

"If ever you should need me, for any reason, send this ring and I shall come."

A small idea entered her head. If she could somehow get the ring included in the letter, it would not take Andy long to figure out she was in trouble and tell Dev. It was the only way she knew to tell Dev the truth, that anything she said in the letter was a lie.

She knew she could not give in too soon or Don Esteban would be suspicious. No, she must spend a few days in this room. Sufficient time to make him believe she was hungry enough and frightened enough to write what he wanted. She did not know if it would work, but in her desperation, she knew it was the only chance she had.

"Three or four days," she whispered to herself as she looked about the dirty hole of a room in which she had been thrust. "Three or four days and I will pretend surrender and do his will."

She knew she would need all her strength and courage if she were to succeed, so she ate another small morsel of the food in the packet, then curled up near the wavering light of the candle and tried to sleep.

She was just beginning to doze when she remembered that Carlos had told her there was a message in the packet he had handed her. Quickly, she grabbed the packet and fumbled through it. She found the small folded paper and unfolded it as fast as her trembling hands would allow. She was stunned by its contents:

Have faith. Do not despair. You have not been deserted by those who love you. There is time to write little else but these words of encouragement, and to let you know that I am watching. It will not be long.

> Your loving father,
> MM

Her father! Not only was he still alive, he was nearby, watching, waiting to rescue her. Angel felt a warm feeling of security. She knew that if she could get the little gold ring home, Dev would find her. She was sure that he would stay on her trail until he did. But until then, just the knowledge that her father was somewhere near was enough to bolster her courage. She put aside all the questions that crowded into her mind. Where could he be, that he knew her predicament? Could she question that twisted little man and somehow find the answers? She lay down and tried to rest. She knew she would need all her strength and her wits to carry her through the days until her rescue could be accomplished.

She slept, but others did not: Don Esteban, gloating over his capture of Miguel's daughter, and another silent figure who waited and watched for the right time to do what he had so long dreamed of doing.

Dev was so exhausted. He could barely move, and the rest of the family, including Andy, were in almost the same condition. When news had been first brought to them that no sailing ship had left the harbor, large or small, on the day Angel had disappeared, none of them could believe it. Since that time, both Dev and Andy had gone up and down the coast in search of someone who might have seen her or the boat she used. Everything turned up negative. It seemed Angel had simply vanished into thin air. It was only after three days and nights of intense searching that Polly suddenly remembered that in the times she and Angel had been together, she had seen Angel in conversation with a man.

"Why didn't you tell us this sooner?" Dev snapped.

"I'd forgotten about it. When I approached them, the man would leave quickly before I would be able to meet him, and Angel said he was only an acquaintance she had made since her arrival."

"Was he anyone you had seen about before?"

"No. But, Dev, there are so many ships putting in here. I thought he was an acquaintance of yours. How was I to know Angel was lying?" she asked.

Dev was so upset at her words, he did not hear the malicious joy in the sound of her voice. But Andy did. He watched her closely and had the urgent nudge to his senses he always had when danger approached. "This girl knows more than she's saying," he thought, but before he could put his thoughts into words, Cap spoke.

"Polly, what did this man look like?"

Polly proceeded to describe, in the exact words Don Esteban had given her, Angel's father. As her description went on, Cap became more sure, and even began to relax a little. "Still," he wondered to himself, "if this was Miguel why would the two of them disappear without saying a word to anyone?"

"Was he accompanied by anyone?"

"No, he was always alone."

"What are you thinking, Cap? Do you know who the man is?" Dev asked.

"I'm almost sure who it is. I'm only confused about why."

"Who, who?" Dev demanded.

"Polly has just described, very accurately, Angelique's father, Miguel Montalban," Cap answered. "But why, why would he just take her away without saying anything to anyone, and more, I don't believe Angel would have gone with him without telling Dev."

"Unless Angel wanted to go," Polly said softly. They all looked at her in silence. "Well, maybe she just decided she wanted to be with her father, and didn't have the courage to face Dev and tell him the truth."

"I'd never believe that," Dev replied. "Angel would not leave me like that, without saying anything."

"Are you so very sure, Dev?" Polly asked gently.

"You have more to tell us?" Andy interrupted. "Why don't you just say everything you have to say?"

"All right," Polly replied. "Angel had been acting funny for a few days, sort of quiet, like she was thinking something over very seriously. Then, one day I asked her what was the matter, and she said . . . well, she said that she wanted to go and see if she could find her father. That what she had was all right but it could not take the place of a real family."

Dev was stunned. Slowly, he sank into a chair, his mind refusing to accept what Polly was saying.

"They were laughing together, and she looked so happy. I just felt there was nothing wrong. But they must have been making their plans all the time," Polly went on, watching Dev. "I'm sorry, Dev. I'm so sorry. If there is anything I can do to help you, please . . . please let me," she said with a whisper. Then she left, closing the door behind her. Once outside, she smiled to herself, proud of the way she had performed her little act. "From the look in Dev's eyes," she thought happily, "when he gets Angel's letter, he will be angry enough to forget her. And when you do, Dev, my love, I'll be here to make you feel better."

It was a good thing then that Polly did not know the anger that was boiling up in Andy. He was sure in his heart that she was lying, but did not have an idea how to get the truth out of her. He turned to Dev. "You don't believe Angel did that do you, Dev?"

"No, not for a second. It looks to me like we ought to take either the *Hawk* or *Lady Angel* and make a trip to Spain as soon as possible. Cap, you'll come along, too."

"That won't be too hard," Andy replied. "I also know of several places that Esteban might be. I was given the information by Captain Martinez."

Cap agreed, but Andy spoke up again. "Dev, I'm going to mark your maps with the places that Don Esteban could be. We'll take both ships to Spain, and if Angel and her father are not there, and I firmly believe they won't be, then we'll split up our forces and hunt him down."

Dev agreed quickly. "We'll leave first thing tomorrow. I don't want to think of Angel being frightened or in that man's power any longer than possible."

Andy had some plans of his own he meant to carry out as soon as possible. He was going to leave the same time Dev did in the morning, but he planned to carry along an extra passenger. *It's time you enjoyed a long sea voyage, Polly, my pet, and it will give us a lot of time alone to talk. Maybe you will enjoy telling me the real truth about Angel.* He mused to himself as he left Cap's house and headed for the *Hawk*. Once there, he took two of his most trusted men aside and gave them swift orders. They were surprised at the contents of those orders, but Andy knew they would do exactly as they were told.

It was in the wee hours of the morning that a bundle was brought on board the *Hawk*, carried below and locked away in a small cabin.

The new morning sun was only a bright rim on the horizon when Andy arrived at Cap's door. Mattie let him into the quiet house, and he waited for Cap and Dev to finish a hasty breakfast. The three of them were preparing to leave when there was a gentle knock on the door. Dev was closest at the moment, so he reached out and opened it. A young man stood on the threshold.

"I would like to speak to Captain Carlisle, please," he said in a voice thick with a strong Spanish accent.

"I'm Captain Carlisle," Dev said.

"I am first mate aboard the *Carlotta*. My ship was intercepted at sea a few days ago, Señor, and we were asked to deliver a very urgent message to you."

"To me? You are sure?"

"It was to be put into the hands of Captain Devon Carlisle and no one else."

"Give it to me," Dev said gently, and the young man reached inside his shirt and removed a small white envelope, and put it in Dev's hands.

"You must take my thanks to your captain," Dev said, "and for yourself."

"You are quite welcome, Señor. I hope it is good news."

"Thank you," Dev replied, but he turned the paper over in his hand and his fingers shook. He didn't want to open it, didn't want to see what was written inside.

"Well, Dev?" Andy said softly.

Slowly, he tore open the envelope and withdrew the paper inside. When he did, a small glittering object tumbled from the envelope and fell to the floor. The four of them stood looking at the small gold ring that lay against the dark wood floor. Andy looked at it and remembered exactly what he had said to Angel when he had given it to her.

"Don't even bother to read whatever lies are written on that paper, Dev. The only message we need from Angel is there on the floor. I gave that to her as a sign of friendship. I told her that if she was ever in serious trouble to send it to me, and I would come. She is in trouble. She must be with Don Esteban at this minute. We don't have to go to Spain. We'll split up now after I've marked your maps. We'll find her. Thank God, she got this message to us before we left."

Dev opened the letter despite what Andy said and read it. Then he looked at Andy. "Yes, thank God. For if this letter had been delivered without it, I might have believed it. And if I had, Angel would be lost to us forever."

He handed the letter to Andy, who read it quickly, then crumpled it in his hand. He and Dev agreed without words at that moment that Don Esteban had Angel at his mercy and that neither of them would rest until Angel was safely back with them, and Don Esteban Ortega was dead!

Chapter 21

Some days earlier, Angel had been jarred awake in her foul cell when something furry and small skittered at her feet. She gave a small scream and struck at the rat, which squealed and retreated to a dark corner of the room. Angel could still feel its presence, though she could not see it, and she was afraid to go back to sleep for fear that it would attack again. She had no idea how long she had slept. There was no way for her to know if it was day or night. She could feel the rise and fall of the ship and knew they were well out to sea. "But bound for where?" she wondered.

The candle had burned down to less than an inch and she dreaded what would happen when the light disappeared and the creatures that lingered in the dark corners found the courage to attack again.

She sat up cross-legged on the floor and ate the remnants of food Carlos had given her. The message, she had wisely burned after she read it.

The scrape of the key in the lock drew her attention, and she watched as the door opened slowly. She almost cried out in relief when she saw Carlos' face peer around the door. He motioned her to silence. He came soundlessly into the room and closed the door behind him. Slowly, with his awkward, shuffling walk, he came to her. His one eye, peering up at her over the hump on his shoulder watched her intently as he pulled another small packet, which, she knew, must contain more food, from beneath his shirt.

"Carlos," she whispered, "can you stay with me for a little while? I must talk to you."

He gave a quick negative shake of his head as he thrust the packet into her hands, then began to back away.

"Please," she said softly. Her hand reached out to him imploringly. There were tears in her eyes. "Just for a moment."

He stood watching her for a moment as if trying to decide, then he moved back to her side. She smiled at him in relief and motioned for him to sit beside her in the wavering light of the candle. "Carlos," she began, "do you know my father?"

He nodded.

"Is he on board this ship?"

Another nod.

"Is there no way I could see him, talk to him?"

Carlos' eye grew wide, and he gave a firm negative shake of his head punctuated by grunts. Pointing to the ceiling, he made an arrogant face.

"Don Esteban Ortega?"

Yes, he made a quick gesture as though sliding a knife across his throat.

"Of course," she said sadly. "I know he would kill my father immediately if he knew he was here. Carlos, has he been with him all these years?"

Yes.

"How did he ever have the courage to stay, knowing if he were found, there was no way to escape?" Carlos pointed to Angelique then to his own chest, then he placed his hand over his heart for a moment and pointed again to Angel.

256

"He loves me," Angel said softly. "To have endangered himself so, he must. Oh, how I long to see him, to tell him how much I love him and appreciate all the sacrifices he has made for me. Tell him, will you Carlos, how I await the day we shall meet, and that I have complete faith in him!"

Carlos came as close to smiling as was possible for his grotesque features, then he rose slowly and laboriously from the floor. Gently, he patted Angel on the shoulder, then he shuffled toward the door. She watched as he quietly closed the door behind her, but this time she did not feel so frightened.

Undoing the new packet, she found three more candles, more food, and another folded piece of paper. Lighting another candle from the sputtering remains of the old one, she unfolded the paper and read:

By the time these three candles are gone, Don Esteban will come for your answer. You must appear weak and despairing. If you must, write your letter to your husband. I shall do my best to find a way to warn him in time. Know that I am watching you, child. Have faith that I will not desert you in your hour of need. I have spent many years thwarting Don Esteban's plans to find you. I have altered his maps and fed him rumors. I would have been content to do this as long as it was necessary, but his capture of you was something I could not stop. Soon we will meet, my daughter, and then both of us will be free.

MM

Slowly, with tear-dimmed eyes, she touched the edge

of the paper to the candle's flames and watched it burn. She thought of the years her father must have lived in fear, of the courage it took for him to live right under Don Esteban's nose. She wondered at the brave way he had kept Don Esteban from finding her. It bolstered her resolve to face Don Esteban with courage. Combined with her love for Dev, and the knowledge that he would be searching for her, she began to formulate what she would say to Don Esteban to convince him that the small gold band she wore had to go with her letter to Dev.

"Forgive me, Dev," she whispered as she slipped his wedding band from her finger and replaced it with the small gold ring Andy had given her. She hid her wedding ring in the pocket of her dress.

The time drifted by slowly, and Angelique's nerves were stretched taut. She lit one candle after the other, and each burnt down to nothing. Several times, she fell into an uneasy sleep.

The last candle had burned nearly to its end when she heard the muffled sound of approaching footsteps. As they neared her door, she inhaled deeply and reached out and pinched the small flame out, then threw the candle to the far corner. Slowly, she rose to her feet and watched as the door was unlocked and pushed open. Don Esteban's face appeared out of the darkness, illuminated by the lantern he held. He was accompanied by Carlos, who watched her with a closed, expressionless face.

Angel bent her head down and let her hair fall carelessly about her. Every line of her body gave evidence of profound despair.

"Are you willing to write the letter now, or am I forced to leave you here a while longer?" he questioned smoothly, sure of her answer.

"Please, don't leave me here, I . . . I'll do anything you ask. Don't leave me in the dark again."

She wanted to curse him for his smugness and overbearing attitude, to hurl herself upon him and scratch the pleased look from his face.

"I knew you would see reason, my dear. Sometimes, it just takes a little convincing."

She stood wordlessly, her head bowed, but molten hatred bubbled through her veins. He came to her side and ran his hand gently up her bare arm. Her skin crawled with aversion, and she pulled away from him.

His next words brought terror to her heart. "Let us hope you do not have to be punished again for not being obedient. You will learn that my word is law. This may be a more rewarding revenge than I thought it would be." He chuckled at the startled fear in her eyes and the way she trembled under his hand.

"Carlos," he ordered sharply, his smile fading, "take her to my quarters. I will be along shortly and we will discuss the terms of your letter," he said to Angel, and watched as Carlos drew her from the dark room into the passageway.

"Carlos," she whispered, her voice filled with fear.

"Sssttt," Carlos hissed sharply. Don Esteban was following close behind them. When they reached his door, Don Esteban passed them by and went up on deck. Now, Angel turned toward Carlos in panic.

"I will die before I let him touch me! If my father is on board, tell him what is happening. I could not bear for him to be near me. Before I let that happen, I will find a way to kill myself." Carlos patted her arm gently then put his finger to his lips and shook his head negatively. Then he pointed to her and with both hands turned palm down,

259

he made a gesture of patience. After that, he pointed to Don Esteban's path of departure and then back to himself.

"You want me to be patient, that you will take care of Don Esteban?"

A violent nod.

"I will try, Carlos, but I am so frightened."

Carlos' eye filled with compassion, and he again gently patted her arm. Then he made a series of gestures which she could not quite understand. He repeated them again, but could not make her understand what he meant. He reached behind her and opened the door. Gently, he pushed her inside, then without another word, he closed the door between them.

She stood alone in the center of Don Esteban's cabin. Her eyes filled with tears and she thought of Dev, how he must feel now, what he would think if he received the letter she must now write. With supreme effort, she calmed herself. Then the click of the latch drew her attention and she backed farther into the room. Don Esteban entered and stood with his cold eyes surveying her abject misery without one trace of compassion or pity.

"You are prepared to write what I dictate?"

"I shall write whatever you say," she answered.

"Good. You may sit behind my desk. There you will find all you need."

She stood motionless, watching him, suddenly seeing that this man was only excited or pleased when he dominated someone. She might have a small grain of knowledge she could one day use against him.

"Well?" he demanded.

She moved to the desk and sat down, pulling the paper

toward her. She picked up the quill and looked questioningly at him.

"'My dear husband,'" he began, "'I find these words difficult to say to you, but nonetheless, I realize they must be said. You were right, before our marriage, to be hesitant about our marrying. You wanted me to find my father and weigh well the life he offered me.'"

Angel looked up at him in surprise. How did he know all this? Then she realized that Polly must have given him all the information he wanted. Her bitterness burned inside her, with the jealous fear that if Dev believed these lies, he might yet end up in Polly's arms. As though he read her mind, Don Esteban chuckled.

"Of course she told me all about you. Do not concern yourself with Mr. Carlisle's future. I have arranged it for Polly to offer him all the comfort he needs to help wash the memories of you out of his mind. One day," he mused, "when I have your father, I may send you back to him. Too late to change what has happened, and," his eyes glittered malevolently at her, "he will not even want you then."

Angel clenched her teeth until her jaw ached to hold down the desire to throw her angry words in his face. Instead, she bowed her head as if she were completely beaten. It seemed to satisfy him.

"Go on with your writing. 'It has weighed deeply on me. I can deny the fact no longer. Our marriage was a mistake.'"

Angel's hand trembled as she wrote the hateful words. But now was her chance, if it could only work. She stopped writing and looked up at him. "Shall I tell him I'm returning his wedding ring? It will probably be the one thing that would make him react the way he should," she added, unable to control the chance to take one stroke at him.

"Wedding ring," he said, his eyes going to the small gold band on her finger. "Yes, that might be amusing."

Angel wrote the words that she hoped and prayed fervently were her means of salvation. He watched over her shoulder as she wrote.

"Good, good. Now add this: 'I do not want to see you again, for it would make it too painful for us both. Make a new life for yourself as I plan to do. I am sure now that I will be quite happy with my father and the Spanish court. The future is filled with great promise for me. Do not spoil it by coming after me in the expectation that I will return to you. It is quite impossible. Good-bye.' Now, sign it," he commanded.

He reached over her shoulder and took the paper and read it over. Then he folded it and put it into the envelope. He picked up the wax in preparation for sealing it when Angel said quickly, "The ring."

"Give it to me!"

She drew the ring from her finger and put it into Don Esteban's outstretched palm. He looked at it and Angel's heart fluttered painfully for the few seconds before he dropped it into the envelope, put the melted wax on and sealed it with an odd object he held in his hand.

She looked at the seal and was stunned by the knowledge that this might be the crest of the Montalban family. Where did he get it? But her good sense told her that the man who stood in this room with her was capable of anything. She must never underestimate what lengths Don Esteban Ortega would go to achieve his ends. Laying hands on the Montalban seal would be an easy task for him.

Now she was truly afraid. He stood and watched her, a slow, evil smile fluttered over his handsome face. With pounding heart, she read in his eyes what he had in mind. He would take her as casually as any whore, then one day flaunt it in Dev's face.

He walked close to her and lifted a handful of her hair, brushing it gently against his face.

"You have lovely hair," he murmured, "exactly like your mother's. She was one of the most beautiful women in Spain. I see now that she will be surpassed only by one other—her daughter. When you are a little older and, I think, just a little more experienced . . ."

She grew desperate for something that would take his mind from her. "You knew my mother well?" she blurted.

He looked down at her, and she sensed that he was not seeing her at all, but the ghost of her mother. She watched his eyes widen as they regarded her, and she realized in terror, she had unlatched the wrong door and opened a flood of memories that could destroy her.

He reached out both hands and took hold of her shoulders and began very gently pulling toward him the ghost of his past love. Angel jerked free of his embrace and backed away until she could go no further. Suddenly, he seemed to shake himself as though awakening from a dream; then he turned from her and left the room, closing the door behind him. She heard the key turn in the lock, then the sound of his receding footsteps.

What had stopped him?

She was completely exhausted. Every muscle in her body trembled so badly that she sagged down on the chair, her knees too weak to hold her any longer. There was nothing left for her now except to worry. Would Dev believe the letter? Would Andy see the ring? Would they find her before Don Esteban destroyed her? How could her father rescue her in any way, when they were miles out to sea and every man surrounding them was under Esteban's command?

Time ticked slowly by, but to her relief, Don Esteban did not return. Instead, Carlos brought her a tray of food and motioned to her to eat so that she could keep her strength. She did as he commanded. After she ate, she paced the floor, waiting for Don Esteban's return. Carlos reappeared and motioned her to go to the bunk and sleep.

"Sleep? How can I sleep when I know he will return here at any time?"

Carlos shook his head negatively, then made a sign of a man sleeping. He pointed to the cabin, then to himself.

"You mean, he's sleeping in your cabin?"

Yes. Carlos made a sign of drinking.

"Is he drunk?"

No. He reached into a pocket of his ragged coat and drew out a small packet of white powder.

"A sleeping powder! You drugged him?"

Yes.

"Why didn't you *kill* him?" she said fiercely. Carlos pointed to the powder and shook his head again. The powder was not strong enough to kill him, only to make him sleep. It was enough release for Angel. She crawled into the bunk and before Carlos could gather the tray and leave, she was asleep.

It was several more days that she was imprisoned in Don Esteban's cabin before she saw him again. The only person she saw at all was Carlos, who came to care for her personal needs.

The gentle rolling motion let her know when they were anchored, but when she looked out, she could see only the ocean. She was on the wrong side of the ship to catch sight of where they had landed. But it was not long before Carlos appeared and motioned her to follow him. She had become accustomed to Carlos' gestures now, and most times she understood what he was trying to tell her. Now he led her on deck, where Don Esteban waited beside the rail. He did not speak to her, but led the way down the gangplank, assured that she would follow. She could not read anything on his face or in his cold eyes. She followed him to a carriage that awaited them, and took the opportunity to look about her as much as she could. It was a small village that gave her the impression that it was entirely out of communication with civilization. The few natives she saw were olive-skinned, small and sturdily built people. Their clothes were mostly shabby but reminiscent of Spanish dress.

The carriage rolled slowly along a dirt road which began to wind away from the village. Once they had passed the last of the village, they were surrounded by jungle. Enormous trees were entwined with great vines and wild undergrowth. The road seemed to go on and on, and, with a sinking heart, Angel realized that if one did not know where he was going, he would soon die here. Anyone coming up the road would only be able to go forward or back, and both ways could be guarded well.

It seemed that they traveled for hours in deep silence before she realized they were slowly going up hill. Suddenly, as though it sprung from the center of the jungle, rose a huge, white stone structure with a green slate roof. It was a sprawling building, rectangular and two stories high, surrounded by a black wrought iron fence with spiked tops.

There was no way for an intruder to find his way here. She may as well be dead as to be imprisoned here.

The twin gates opened under the combined strength of two men, then clanged firmly shut behind their carriage after they drove through. The sound vibrated through her like a death knell, and for the first time, Angel came close to giving up the hope that she would see Dev again.

They stopped in front of the tall doors. She saw that they were heavy enough to withstand any force. Don Esteban stepped down from the carriage and put his hand out to help her. Tilting her chin stubbornly in the air, she ignored it and climbed down to stand beside him. She could not help but be overwhelmed by the size and impregnability of the structure that seemed to overpower her and drain her will.

"Do you believe it takes a place so strong and secluded to imprison me?"

He ignored her question, and laughed. Then: "The word is already being spread. Your father will find out that you are still alive and in my possession. Then he will surrender to me. But by that time, it will be too late to return you to a husband. Perhaps," he mused, watching her reaction to his words, "perhaps I shall put you on the docks, sell you to the highest bidder and let you earn your way in the world."

If he had intended to reduce her to pleading, he was disappointed. The proudly raging Montalban blood would not let her surrender to him. She stood erect and returned his cold glare. "I am powerless to stop whatever you would do to me, Don Esteban Ortega," she said proudly. "But I ask you in the name of God and humanity to forget this vengence. You are wasting your life, as well.

Will it take all our lives to repay what you think is owed? For you also will die of this vengence. What will you do when my father and I are gone? What will become of you when there is no longer anyone to hate? The empty shell of your life will be worthless. When—"

"Silence!" he snarled. "I don't want to hear your prattle! Your father will pay the price of taking from me the one thing in life I loved. To say nothing of the position and wealth I have lost because of him."

"My mother?"

"Your mother should have been mine, and all the wealth that went with the D'Santiago name. Honor! Position! Wealth and the one woman I have ever loved! The debt is great and I will see him beg for mercy, both for himself and for you before I have finished."

Angel opened her mouth to reply, but Don Esteban reached out and struck her across the face. It was not a hard blow, just enough to make her stumble back against the door and to bring tears to her eyes.

"I want no more words from you," he said, and reached behind her and opened the door. "Go inside, and do not have enough folly to speak to me so again."

He led her up a flight of stone steps to another door. Opening it wordlessly, he pushed her inside and closed the door behind her. She could hear the key grate in the lock, then, silence.

She looked about the room. It was large and quite comfortable, with a huge double bed in the center. The windows were barred with the same iron bars that formed the fence about the house. Walking to the window, she looked out through the bars at the wide expanse of jungle and ocean that separated her from freedom.

As the hours went by, she began to wonder if Carlos or

another would come with food. She had not seen Carlos since she left the ship.

The closet in the room was filled to overflowing with beautiful gowns, and the dresser and chests, with every sort of lingerie. Alarms rang in her mind. If all those things were for her, it they looked as if they were, then Don Esteban must plan for her to stay here a long, long time. Perhaps forever.

When night fell, a young woman came in to light the candles. No matter how Angel tried, she could not engage her in conversation. The girl seemed filled with pity, but she would not reply to her questions.

After the girl left, Angel browsed through the drawers and found a nightgown she could wear. The fit was perfect, but the gown was terribly sheer. She extinguished all but two of the candles and was about to crawl into the huge bed when a sharp click told her the door was being unlocked. She stood in shock as Don Esteban entered the room. Without a word, he locked the door behind him and put the key in his pocket.

Chapter 22

Dev and Andy's ships left the harbor at the same time, but headed in separate directions. Andy had marked Dev's map with all the places that Captain Martinez had given him. There were eight marks. Two had been eliminated because they were both Don Esteban's houses in Spain and both of them knew the last place Don Esteban would have taken Angel now would be to one of his houses, the political winds had drifted in Miguel's favor, and against Esteban.

They had each taken two of the other four places to investigate, and made a rendezvous point, with an agreement that if either was not at the rendezvous after a specific time, the other would go in search, starting with the other's last stop.

Andy left with only one advantage over Dev. He had a captive locked in his cabin who might be able to shed some light on the situation.

He stood at the wheel, guiding his ship toward the first place marked on his map. It was an island, mostly covered with jungle. But Captain Martinez had informed him that Don Esteban had a sanctuary up in the mountains in a remote area. He had also told him that the people in the small village there were loyal to him only out of terror of his wrath. Andy did not know exactly how he would find a way into the well-armed sanctuary of Don Esteban, but he knew he would find some way. "We'll find you, Angel, no matter where you are. I'll find you and when I do, that devil's heart will be consigned to hell where it belongs."

"Sir?" Briggs asked.

Andy glanced at him in surprise before he realized that he must have spoken aloud.

"Nothing, Briggs. Just some evil thoughts."

Briggs remained silent. In all his years with Andy this was the first time he'd seen him so angry and so determined to do something without explaining to him what was going to happen. He wondered at this change in Andy. Somehow, he felt there was a connection between Andy's unexplainable anger and the disappearance of his best friend, Captain Carlisle's wife. He prayed he was wrong, for this was the only thing he knew could destroy the man who was his captain.

One of the seamen approached him after they had been well on their way for over two hours.

"Mister Briggs?"

"Yes, Tucker. What is it?"

"Captain wanted to know when the lady was awake, Sir."

"Lady? What lady?"

The man forced himself to control the grin. It was the first time that Briggs was not on top of what was happening.

Briggs glared at Andy who was laughing unashamedly. "What lady?" he repeated to Andy.

"All right, Tucker. Make sure the cabin doors are locked, and prepare yourself. I think an explosion is about to come. Under no circumstances are you to unlock that cabin door. Is that understood?"

"Yes, Sir," he answered. Then he retreated rapidly under Briggs' angry stare.

"What are you up to Andy? Taken to kidnapping women now?"

"Not exactly, Grandma Briggs," Andy chuckled. "If you'll let me explain all that's happened, I'm sure you'll see that what I've done is necessary." Briggs' look told Andy that he wasn't sure of that, but he would listen to the explanation. Andy told him the story, from the beginning, leaving out only how he felt about Angel. When he was finished, Briggs was quiet, contemplating Andy's words—the spoken and unspoken ones. He knew without doubt how Andy felt about Angel. To know that the one and only woman Andy had ever given a second thought to was wife of Andy's dearest friend made him wonder just how far Andy was intending to go.

Andy stopped speaking and smiled at Briggs awaiting the explosion he thought was coming. He was surprised and unsettled when Briggs said, "You aiming to save her for Captain Carlisle? Or for yourself?"

Andy's smile faded and he stood and watched Briggs' face. He knew he could not fool Briggs about much. There was no sense to him lying now. "If I thought that I had a ghost of a chance of making her care for me as she does Dev, I would keep her on the *Hawk* once we find her and run to the ends of the earth to keep her."

"It's like that?"

"Yes, just like that. I'll go wherever needs going and do whatever needs doing to get her to safety. Where I go, the *Hawk* goes. What about her first mate?"

Briggs grinned. "I wouldn't let you take the *Hawk* into deep water without me. I'll go along on your merry little chase. I think you need being looked after. You've lost all your senses. What makes you think you know where to look?"

271

Andy explained about Captain Martinez' map. "And below I have a young lady who knows more about Angel's disappearance than anyone. So, will you take the wheel, Briggs, while I face the ultimate danger in a man's life— an angry woman?" Andy laughed.

Briggs took the wheel and watched Andy's broad retreating back as he made his way to the cabin in which Polly was a prisoner.

Polly had come awake sluggishly and for several minutes could not understand where she was. Then the night before came flooding back to her. She had promised to meet a handsome young sailor from the *Hawk*. He had brought along some drink, for which Polly developed a taste. She had drunk with him—but never noticed that he did not drink. Her memory of the night was vague; after he had opened the bottle, she remembered nearly nothing. Now, she realized exactly what had happened. She had been drugged and carried on board a ship. And that ship could only be the *Hawk*. She knew immediately that Andy must be suspicious about her. What other reason could he have for having her brought aboard. She rose from the bunk and walked to the door, but she knew before she touched it that it was locked. She panicked and began to pound on it. But quickly getting herself under control, she backed away from it and gathered herself to be ready to face Andy.

She was still standing there, facing the door, when Andy unlocked it, stepped inside, and locked it behind him.

"Well," he smiled. "I see you've finally decided to wake up."

"Why am I here?"

"You don't know?"

"I've no idea at all. I thought you would be out trying to help Dev find his runaway wife."

"Runaway!" Andy's eyes glowed wickedly. "I think not, Polly. Rather, *carried away*, wouldn't you say?"

"How would I know? I only know what I saw. Angel left of her own free will. The letter she wrote to Dev proved it!"

Slowly, deliberately, Andy told Polly about giving Angel the ring and why. "You see," he said softly, "if she sent that ring, it was because she was in trouble."

Polly's face became pale, and she backed away from him. Andy followed her, step by step.

"And now, Polly, you're going to tell me what really happened to Angel."

"I'll tell you nothing, Andy Ryan!"

He went on as though she had not spoken. He grabbed her by the shoulders and almost jerked her off her feet as he pulled her against him. "First, little Polly," he said with deceptive gentleness, "I am going to strip you and use you as one uses the filthiest whore, then I'm going to share your lovely charms with every man on the ship, as often as they like."

Polly trembled in his arms and her eyes grew wide with dawning fear. "You wouldn't dare."

"Oh, wouldn't I? Who's to stop me? I'm captain here, and if I want to share you with them, why they will accept my charity in the manner it is offered."

"Andy . . . please."

"Tell me what I want to know," he said.

"I don't know anything else," she almost screamed. Andy wrapped one arm about her, and grabbed her bodice. With one violent tug, he ripped it from her breasts. She began to fight, pelting him with her clenched

273

fists before he held her tightly against him. Brutally, he massaged one breast, knowing he was hurting her, then he let his hand slip down to her skirt and pulled it away from her. She slapped and kicked at him and tried to bite him until he slapped her, just hard enough to daze her and tumble her back onto the bunk. She sat up weeping softly and looked up to see him slowly removing his clothes.

"Andy . . . don't, please," she cried. "I only did it because I loved Dev. You don't know how it is to love someone who cares only for someone else. I just couldn't bear it any longer." She buried her face in her hands and sobbed brokenly.

She had struck Andy a terrible blow. "To love someone who cared only for someone else." Of course, he knew how she felt and he suddenly realized that not only could he understand how she felt, he began to feel pity for her. He went to the edge of the bunk and sat beside her. Then, gently, he drew her against him and held her to him.

After she had her tears under control, Andy began to talk to her softly. He told her the whole story, and from the look in her eyes, he could tell that she had never known the truth.

Then she began to talk, to tell him how she had been fooled and used. How Don Esteban had convinced her that Angel would not be harmed, that all he wanted was to contact her father. He had made her believe, first out of gullibility, then fear, that he would get Angel out of Dev's life and make it possible for her and Dev to be together.

Andy questioned her, and after some time, he began to believe that he and the *Hawk* were closer to Angel than Dev was. Once, Polly said, Don Esteban had referred to his "sanctuary" and at another time, to his "island."

"I'm on the right track. Angel must be there. But how do we get to him? I'm sure he has lookouts all over the island."

Polly watched him closely while he contemplated possible plans, then suddenly her eyes widened and she said, "How can you condemn me for loving Dev, Andrew Ryan, when you are in love with Angel? We are in the same boat in more than one way, for each of us knows his own cause is lost."

Andy looked at her. Yes. How could he condemn her for harboring the same thoughts that he, in secret, had. She was a woman, defenseless against a man like Don Esteban. She had done what he might have done if the opportunity had arisen. He could not know that he would not have.

There was no anger left in him for Polly now. To condemn her was to condemn himself. He reached down and picked up a blanket and wrapped it about her as gently as he could. "I'm sorry, Polly. You are right about both of us. Neither of us can be blamed for loving and losing, or for fighting for what we want."

"If I could do something to make up for it, Andy, I would," she said and her eyes spoke the truth. For the first time, Polly was beginning to know what love really was. What Angel and Dev had was something so very special and in all possibility it could have already been destroyed.

"Tell me everything you know, every word that Esteban has ever spoken to you. Somewhere, somehow, there might be something we can use. Perhaps we can both make up for things."

Polly talked for hours while Andy paced the cabin

floor. At length, he saw that she was trembling from exhaustion and that her face was wet with tears of humiliation at her complicity.

He stepped to the bunk and, taking her hands in his, sat beside her.

"Oh, Andy," she sobbed. "I'm so sorry. Now there is no way to tell either of them that I'm sorry for all the harm I've done." She began to cry, warm clean tears of penance.

"We'll find her and somehow we'll get her back," he said gently. "There is much in what you told me that is helpful. You sleep now. I shall bring us in on the opposite side of the island from Don Esteban's village. We'll drop anchor there. Perhaps, when we get there, I will have devised a plan for getting Angel out, if . . . if she's there."

Polly nodded and lay down on his bunk, and Andy closed the door behind him and went up on deck. There he gave Briggs the coordinates for their destination and told him as much of Polly's story as he thought it useful for Briggs to know. He stood at the wheel most of the evening and halfway into the night. He had studied the island for a long time and knew how much rough terrain and jungle stood between him and Don Esteban's village on the island. It would take a long time to cross that on foot, if it were possible at all. He didn't think he had that much time to spare. Every moment Angel spent with Don Esteban would be filled with fear and despair. The thought of her in such a state was unbearable.

If the winds had been with Dev, he should be at his first point by now. The more Andy considered it, the more he was convinced that Esteban could only be on the island. Dev would be sailing from his second destination

276

to the rendezvous point, and if Andy wasn't there, to the island. Andy calculated how long that should take.

Perhaps, if Andy anchored on the far side of the island and took a longboat around the tip of the island, he could hide the boat a little below the village and find out if Don Esteban really was there and if he was, exactly where. Then he would come back to his ship, and—although it would be difficult—wait for Dev. By that time, he could possibly have made some kind of plans for Angel's rescue. He sighed deeply. It was poor planning, and so weak it irritated Andy. To just sit here on his ship and twiddle his thumbs went against Andy's nature. He was a man of action, and waiting would be hard.

It took them almost a week to reach the small cove Andy had picked out. During this time, there had not been much communication between Polly and him. He had left her his cabin and had shared Briggs'. They had had some of their meals together, though, and being in such close quarters, it was impossible for them not to have some time alone with each other. Andy had always found Polly attractive and would have been drawn to her, but Dev and Angel stood between them like a silent wall.

Polly did nothing to try to force Andy's attentions, either. She kept to herself most of the time, her thoughts turned toward her past and her future. She came to understand that what she had felt for Dev had not been love. Love, she knew now, could not have hurt as she had hurt Dev and Angel. She vowed in her heart if God would grant Angel's safety, she would do everything in her power to repair the damage she had done. She was prepared to throw herself on Angel's mercy; but if anything happened to her, she wondered if there would be any mercy in the heart of Devon Carlisle.

It was early in the morning of the second day they had been anchored in the quiet little harbor, that Polly came on deck to find Andy making preparations to leave the ship in a longboat. He was dressed roughly as a common sailor, and she stood at the companionway admiring him for a few minutes before making her presence known. His height was accented by his clothes. Dark pants and shirt with a heavy jacket. His red hair gleamed in the early morning sun and she could see his smile flash as Briggs said something to him. Polly walked toward them and Andy stopped talking in the middle of a sentence when he saw her coming.

"Good morning, Polly. Sleep well?"

"Yes . . . Where are you going, Andy?"

Andy and Briggs exchanged quick glances which did not pass Polly unobserved.

"One of you answer me," she demanded. "Are you going after Angel alone? You can't, Andy. You'll be killed!"

"I'm not going after her yet. I plan to wait for Dev. I want to acquaint myself with the territory a little better."

"Take me with you," Polly demanded.

"Impossible!"

"Andy, please, I can help."

"No, Polly. It's too dangerous for you and it would slow me down considerably if I had to look after you."

"You won't have to look out for me! I'll take care of myself. I won't slow you down. At least, let me watch the boat for you. If someone should find it, they would know you were here."

Andy gave her a doubtful look, but she could see that he was considering her plan.

278

"Please, Andy," she said, and put her hand on his arm. "Can't you see I have to try to do something to make up for what I've done?"

Andy sighed. "All right, but if we have to get out of there in a hurry, I'm not stopping for you."

"Agreed," she replied.

"You have to wear something else. You can't go traipsing around in that dress."

"Give me a minute," she called back over her shoulder as she whirled away from him. Andy turned to see Briggs with a thoroughly displeased look on his face.

"It's her choice, Briggs," he replied defensively.

"Which you don't have to take," Briggs replied.

"Goddamn it, man, she started all this off. She should at least do her part to help us straighten it out."

"Who do you think you're fooling, Andy? What could a little mite of a thing like that do if something goes wrong. Face it, man, you don't really want to leave her here, flirting with the men. She's got you wondering about what she'll do while you're gone."

"You tryin' to tell me I'm jealous of her? You're out of your head, Briggs. I don't care what happens to her one way or the other."

"Then leave her here. If you're to be gone a couple of days, she'll have better company here than you are." Briggs grinned.

Andy's eyes widened in surprise as he saw the companionway door open and Polly step out. She had gone to the cabin boy, who had given her some of his clothes. The pants were snug and hugged her hips like a second skin. The shirt, too, was too small and was laced across a chest built much differently than the one for which it was made. She had braided her hair in one long

279

braid and let it hang loose. Her feet encased in the cabin boy's best boots completed a most astonishing and, in Andy's eyes, pleasing outfit.

"You mind your own business and take care of the *Hawk*, Briggs. I'll take care of Polly," Andy whispered as Polly approached them.

"I'll bet you will," Briggs replied. "That's exactly what's worryin' me. Seems to me she needs some protection from you."

Andy chuckled, but the laughter died quickly as Polly came nearer. "Briggs is right," he thought. "I should leave her here. There's too much danger out there, from Don Esteban . . . and from me." But he wanted her along and he knew it, just as Briggs knew it. Polly reached his side and smiled at him.

"Is this better?"

"Not really," he laughed. "Now I have to keep my mind on two things at once."

He was surprised when Polly blushed and turned her eyes away from his. "Don't worry about me, Andy," she said coolly. "You keep your mind on what you're after, I'll take care of myself. I would just as soon you and any other man would leave me alone. I owe a debt and I intend to pay it; and it does not include being a bed mate to any other man as long as I live." With these words, she climbed over the side and descended the rope ladder to the small boat below. Andy cast a glaring look at Briggs who tried to suppress the laughter, then climbed over the side and joined Polly in the boat; but Briggs' parting laughter rankled, and he was silent as he headed the boat closer to shore where they could creep along and come close to the small town unobserved.

Polly sat in silence watching him maneuver the boat.

When they could barely see the outline of the small village ahead of them, he headed for shore. Together, they pulled the boat up onto the sand.

"Could you push her off, if necessary?" he asked.

"Yes, I've done it before."

"Good. Wait here. I should be back by nightfall. There's food in the boat. If you see signs of strangers, shove off and wait a few minutes. If I don't come, get back to the ship as fast as you can. Do you understand?"

"I understand, but I don't intend to do it," she replied.

He stared at her and his face flushed with anger. "Just what do you think you're going to do?"

"I'm going with you," she stated firmly.

"Like hell you are!" he almost shouted.

"Andy," she said with a cool grin. "If you don't take me, I'll follow you and that would be twice as dangerous. I want to help, and I can't do that squatting here beside this boat waiting and worrying about you. I'm going along."

"You're not! That's final, do you understand?"

She smiled, but slowly shook her head. He was so furious at her, he could have slapped her. She could see it clearly in his eyes, but she stood her ground and would not shift her eyes from his.

"You're the most infuriating bitch it's been my misfortune to run across," he stormed. If he intended to intimidate her with his anger, he failed, for she did not reply but merely stood and waited patiently until he realized how futile it was to rave at her.

"You're wasting valuable time," she reminded gently.

"Damn you, woman," he raged. "If we get out of this all right and I get you safely back to the ship, I'm going to knock some sense into that head of yours. Don't you

281

know what would happen to you if Don Esteban found you? He would know you betrayed him. How long do you think you would survive if that happened?"

"About as long as you will if you're caught," she said calmly. "Together, we might be able to help each other. Alone we're both vulnerable. Andy," she added, "I don't think I could stand it, sitting here worrying if you're all right or not. If something is going to happen, I . . . I'd rather we were together when it did. If I'm going to die, I don't want to be alone, and I don't want you to be alone, either."

There was nothing he could say to this. He knew he was defeated. Slowly, he lifted the bundle of food and two rolled blankets from the bottom of the boat. Then he turned away. "All right, Polly, come along. I can't argue with you while our time is slipping away."

They walked across the sand to the edge of the jungle. Suddenly, the bright sun disappeared and they seemed to be cut off from the world in a semi-dark, damp green jungle. They did not go too far into the jungle, for Andy knew he would soon be lost without the sun to guide him. Polly followed closely as he cut his way through the undergrowth. It seemed that they traveled one exhausting mile after another. She was sweating and the damp shirt clung to her body. Small, evil bugs attacked her skin. She was gasping for breath in the thick humid air and silently longed for the cool ocean breeze. She was concentrating so hard on keeping up that her attention was all on making her body move forward one step after another. She didn't realize Andy had stopped until she came up against his broad back with a solid thump. She stifled the words that were on the tip of her tongue as Andy turned to face her, a malicious gleam in his eyes.

"Tired?" he asked, his voice thick with sarcasm.

"I'll keep up," she gasped. "I can go as far as you can and I will."

"I bet you would too, you stupid female," he said between gritted teeth.

"Damn you, Andy Ryan, who do you think you are to call me names," she shouted angrily. "I only want to do the same things you do. If that makes me stupid, what does it make you, you arrogant bastard?"

They stood glaring at each other, then Andy began to laugh. There they were, in the middle of a jungle, dependent on one another, yet shouting at each other like children. He wrapped his arms about her and held her against him. "All right, Polly. I give in. Let's have a truce until we're on board ship again. What do you say?"

She nodded, and, slowly, they began to move forward again. But this time Andy slowed his pace to Polly's.

Chapter 23

Dev paced the deck with slow, measured steps. He had been doing so for more than three hours, and the first mate who stood at the wheel could feel his nerves stretched taut. Since they hadn't found any trace of Angel or Don Esteban after they had searched for days in the two places he was to cover, Dev had gone to their rendezvous point and waited in vain for Andy for over two days. Sure now that Andy had found Angel's location, he had stared hard at the map with the two small *x*'s on it. "Which one was the right one? Just where was Andy anchored and waiting for him?" With his first mate standing beside him, Dev had pointed to the small island marked on the map.

"There's our destination. There's a small cove on the side of the island away from the village. If I know Andy, that's where he'll be."

They had turned the ship about and were now headed toward the island as fast as the wind would carry them, but it wasn't fast enough for Dev. He paced silently as if that would move the ship faster. His mind forbade him from thinking of where Angel might be at that moment. He knew he would lose his sanity if he allowed himself to dwell on it. Instead, he directed his thoughts to what type of rescue might be needed. If he joined forces with Andy, surely his crew and Andy's would be enough to take over that small village. "Then," he thought, "then I shall give

Don Esteban all the thought he deserves." For a moment, he allowed himself the luxury of letting Angel creep into his mind. The softness of her, and the feel of her fingers against his skin . . .

"Angel," he whispered.

Davy turned to look at him. "Did you say something Sir?"

"No. No, Davy. How much longer to the island?"

"Mornin' sun should find us droppin' anchor in the cove you pointed out. But . . ."

"But what, Davy?"

"But what if Captain Ryan ain't there?"

Dev's jaw clenched firmly and Davy could see the darkening of his eyes and the muscles that jumped spasmatically in his cheek.

"He'll be there," he answered firmly his voice like the grating of iron upon iron. "He has to be there, there's no other logical place he could be."

"Why don't you go down and get some sleep? There's a lot of hours before we arrive and if you keep on like you are, you won't be able to rescue her even if she is there."

Dev knew Davy was right, just as he knew how impossible sleep would be. But to ease the tension, he agreed. He went below and closed his cabin door. The confines of the cabin were almost too much to share with Angel's memory.

He lay for a while on the bunk, but as he knew, sleep was an elusive thing. Half faded segments of the past crept in—the short time they were together, and the miracle of love they had shared. He found it impossible to lay still. He rose and poured himself a substantial glass of brandy, then stood gazing down at the map. Slowly, he reached out a finger and placed it on the x that marked the island.

"I pray God you're there, Angel," he said softly.

Angel stood staring across the room at Don Esteban as he moved toward her. His eyes had the same glazed, faraway look they had when he had spoken to her before. With a shock, she saw that he was completely drunk. She backed away a few steps, but the bed blocked any further escape.

He was only inches from her, the deep gleam of lust in his eyes. Slowly, he reached out and with surprisingly gentle fingers, touched her hair, then whispered words that froze her heart. "Anna . . . mi Anna . . . mi Alhaja . . . mi Vida." He caressed her hair, then slid his hand to the nape of her neck and began to draw her to him.

For a moment, she panicked. He thought she was her mother!

Suddenly, she regained control of her senses and, putting both hands on his chest, she pushed with all her strength. Don Esteban stumbled back a few steps, and Angel moved quickly. Jumping on the bed, she rolled across it and came up on her feet on the opposite side. She looked about desperately for something, with which she could defend herself. A heavy gold candlestick stood on the stand beside the bed. Quickly, she threw the candle aside and grabbed the heavy candlestick in her hands.

"Don't come near me!" she shouted. "I'm Angelique Montelban. Not Anna D'Santiago. My mother is dead. Dead because of you, you foul, evil man. You shall never have me. If I cannot stop you, I will find a way to kill myself. I would sooner die as my mother did than surrender to you."

"You little fool," he snarled, seeming to recover from his drunken trance, "do you believe you can stop me from taking you if I so desire? What will you do?" He laughed.

She wanted to cry, for she knew he was right. Slowly now, he stalked her, a half smile curling his lips, for they both knew the only way things could end. When he finally attacked, she battled the best her strength would allow, but within seconds, the candlestick was tossed aside and she found herself held helplessly against his hard chest and unable to struggle against the two strong arms that held her so tightly, she could only struggle for breath and try to turn her face away from his seeking mouth. He twined his hand roughly in her hair and jerked her head back, ignoring her cry of pain and anger as his hard mouth descended on hers and took it brutally, bruising her lips and face. He ravaged her mouth with slow, deliberate pressure. When he lifted his mouth from hers, he looked into her angry eyes and laughed at her helpless struggling.

She spat in his face and shouted in wild anger at him. "You foul bastard. Kill me now! Kill me now! Don't make me suffer the agony of your rotten hands on me."

His face blazed with fury and he struck her, knocking her to the floor. She saw a blinding flash of stars and felt her world spin. Then as she rose to her feet, he deliberately and calmly struck her again. Her world darkened for a moment then she felt him jerk her to her feet. He lifted her into his arms, walked the few steps to the bed, and threw her on it. She felt the bed sag for a moment as his weight landed beside her. Pulled into his arms, she whimpered as she felt the pressure of his mouth against hers and his hands ripping away her gown.

Her struggles were useless, and she began to cry Dev's name in soft, gasping sobs as he began to master her.

Suddenly, Don Esteban froze as a familiar voice from across the reach of time called out to him. "Don Esteban! Murderer! Foul fiend from hell. Stop the monstrous thing you are doing. Turn to me and fight a man who has waited a long time to put an end to your miserable life."

Don Esteban had risen from the bed at the sound of the voice and stood now, rage darkening his face. Angel looked through a bleary veil of tears and saw Carlos, then watched a miraculous transformation. Carlos stood slowly erect and unbuttoned his tunic. He let it fall with a solid thump on the floor. With it, fell the heavy, padded hump he had been wearing all these years. He tore the black patch from his eye, and with a quick gesture, he brushed the hair back from his face. Features that had been grotesquely twisted slowly began to straighten. Dark, purple-blue eyes that mirrored her own, looked at her now with pride and compassion as he saw the realization suddenly dawn in her eyes.

"Father," she whispered.

"Yes, my child. I'm your father. Come to me, Angel," he said gently.

Quickly, Angel slid from the bed, grabbing a sheet to wrap around her. She took a few steps toward her father, but suddenly a strong iron hand closed about her waist. Don Esteban jerked her toward him as he drew his sword from its sheath. With one quick movement, he pushed her behind him and stood facing Miguel Montalban.

"For eighteen years I have sought you. You will never leave this room alive." He lifted his sword and advanced slowly toward Miguel.

A soft note of humor was in Miguel's voice, as he said in a taunting reply, "For five years, I have lived in your shadow, Don Esteban. The only reason I did not try to kill you long before this is that I was afraid that if I failed, my daughter would be at your mercy. And so I waited and watched, misleading you at every turn, altering your maps, feeding you rumors in many roundabout ways. After a while I began to enjoy the game. As long as my daughter was safe from you I was contented to watch your frustration and anger. If it had not been for that little wench Polly Dillon, my daughter would still be safe with her husband and you and I would still be enjoying our little game. I am taking my daughter from here."

"You are a very clever man, Miguel. Having known you before, I should have known that you were near, that you were not in hiding. But you have drawn the game to a conclusion that is satisfactory to me, for I will kill you now and I will make your daughter pay, day by day, for your little charade."

The two swords rose and touched. Steel clashed against steel. Don Esteban smiled grimly as Miguel retreated under his attack. Miguel seemed to be defending himself poorly, until their eyes met over the swords and Esteben realized that Miguel was retreating purposely, allowing him to attack and tire himself. It was then he began to control his anger, and it was then Miguel realized he was engaging a truly remarkable swordsman. Both men were concentrating so thoroughly on each other that neither of them noticed that Angel was edging toward the table that held the mate to the large candlestick she had defended herself with before. She lifted the heavy candlestick in both hands and crept slowly behind Don Esteban. Within two paces of him, she lifted the candlestick high over her head and brought it down with all her strength on Don Esteban's sword hands. He cried out in pain, and his sword clattered to the floor. A second later, he felt Miguel's sword point at his throat.

He glared at Miguel with unrestrained hatred. "Kill me now or you will regret it. For this will be only another debt to add to your account."

"Oh, no, Don Esteban. I will not make it that easy for you. I will take my daughter from you, and we will return to Spain where I will reclaim what has belonged to the Montalban and D'Santiago families all these years and is now rightfully mine and Angel's. We will be out of your reach."

"And just how do you expect to get out of this castle alive? I shall raise the alarm as soon as you are out of this room."

"Again you are wrong, Don Esteban." Miguel reached into his pocket and took out a small packet.

"Angel, go to the table and pour a glass of wine."

Angel did as she was instructed.

"Bring it to me, now."

When Angel came to his side, he handed her the packet. "Pour the contents of this packet into the wine and stir it well."

Again Angel did as she was told, watching the white powder dissolve in the bright red wine.

"Do not go any closer than necessary, but give the wine to Don Esteban."

As Angel handed Don Esteban the goblet, she could feel his cold fingers as they touched hers, and she glanced up into the cold hard fury of his eyes. Quickly, she went back to her father's side. He put a protective arm around her shoulder. Don Esteban looked at the goblet, then at Miguel.

"Poison, Miguel? I would rather die at sword's point than from poison."

"I will not give you the pleasure of either one. This is merely a drug that will make you sleep until we are safely on our way. By the time you awaken, both Angel and I will be beyond your reach."

As he looked at him, Miguel's eyes became cold and hard. And he pushed his arm forward slightly, just enough so the sword point nicked Don Esteban's flesh.

"Drink!"

Slowly, Don Esteban raised the goblet to his lips. Burning hatred could be felt in the room like a live thing. The air hung thick with it. Don Esteban drained the cup, and it fell from his fingers to the floor. Within moments, he began to weave slightly on his feet. Angel and Miguel watched as, slowly, Don Esteban crumpled into a silent heap. Miguel sheathed his sword and turned to face Angel. With a soft cry, she threw herself into her father's arms. He held her close to him, gently rocking her in his arms, caressing her hair and murmuring her name over and over. Then, taking her by the shoulders, he moved her away from him and looked down into her tear-filled eyes. "Angel, we must get out of here now. Go to the closet and find some clothes and get into them as quickly as possible."

She moved rapidly to do as he said. While she was doing so, Miguel moved to Don Esteban's side, lifted him from the floor, carried him to the bed, and dropped him on it, pulling the covers up over him as though Don Esteban were asleep.

"How will we ever get out of here, Father, and pass all of Don Esteban's guards without them raising an alarm?"

Miguel smiled and motioned Angel to follow him. "I have been in and out of this castle quite often. I would wager that I know more ways in and out of it than Don Esteban himself."

As he spoke, he walked, it seemed to Angel, toward a solid stone wall. Slowly, methodically, his fingers ran up the crevices between two large stones. Angel gasped as, silently, a small portion of the wall gave inward. They stood facing a small doorway..

"Come, quickly. Someone could come here at any time, and I want them to think he sleeps, and that he is alone."

Angel stepped into the small dark tunnel and Miguel followed. The doorway closed silently behind them and they stood in the dark. Angel felt her father grip her hand firmly.

"Don't be frightened, child, I know my way about these corridors very well. We will wait one minute until my eyes become accustomed to the dark and then we will make our way out of here. There is a small portion of the jungle for us to cross and then we will both be free. A friend is waiting on the other side of the island with a ship. In a matter of a few days, we will be on our way to Spain."

"Spain? Father, I must return to my husband. He is probably beside himself with fear for my safety." She sensed resistance though she could not see his face.

Miguel remained silent for a few minutes. Then: "In time, child, first we must get out of here. Come," he said as he began to move slowly forward, drawing her with him.

It seemed like hours to Angel as they moved slowly and steadily forward. Then she realized that not only were

292

they moving forward, they were steadily going downward. Before long, she heard the sounds of the surf, and the breeze lightly touched her face.

"The ocean!" she whispered. "That is the air from the ocean."

"Yes, we are not far from the exit. There is a small inlet from the sea that runs almost directly beside the back of the castle. We shall follow it across the jungle to safety. I've hidden some food and blankets near the river."

Suddenly, they were out in the night. Bright silver stars glittered against the black sky and she could feel the softness of the ground against her feet. Miguel led her at a quicker pace now, although she could barely see him against the dark foliage at the edge of the jungle. He seemed to have eyes like a cat and was sure of where he was going. She sensed when they were near the river, for Miguel stopped and took a bundle he had hidden and slung it over his shoulder.

They changed direction and began to follow the narrow, twisted stream. They walked as rapidly as the undergrowth would allow. Slowly, nervous strain and exhaustion began to tell on Angel. Her pace slowed until she could barely keep up with Miguel. She stumbled over the large root of a tree and fell flat on her face. She was bruised and dirty when Miguel helped her to her feet. But despite the miserable condition she was in, they had to move on. Don Esteban would regain consciousness soon, and they had to put enough distance between them that they could not be overtaken.

"Angelique, I know how hard it is for you, but we cannot stop here."

"I know," she said miserably. "I can go on. I am fine."

"Brave girl," he murmured as he gave her shoulders a

293

quick hug. "You are so like your mother, it is hard for me to believe you are not she. I'll make up to you for all the pain and misery we have caused you. Soon, we will be free."

Angel rested her head against the hard strength of his shoulder for a moment, then she stood erect again.

"I'm ready. We can go now, Father, and I will keep up with you."

He kissed her quickly, then began to move ahead, but Angel realized he was slowing his pace for her.

Minutes turned to hours, and Angel became numb with exhaustion, unaware of anything except the necessity of putting one foot before the other and to go on and on and on.

A pale ribbon bordered the horizon, heralding the first light of dawn. Miguel thought it was safe to stop and rest. He turned to face Angel, and his eyes filled with pity. She swayed on her feet from fatigue, her clothes were torn and dirty, and her arms and face were scratched in hundreds of places and bleeding. Her hair had become loosened and fell in a damp, tangled mass about her. She was panting as though each breath would be her last.

"Come, child," he said gently as he spread one of the blankets on the ground. "Sit here and I'll get you something to eat, then you can get some rest."

Angel sagged gratefully to her knees and lay her head against the tree by which Miguel had spread the blanket. He unwrapped the bundle of food. With a sharp knife he cut a piece of bread and turned to hand it to Angel, but her eyes were already closed in deep sleep. He gazed down at the child he had protected for so long, then knelt beside her and eased her body to the ground and covered her with a blanket.

He sat on the ground beside her, his back against the tree, and slowly, thoughtfully, chewed the crust of bread. If Angel had known his thoughts at the moment, she would have been alarmed. He was grateful to Robert Cortland for protecting her for so long, and to Dev. But he wanted her for himself now. He wanted to show her what life as a Montalban could be. He had no idea of the love that existed between Angel and Dev. "Once I get her home, we will set about annulling this marriage. One day she will be able to choose from among the royalty of Europe a perfect husband."

Angel slept on peacefully unaware that the hand of fate was about to reach out and turn her world upside down.

The day grew unbearably hot and Angel came awake with her body soaked in perspiration. Her father was already gathering their things together and preparing for them to move on. Every muscle and bone in her body complained in agony as she rose to her feet. She and her father faced each other.

"Can you go on, child?"

"Before I would fall into the hands of Don Esteban again, I would rather die here. I will go on," she said with determination.

"We will make it. Another two nights of traveling will see us safely aboard my ship."

She nodded, and he reached out and took her hand and together they moved forward.

They traveled the rest of the day and deep into the night before they stopped again. They ate as they walked. Several times, Miguel had stopped, but Angel insisted upon going on. The next day, Miguel became alarmed at the glazed look in her eyes. In the early afternoon, he stopped again.

"Don't stop," she gasped. "We must go on until we are safe on the ship. I must get out of this terrible place."

"Angelique," he replied softly, and reached out to touch her, only to discover she was burning hot. "You're running a fever. We must stop for a while."

"No," she said and was about to say something else when slowly her body collapsed and she fell forward into a small heap at his feet. Miguel spread a blanket down and lay her slight form on it. He carried water from the river and bathed her tired dirty body in it. Then he wrapped her in another blanket.

As the hours passed, the fever began to rage higher and higher, and she moaned and cried in delirium. Hour upon hour, he bathed her in the cool water, trying to reduce the fever. He was helpless against this illness and angry with fate.

Hours turned into days and for the first time, Miguel began to believe he might loose her completely.

He almost cried when, on the fourth day, her fever began to break. He didn't want to tell her that there was now no possible way their escape ship could still be waiting. He had told its captain to wait three days and if he was not there, he would have failed and they were to leave.

The fever broke completely the next morning, and Angel opened her eyes and for the first time, they were clear. Miguel's hopes soared, only to be dashed at the first words she spoke. "Who are you? Where am I?"

Chapter 24

Andy squatted back on his heels and he watched, from the covering of the jungle, the comings and goings of the people of the small village. He grinned, pleased with himself. There was a pattern in their movements, and now he knew what it was. Three or four times a day, a wagon covered so that he could not tell what its contents were, left the village and proceeded up a small road that disappeared into the jungle. It was clear that the road led to Don Esteban's hideaway, and he was determined to find it.

He moved back into the small clearing where he and Polly had been staying for the past two days. It was early morning, just after sunrise, and Polly was still asleep, wrapped in a blanket. He eased himself to the ground beside her and sat quietly allowing her to sleep as long as possible. Andy had developed a grudging admiration for Polly. She had stayed with him, taking her turn watching without complaint. She had slept on the ground, endured the terrible food and the discomforts, and could still smile when Andy found it quite difficult.

After the first night, when he had suggested they share the blanket to stay warm on the cold nights, he had not broached the subject again. Polly had turned on him in fury, and made it clear that not only could he keep his blankets, but if he tried to put a hand on her she would cut his throat in his sleep and let him choke on his own blood.

Now he was surprised at himself when he felt the sudden surge of desire flood over him. It was something Andy had never been faced with before. Women were always drawn to him. Well, once they were out of this jungle and back to civilization, there would be no more such problems. He would find himself a willing woman.

He looked down on Polly's sleeping face and watched the sunlight touch the pale ivory of her skin. Her pink lips formed a half smile as if she were dreaming something pleasant. Her disheveled hair fell about her shoulders in wild abandon, and for the first time, he noticed how thick and soft it was, and the streaks of pale gold that threaded through it. He leaned down near her and gently brushed the hair from her shoulders, feeling its satin softness between his fingers. At that moment, she opened her eyes. Neither of them moved. Neither of them were able to move.

Andy could feel some invisible thing draw him closer and closer to her. She did not resist, for she was bound by the same force. She felt a warm lethargy overtake her and watched, fascinated, as his eyes widened and darkened as he looked into hers. Slowly, he lowered his head as if any sudden movement would break the spell they were under. His lips touched hers, and he could feel her mouth tremble under his. She stirred in his arms, and a soft, alarmed murmur escaped her. He lifted his lips slowly from hers, reluctant to leave her.

They looked at each other in shock. This warm gentle emotion that washed over Andy was something completely alien.

She rolled away from him and scrambled quickly to her feet. Andy got to his feet and stood inches from her. His eyes questioned hers, and were answered by an unwilled acceptance—acceptance that she belonged to him, that she wanted him in a way she had never wanted any other man. And he was as shaken as she was. Many women had been his, for a day, a week, but none had looked at him in this way.

"Polly?"

"Don't, Andy," she whispered. "Don't touch me." Her voice broke and she inhaled deeply. "I'm not a toy, Andy, I'm not to be taken and discarded, not again . . . not ever again. I'll not belong to any man again unless he offers me more than a quick touch and a quicker goodbye."

"What is it you want, Polly?"

"I *don't* want you to reach out to me just because Angel can never be yours. I need more than to be your consolation for your loss."

"Polly, it's not that."

"Don't lie to yourself, Andy."

Andy was miserably confused. He did not know at this moment how he felt about Angel. He knew he wanted Polly, but was that all there was to it? Was it as she said, to use and discard or was it something else? "I don't know what to say to you, Polly. I want you, you know that, you've known it all along."

"I don't want you to say anything you don't feel. We'll be out of all of this one day. You can make your decision when you feel it is right. For now, we will concentrate on trying to find Angel. Now, more than any other time, I want her to be free. Maybe then, she can set you free. Free to return the love someone else can offer you."

"You're saying that you love me?"

"I realized that quite some time ago. What we do about

299

it is up to you. But I'll only give you two choices. You can come to me as a whole man ready to give me all your love, or you can go on loving a ghost. But if you do, then leave me alone. I won't share you with Angel or any other woman."

"You've certainly changed a lot in the past few months, Polly," he said bitterly.

"Yes, I was a soft giving creature, and everyone, including Dev took all I could give and returned nothing. Now, I will no longer allow myself that pain again."

He sighed deeply. "All right, we'll do what we came here to do. But one day soon, we will talk about this again. In a time when there are no ghosts between us. We'll give each other time, enough time, so that we both know what we really want."

Polly nodded. She could not say anything. Words of surrender hovered too close. She started to turn away from Andy, but his voice stopped her.

"Polly?"

She looked up into his clear green eyes. He was smiling at her. "This is just a little reminder," he said gently, and suddenly his two large hands encircled her waist, and he lifted her almost off her feet and against the hardness of his body. His mouth covered her exclamations of surprise as he kissed her thoroughly and expertly.

When he finally released her, she was trembling. She stepped away. Kneeling beside her blankets, she began to roll them into a bundle. Andy watched her for a moment, then began to gather his things together.

They moved quietly through the tangled underbrush until they came to the winding dirt road that led through the jungle. They walked along the road where it bordered the jungle.

It was with open-mouthed wonder that they gazed at the enormous edifice that loomed before them.

"My God, what a fortress!" Andy muttered.

"If Angel is in there, we'll never be able to get to her," Polly said, despair in her voice.

"There are a lot of men on my ship, and when Dev's ship arrives, there will be enough of us to overrun this place. We'll get in, and we'll find her, if she's there."

"Yes," Polly said quietly, "if she's there."

"Polly, are you willing to stay here a little longer, before we return to the ship? We could watch the comings and goings, maybe find out for sure if Angel really is here. By the time we get back to the ship, Dev may already be there. At least, we would be able to tell him something for certain."

"Good heavens, Andy, we're almost out of food. What will we eat?"

"Well," he grinned, "I thought I'd forage in the village some time after dark, maybe find something. If you don't agree, we could go back to the *Hawk* and I could always come back later, alone."

Polly chuckled at the challenge in his voice. "You know I wouldn't leave you out here alone," she laughed. "I wouldn't put it past you trying to get into that huge pile of rock by yourself. No, I'll forage with you, wait with you, and we'll both go back to the *Hawk* and get help from Dev, or we don't go back at all."

"Stubborn wench, aren't you?"

"As stubborn as you. I owe a greater debt than you do."

Andy made a sharp sound of exasperation and drew her off the path and into the edge of the tangled underbrush. "We can stay here until nightfall. We're not too far from the village now. After dark, we'll see what we can find."

Polly nodded agreement and dropped the bundle she was carrying. She felt absolutely dirty, and she knew she looked no better than she felt. Spreading her blanket down, she sat cross-legged on it and thought wishfully of a hot tub of water, some nice smelling soap, and a good hot meal.

Andy lay on his blanket beneath a tree and closed his eyes. Polly watched him. He certainly was a handsome man, she conceded, regarding his long lean body. She grew warm as unwelcome thoughts invaded her mind— the way his moustache tickled her mouth when he kissed her, the hard strength of his hands. It would be easy, so very easy to succumb to Andy's charm.

The small gurgling noise she suddenly became aware of must have been on the edge of her consciousness for a long time. Now, with a wild leap of her heart, she put a name to it. Water! Fast moving water! Which meant either a small waterfall or a river. At that moment, she didn't care which. Slowly, so as not to waken Andy, she got to her feet and moved in the direction of the sound.

She came out of the tangled underbrush and gasped at the remarkable beauty before her. She faced a small pond about forty feet across that was fed by a waterfall which fell straight down from high, jutting rocks. The water was clear as crystal. She could look down to see its rocky bottom. It looked to be considerably deep.

Quickly, she removed her clothes and, bending over the edge of the pond, she washed them as best she could. Then she spread them on bushes in the hot sun to dry. Without hesitation, she unbound her hair from its confining braids and dove into the pond, feeling the velvety, sun-warmed water against her skin. It was the most delicious sensation she had felt in a long time. She came to the surface when she could stay under no longer. Joyfully, she floated on her back, letting the sun touch her body. It felt so good to feel clean again. She swam in the warmth of the water, occasionally diving again to see if she could reach the bottom, but it must have been far deeper than she had thought, for her lungs begged for air before she could reach it.

Finally, she began to tire and decided to see if her clothes were dry enough to wear. She would lie in the sun for a few minutes if they weren't. Swimming to the edge of the pond, she rose and was about to step out when she looked up and came face to face with Andy's warm appreciative gaze.

"You are without a doubt the most beautiful mermaid I've ever seen." He made no effort to hide the physical evidence of his desire.

She made a lovely picture, her wet body glistening in the evening sun. Her hair hung in damp tendrils over her shoulders, caressing the soft, milky breasts that he yearned to reach out and hold. Her amber eyes were wide and frightened, and he could see the trembling of her body as his eyes devoured her. "Polly, I shall tell you one thing about me that has always been truth and always will be. I do not lie. I have never lied to any man or woman. Any woman who has ever been with me has known from the beginning just where we stood. Now, I will tell you how it stands with us. I want you to be my wife. That is the truth. I will not say anymore. If you believe, then come here to me."

He held her gaze with his as he waited for her to bridge the gap which separated them. Very slowly, she stepped out of the water and walked slowly and seductively across the soft grass to him. She stopped a few inches from him and reached out and lay her hand gently against his chest. Without a word, he put both hands about her waist and drew her into his arms. She raised her parted lips to meet his.

"Oh, Andy," she whispered. "Love me . . . love me."

"I do," he answered softly as he drew her down to the soft grass. Andy's expert hands slipped across her body and his hungry mouth stormed hers, parting her lips with demanding force. He left her side only to discard the clothes he wore. Then he was beside her again, drawing her water-cooled flesh against his desire-heated body. His lips traced a line of feather-light kisses down her throat, then to the hardened nipples of her breasts. She gasped in surprise as they roamed further down the soft flesh over her ribs to the curve of her waist and across her taut belly. He nibbled her tender skin gently, and she moaned, wildly aflame with need for him, to hold him within her, to know he belonged to her.

He could feel her body writhe beneath his touch, ready and warmly willing to accept him. But he wanted to carry her higher. His lips traced a heated path to the soft inner flesh of her thighs. He heard her moan in pleasure as he tasted the honey sweet depths of her, and when he knew that she could bear the agony no longer, when she called to him in a voice thick with passion and urged him to possess her, he rose and lowered his body against hers. As he entered her, he took her mouth with his. Pressing himself deep within her, he felt her twine her long slender legs about him like clinging ivy to an oak. His movements, slow, deep, and steady, drove her to distraction. She arched her body to meet his, matching his increasing rhythmic movement. He heard her murmur his name over and over again in a wild passion and felt her slender fingers caress his back, urging him to deeper and deeper fulfillment.

Andy was as deep in wonder at what was happening to them as Polly was. He had loved many women before, but none of them had met his flaming desire with a fire that burned as bright. He felt himself devoured by the flame and fell willingly into it. Both were lost to time and place as their need for each other surpassed the highest pinnacle and soared beyond.

They lay, entwined, neither of them wanting to move, neither of them yet believing their own miracle. Slowly, Andy raised himself and looked down into her half-closed eyes.

"I know now I've never loved before in my life until you," Andy whispered.

Small, glistening tears appeared at the corners of her eyes and fell down her cheeks. "Oh, Andrew Ryan, you break my heart with your gentleness and your love. After this, I don't think I could live if you did not love me. Say it, say it again," she said softly.

"I love you, Polly. For the first time in my life I can believe in it, feel the need for it."

Slowly, he stood up and drew her up beside him. They stood barely touching with their bodies, yet holding each other.

"When we leave this place, when all this is over, will you stay with me Polly? There is not much wealth in my life. I have the *Hawk* and me. Is that enough for you?"

"Yes . . . oh, yes, Andy."

He smiled. "Put your clothes on, love," he threatened. "Or you shall find yourself flat on your back again, and right now, my stomach is reminding me of my lack of attention."

"Beast, to think of food at a time like this," she laughed as she began to dress.

They walked slowly back toward the road. It was nearing dusk, and they wanted to be on the outskirts of the village by nightfall.

Polly was just about to step out onto the road when Andy grabbed her arm and drew her back into the shadows of the trees. She looked at him questioningly, and he put a finger to his lips, motioning her to silence. Soon the creaking of leather and the clopping sound of horses could be heard. They watched as two men on horseback came up the road. But that was not the cause of Polly's gasp or Andy's cursing under his breath, for tied tightly and being dragged along behind the horses was a dirty, bloody, half-conscious Devon Carlisle.

Chapter 25

Dev had struggled to control his desire to storm the island with what men he had and search for Angel. But a premonition had held him as he watched the vague outline of the island on the horizon.

"Swing around the edge of the island, Davy" he said. "I want to come in on the far side, away from the village."

"Aye, Sir."

They had sailed wide of the coast to keep from being seen, and therefore, Dev had not seen the ship that still waited for Miguel Montelban. If he had, much of the grief and pain that were in store both for Dev and for Angel would never have happened. But it was not meant to be.

The ship, whose captain had refused to go and leave Miguel there, had been waiting for them many days after they were due. Miguel had cried in relief at the sight of it swaying gently in the harbor when he came out of the jungle carrying an exhausted Angel in his arms.

On board the ship, Angel had been taken directly to the captain's cabin where she was brought food and encouraged by her father to get some much needed rest.

Within half an hour after Angel and her father were on board, the *Marie Elana* had unfurled her sails and left the island on a direct course for Spain.

It was just as the *Marie Elana* slipped over the horizon out of sight that Dev's ship had rounded the tip of the island, eased into the calm harbor, and dropped anchor.

When Don Esteban had regained consciousness, he was furious, not only at their escape but that the man he had searched for, for so many years, had been laughing at him while he sat directly under his nose. He gathered together a search party of over thirty men. There was no doubt in his mind that Miguel and Angel had escaped through the jungle, for he knew it would have been impossible to have reached any escape through the village. If Miguel had planned this escape well, there would be a ship waiting for them somewhere closeby.

He paced the floor of his study until the men he had sent for came to him. "How many of my ships are in the harbor now?" he demanded.

"Two, Sir," came the quick reply.

"Good. Have them both circle the island. There are two locations that have safe depths for a ship. They are to go together and close the entrance of any harbor they find another ship in. We will follow their trail across the jungle. If you are in time, since they have not had enough time to have reached safety, we can trap them between us."

Don Esteban's orders had been carried out exactly as he had given them, with the exception of two things. It was not Miguel's ship he trapped in the small harbor, but the *Lady Angel*, and it was not Miguel he took captive, but Devon Carlisle. Still, his white hot rage at Miguel and Angel's escape would soon find an outlet for its violence.

It was impossible for the few men Dev had with him to defend themselves against two ships of men.

Don Esteban walked across the white sand to stare

with a grim smile at the ship that sat helpless before him.

"Cap'n, Sir," Davy said, "we can fight our way out of here."

"And have my men killed?" Dev said grimly. "No, the only way for me to find out exactly where Angel is, is to allow them to take me there. If it is possible, I'll make a deal with him."

"A deal! To save our skins at the price of yours? The men would never stand for it. We would rather fight to the death like men than to sneak out of this harbor with our tails between our legs."

Dev turned to look at Davy, his eyes like two frozen pools of blue ice. "Mr. Halt, I'm still captain of this ship. You and the men will follow my orders. If I can make a deal with him, if I can get you safely out of this harbor, you will do your best to find Captain Ryan and the *Hawk*. With his help and Cap's from outside, we will find some way to escape. If we fight now, Davy," Dev softened the hard timbre of his voice, "I might never have a chance to get Angel out of there."

Davy nodded with a deep sigh of surrender. Both of them were drawn to the rail as one of the men in Don Esteban's group shouted from the shore. "Ahoy, *Lady Angel!*"

"Get your ships out of my way and let me pass," Dev shouted back, and his hand tightened on the rail as he heard the murmur of laughter from the group.

"You and your men will come ashore, Captain Carlisle, and my men will take her to a safe harbor."

"We'd rather fight our way out."

"Against impossible odds, Captain. How very foolish."

Dev watched in silence as a longboat was lowered from one of the ships guarding the harbor, then went to pick up Don Esteban, and was rowed from the shore to the *Lady Angel*. He stood by the rail as Don Esteban climbed the rope ladder and stepped onto the deck.

The two men contemplated each other in silence. Each was trying to take the measure of the other's strength and weaknesses. Dev looked into the cold, calculating eyes of Don Esteban and knew immediately this was a man who gave no quarter. Don Esteban would not let one man get to freedom.

Don Esteban, in return, read Dev's cool, blue gaze and knew without doubt that this was an estimable foe, one who would not back down.

"You are Don Esteban Ortega?" Dev asked quietly.

"And you, of course, are Captain Devon Carlisle." Don Esteban smiled mirthlessly and watched with pleasure as the anger quickened in Dev's eyes. If he played this well, he would have the one thing that Angel would return for. He would have the bait that would trap both father and daughter.

"You were very foolish to come here, Captain," Don Esteban said softly, his lips curling in a sneering smile.

"Where is Angel?" Dev said, just as softly, and just as venomously.

"Safely in my little hideaway on the island. You needn't worry, Captain. After I have disposed of you, I shall take good care of her. She is quite a lovely woman and I'm sure you have taught her the ways of love well. I imagine there are some things I could still teach her, and it will be an excellent pastime. When I'm tired of her, the men on my ships will enjoy her company." He felt a surge of satisfaction as Dev's face became white with rage and his eyes darkened to a deep blue fury.

"You bastard! If you have harmed her in any way, I

will kill you."

"And just how do you propose to do that? You are sur-rounded by my men. Your ship, your men, and you are at my disposal."

Dev choked down the rage that almost consumed him. "I'll make you a bargain," Dev said.

"What," laughed Don Esteban, "have you to bargain with?"

"My life. I want to see my wife. I'll go back with you willingly if you let my ship free of this harbor."

Don Esteban appeared to be considering what Dev had offered. But he had made his plans long before.

"Ah," he said smoothly, "perhaps I should reconsider uniting you two lovebirds, even if it is only a temporary reunion."

"Then you accept my offer?"

"Yes. Yes, I believe I will. I accept your so gallant offer."

"Good. Send a signal to your ships to clear the neck of the harbor, and we will watch that they don't follow until my ship is safely away."

"My, my, you are not a very trusting soul, are you?" Don Esteban gave a quick order to one of the men who had accompanied him, then turned back to Dev. "He will signal the ships. You will come ashore with me now and your ship will be given safe passage out of the harbor."

Dev nodded, then gave one last look at Davy's distressed face. "Do what needs doing, Davy," he said softly.

"Yes, Sir."

"Yes," thought Don Esteban. "Do what I want you to do. Warn Miguel and his daughter that I have Carlisle."

Dev climbed down the ladder and, soon, he and Don

Esteban were being rowed ashore. The two of them stood and watched as the *Lady Angel* moved gracefully and safely out of the harbor. Soon, her sails were a speck on the horizon.

Don Esteban smiled at Dev. "Are you satisfied, Captain?"

"Yes."

"Good. Now I shall tell you just what a fool you are. Your wife was rescued by none other than her father just a few days ago. They are the reason I was here to meet you. Now, your own ship will carry the news that I have you. So you see, Captain, you have given me all the aid I need to recapture the both of them and this time there will be no escape for any of you."

Dev looked at Don Esteban as the realization of how well he had been tricked triggered a burst of anger. He would be the means by which Angel and her father would be back in Don Esteban's power! He leapt at Don Esteban, his hands gripping him about the throat. A quick blow came from behind, and Dev fell in a heap at Don Esteban's feet.

The trip from the beach back through the jungle was agony. His hands tied together, he was dragged along at the end of a rope by one of the men. Whenever he stumbled or fell, the heavy blow of a whip brought him to his feet. The three days and nights of the nightmare journey blended together. A nightmare, for along with the beatings came the taunting of Don Esteban. Dev did not know which was worse, the physical misery or the mental pain as Don Esteban's voice went on and on about what he had planned for Angel and her father.

"If . . . *if* they come to me," he said softly, "for, after all, my friend, who would put themselves in the hands of

312

sure death for one who means little in their lives?" Don Esteban had been riding beside him as he said those words. Dev looked up at him through reddened, weary eyes.

"How would an animal such as you know of love. I hope they do not believe you. I hope Angel and her father stay safely out of your hands!"

"Then you shall die in their place."

"But I will know, even if I die, that you have failed, and the thought will accompany me to my grave."

"You are stupid. What are their lives to you? You don't even know Miguel Montalban."

"I love Angel. And she loves me. That is something a pig like you cannot touch."

Don Esteban put his booted foot against Dev's chest and kicked him off his feet. Then he was dragged several feet before he could get up again. He glared at Don Esteban, his blue eyes flamed with a hatred that could be felt in the heat-thickened air. Then, deliberately, he spat at him, the saliva landing on Don Esteban's jacket. At an angry signal from Don Esteban, he was jerked off his feet and dragged, his body striking the stones and underbrush. He was half conscious before they slowed their pace and allowed him again to stagger blindly to his feet. Then they pulled him along. By the time they arrived at Don Esteban's sanctuary, he was beyond caring or feeling. When he was finally locked in a dark cellar room, he collapsed on the damp stone floor and let merciful unconsciousness overtake him.

He was soon to discover true agony. He was to learn first hand about Don Esteban's methods of revenge.

The first two days of his occupancy in the small, dark, damp cell were spent in complete isolation. What he was

313

given in the way of nourishment was an inedible gruel and a small cup of tepid, blackish water.

Then Don Esteban began to make several appearances a day.

The first visit to Dev's cell satisfied Don Esteban, for the strain was beginning to show. A man carrying a lantern went into the cell with Don Esteban. The sudden brilliant light blinded Dev, and he raised one hand to shade his eyes.

"Ah, good evening, my friend. Are your accommodations comfortable?" Don Esteban chuckled.

Dev glared at him, but refused to answer. Don Esteban ordered the lantern be put on the wooden table that, along with a pile of filthy straw for a bed, were the only concession to comfort. He rested one hip on the table, his immaculately booted foot swinging nonchalantly back and forth.

"I want you to know that messages have been sent to your wife and her father about your presence here, but I have some serious doubts as to whether we will receive any reply."

"Don't waste your breath on me," Dev grated through clenched teeth. "I don't believe a word you say. If Angel knew I was here, she would have her father raise an army to get me out of here."

Don Esteban threw back his head and laughed heartily. "My dear friend, this is a test in the game Miguel and I have been playing for years. Angelique Montelban, if my guess is right, will never know from her father that you are here. We are experts at this game, Miguel and I. We know who is expendable and who is not, and believe me, Señor Carlisle, you definitely are. You form as much of a threat to Miguel as I."

"You are insane, nothing more than a base animal!"

Don Esteban's face flushed with anger and he raised the riding crop he held in his hand and struck Dev, laying open his face from the corner of his eye to his jaw.

With a low animal growl deep in his throat, Dev leapt at Don Esteban. The force of his body sent them both crashing to the floor.

Don Esteban fought, but Dev's hands were closed tightly about his throat, trying with all his strength to kill him. He would have done so if the man who had accompanied Don Esteban and waited outside, had not heard the crash and come in, to strike Dev a stunning blow from behind and knock him almost senseless to the floor. Don Esteban was now so furiously angry, he ordered the man to bind Dev, face toward the wall, with chains that were deeply imbedded in the stone. Dev began to rouse as he felt the cold chains close about his wrists. He was held spread-eagled against the damp cold stones. His eyes could barely focus and he felt warm blood drip down his face and neck.

"I will break you, my friend," came a soft velvety voice. "You will crawl at my feet like a begging dog before I am through with you. You will be a thing. A thing that would never dare raise a hand to me again."

Don Esteban was speaking to the man who had accompanied him, but Dev could not hear the words, for his head was still spinning from the blow he had received. Minutes passed in silence. Then hands grasped his shirt at the neck and ripped it from his body. He strained to see who was standing behind him, but his arms were stretched out so tight he could not turn his head. Then his body and all his senses were jarred awake at the burning slash of a thonged whip as it cut across his back.

He almost cried out at the sudden pain, until he heard the deep-throated chuckle from behind him. He clenched his teeth together, refusing to give Don Esteban the pleasure of his cries or pleading.

The whip cracked again and again with an even-paced rhythm. After he could no longer count the blows, or prepare himself for the next one, from far away he heard a deep moan and did not even realize that it was his.

Blackness swirled mercifully about him and he sagged, his weight being held up only by the chains about his wrists.

"You may stop now," Don Esteban said in a voice as cold as ice.

"What do we do with him?"

"Why," Don Esteban said, "we are going to give him to Jacobi for a few days."

The man's eyes widened in fear at the mention of a hated name. He almost felt pity for the young man who hung chained to the wall. Jacobi was not only an expert torturer, but he had a taste for young men. The man knew what Dev would go through as Jacobi began to break him, for there was no doubt in his mind Jacobi would succeed—he always did.

Dev was taken down and dragged to another room where he was dumped on the floor. Slowly, consciousness returned and he blinked his eyes open to blinding agony. Slowly, he turned his head and looked up at the huge man who hovered above him.

Chapter 26

Angelique Montalban stood in front of a full-length mirror and admired the new gown her father had given her. It was one of many that hung in her closet. She had the best of everything.

"Why then," she thought, "do I always search for something?"

And there were the headaches that plagued her. They would catch her unprepared and at the worst possible times. Her father had introduced her to several young men whom he considered eligible for marriage. Some of them she even liked herself. But each time one of them made even the smallest overtures toward her, she would develop a terrible headache. When one would catch her, she would try to rest, only to find that they led to the most unbelievable dreams.

The dreams had started to come quite often now, and they were not always heralded by the headaches. Dreams, confused and blurred, people without faces. The only thing that stood out clearly was the presence of the man who always appeared. He was tall, and his hair very dark. She could not make out the features of his face no matter how hard she would try, but she knew that he was asking her for something. He would put out one hand toward her as though in supplication, and she would begin to cry as if what he was asking was something she wanted to give but could not. Sometimes, she would awaken to find her pillow wet with tears.

Afterward, she would lie awake wondering about the man in her dreams and why it caused her such pain when she could not help him.

Now she stood, looking at her reflection with the same curious look, for she did not know anything about herself or her past. Her whole life began six months ago when she had awakened in this beautiful room with her father at her bedside. She had not even known who he was until he explained and told her that she had been quite ill and was not to worry or think about her past. That it would return. She was, he urged, only to think about the future. He had told her some things from her past, but much of it seemed not to ring true to her.

There were times when she would lie awake in the middle of the night and try to put substance to the things her father had told her. She could not remember any of the things he said she had done. She would have obeyed her father's wishes about not trying so hard to remember if it weren't for the constant nagging feeling that she had lost something very valuable in the dark shadows of her past.

The door opened, and a woman walked into the room. Angelique's eyes and hers met in the mirror, and they smiled at one another. The woman was dark and beautiful. Her black hair was braided and wrapped about her head like a coronet. She was tall and slender. Her age, Angelique had judged, was somewhere in the late thirties. Her eyes were large and golden brown. They were kind eyes, and now they looked intently at Angelique.

"Angel, are you feeling well?"

"Yes, I'm fine, it's just . . ."

"Another headache?"

"No, just that strange feeling that something or someone is calling to me and I can't hear. Do you think I'm mad?"

"No, child. It must be difficult when you cannot remember your past. But you should take your father's advice and look only toward the future. He can supply you with all the past you need."

"My father is very good to me."

"He loves you, and he has been away from you a long time. I imagine he's trying to make up for all the time he has been without you."

Carlotta Armondo had met Miguel herself only in the past six months. She had been present at court when Miguel had presented his daughter and had been quite impressed with both father and daughter. She and Miguel had been drawn to each other almost immediately, and three months ago she became his mistress. He spoke to her freely of his own life, told her of his emnity with Don Esteban and of his and his wife's flight. He told her of Angel's birth and then that she spent her life in a secluded convent, where he had just recently, since his name had been cleared, gone to bring her back.

"I feel so very ungrateful, Lotta, but, I must remember. One cannot go into the future without taking along something from the past. I feel that I must remember something."

"Well, Angel, put it out of your mind just for tonight. Your father has been ready and waiting and we should have been on our way before this. Do come along or we shall be late."

"All right, Lotta, I'm ready." She gave her hair one final pat, looked herself over critically. Her dress was a deep green velvet. It draped her shoulders and was cut low. Tiny silver roses trimmed the neckline and silver thread glistened along the border of the full skirt. Her hair had been braided and then coiled at the nape of her neck. A black ivory comb was her only adornment.

Angel walked with Lotta to the door. They went down the long corridor to the stairway that led to the ballroom. Angel's father stood at the bottom of the staircase, waiting impatiently for them. Miguel was handsome in his black velvet jacket with ruffles of white lace at wrists and throat. He looked many years younger than his forty-two. He turned and looked up, and his eyes brightened as he watched Angel and Lotta descend to meet him.

"Father," Angelique smiled as she reached up to kiss him, "don't be cross with Lotta. She's been ready for quite some time. It was me, dawdling in front of my mirror, trying to make myself look good enough not to shame you in front of your friends."

"Angel, my pet," laughed Miguel, "I do believe you are maneuvering a compliment and I refuse to fall into your trap. You will receive enough compliments tonight."

"Oh, but, Father," Angel pouted prettily, "none of them are as important to me as yours."

Miguel cast a glance of mock exasperation at Lotta. "What am I to do with this impossible child? She has the ability to wrap everyone about her little fingers."

"Like father, like daughter," Lotta replied. "She inherits it honestly, Miguel."

"I can see I'm going to lose the battle here. Let me escort you both to the ball before I have to retreat in shameful defeat."

They laughed together as they boarded their carriage. They were driven slowly through the streets of Madrid to the house of an influential and wealthy count.

Music flowed through the open windows as Miguel assisted both women from the carriage, then walked proudly inside with a beauty on each arm.

Word of the beauty of Miguel Montalban's daughter spread like wildfire upon their entrance. She was completely surrounded by admirers. Angel felt the first glimmer of annoyance when she began to wonder if they were drawn to her or to her father's wealth. She took the advice that Lotta had given her before the ball.

"Flirt with them all, enjoy yourself, laugh and dance and have fun, Angel. But be careful where you put your heart."

She did exactly that, and it never ceased to surprise her at the passion and enthusiasm she seemed to rouse with only a smile or the light touch of her hand.

She and her father, Lotta and an old friend of Miguel's, Antonio Perez, were standing together sipping champagne and making light conversation when a sudden, eerie feeling that someone was watching her swept over her like an icy wind. Slowly, she let her eyes travel over the crowd of merrymakers until, with a gasp, she saw him. He stood far across the room in the shadows, just outside the light. But without doubt, and with a sudden feeling of impending disaster, she recognized him. The man from her dreams! She knew, without clearly seeing his face, that he was watching her intently, and with a deeply malevolent gaze. He did not move a muscle when he saw that she was looking at him, but stood like a phantom and returned her gaze as though he expected her to know him.

Angel felt the blood drain from her face and a violent trembling overtook her and suddenly, like a blinding explosion, she was caught by the severe pain in her head. Her trembling hand dropped the glass of champagne she was holding and her knees weakened, and she almost fell. Her father and Lotta both reached for her at the same time and supported her between them.

"Angelique!" Miguel said, alarm deep in his voice.

"What has happened? What is the matter with you? Are you ill, Angelique?" Lottie said gently. "Do you want me to take you home?"

"Please?" Angelique could barely whisper. "Lotta, please get me out of here."

"Of course, child," Lotta said quickly. She took Angel's arm and, half supporting, half guiding, she climbed the stairs to a small guest room. Miguel followed close behind and stood over the bed while Lotta held Angel's hand.

"What is it, Angel. Another of those terrible headaches?" her father asked, his brows furrowed in worry.

"Father," Angel laughed rather shakily. "It's just a temporary female indisposition. I'll be all right in a few moments. You should go back to your friends and explain to them that I am fine."

"I'm not too sure you are," her father answered gently. He watched her in an odd way. "What caused you to go pale and almost faint like that? Was it . . . was it someone you saw or something that might have been said?"

Now it was Lotta's turn to examine Miguel closely for some hidden meaning. She watched him under her lashes and had a strong premonition that not only did Miguel suspect what had happened, but that he had lied both to her, and to his daughter. She wondered what thing from their past could frighten Angel so, and her father, for she realized that Miguel's hand also trembled and that the color had faded from his face.

"Miguel," she said soothingly, "I'll take care of Angel. I'm sure she'll be fine soon."

"No. I shall go down and have the carriage made ready. I'm going to take her home immediately."

"But, father . . ."

"Angelique," her father said in a voice that stopped all argument, "I am taking you home now, and tomorrow we will go to our home in Granada. You need rest, and I shall see that you get it."

Lotta was shocked, but she did not let any expression cross her face. Miguel was running away from something, or someone. He was more frightened than she had imagined. He left the room, and Lotta turned to meet Angel's eyes.

"All right, Angel," she said gently, "now, suppose you tell me what frightened you so?"

"Oh, Lotta. The man in my dreams, the one I told you about. He was there . . . he was watching me."

"It was your imagination."

"No!" Angelique said vehemently. "I saw him, as clearly as I see you now, except he stood in the shadows so I could not see his face. But, Lotta, it was him! I know it was him!" Angel's voice broke as she clutched Lotta's hand.

"Why does he frighten you so? Do you know him?"

"No . . . Oh, Lotta, he looked at me and I could feel he hated me!"

"Angel, that is ridiculous."

Angel began to cry, and for the first time Lotta realized that this man truly terrified her. "Lotta, there is so much I don't know. What if . . . what if he wants to kill me, what am I to do when I don't even know what I'm protecting myself from or when he will come again?"

"Angel, your father and I are going to take you home now. In the morning, we will leave for Granada. Both of us will protect you. Have no fear. You will never see him again." She patted Angel's hand, then rose. "I'll go get our things and see if the carriage is ready. Don't leave this room. I'll be right back."

Lotta left the room. Halfway down the stairs, she met Miguel coming up with their cloaks in his arms.

"Go and get Angel, Lotta. The carriage is ready."

Swiftly, they bundled Angel into the carriage and drove away, unaware of the man who stood in the shadows at the edge of the garden, his cold gaze watching the departing carriage until it disappeared. Then he turned away and faded silently into the night.

The night was long and sleepless for Angel. She was afraid if she went to sleep, she would dream again of the same man and this time, since she knew the phantom of her nightmares really existed, the dream would be more terrifying than it had been before.

The morning finally came. Their baggage was carried out to the carriage, and they were prepared to leave. Angelique searched the surroundings with her eyes as they walked to the carriage, but there was no sign of any stranger.

The drive to Granada took them two days. They spent the night at a small inn along the way and were back on the road by dawn the next day.

They arrived in Granada in the early evening. Exhausted from the journey, both Lotta and Angelique decided to forego a heavy dinner in deference to some cool fruit and cheese and some chilled wine on a tray in their rooms. After a hot bath, they sat together on the veranda outside Angelique's room and nibbled on their food. The breeze from the ocean cooled the air and the towering Sierra Nevada gave them a breathtaking view.

"Do you feel more at ease now, Angelique?"

"Yes, Lotta, I feel much safer here. I'm sorry to have acted like such a child."

"Nonsense! You were frightened. It is best you get away and get your nerves under control. Why don't you try to get some sleep? With this beautiful full moon and that lovely breeze, you will sleep well."

"Yes, I am tired. If you don't mind, I think I will go to bed, as soon as I go down and say good night to Father. Lotta, shall we ride together before breakfast tomorrow?"

"Wonderful. I'll leave orders that we are to be wakened early. It would be good for both of us."

Lotta extinguished the candles after kissing Angelique good night. Closing the door behind her, she walked down the hall toward her room. To get to her room from Angel's she had to pass the top of the stairway. As she did, she looked down. The door to Miguel's study was at the bottom of the stairs. It was open several inches and a beam of golden light lay across the tile floor. The soft murmur of voices drifted up to her. She did not know why, but she was careful to make no noise as she descended the stairs and stood a few feet from the door. What she heard shocked her into silence and led her closer to the door. She stood outside and listened as a different Miguel than she knew gave incredible orders that caused a cold numbing fear to crawl up her spine.

325

"Si, Señor, I have made absolutely sure no one followed us, and I left word in Barcelona, Valencia, and Alicante to widen the search for the two ships you have named. But how could he have got away from Don Esteban's stronghold. That was where he was when Don Esteban sent you the message, wasn't he?"

"Don Esteban had him prisoner there," came Miguel's hardened voice, "and we know what becomes of Don Esteban's prisoners. I know that Don Esteban arrived in Spain only a month after we did and I am sure he has eliminated one of my problems, namely Angelique's husband. Now, I suspect that my daughter has seen one of his friends, perhaps his step-father. I want you to see that they do not get near or send a message to Angelique."

"We will let no one close to her Señor, believe me. There is no way he can contact her. The house is completely surrounded and we will be watching them closely every minute."

"Good. Don Esteban will make another attempt one day soon, and I don't want to have my attention on other things when he does. The game is almost played out. This time it will reach a final conclusion and I shall come out the victor. Until I have finished with him, I want no interference."

Lotta barely had time to step back into the shadows when the man to whom Miguel was speaking opened the door and walked across the foyer out the front door. Slowly, she walked across the floor and stood in the doorway of the study, her face very pale, but her eyes alive with anger. Miguel looked up from some papers he had been reading and smiled at her.

"Good evening, Lotta. I was afraid you had gone to bed without me, I was going to . . ."

His voice faded when he saw the distaste on her face. "What is the matter, Lotta?" he asked coolly, but he knew that she had heard the conversation he had just had.

"I thought I knew you," she whispered. "I thought you were the kindest and most wonderful man. I admired your devotion to your daughter. Now, after what I have just heard, I think you are a most abominable animal. You are using her, using that child to flush out your enemy so you can kill him. What of her husband? What of a life and love they must have shared? How can you do that Miguel?"

"Love! I love Angelique more than my own life. Didn't I risk my life for years living under Don Esteban's nose to set her free?"

"Why didn't you kill Don Esteban when you had the opportunity, Miguel?" she asked calmly.

Miguel slammed his hand down on the desk and glared at her. "Stay out of my affairs, Lotta!"

"Miguel, what has happened to you? You say you love your daughter, yet you let her be bait in . . . in a thing you consider a game. You didn't kill Don Esteban when you had the chance, because you wanted him to come after you on equal ground, just to prove that you could beat him, that you are superior."

"You needn't worry about Angelique. I can protect her from anything or anyone."

"Except yourself. Miguel, listen to me. You are as mad with this vengeful thing as Don Esteban is."

"I am well! I am as sane as you, and Don Esteban

deserves whatever he gets and I intend to see that he receives full value. The next move is his."

"Listen to yourself, Miguel. A game. Don Esteban the prize and Angelique and her life and her husband are pawns."

Miguel turned away from her and poured himself a drink from a crystal decanter on the table behind him. He presented his back to her as he drank it, as if he expected her to be gone when he turned around again.

"Some time ago, I received a message from Don Esteban. He told me that he held her husband and if I did not come to him, he would kill him. He gave me two weeks. Angelique's husband is dead. He *is* dead!"

"And out of your way," Lotta said.

"Yes, out of my way. He didn't deserve her. A sea captain, a nothing. Angelique will marry well when the time comes."

"What of love, Miguel," she said softly. "What if she loved him and he loved her?"

"She doesn't even remember him and I will see that she never does."

"She dreams of him. You knew all along who the man in her dreams was."

"She'll forget!"

"You are wrong, Miguel."

"You think I can't keep her from knowing?"

"That's right. You see, I intend to tell her. She has the right to know."

"You wouldn't dare," he whispered.

"How will you stop me? Would you kill me, Miguel? That is the only way you can keep me from going to her with the truth. You see, I love her as a daughter."

"Don't try this, Lotta. I will be forced to stop you."

Lotta stood staring at Miguel. She could not believe what she heard or what she saw. Miguel's cold eyes and the sound of his words. Would he really harm her? If she turned from him now and went up those stairs and told Angelique all her past, would he go to any lengths to stop her? She knew, that no matter what the cost, she was going to do just that.

"Miguel," she said softly. Her eyes held his calmly as she spoke the words, "I'm going to leave this room, go up those stairs, and waken Angelique. Then I'm going to tell her everything. There is no way to stop me unless you kill me, and I do not think you are a man who commits murder. Look into yourself, Miguel, and see if your little game is worth the price you are paying. All that has happened in the last nineteen years have cost you a whole happy lifetime. Think, Miguel, and decide for I have told you how it is with me."

Lotta turned toward the door.

"Lotta, don't do this," he warned.

Slowly, step by step, she neared the door, giving Miguel all the time he needed to make his decision.

"Lotta, don't force me to do something we will both regret. Stop!"

Her hand was on the handle of the door and she smiled to herself as she realized that despite his threats, Miguel was no cold-blooded killer.

She was about to open the door when a soul-shattering scream pierced the silence. Both of them were so shocked, they were frozen. Then Lotta flung open the door, and, lifting her skirts, ran up the stairs, hearing the thud of Miguel's booted feet as he raced up behind her.

She flung open the door and ran into the room. It was empty. The windows stood open as they were when she left the room. Obviously, Angelique had not been able to put up any fight against whomever it was who had taken her. She turned to Miguel and felt the sting of pity at his unbelieving face.

"It's too late, Miguel."

Chapter 27

Andy had pulled Polly into the safety of the trees when the man who had Dev in tow had passed by. Both of them had stood in stunned silence and watched as they dragged Dev along headed for Don Esteban's stronghold.

Andy realized immediately what had happened. Dev must have anchored in a harbor watched by Don Esteban's men, but where was Dev's crew, and in what harbor was the *Lady Angel?* Most important of all—how was he going to get Dev out of that imposing fortress?

Polly read every thought in Andy's mind like an open book.

"Don't be a fool Andy, you're only one. You have no idea how many are in that place. There's no way of you getting in without getting caught." Her voice had risen in alarm as she watched the wicked adventurous glitter fill Andy's eyes and the slow grin curve his lips.

"You fool. You can't go in there alone."

"I've always discovered that a man can go more silently and unobserved if he's alone, rather than in a crowd. If they're looking for any kind of rescue, and I'm sure they're not, they'll be looking for a group of men instead of one. I stand a better chance if I try it alone."

"We can't, we just can't. You reckless idiot, we'll never get away with it."

"I didn't say anything about we," he said firmly.

"If you think for one moment you're leaving me here,

you are sadly mistaken. I came to help you find Angel, and just because the prisoner has changed does not mean our plans have. I'm here to stay Andy, right by your side. Live or die, that's how it is."

"God you are an impossible woman. I can't drag you in there. It's too dangerous." He stepped close to Polly and cupped her chin in one hand. "I couldn't stand the thought of you in Don Esteban's hands. If you stay here and anything goes wrong, you can make your way back to the ship for help."

"And I can't stand the thought of not knowing if you are alive or dead. It's no use to try and sweet talk me just to keep me safe Andy. I'll not get in your way and I'll keep up with you, just don't get the idea of planting me in a safe place while you go off like all kinds of a fool and put yourself in Don Esteban's hands."

"Christ woman, when I get you safely out of here, I'm going to beat you black and blue. Don't you ever listen to what's best for you?" Andy was almost shouting now, his eyes blazing like green fire.

"Do you?" Polly replied softly.

Andy finally chuckled in defeat.

"We should have the damnedest kids," he laughed.

Polly laughed with him and slid her arms about his waist. She felt, with relief, his strong arms come about her and pull her tight against him.

"Andy, what are we going to do?" she whispered against the broad expanse of his chest.

"It's going to be night soon, and we're in need of some food and some plan. I suggest we go on to the village and scavenge some food, then we can come back to our camp and make plans on how to get Dev and Angel out of there."

"Dev and Angel," she replied. "I wonder if they're being held in the same room."

"Hardly. I don't imagine he's the type of man who would let them have the satisfaction and comfort of consoling each other. He won't let Angel even know Dev is there unless he plans to use him to make Angel do what he wants."

"To bring her father here?"

"A message from Angel to her father would bring him on the run don't you think?"

"My God Andy, once he had all three of them he could do as he pleased with them and no one would be the wiser."

"You're right, and that means we have to do something pretty damn quick, or it will be too late."

"What's first?"

"Food, I'm starved."

"Then let's go. I wouldn't want you to go collapsing on me from lack of nourishment." He laughed and held her even closer, his hand roaming gently down her back and over the soft curve of her hips. He bent his head and touched her lips lightly with his once, twice and again.

"If I die from the lack of anything, it won't be lack of food," he said softly against her lips.

"You're a man of strong appetites, Andy" she laughed lightly.

"You've created an appetite in me I'm afraid will never be eased. If we go now we can raid the village and be back here before the night is gone. Then we could put the balance to better use."

She nodded her approval and they walked together through the jungle toward the village. Keeping just inside the overgrowth of jungle, they followed the narrow winding dirt road to the village. By the time they reached its outskirts, the bright silver moon was high in the night sky, and the village slept.

The village had one wide dirt road that ran down the center to the harbor. Any paths that led from this could not, in the widest sense, be called roads. They were dirt paths that had been beaten into the ground by the feet that trod them. There were about twenty to twenty-five dwellings, each made from poles cut from the trees surrounding the area, then thatched. They were resistant to the heavy rains that fell in the area in spring and kept cool in the strong heat of the mid-summer sun. At the edge of the village were two long narrow buildings made of a rather muddy colored stucco that, to Andy, resembled the low white haciendas of Spain.

This he contributed to Don Esteban's influence here, and suspected that Don Esteban was exporting something from here as he first thought.

"Some small contact with someone in the village would give them the answers they wanted," he mused.

"Where do we go Andy?" Polly whispered.

Andy pointed toward the center of the group of buildings.

"That larger place seems like some kind of storage space to me. Maybe it's a place for community food. Anyway, it's a good place to start."

"But we'll have to go straight to the center of the village. What if we wake someone up?"

"Then," he said drily, "we'd better hope it's someone friendly, if not . . ." He shrugged, for he had no idea of what would happen then.

"You must have been the wildest little boy in God's creation, Andrew Ryan. Doing a thing like this doesn't disturb you one little bit. You must have nerves like iron."

"Remind me, when we're out of this mess, and I'll tell you the story of my childhood. It's not the prettiest story in the world, and I'm not exactly proud of everything I've done. You are probably the only person in the world I would tell, outside of Cap and Dev."

"Nobody is pleased about all the things they were forced to do to survive in this world. I don't care what you've done Andy, I care about you."

He turned and looked down into her wide eyes and knew she spoke the truth that she felt.

"I'll remember that," he said softly. Then he grinned, his teeth flashing white in the semi-dark.

"I'll go on ahead to the first house. If it's all clear, I'll motion you on. If we run into any trouble at least you will have a few minutes to run. If you have to do it, you do it. Do you understand? If one of us gets caught, the other has to get back to the *Hawk* and bring help."

She nodded. He bent his head and kissed her swiftly, then suddenly he was gone. She watched him work his way like a silent ghost. Andy was constantly filled with surprises for her. He held himself against the side of the first dwelling that stood between them and their destination and motioned her to come to him. She did, as rapidly and silently as she could manage. They stood together and listened to see if their movements had been detected by any sleepers. All was silent. Again she saw the quick glimmer of his smile and realized that Andy was enjoying himself.

"Good, no one has heard us. Ready for the next try?"

"Yes."

Andy was gone from her side in seconds and reappeared at the shadowed side of the next house. He looked about him, then motioned her forward again. They continued this way until they stood against the deep shadows of the largest building. Slowly, watching intently about him, Andy made his way toward the door. He held Polly's hand in his. The door was unguarded and to their surprise pushed open easily.

"These people certainly aren't afraid of anything," Andy whispered. "Nothing around here seems to be guarded."

They stepped inside, closing the door quickly behind them. Then they stood still for several minutes allowing their eyes to adjust to the dark. Slowly, vague outlines took shape. Large earthenware jars stood against one wall, and against the other were stacked even larger containers. From low rafters hung herbs, spices and dried meats.

"I was right, this is a food storage place. I hope those jars contain some liquid refreshment. I'd like to see what these people can brew." He chuckled at the sharp click of Polly's tongue, her small way of showing her displeasure. Polly began to go through the room, collecting things as she went, while Andy pried loose the lid of one of the jars. Using it like a shallow dipper, he tasted the liquid inside.

"Christ, this stuff would fell an ox!"

Andy found a container and filled it with the liquid. He wondered wickedly, if one sip had sent the blood flowing in his veins and warmed him, just what it would do for Polly.

Once they had enough gathered together for several meals they faced the problem again of slipping safely out of the village, past the huts filled with sleepers. Andy

336

opened the door a crack and looked in every direction. There was no sign of life. Slipping out the door, drawing Polly with him, he bent his head close to hers and whispered in her ear.

"It might be safer if we just made this as quick as possible. We'll cut a straight line from here to the jungle. Move as fast as you can, and make as little noise as possible."

Polly nodded silently. They moved quickly and reached the edge of the jungle with no mishaps and no sign of pursuit. Working their way back to the camp they set about preparing some of the food. Neither of them had seen the shadowy form that had stood in the darkened doorway of one of the huts, nor knew of the shadow that followed them and stood in the protection of the thick underbrush and watched them eat.

Andy relaxed beside the small fire and watched as Polly wrapped the rest of the food to preserve it for the next day.

He poured each of them a drink and offered hers to her with a half smile. "Come and taste this potent stuff. It should take off the evening chill."

Polly came and knelt down beside him, but to his surprise she did not take the offered cup. Instead her eyes held his as she spoke softly. "I really don't need anything to warm me Andy. You are all I require. If you feel the need, you drink it."

Andy's eyes held hers for a few seconds, then slowly he tipped both cups and let the liquid trickle to the ground. Both cups followed as Andy reached for Polly, and with a soft sound she came willingly to his arms.

The man who stood in the shadows gave a small soundless laugh and melted away into the blackness of the night.

Polly sighed with a deep sound of pleasure as Andy's hungry mouth claimed kiss after kiss, each deeper and more demanding. His hands caressed the softness of her body with gentle feather touches that set her aflame and created the urgent need in her for more and more of him. Andy felt the blood pounding in his ears as Polly came to him in wild abandon, swirling his senses in a blinding malestrom. "God," he thought passionately, "She is a more sensual woman than I've ever known before," and he vowed at that moment that Polly would remain his for as long as there was a breath in his body.

Andy lay awake long after Polly had fallen asleep against his shoulder. He looked down on the creamy length of her lying against him. He thought back over his life, of both the good and the bad things that he had done, of the women he'd had, and he realized that Polly was a beauty among them, a woman who came to him asking nothing but his love in return.

"It's a small thing to ask for what you've given me," he whispered gently against her hair, "but it's yours for as long as you want it." He smiled as his voice disturbed her and she whispered his name and clung to him. It was with a sense of profound tenderness that he held her close and drifted off to sleep.

When he wakened Polly was no longer beside him, and a bright morning sun was already cresting the trees. He heard the splash of water and knew Polly had left him to go for a morning swim. He rose to his feet, intending to join her when a muffled scream reached his ears.

"Polly!" he shouted, and broke into a run in the direction from which the scream had come. He charged through the underbrush and into the clearing around the pond, then he froze in his tracks. Polly was being held helpless in the arms of a huge black. His arm, like a thick tree limb, was about her waist and the other hand covered her mouth. She writhed in helpless frustration and her movements went completely unnoticed by her captor who held her as if she were a child in his arms. Andy took a hesitant step in their direction when a soft voice stopped him.

"Man, I can tear this woman's head from her shoulders before you take another step. Think well before you do."

Andy stopped and for the first time Polly's eyes filled with fear.

"What do you want with us? Are you one of Don Esteban's trained animals?" Andy replied coldly.

The man's eyes glittered with amusement, then he lifted his head and gave a shrill whistling call, a sound Andy had mistaken for some exotic bird earlier. Without a sound, two other men stepped from the brush and went to Andy's side. Quickly and wordlessly they drew his hands behind him and tied them firmly. The same was done to Polly. No matter how hard Andy tried to engage them in conversation, they gave no reply to his questions. They merely urged him and Polly ahead of them toward the village. There they were pushed into a hut and the door was pulled shut.

"Andy," Polly whispered. "Do you think their Don Esteban's men? What are they going to do to us?" Her voice filled with fright.

"No," he answered quietly. "There's more going on here than we know. If they were Don Esteban's men we would have been taken to the fortress."

Before Polly could speak again, their original captor opened the door and came in. He waved to two stools.

"Please sit down, I'm sure you will be more comfortable. I would like to ask you some questions."

Andy bristled, "Is this the way you welcome people to your island. Untie us, then you can answer a few questions of mine."

The man chuckled, and went to Andy's side and began to loosen the bonds. "I would suggest that you did not try anything foolish my friend. You would be dead, and your woman also, before you took three steps from this hut."

After he released Andy he did the same for Polly, who went immediately to Andy's side.

"What are you doing here?" the man asked.

"None of your damn business. I have no intention of interferring with you or your people. Let us go and we'll be off your island in a few hours."

Again the man gave a soft amused chuckle. "That is impossible until Suantee returns. He will decide what is to become of you."

"Who is Suantee?"

"Do not ask so many questions my friend. None will be answered until Suantee decides.

"What are you going to do with us now?"

"You will remain here unharmed until Suantee returns."

Andy stood relaxed with his arm about Polly to ease her fears. He felt no alarm. There were enough men on the *Hawk* to get them out of here when the time came. Briggs would be on their trail before too long. His thoughts seemed to be read by the man.

"Do not expect help from your ship Señor Captain, they have long since been taken prisoner and are also our guests waiting for Suantee's return."

Andy cursed as the door closed on their host's

retreating figure. He could still hear the soft laughter which made him even angrier.

"What are we going to do Andy?" Polly asked. Her voice had lost some of the fear when she was unbound and safely at his side.

"What choice do we have? If they have Briggs and the *Hawk* we certainly can't get away. Besides I'm beginning to get curious about what's happening here, and just who the hell this Suantee is."

"Andy, what about Dev?"

Andy sighed helplessly. "I don't know Polly. I'm sure going to try to convince this . . . Suantee that we need help to get him out of there, but. . . ."

"But what?"

"Who knows just when this Suantee is coming back, what Dev is going to face in there and just how long Dev can hold out. He has no way of knowing there's anyone here to help him."

"Andy, I know Don Esteban. I've seen his anger. He will make Dev's life hell in there."

"Polly, there's nothing we can do but wait . . . wait and pray that Dev has enough strength to hold out until we can get to him."

As the day wore on no one was seen except a young girl who brought them food, and though they tried to question her she refused to speak. They curled together on matts on the floor that the girl had brought and unrolled for them. The night passed and Polly slept restlessly in Andy's arms while he lay awake trying to put some order in the things that had happened. It was obvious they were not in Don Esteban's hands or they would be in the fortress by now. But how did they get hold of the crew of the *Hawk*, and for that matter, why?

And who was this mysterious Suantee who was spoken of with such reverence? Somehow he got the feeling that these islanders were not as friendly to Don Esteban as he might believe, and that maybe they had unwittingly stepped into something that had been brewing for a long time.

They were kept prisoner in the small hut for almost a month. They slept, ate, and were taken out only to relieve themselves and bathe. Andy had to laugh at the way their every whim was cared for without a word.

It was well over a month when their original captor reappeared one morning. He walked in with a pleasant smile as if it had been only hours since they had spoken.

"Good morning. I see you are well. Have all your needs been taken care of?"

"All but one." Andy replied.

"Ah, and what is that?"

"The need to know how my crew and my ship are, why you're holding us, and just how soon we'll be set free."

"But you said one thing, my friend," the man replied humorously.

Andy laughed. "Then at least answer one."

"All in good time, my friend. What I have come for this morning is your young lady friend." He smiled at Polly. "You will come with me."

"Like hell she will," Andy replied angrily. "She's staying right here with me."

The man's smile faded, and for the first time he became cool and firm.

"I would hate to have to use force, my friend, but I will if necessary. The young lady will not be harmed, but temporarily she is to be held in a place unknown to you. It is a way to get your undivided attention when we talk."

342

The man barked a sharp command and two men appeared behind him with long wicked-looking spears in their hands. Then he smiled again at Polly and repeated softly, "You will come with me."

Polly looked at Andy. He smiled as reassuringly as he could. She went to the door and the two men left with Polly between them.

"Now my friend. We will discuss your connections with Don Esteban, and your presence here."

"I have your word you won't harm her?"

"The only way she or any of your crew would be harmed is if you refuse to answer my questions."

Andy sighed resignedly and sat down on one of the stools. The man sat down opposite him and listened intently and without interruption as Andy told him the whole story. After he had finished the man rose.

"For now, you, your woman and your crew are safe. When Suantee returns and hears, he may wish to speak with you further. Until then you are free to move about within the confines of the village. Do not be so foolish as to try to contact either your woman or your men. It would only succeed in causing their deaths."

"Then this Suantee is back?"

"I will leave you to enjoy your breakfast my friend. Please keep my warning in mind."

He left the hut before Andy could ask any more questions.

Several days passed. Although Andy did take the advantage of looking about on his short excursions outside he could not find out where his men or Polly were being held. He did begin to see how organized and well run the village was. The people were extremely attractive—a deep chocolate color with raven black hair and golden amber eyes reminiscent of the Egyptians. The men were strong and muscular and the women pretty, in a shy way. There was no one, Andy found, who stood higher than the mysterious Suantee. Next to him was the still unnamed man who had captured him and Polly. After these two, there was the council of four. These men were quite old and sincerely venerated by the whole people. After this came the family unit, of which the man was the complete head. The women seemed to enjoy their way of life, and when Andy questioned what would happen if a man abused his wife or children he was told, matter of factly, that man would be brought to the council of four, and if the charge was proven he was put to death. When Andy registered surprise at this he was asked, "If a man does not have the honor and pride to care for his wife and children, how then could his friends and family trust in him. Of what use then was he to his People?"

Andy did not have an answer for this.

The children were most obedient and well behaved. Recourse for their disobedience was also the council of four, and although the punishment was not as severe, it was enough to deter any severe problems.

They were an extremely clean people. They bathed daily and their facilities for sanitation amazed Andy. He knew one thing for sure, the man who ruled this village, the mysterious Suantee, was a man of high intelligence and must have been educated far beyond what the island had to offer. He found himself impatient to meet the man. He became quite friendly with the men of the village and often sat with them at their homefires and shared a cup of the potent drink they brewed. Another thing happened that was more of a surprise to Andy than anything before. Several of the young girls found him attractive and smiled warmly at him. At any other time Andy would have taken advantage of this and quickly. What surprised him was the fact that his thoughts were only on Polly, where she was, if shé was safe and if she missed him as much as he missed her.

What plagued his dreams was Dev and what was happening to him while Andy sat twiddling his thumbs and waited for word from the elusive Suantee.

From the time of their capture it was well over two months, and Andy was becoming frustrated with the knowledge that Dev must feel completely deserted by now. He rose quite early one morning and left his hut to enjoy the sunrise. He was surprised to see the main hut was lit with torches. He stood silently watching, until the portent of what must have happened last night came to him. Obviously, while he slept, someone of great importance had come, and he knew just who that someone might be. He hoped he was about to meet Suantee. He went back in his hut and waited with impatience until the messenger finally came. It was their original captor.

"You will come with me," he stated.

Without any argument, or any of his usual attempt at flippancy, Andy rose and accompanied him to the main hut. The man who led him stood aside and let Andy go in. Andy was tall and he had to stoop a little to enter the door. When he stood erect his eyes widened with surprise at the first sight of the only other occupant of the hut.

Suantee was huge. It was the only word that came to Andy's mind to describe him. He was well over six feet tall, which surprised Andy, for the other islanders were quite a bit shorter. He must have weighed at least two hundred and thirty pounds and that was well distributed muscular weight. Eyes of gold flecked amber assessed him as thoroughly as he was being assessed. They were bright intelligent eyes. His face was strong and heavy jowled. The nose straight and narrower than the other islanders. His hair was black and long, tied back with a piece of leather. His skin, a few shades lighter than the others, convinced Andy that maybe one of the parents was an islander, but the other wasn't. Suantee remained silent, watching Andy closely.

"I take it I am in the presence of Suantee?" Andy laughed. "You are a very difficult man to see."

"Why are you here?" came a soft melodious voice. "You have no reason to be here. I want to know what you are after?"

"Straight to the point," Andy replied coolly, "There certainly is no overabundance of good manners here."

The swift flash of anger touched Suantees eyes for just a moment, then they were just as quickly filled with amusement.

"Touché, my friend. I'm sorry for my lack of hospitality. I'm quite tired from a very long trip, and I return to find another thorn in my side. Will you sit please and I shall send for something to drink."

Andy sat down and Suantee made a small sound with his fingers and two girls appeared.

"Bring us something to drink," he ordered. Obediently they were gone and in a few minutes they returned with two drinks. Suantee eased himself down slowly in a chair opposite Andy.

"You referred to *another* thorn in your side. Would I be safe in saying that one of your thorns could be Don Esteban Ortega and his fortress?"

"How are you connected with Don Esteban?"

346

"Do you always answer a question with a question?"

Now Suantee chuckled, a heavy rumbling laugh from his massive chest. Then he leaned back in his chair and his white teeth gleamed in a broad smile. "You are in no position to spar with me. I have something you value highly. From what I understand from my men, who spied on you during your stay in the jungle, the woman is your mate. You would not want irreparable damage done either to her or to the crew of your ship." He could tell by the narrowing of Andy's eyes that he had struck home. He leaned forward. "Tell me your story as you told Teeata."

"Teeata was the one who captured us?"

Suantee nodded.

"Why should I repeat the same story twice?"

"I want to see your eyes as you speak. Teeata and I will then discuss it with the Council of four. If they and I find in your favor all will go well with you."

"And if not?"

Suantee shrugged. "We will kill you," he said softly.

Andy repeated the story he had told Teeata, and not once did Suantee's eyes leave his. When he was finished he remained silent. After a few minutes, Suantee rose. "You may go back to your hut. Teeata and I will meet with the council of four. After that I will come and speak to you again." The words were said with such firm dismissal that Andy realized there was no point in arguing. He rose and went back to his hut. He threw himself on the small matt that served as a bed and prepared to wait. Minutes turned to hours and hours finally turned to days. Andy's temperament went from annoyance to anger. They had been on the island now for over three months, and were no closer to rescuing Dev than they had been on the first day they arrived.

Andy was pacing his hut like a caged animal one evening when a young girl appeared.

"Suantee wishes to speak to you," she said.

"It's about time," Andy snapped. He was sorry immediately that he had spoken so to her, but his patience was at an end. He walked swiftly to Suantee's hut and was ushered inside by two men he had not seen before. Suantee stood almost in the same position in which Andy had first seen him. The only thing that was different was that he seemed more disposed to friendliness.

"The council of four, Teeata and I have all come to the same conclusion. We believe what you say."

"Thank you," Andy replied dryly.

"Your men and your woman all tell the same story."

"You questioned all of them?"

"But of course."

"Are they all right?"

"Your men will rejoin you tomorrow, and your woman will be returned to you tonight. Until then, would you join me in the evening meal?"

Andy nodded and, with the same quiet signal, Suantee sent for their food. They ate while Suantee talked. He explained just what his situation was and what kind of help he wanted from them.

"My father was King here when Don Esteban first found the island. He greeted Don Esteban with open friendliness and made him a welcome guest here. All went well until Don Esteban found a treasure. Then he betrayed my father, killed him, and took control of the island."

"A treasure?" Andy questioned.

"Useless things to us, but Don Esteban and his men put a high value on them. So high they would kill and keep a whole people slaves."

"I don't understand. What is this treasure?"

Suantee reached down and loosened a small bag that hung at his waist. Pulling the bag open, he poured the contents in the palm of his left hand. Andy gasped at the fine, beautifully matched, exquisite pearls that lay before them.

"Pearls," Andy said softly. "In our land, Suantee, there is great value in these. A man could wield great power if he had enough of them."

"So? And he has great power in your land?"

"No, but he does in his own. He and I are from different lands."

"You and your friend are from the same land?"

"Yes, we have to get Dev and Angel out of there. When we do, we will help you in any way to destroy Don Esteban. Then we will return to our own land and leave you in peace."

"The treasure does not appeal to you?"

"I'm not going to lie to you. It would make me a rich man, but I'd rather take my friend, our women and my men. That's enough for me."

"I'm afraid the woman of your friend is already gone. She has been gone for almost three months."

"Angel? How?"

"Months ago Don Esteban was quite upset by the escape of the young woman accompanied by her father. We were set upon their trail. Needless to say, we let them both escape."

"Her father?"

"Yes. He had been a friend among us for a long time.

349

We helped him get his daughter free. We did not know of the capture of the other one. How long has he been a guest of Don Esteban?"

"Since the day we were brought here."

"There are several men in our village who have had the experience of Don Esteban's enforcer. Some of them have not been the same since. I am afraid your chances of finding your friend in rescueable condition are very slim."

"Then we must do something now," Andy said grimly. "If I find Dev dead, Don Esteban will not live much longer."

"My friend, had you noticed the ship at the mouth of the harbor when you paid your visit that first night?"

"No."

"It was a ship belonging to Don Esteban. He set sail that morning. He is on his way to one of his palatial homes in Spain where he will live in luxury while your friend lives in hell. If I know what is going on at this moment, he is in the hands of Jacobi. If so . . . well, Jacobi takes some malicious deviate pleasure with young men. By the time we can reach him, I'm afraid it will already be too late."

"Suantee, I'll do anything you want. Whatever help you need, only you've got to help us get Dev out of there."

"In any condition?"

"I don't care. We've got to get him out of there."

"Maybe he would rather die than face the world again when his pride and his manhood have been destroyed and he has become a whimpering plaything for a beast such as Jacobi."

"Dev is too strong for that. He knows that Angel and her father will send help. He knows also that I cannot be too far away and that I would search for him until I found him."

"What one knows before Jacobi begins is not always what one retains when Jacobi is finished."

"You can go to hell before I left a finger to help you if you don't agree to help get Dev out."

Suantee smiled broadly. "I'm glad to know just how far your loyalty extends. Now I know you are a man of strong convictions. I will explain the situation and how we can help each other."

Andy followed as Suantee led them past their camp into what they thought was the dense part of the jungle. Paths that neither of them could see were found by the huge sure-footed man. Suddenly they reached a small clearing in the center of which stood a hut that was an exact replica of all the others in the village. He opened the door and stood aside to let Andy enter.

Inside he was greeted happily by Briggs and the crew of his ship. Also by a happy Polly who threw herself into his arms. He held her against him, enjoying the soft feel of her in his arms. Reluctantly he let her go and turned to Suantee.

"Suantee, let's get on with what we can do about this. The longer Dev is in there the worse it is."

"No matter, it is still going to take some weeks to complete our plans."

"And just what are your plans?"

"Aboard your ship you have some black powder?"

"Gunpowder? Sure."

"There are passages into the castle that Don Esteban knows nothing about. We will carry the gunpowder through these in stages, and put it in several places. I will then help you get your friend free. After that we will blow that terrible place off the island and kill all of Don Esteban's people. It is the only way my people can be free. They are terrified of the strength of Don Esteban's men and their weapons. The only way for me to free them is to destroy the source of their fear completely. Do I have your help?"

"Once Dev is free, you bet your life you have all the help and the gunpowder I can get."

"Thank you my friend."

"Why can't we start now?"

"It will take us two to three days to get back to the ship, another to unload the gunpowder, and another three days to get back to the castle. Then it will take us some time to get it all placed in strategic points that I have marked. When it blows I want the whole place to go at once."

"Two to three weeks more," Andy said.

"Andy," Polly said softly, "that will be an eternity for Dev."

"I know. I hope Dev has the faith to know that his friends will not desert him there." Andy reached out and took Polly's hand. "We'll get him out of there as fast as possible to Angel. Everything will be all right love."

"I know we'll all try our best Andy." She smiled, but her eyes were wide with fear, "I hope we're not too late for Dev."

Chapter 28

Pain, bone-wracking pain, brought Dev up from the sea of darkness he had fallen into so gratefully. He had no idea how long it had been since he had awakened at Jacobi's feet. He tried to move, but found he was tied to two posts, one at the top and one at the foot of the thick pad he was lying on. After a while, he lay still and ceased to fight. It was only then that he realized he was completely naked. He stared about him. The cell in which he lay was a different one from the first he'd been in. It was not as cold, or as damp. Why had he been moved?

Every move brought pain to his back, which was criss-crossed with flaming welts from the whip. Since there was very little light, he had no way of knowing what time of the day it might be. In fact, he no longer knew how long he had been here at all.

During the worst of the time, when the pain of the whip was almost too much, he had concentrated all his thoughts to Angel. Angel would send someone to help him, there was no doubt in his mind. Angel loved him, and now that she and her father were both free, it would only be a short while until she sent someone to help him. That knowledge, plus his faith that Andy, too, would be looking for him, helped him to endure. How long would it take the two people dearest to him to set him free from this hell hole? All he had to do was to hold out until they came. He closed his eyes and could feel the soft touch of

Angel's breath against his shoulder, the warm velvet of her skin under his hands. The way she had given herself to him so freely and openly—she loved him! Now, his whole world depended on that. It held his heart and his mind and gave him some control. There was not a doubt in his mind that rescue would come and he and Angel would be together again . . . this time forever.

He heard the sound of the key in the lock. The door grated slowly open and Jacobi entered, holding a lantern. The yellow light spilled into the room. Dev blinked against the brightness, then watched Jacobi turn and close and lock the door behind him. He watched Jacobi turn and face him, and, for the first time, he felt fear. He had believed he was able to endure whatever physical pain Jacobi could give, as long as he had the images of Angel and Andy to cling to. But if any man could strike terror in another man, it was Jacobi. He was as immense as he was ugly. His eyes, narrow slits, looked out of place in his large face. His nose was flattened with wide nostrils. His lips were thick and Dev was sickened by the continuous stream of saliva that clung to them.

He walked slowly to Dev's side, and as he did he picked up a small stool and carried it along with him. He did not say a word as he stood the stool beside the pad on which Dev lay and sat down on it.

Anger filled Dev at the way he examined him, letting his eyes roam over Dev's nakedness. He licked his lips and grinned evilly, the smile showing blackened stubs of teeth. The urge to hit him, to smash that evil face, to put a stop to that knowing smirking grin swept over Dev. He fought against the bonds that held him and only stopped to glare in helpless, frustrated fury at Jacobi's guttural chuckle. Slowly, Jacobi extended one stub-fingered hand

and ran it lightly down Dev's chest and belly and nonchalantly fondled him.

"You filthy bastard!" he shouted.

Again, Jacobi chuckled. It was not a sound of mirth, but of sure knowledge that at that moment he could do anything he pleased and Dev could do nothing about it.

"Pretty soon, you beg Jacobi. I just come to tell you when you have enough, when you ready to come to Jacobi and be obedient, then the pain will stop. You belong to Jacobi now."

"You filth!" Dev shouted. "I'll die before I come to you. You'll never see the day I'll beg."

Again, the soft gutteral laugh. "You don't know the ways Jacobi has to train his puppies. Soon, you come to me, you beg. Jacobi will enjoy you. You are young and very pretty."

Again, he reached out and fondled Dev's body. Dev writhed in vain against his bonds, his eyes blazing in fury. Then, Jacobi got to his feet and smiled down at Dev. Lifting the lantern without a word, he left the room, locking the door behind him. Dev lay again in the almost dark room. For one panicked moment, he allowed fear and despair to creep into his mind. No! He would not allow that animal to defeat him this way. He forced himself to regain control.

He lay on the pad for two days without food or water or a sign of another human being. He dreamed, the few times he fell into light slumber, of warm water and soap, of hot food, Mattie's cakes. No matter how he controlled his waking hours, he could not do anything about his dreams. He could feel the extreme weakness from lack of nourishment and began to wonder if Jacobi intended to starve him to death. He laughed at himself. If that was

355

what Jacobi thought would bring him to his knees and make him beg for his favors, he was sadly mistaken. It would certainly take a lot more than hunger to give in to what Jacobi wanted. Dev was sure of his own mind, and certain that he could stand anything that Jacobi could hand out. What he did not know was that he thought with a normal mind and Jacobi did not. He thought only of the things that one sane man could do to another, and did not take into consideration Jacobi's insanity. He was soon to find out the depths to which a mind as twisted as Jacobi's could sink.

The beginning of the third day, when he became dizzy and cloudy-minded from lack of food and the odors in the room, he heard the door squeak open. Two men came in—large, vacant-eyed men. They must have come from the village; their skins were dark and they resembled the other natives of the island. They untied him and, without a word, took him by the arms and half dragged, half carried him from the room. The room they carried him to was so brightly lit that he had to close his eyes and turn his head away from the blinding radiance.

By the time he adjusted his eyes to the light, they had already dragged his arms above his head. The bonds about his wrists were pulled taut and he hung so that his feet could only support him if he stood on his toes.

Jacobi stood in front of him, his arms folded across his broad chest, and the same evil grin on his face.

"You choose now," he said. "You will be obedient or must Jacobi teach you?"

Dev gathered what saliva he could in his mouth and spat at Jacobi, who jumped back from him, anger clouding his face.

"You must be taught, young friend," he said. "You

356

will learn to be my most obedient pupil. We begin now. When you can bear no more, when you are willing to obey and want us to stop, you need only say, 'Please Jacobi,' and I will take you into my tender care."

"I will die first."

"I think not, you will merely wish you were dead."

He nodded his head to whomever it was who stood behind Dev, and it began. A nightmare of agony that Dev would remember for the rest of his life. After a few hours, he slipped away from time; there was no way for him to know how much had passed. Each agonizing moment blended into the next. Through sweaty, tear-filled eyes, he could see only Jacobi's smiling face in front of him. Occasionally, he was questioned again. Each time, he refused to answer. The last time he was questioned, he lashed out at Jacobi with his foot, but Jacobi seemed to fade away and his own movement caused his arms to feel as though they were being wrenched from their sockets.

At the end of the day, he was taken down, dragged back, and thrown upon his filthy pad. He was not tied this time, for they knew it was unnecessary. He was incapable of going anywhere. He lay still. Movement was so painful, he did not try it again after the first attempt. He slept. He thought it was only a short while, but in reality, he lay for almost six hours. What wakened him was the return of the two men who had taken him out before. Again, they took him to the same room and he could no longer control the cry of pain that was wrenched from him as his arms were pulled over his head and he hung in the same position he had before. Again, Jacobi paraded slowly in front of him.

"Are you ready, my stubborn one, or must your lessons continue?"

"Roast in hell, you maniac," Dev groaned hoarsely, "I'll never come to you."

"Ah, my dear boy, you are hard to break, but be assured Jacobi will enjoy you even more because of it."

"You'll have to kill me, Jacobi," Dev snarled. "If you don't, the day will come when I'll kill you."

"No, no, it would be such a pity to kill one like you. I will enjoy you at my leisure," he chuckled, then his face grew serious as he looked past Dev and slowly nodded his head. Again, Dev's world exploded into a pain-filled blackness. By the time the day came to a close, Dev did not respond to anything they did to him. He was carried, unconscious, to his prison and left.

Sometime during the long dark hours of the night, Dev's mind regained some semblence of conscious thought. He realized then that if he did not have the solid rock of the knowledge of Angel's love and Andy's loyalty, he would no longer be able to stand what was happening to him. He clung to thoughts of her in sheer desperation. It was the only thing he had, the only thought that held him above turning into the beast that Jacobi wanted. There was nothing else in his mind but Angel. Angel with the purple eyes. Angel with the love that kept his mind from breaking. Angel, Angel, Angel. The night was short, and with the dawning of a new day, Jacobi's men returned.

Carried to the same room, tied in the same position, Dev was only half aware of Jacobi now.

Then Jacobi spoke. And this time, Dev's world collapsed.

"You have had another night to think. Now, I will give you another thing to think about before we begin again."

"I . . . don't . . . want . . . to . . . hear . . . you," Dev groaned.

Jacobi came close to him and, reaching out, lifted Dev's face in his large hand. Almost gently, he brushed the hair and sweat away from Dev's face and looked into Dev's half-focused eyes.

"Listen to me, and listen closely. A message was sent to Miguel Montalban and his daughter, Angelique Montalban . . . your wife. They were told of your position here, your capture by Don Esteban. They were even told of what you might suffer."

Dev's eyes glowed with the first small ray of hope. Then Jacobi sneered and went on:

"They are no longer interested in you. Montalban has informed us that your marriage to his daughter has been annulled. She is dancing, eating, laughing and flirting with every bachelor in Spain. You are the last thing in her thoughts, if you are there at all."

The words echoed in Dev's mind, and for the first time he lost all control. He cried out a harsh broken cry. Blackness overpowered him, and a slow, seeping madness overtook him. Jacobi smiled in deep satisfaction as he heard the strangled, insane words he had been waiting for. "Please . . . please, Jacobi."

Dev's world crumbled. His shell was dragged to Jacobi's room, the shell that shared that night and many others to follow with Jacobi and did not really even know or care what was happening to him. They were blank, black shrouded days and nights. Days and nights when he moved like one dead, and obeyed without question everything Jacobi told him to do.

The degradation of his own body and the way Jacobi

used him did not reach his conscious mind at all.

Then, slowly, his mind began to search for his soul. One day without Jacobi realizing it, Dev awakened from his dreamlike state.

He came awake to the feel of a soft comfortable bed and was unable to realize for a minute just where he was. Then, as if flipping rapidly the leaves of a book, bits and pieces of his memory returned. He wanted to scream out in anguish, and turned his face into the pillow to muffle his cry. Black, boiling hatred bubbled through his blood. He flexed his hands at the thought of being able to murder Jacobi for what he had turned him into. Then, as his control returned, his thoughts and heart turned to ice as he dwelt upon another memory. Angel.

Angel and her father had deserted him. He thought of Miguel Montalban, and the thickness of the hatred in him almost stopped his breathing. Miguel Montalban would not enjoy his success. Both he and Don Esteban were going to pay full price for all he had suffered. There would be a way for him to destroy them both, body and soul as he had been, and Dev vowed to find the way and to take full measure of revenge. Then he smiled, a cold twisted smile and said softly to himself, "And for you, Angel, my dear, dear wife, for you, there will be special payment."

At the same moment that Dev awakened to reality, Andy, Polly, Suantee and three of the islanders who were loyal to Suantee and less afraid of Don Esteban's power, were making their way toward the castle from the *Hawk*. Each of the men carried two large barrels of gunpowder.

Suantee led the procession, for he knew the paths of

360

he jungle well; but more—he knew of the secret entrance to the castle and the hidden passages through it. They were now less than a day away from the castle.

They had planned exactly where they would plant the gunpowder. Suantee had drawn a plan of the castle's rooms, and the powder would be put in such strategic places that, if their plan worked well, they would blow the castle completely apart. None of Don Esteban's men would survive. Suantee's people would be free. Suantee had rewarded Andy with a large bag of the pearls for himself, one for Polly, and one for Dev when he was found.

They made their way in silence. There was no need for words now.

When Suantee raised his hand for them to stop, Andy came to his side.

"We will rest for a few minutes while we go over our plans for the final time. We have no room for any mistakes." With a swift motion, Suantee gathered everyone to him. With a stick, he quickly sketched the castle. With quick motions he stabbed the stick into the ground as he spoke to punctuate each word.

When he had finished, Andy whistled under his breath. "We're not going to have much time to set off the gunpowder and get Dev out."

Suantee said softly, "As I have said, be prepared to accept that your friend might be dead." He and Andy looked at each other.

"Andy," Polly said fearfully, "you don't really believe that Dev might be dead?"

"Not on your life, Polly." He put his arm about her waist and drew her tired body against him. "We'll get to him in time. And we'll get him out of there."

When at last they could see Don Esteban's towering building, Suantee led them on a path that ran parallel to the castle. They followed it until they came to a small stream along whose bank they walked for another half an hour. Then they came to a thickly overgrown mound. Andy watched as a sure-footed Suantee walked to the mound and, moving aside some of the overgrowth, revealed a cave entrance.

"We enter here. But we must be quiet. The sound of voices will echo in here. When we work our way up the secret passages to the first floor, we will begin planting our powder."

They made their way quietly through the damp corridor. At length, they entered the castle. Small narrow steps between the walls led to every room on every floor. As they proceeded, Suantee motioned here or there for a cask of gunpowder to be deposited. They made their way slowly, taking great care now not to make a sound.

Suantee stopped before a door and motioned for Andy and Polly to join him. With sign language, he made his meaning clear: If he was alive, this was the room where Dev most likely would be. Suantee felt about with his fingers until he found the lever which silently slid the hidden door open.

What greeted their eyes froze them all. Polly turned away with an anguished cry and both Andy and Suantee were held motionless by the horror.

Dev, in his madness, lay on the bed and waited for the return of Jacobi. An hour or so before, he had willed himself enough strength to get out of the bed and search about the room for a weapon. He found what he was looking for. On the wall hung trophies of war and destruction. Among them was a double-edged battle axe. He took it down; caressing it as though it were a child, he carried it back to the bed. There he lay in wait, every muscle controlled by only one thought.

The door opened, and Jacobi came in. Dev turned his face toward him. With narrowed eyes, he watched Jacobi come toward the bed.

"Ah, little puppy," Jacobi said softly, "you are awake. Good. I have need of you."

Bile rose in Dev's throat and the black hate almost made him rise from the bed and attack at that instant. But he knew Jacobi was too strong for him in his weakened condition. He took hold of the axe with both hands. There would only be one chance.

Jacobi removed his clothes, and Dev stared at the obscenity of his immense, dead white body. Then Jacobi moved again toward the bed. Dev held the axe tightly. Jacobi reached for the blanket and lifted it away from Dev with a grin. It was a grin that was to remain on his face forever. With every ounce of strength he had, Dev swung the axe upward and out. The force of the blow severed Jacobi's head from his shoulders. His head rolled away, and his blood-spurting body collapsed across the bed, covering Dev in the hot sticky blood. There was no grain of sanity left in Dev. He kicked the body to the floor. Rising up from the bed, he slowly and methodically swung the axe and began to laugh as he chopped Jacobi to small pieces.

He looked up in blind wonder as the hidden door in the

wall slid open. For a moment, he did not recognize any of the people who stepped into the lighted room. He stood spattered with blood, his red-rimmed eyes glaring like a maddened animal. It was Andy who recovered his senses first. He took a step toward Dev and began to speak softly.

"Dev, it's me, Andy. We've come to get you out of here. Dev, do you hear me? Put down the axe. The *Hawk* is in the harbor. We've come to take you home."

Dev blinked. Then recognition came. Andy! Polly! He collapsed to his knees, closed his eyes and began to cry. Andy ran to his side, knelt beside him, and wrapped his arms about him.

Suantee took a blanket from the bed, wrapped it about Dev, and lifted him as though he weighed no more than a child. They made their way back through the door and let it close behind them.

"Now," Suantee said, "we begin. Once we are started there is no way we can stop. Each barrel is ready to be exploded. Are you ready?"

They all nodded. They made their way to where the first barrel had been prepared with a long stream of the powder as a fuse. One of Suantee's men knelt and struck his flint to light it. As it flared up, they ran toward the second. By the time they reached the third, a reverberating echo told them that the first barrel had exploded.

By the time they reached the exit, the last barrel exploded, and they stood and watched the remains of Don Esteban's castle collapse and crumble into debris—the castle and all the evil that Don Esteban had brought to the island.

Dev was still in shock when they reached the *Hawk*

There, they washed him and put him in a bunk, where he remained in a deathlike slumber.

"Let him sleep as long as possible," Suantee said. "It is the only way now that his body and mind can heal themselves."

Andy brought the *Hawk* into the main harbor, and Suantee went to his village to tell his people that they were now free of Don Esteban. He chose a council of five men to organize a government for his people.

"Aren't you king here?" Andy asked.

"When I return."

"Return? Where are you going?"

"To Spain with you. After you take your friend home, I must make sure myself that Don Esteban is dead and will return here no more."

They waited in prayerful silence while Polly did her best to nurse Dev back from the depths of hell.

It was very early in the morning. Stars hung brightly in the black night sky. Andy walked the deck of his ship in thought. Both Polly and Suantee slept below. But for Andy, sleep would not come. He thought about Dev and how changed he was since he had awakened from his sleep. He had begun to regain his strength slowly. The fresh sea air seemed to help. But he refused to talk about what had happened to him. Once Andy had come upon him unaware; he was standing by the rail looking at the horizon, and the look of black hatred on his face struck Andy like a physical blow. Andy leaned against the rail and stared out to sea now, wishing there was something he could do to reach Dev. He was so deep in his thoughts, he did not hear the approaching footsteps.

"Andy?" came a quiet voice from the shadows.

Andy turned quickly. "Dev? What's the matter, can't you sleep?"

"No more than you can." Dev stood beside Andy and looked out over the star-kissed sea, his face a frozen mask. Then he said, "Andy, do you have something to drink in your cabin?"

"Yes," Andy replied, a puzzled frown on his face.

"Would you get some? I feel the need for some courage, and you will need it when I've finished this pretty little story."

Andy questioned no further. He went down, got the bottle and two cups, and returned to the deck. He and Dev found a seat on the hatchway. Andy poured them each a drink, and Dev drank his quickly and reached out his cup for another. Then he began to talk. The story poured out of him as if he were washing the evil away with his words. Andy did not interrupt until the end when Dev explained what Jacobi had said about sending a message to Angel and her father.

"Dev, you don't know that that isn't a lie! You don't know for sure if it wasn't just Jacobi's twisted way of breaking you. At least, you've got to find out for sure before you do anything."

"You're right, Andy," he replied.

"What are you going to do?"

"I'm going to Spain, but I am not going to make my presence known until I've waited and watched. If what Jacobi said is true—if Angel and her father did deliberately leave me there—then I intend to kill Don Esteban *and* Miguel Montalban."

"And Angel?"

"For Angel, there is something special. If what Jacobi said is true, Angelique Montalban will curse the day she was born."

He spoke calmly and quietly, but Andy felt a chill of fear from his tone. He could see the frozen determination in Dev's eyes. Andy said nothing, for he knew in the state Dev was in, his words would not be heard. Instead, he vowed to find out some truths for himself. If not to help Angel and her father, then to help Dev.

Chapter 29

The moment they set eyes on Dev, Cap and Mattie knew that something terrible had happened to him. Andy took Mattie and Cap aside and tried his best to explain everything that had happened. Both immediately resisted any idea that Angel had abandoned him deliberately.

"She is not that kind of a child," Mattie said. "Wealth and position don't mean that much to her. She adores Dev!"

"I agree," Cap said. "There must be some way to get through to Dev that Angelique would have died before she would have let him be hurt like this. We must make him understand."

"I've tried," Andy said. "I've argued with him day after day. His mind is still unsettled, and I cannot change it. Even Polly has tried. He simply does not let anything we say penetrate. I hope he finds out Angel was not responsible. Then, maybe this nightmare will be ended."

"Well, he's supplying the *Lady Angel* now. I imagine he'll be leaving for Spain by the end of next week."

"Are you and your friend Suantee going with him on the *Angel?*" Mattie asked.

"No. Dev doesn't want any company on this trip. He made that quite clear when I offered to leave the *Hawk* here and go with him."

"You letting that stop you, Andy?"

"Nope. When the *Angel*'s on the horizon, the *Hawk* will be right behind her."

"Good. I knew you'd be there." Cap answered.

"Where has Polly gone today?" Mattie asked. After a shocked first meeting, she had come around to forgiving Polly her part in the situation.

"Down to visit her folks. She'll explain some of where she's been and the presence of the new man in her life. I wish we had time for the wedding before we go, but I have to keep an eye on Dev. If he slips out of the harbor while I'm not watching, I'll have a hell of a time keeping an eye on him."

"I'm sure Polly understands," Mattie said.

"She not only understands. She wants to go along."

"Why not?" Cap replied.

"Cap, me bringing Polly back with me alone was enough to have all the tongues wagging now. If I took her with me without marryin' her, there would be no doubt in anyone's mind. She'd be branded for the rest of her life. We'd have to leave here permanently. I don't want life to hurt Polly any more than it already has."

At that moment, the door opened and Polly came inside. Her cheeks pink from the ocean breeze and her eyes shining with love when she looked across the room at Andy were proof enough to Cap and Mattie of how these two felt about each other.

"Andy," Polly said, "I have to tell you something."

"What is it, child?" Cap replied.

"I walked past the docks on the way home. Dev and his crew are working on the *Angel*."

"What do you mean, working? Andy inquired.

"They've scraped off the name *Lady Angel*, and

369

painted on another."

"What!" Andy said as he rose to his feet. "What name?"

"*La Muerte Negro,*" Polly said.

"Oh, God." Andy slowly sat back down in his chair.

"Andy," Mattie asked quickly, "what does *La Muerte Negro* mean?"

"It means 'The Black Death.'"

"I'm afraid for him, Andy," Mattie said, tears forming in her eyes. "Dev was never this kind of person. It will kill him. Sure as there is a God, it will kill him."

"What can we do to stop him?" Cap said almost to himself.

"Nothing, Cap."

It was near midnight. Suantee, who had helped Dev with all the information about Don Esteban, was standing with Dev at the rail of the ship. A companionable silence hung between them. Dev knew instinctively, without his saying so, that Suantee understood what he had been through and why he was so determined to follow the trail he was on.

The only course Suantee himself had set was the death of Don Esteban. He wondered what the real reason was behind Dev's wife's betrayal. Having heard the whole story about Angel's life from Andy, he wondered if there were not more to it than what Dev knew. "You go soon?"

"Yes. The ship is well supplied. It's time," Dev replied quietly.

"Captain Carlisle, may I ask you a great favor?"

"Of course."

"I would like to accompany you to Spain."

"Why? Why not go with Andy?"

"Then you know he is going also?"

Dev chuckled, but the laugh, like all of Dev's laughter now, was cold and lifeless. "I've known Andy most of my life. I don't think there's a time when I could not tell you what Andy would do."

"Like his determination in saving you from the island?"

Dev turned to face Suantee. The moon made dark shadows on his face, but Suantee could see his eyes clearly. Dev had grown a short beard and a full moustache and to Suantee he looked like a large, dark, frozen-eyed statue.

"You're trying to make a point, Suantee. I don't know what it is, and at this moment, I do not care to guess. Just what is it you are trying to say . . . in plain English?"

"All right, my friend . . . in plain English. Your friend is very worried about what you intend to do. You've altered your appearance so that someone who has not seen you before, or not seen you often, would not recognize you. You've altered the name of your ship, and I must say to a rather debasing name. I know you sold the pearls I gave you for a great deal of money. To me, it seems you have a definite plan in mind. We both agree that Don Esteban must pay for the evil he has done and I am sure your plans and mine correspond there. But . . ."

"But?" Dev supplied gently.

"From all that I have been told about your wife and her father, I am not sure that things are as they seem to be. Especially your wife."

"Suantee," Dev interrupted, "as far as Don Esteban is concerned, I welcome your company, even your help. But—" his eyes were two chips of blue ice—"what concerns me and my wife is none of your business. I do

371

not want your—or anyone else's opinion or interference. I know that Andy means well, but I must do what I have to do."

Suantee watched Dev closely for several minutes. Then, quietly and after deep thought, he said softly, "I should like to go with you if you permit me. I shall ask you no more questions about your plans."

"Then, welcome aboard, Suantee."

Suantee grasped his hand firmly and smiled. "It is a pleasure to serve with you. I shall go and get my things. When do we sail?"

"On the early evening tide."

"Good. I shall be here."

Dev watched Suantee walk down the gangplank and knew that he would be telling Andy exactly what had transpired here. That is why he intended to sail not in the early evening of the next day, but as soon as Suantee was back aboard. He smiled grimly. He was not going to be stopped by anyone. He admitted to himself that he could use Suantee's help with Don Esteban, but he would keep his own counsel about Angel . . . Angel, with the silver hair and deep violet eyes . . . he closed his eyes and willed her out of his mind. He would not allow her soft deception to undermine all that he had planned.

Dev was right about one thing. Suantee had gone to find Andy.

"I am glad to know you'll be with him, Suantee. At least I know he has a friend at his back . . . until he comes to his senses. Now, I shall be going to Spain after you. I shall find a port in Cartaginea. I will stay there, out of sight. If I am needed, will you send for me?"

"I shall send you a message as soon as we land. Then you will know where we are. From that time on, I shall inform you, both of his progress and of mine."

Suantee gathered what few belongings he had and made his way back to Dev's ship in the first gray light of dawn. Once on board, he went down to Dev's cabin and knocked lightly, expecting to find Dev asleep. But Dev opened the door, fully dressed.

"Come on in, Suantee. Throw your things on the bunk over there and come on deck with me if you want to see the last of the English shoreline."

"The last of . . ." He left the sentence unfinished as he felt the change in the roll of the ship. She was moving. He stared at Dev who returned his gaze calmly.

"Just a little change in plans," Dev remarked quietly. "So we won't have too much unexpected company."

Suantee smiled, and Dev returned it. "It is the first time," Suantee thought, "that I have seen a genuine smile on his face. Perhaps the idea of doing something besides that dreadful thinking has stimulated him."

Suantee threw his things on the bunk without another word and left the cabin with Dev. Standing at the rail, they watched the English shoreline recede in the first rays of the morning sun.

"I've ordered breakfast for the both of us and plenty of hot coffee. Would you like to join me?"

Suantee agreed. "As long as the breakfast and the coffee are accompanied by some conversation."

"It is time for that too," Dev answered.

They ate together and talked long over their coffee. The longer they talked, the more Suantee began to believe that he understood Dev better than Dev understood himself. Of one thing he was certain: whether Dev would admit it or not, he still loved his wife deeply and the belief that she had betrayed him was the only real hurt he carried.

Dev and Suantee were playing a game of chess, just two days before they were to reach the coast of Spain. A bottle of whiskey sat beside the chess board, and Suantee kept Dev's glass filled until Dev hovered near drunkenness.

Suantee had been accepted by Dev as an educated, civilized man. Suantee realized that Dev had no idea of his real background. Reared in the culture background of the jungle, Suantee had acquired powers of which Dev had not the slightest notion—the powers to captivate another person's mind and hold it, search it, suggest to it.

When he thought Dev was in the best condition for his purpose, he leaned back in his chair and, in a soft melodious voice, began to speak. At the strange sound of his voice, Dev looked up into his face and was caught suddenly in the deep amber depths of Suantee's eyes. They held him immobile as the soft voice washed over him. He felt himself slipping away into a warm, dark place where only Suantee's voice existed.

"In the depths of every man's soul there is a black place where man should not go. In that place, no man can live. It will drain the mind of all love, of all kindness, of all gentleness. When one finds a friend there, he should do everything in his power to reach in and ease the pain of his nothingness. You were pushed into this darkness, and I know that without the help of those around you, you will take the last step and destroy the only other person besides me who can touch you there . . . the woman you love despite what you say."

Dev sat frozen in his chair, his eyes blank as he listened to what Suantee was saying.

"I, and the others who care deeply for you, know that the love you have for this woman is so deep that by destroying it, you will also destroy yourself. I cannot stop you from everything you intend to do, that is beyond my simple powers, but I can suggest to you small ideas that may turn the tide of your vengeance in time. First, you will tell me, young friend, all that you plan to do."

Held in the thrall of Suantee's power, Dev told him everything he wanted to know. Of Don Esteban, he spoke easily, and the same of Miguel Montalban. But when he came to Angelique, his voice slowed and filled with anguish. Suantee could feel the pain that emanated from Dev, but he sat still and said nothing, holding Dev in the depths of his eyes. Dev spoke of Angel as if the word were being torn from him, and when the flow of words stopped, there was a deep silence in the room for several minutes. Then again Suantee began to speak in a voice deep with sympathy.

"I know how you feel, young friend, and it is impossible for me to stop you. I only put this suggestion deep into your mind, that when the time comes, and you are face to face with your woman, you will listen to her reasons and treat her with compassion and understanding. You will give her a chance to redeem herself in your heart.

"Now you will go to your bed and sleep a deep sleep from which you will awaken refreshed and with no memory of the words we have spoken."

Dev rose from the chair and went to his bunk. He lay down with a deep sigh of relaxation. It would be the first comfortable full night's sleep he had enjoyed in a long time.

Dev was surprised when he awakened the next

morning, for he could not remember the end of the chess game. "I must have got drunk," he thought angrily. "I wonder if I said anything I will regret?" He had to admit it was a good night's sleep, for he felt better than he had in a long time. He rose, dressed, and was getting ready to go on deck when the door opened and Suantee came in.

"Good morning, my friend."

"Morning, Suantee."

"It is a lovely day outside. We've a full wind and your ship is a miracle of speed. By tomorrow, we should arrive."

"Funny," Dev laughed hesitantly, "I don't even remember who won our chess game last night."

Suantee chuckled. "Last night, you were the winner."

Dev sensed some double meaning in Suantee's words, but did not question them. He spent the next few hours watching Suantee covertly, but he could see no change in his attitude. After a while, he began to relax. He felt well, and for the first time allowed his thought to flow freely.

They reached the port of Alicanti in the early evening hours. When the ship had dropped anchor, Dev and Suantee rowed ashore. Suantee was surprised that Dev knew exactly where he was going, and the right people to contact.

Before the night was out, they had acquired a small house on the outskirts of the city. It set well away from its nearest neighbor and was surrounded by a large stone wall with a high, iron gate. Dev arranged to have their possessions brought, and hired a woman to care for the house.

Once they were settled, Suantee asked Dev what his next plans were.

"Why, Suantee," Dev smiled, "we are going to Madrid

and look up some old friends. The Montalbans. I'm deeply interested in how they have been passing their time for these past months."

"That is several miles from here. We cannot go and come back here every day."

"I've no intention to do so. There is a small house in Madrid waiting for us. *This* house is to be kept in the event of . . . ah . . . unexpected house guests."

Suantee said nothing more. He already knew the rest of Dev's plans.

A hired carriage was brought about the next morning, and they were on their way to Madrid. It was two days of hard travel before they entered the city. When they arrived at the house, Dev dismissed the carriage. Inside the house, they found a warm fire, a hot meal, and a stranger who awaited them. Suantee listened to the conversation between the stranger and Dev. He told Dev of the locations of Don Esteban and Miguel Montalban and his beautiful daughter, who, the man said with a bright smile, "is the loveliest woman in all of Spain. The world is at her feet."

Suantee watched Dev's impassive face as he questioned the man about Angel and her father. Their comings and goings, who their friends were. It was obvious the man had done his job well for by the time he was done, Dev knew all there was to know about the lives of the people he had come to find.

The man was dismissed with orders from Dev to continue his vigilance.

The next morning, Suantee was surprised to see Dev come downstairs dressed for riding.

"Where are you off to?"

"I'm going riding. Want to come along?"

"Yes," Suantee replied. They hired horses and rode through a tree-shaded park. Suantee noticed that many others rode as well. He was about to question Dev but when he turned to look at him, he saw that all his attention was riveted elsewhere. Following his gaze, he saw a man and two women riding toward them.

From the look on Dev's face, Suantee knew immediately that the lovely silver-haired girl must be Angelique. He watched her also. She was, he agreed, one of the most beautiful women he had ever seen. She was laughing at something the gentleman had said to her. It drew Suantee's attention to the man. Miguel Montalban. Then, of course, the woman had to be Angelique. He wondered also who the other woman was who accompanied them. She also was very attractive.

"Dev, I must stay out of sight. Miguel knows me too well."

Dev nodded, but he still had not taken his eyes off Angelique. Whether he would admit to it or not, the look on Dev's face was not hatred. It was hunger. The deep need of her showed plainly in his eyes for a moment, then, with a tremendous effort of will, he got himself under control and wiped all expression off his face. He urged his horse slowly forward.

The riding path was too narrow to allow all three of them to pass the dark man ahead of them at one time. Lotta took the lead and Miguel followed. Angel was the last to pass him. When Dev was abreast of Angel's horse, he looked directly at her.

It was probably this occasion that had impelled Angel's dreams; she looked up at Dev and a smile started on her half parted lips. Then her eyes widened and her face went pale. But she urged her horse on and passed Dev quickly.

378

This was the first of many such occasions. Dev made it his business to be at every ball or party or theater attended by the Montalbans. Now and again, Angel would catch a glimpse of the dark, bearded man who haunted her dreams.

On the night of the ball, Dev returned to the house and told of Angel's reaction to his presence there.

"She collapsed, Suantee. The guilt has become too great a burden for her to bear. To have a husband, whom she assumes is safely dead, to reappear just when she is on top of the world, would hardly be called a happy affair."

"What will you do?"

"I am paying my lovely wife a late-night visit. I am going alone," he added hastily, as Suantee prepared to rise. "I am expecting some visitors in Alicante soon. I would like you to be there to welcome them and make them comfortable."

"Who are you expecting?"

"You will know our visitor when he arrives. I expect he will come alone and be very curious. Keep him here until I return."

"All right, I will do as you say, but I am worried about you, my friend."

"Don't be, Suantee. What needs to be done will be done, then it will all be finished."

"That is what worries me," Suantee replied. "When this is all, as you say, finished, what of you? Of the rest of your life? Sometimes revenge is not always that easy to forget once it is an accomplished fact."

"I'll be all right," Dev answered shortly.

Dev rode alone to the home of Miguel Montalban. He had long ago marked the room that belonged to Angelique.

Like a dark shadow, he climbed the high wall that surrounded the house and moved rapidly across the lawn to the side of the house just below her window.

Angelique's windows stood open to the evening breeze. To the left of her balcony was a large tree whose branches touched the balcony railing. Now, silently, he climbed the tree and dropped lightly to the balcony. Slipping inside the room, he stood in the shadows until his eyes adjusted to the dark room. Suddenly the sound of approaching footsteps reached him and he barely had time to step into the shadows of the balcony when Angel came in, carrying a lighted candle. He stood, watching her prepare for bed. She was still pale and nervous from her encounter with him in the ballroom. Her hands trembled as she removed her clothes.

Dev watched her undress, and, despite himself, was flooded with memories. He could almost feel the softness of her skin and the silkiness of the hair she loosened and let fall about her in a silver cascade. His body reacted to the need for her, giving no heed to his thoughts that shouted for it to be calm. He wanted her, and he cursed her for still possessing the power to reach him.

He had intended to remove her from the house, take her to the docks, and put her on a ship that was bound for the open sea. He knew just what her life would be like there and he thought it justice that she would pay in coin for what he had suffered. He would keep her prisoner and take her when he chose. He reminded himself now, gritting his teeth and forcing himself to remain intent on his revenge . . . take her and enjoy her, and when he was tired of her, he would inform Miguel he had her and bring the game to a finish.

Angelique had set the candle on the small stand by the

bed and was pulling the covers of the bed aside preparing to get in it when she heard the small noise from the balcony. She turned about. There was not enough light to see anything, and she took a few tentative steps toward the balcony. Suddenly, Dev stepped into the ring of light. She had time to scream only once before his large hand clamped over her mouth and his iron-muscled arm came about her, holding her immobile. He lifted her and carried her to the balcony, then stuffed a piece of cloth into her mouth and tossed her over his shoulder.

For hours, Suantee set alone, watching the fire and wondering not only what Dev intended to do, but who his late guest would be. He hoped his hypnotic suggestion would keep Dev from hurting Angelique.

It was almost three in the morning before Suantee began to give up hope. Then a knock sounded on the door. He walked slowly toward it wondering who he would find on the other side. No one could have been more surprised than Suantee when he came face to face with Don Esteban Ortega.

Chapter 30

Angelique felt waves of nausea almost overcome her from the cloth that was stuffed in her mouth and from the arm that bound her so tightly against her captor that she could barely breathe. They kept up their headlong flight until she moaned softly from the pain and stiffness from her enforced position. They came to a stand of trees and he brought his horse to a stop. She felt him slide from the saddle; then he reached up and lifted her down beside him. She staggered and almost fell against him when her cramped legs refused to hold her. He slid both arms about her and pulled her against him.

"My, my, we *are* anxious to be loving after such a long separation, aren't we?"

Angelique stiffened and stood erect and pulled her body as far away from him as she could. She looked up into that familiar, haunting face and met the gaze of the coldest blue eyes she had ever seen. He reached out and pulled the cloth from her mouth.

"Who are you?" she gasped weakly. "Why do you haunt me? What do you want with me?"

Dev looked at her, his blue eyes clouded with anger. Was he such an unimportant memory that she no longer even remembered him? He wanted to strike her, to hear her cry out in pain, but something deep inside him cautioned him to more control—to listen to what she had to say.

"That, my love," he said softly, "is a terrible way to great a long-lost husband."

Angelique stood stunned. "Husband!"

"Ah, Angelique, I don't know what your game is, but how can you pretend you don't even know me?"

His voice was so calm, so cool and unfeeling, she could not believe what she was hearing. "I . . . I don't know who you are. Please, take me back to my father . . . please."

"Oh, you will see your father soon enough. He will come; and when he does, we will find the answers to all our questions. We have a long way to travel yet, so I cannot give you any more time to rest."

Angelique began to tremble, both from fear and because the thin nightgown she wore was very little protection from the cool night air. And he, too, was aware of her lack of clothing. He looked at her, and his body reacted to her near nakedness. Again, that quiet voice nudged his conscious: "Listen to her, hear her," but he did not want to listen, to hear. He wanted to feel, to taste. Angelique's eyes widened as his hands again slid possessively about her and drew her body close to his. He brushed her lips lightly with his, and at the soft sound of fear from her, they suddenly took demanding possession of her mouth. She moaned and tried to struggle, but she accomplished nothing more than stirring him even more. His hands slid over her, pulling the sheer bodice down to her waist and exposing her breasts. His mouth roamed to the pulse that beat wildly in her throat, then down to the soft creamy rise of her breasts.

"No," she gasped, "no, please, no. My father is wealthy, he will give you anything you want. Listen to me," she cried, "he will give you any amount of money you ask for, but only if you bring me back to him!"

Again, the cold blue eyes held hers and she could see clearly that her words meant nothing to him. "Your father does not have enough money to keep me from having you. I intend to have you quite often before I'm done with the Montalban family. Any time I choose and as often as I choose. Do you understand me?"

She nodded, the tears too thick in her throat for her to speak. She expected him to throw her on the ground and take her there and prepared herself for his attack. She was not prepared when he removed his jacket and placed it about her shoulders. She looked up in surprise, only to find that the blue gaze had not warmed at all.

"When the time comes, I will do with you as I please. For now, we have a long journey."

He mounted his horse again, then reached down and effortlessly lifted her in front of him. She again felt the hard strength of his arm close about her. No words were said again as he kicked the horse into motion and continued the journey away from everything she knew and into the black unknown.

Angelique blinked her eyes open. It was early morning and a gray half-light filtered into the room. The rocking motion of the ship eased her. It was a familiar feeling, yet she did not know why. She tried to turn over, and realized that her hair was being held. It was only then that she saw the long hard body that lay next to her. She pulled her hair away from him and rolled over, then saw that her nightgown was gone. She lay beside him completely naked.

"Good morning. Did you sleep well?" came the taunting question.

"Let me go! Why do you torture me like this? Who are you?, What do you want with me?"

He pulled back the covers that protected her and cast a cool, appraising look down the length of her body. When his eyes again met hers, he smiled and said softly, "As lovely as you are, what would any normal man want? And as for torture, my love, you haven't begun to know what that word means."

He reached out and cupped one breast in his hand.

Angrily, she slapped his hand away. "Don't touch me!"

"Go ahead, try to fight me. It's better that way." His eyes hardened. "Then I can prove to you that I can and will have you whenever I want you."

She gasped at his vehemence, yet knew that he spoke the truth. There was no doubt that he was large enough and strong enough to do what he said. "Why don't you tell me what it is you think that I or my father have done to you? Whatever it is, you are wrong. I do not know you."

If ever Angel said the wrong thing at the wrong time, that was it. She saw her error when his eyes blazed with fury and his arm reached out and bound her to him. "Bitch," he murmured, "before I'm done, you will admit you remember."

His mouth possessed hers in a brutal kiss that told her of the futility of any fight. With a small sob, she tried to turn her face away from him and heard his light chuckle as he twined his hand in her hair and held her head immobile.

Then, suddenly, things began to fade from Dev's control. *This is Angel*, his mind roared. *You loved her before, and no matter what she has done, you love her still.*

She was surprised when his hard mouth softened against hers, and his hands became suddenly gentle. She was even more surprised at the burst of familiar sweetness that flooded through her as she tentatively reached out and touched the hard muscles of his shoulders. She slid her hands down his back, then gasped in surprise at the raised scars that crisscrossed his back.

"My God, what has happened to you? Is this the reason for your anger?"

But Dev was beyond anything but knowing again the sweetness that was Angel. He rolled above her pinning her to the bed. She looked up into his impassioned eyes. Very slowly, he touched her lips with his, again and again and again, until despite everything, she lifted her mouth to his. He took her mouth in a slow kiss that sent her world careening out of control. He held her face between his hands and leisurely kissed her forehead, cheeks, and mouth until he heard her murmur softly and felt her stir to life beneath him. Her body was warm and soft, as he remembered; her giving was free and abandoned, as he remembered; and he wanted her more than anything at that moment, as he so well remembered.

He knew she was still fighting him with the last of her strength, but he also knew the battle was lost. His hands traced the curves of her body and his lips followed, and now her world was upside down. Something deep within her stirred to life, something she had known before, something she clung to.

"Oh, damn you," he whispered against her throat, "you have the power to shake my world as no other has ever had."

Then, suddenly, he was deep within her, filling her, touching a need that only he had been able to reach. The low deep movement of his body drove her to passion. She moved against him, searching for the fulfillment she needed, and she found it as the wave of desire carried them both away as it had done so often before. Her legs entwined him and the urgency in her trembling hands drew him closer and closer until they were one breath, one movement, one heartbeat. He wanted to hold himself within her forever, to forget all that had come before this moment.

They lay still, finally, each too filled to move or to speak.

Slowly, Dev's world righted itself and he looked again into the wide purple blue eyes he had been determined to hate. He was defeated, and he felt the urge to bury his face in her soft hair and cry for all that they had lost; for the first time, Suantee's words took complete control. There was no way he could justify the plans he had already set in motion. In silence, he stood and looked down on her face. Then he turned away, dressed, and left the cabin.

Angel could hear the turn of the key as he locked the door behind him. She turned her head into the pillow and wept. He had done as he had threatened to do. He had used her, used and discarded her. She was lost, for she knew that she could never resist him again, that she wanted to feel the magic he wrought, and yet she knew to him she was only a method of vengeance, and the worst of it was that she did not know for what.

If Angel was confused, Dev was even more so. He had laid his plans so carefully. He would find her, take her, then cast her aside into a world that was the same kind of hell he had lived in. Why, then, with one touch of her satin skin, one wide-eyed look from her oh so innocent eyes, could he forget his plans? There was that constant pressure somewhere deep within that held him back.

Temporarily, he forced Angel from his mind and turned his thoughts toward her father.

Miguel Montalban at that moment was pacing the floor of his library. His face a mask of anger and frustration. Lotta set curled up in a large chair and watched him in silence. Although she tried to keep her feelings to herself, her eyes were silently condemning and Miguel refused to look at her.

A soft rap sounded on the door, and three men came in. They had been in Miguel's employ for several years. He trusted their loyalty.

"Well?" Miguel demanded, his voice hoarse with worry.

"There is no sign of her. We have searched all the grounds. Whoever it was, came alone, like a ghost. We found the place where he tied his horse and came over the wall. The tracks were traced for a few kilometers, then vanished."

"A ghost," mused Miguel. "You have done well. Keep up the search. Get more men if you need to, but stay on the trail until you find some trace of them. And when you do, I want whoever has her to be killed without any questions. Is that understood?"

He heard Lotta's sharp gasp, but he refused again to turn his head and meet her eyes.

The men left and a heavy silence descended in the room. Miguel walked to the chair behind his desk and sat down.

"Miguel, you and I both have a good idea who Angelique's captor is."

"Her damned husband! The man must possess the nine lives of a cat."

"Most of which you have personally tried to extinguish. Can you blame him for being angry with you? Were I he, and I had suffered so, I should strike you where you are most vulnerable. He gets his revenge both ways. On Angel, for abandoning him, and on you for taking her away from him. Of the two of you, you are the only one who carries blame. But I think it is Angel who will pay the debt."

"He won't hurt her. It is me he wants!"

She watched his eyes, and just for an instant she saw his loneliness and his longing. Then the light faded and the cold hard gaze returned.

"It is past dawn, Lotta, and I must join in the search. I suggest you go to bed."

She rose slowly, and without another word, gave a deep sigh of pity and walked to the door. She was about to reach out and open the door when someone rapped on the other side. Lotta swung the door open and saw one of Miguel's servants.

"Yes, Fredrico, what is it?"

"A message for Señor Montalban, Señora."

Miguel called out from behind her, "Bring it to me, Fredrico!"

He read it with an impassive face. Slowly, he folded it and put it in the top drawer of his desk, then he looked at Lotta and said quietly, "Good night, Lotta."

Lotta inhaled deeply. For a moment, she was going to demand to be able to stay, then she realized the futility of any argument. She left the room closing the door quietly behind her.

Once she had gone, Miguel paced the floor, trying to

come to a decision. When he had finally come to a conclusion, he left the room, went to the stables, and waited impatiently for his horse to be saddled. In a few moments, only the receding sound of hoof beats could be heard.

As soon as they faded into the night, Lotta left her room and crept downstairs, trying to remain unseen by any of the servants. She went to the study door and turned the handle.

"Locked!" she whispered angrily. Then she whirled about and went soundlessly to the rear door of the house. Outside, in the back garden, she had to move slowly and carefully because of the darkness. She moved to the windows hoping to find them unlocked. She sighed with relief when the right one opened under her hand. She moved across the room, took the candle and lit it from the embers of the fire, then walked to the desk. She slid the desk drawer open and removed the message. She unfolded it and bent close to the candle.

Your daughter is my prisoner. She will remain so for the few days it takes you to get to Madrid. The address contained here is where we will meet. Rest assured, I shall enjoy my wife's company since our enforced separation. There are things that have to be settled once and for all. Debts are owed and the time for payment is now. You are being watched. If you bring anyone with you, you will sign your daughter's death warrant. What has to be settled must be done only between us. I await you, Miguel Montalban, and your daughter awaits you also. The days and the nights, I'm sure, will be long for her so do not waste time.

The letter was signed by Devon Carlisle, and contained an address in Madrid. Lotta sat down in the chair behind the desk to consider what was the best move for her to make. She knew that she loved Miguel Montalban. She even understood his hatred for Don Esteban. But there were too many unknown things, too many shadows from the past that Miguel had kept hidden.

She pulled the drawer open and pushed the letter back inside, and when she did, her fingers touched a leather-bound book that had been pushed to the rear of the drawer. She drew it out. It was a thick book and engraved on the brown leather were the gold initials M.M. It was a diary. She leaned back in the chair and opened it. Slowly, she leafed through the pages, then, suddenly, sat bolt upright. Turning back to the beginning of the book she began to read. The candle burnt down and sputtered out without notice. The morning sun found her before she had closed the book and returned it to the drawer.

It was unsure who was more surprised, Don Esteban or Suantee. They stood and looked at each other in shock. It was Suantee who first regained control. He did not know how the feat was accomplished, but he knew Dev was responsible for him being here.

"Don Esteban, please come in and make yourself at home. Your host is not here at the present, but he will return. I am sure you are not in a hurry to leave until you find out what this summons is all about."

Don Esteban's eyes narrowed as he gazed at Suantee. He knew the familiar face, but he could not at first put a connection between a man he thought of as a helpless puppet, and Dev Carlisle. His curiosity, both over the letter he had received and Suantee's presence here, was more than he could easily ignore.

"I suspect you are responsible for Carlisle being free
from the island. You have changed since I last saw you
Suantee, and, I must say, the role you are playing now
suits you better than that of a feeble-minded islander."

"Thank you. I was sure you would appreciate it."

"I am obviously not going to leave here until I find out
just what Carlisle meant in his letter to me, that I would
find what I had been looking for for years in his possession. I hardly expected to find you here. How long must
we wait until Carlisle presents himself?"

Suantee eyed Don Esteban with a calculating gaze.
"You are not afraid of anything are you?"

Don Esteban laughed. "Afraid? What is there for me
to be afraid of? Once he has brought Miguel and
Angelique to me—and I am sure of that, my friend—I
can offer him riches and power beyond his wildest
dreams. He knows already the strength of my arm. He
will give me what I want in return for what I can give
him."

Suantee's eyes grew hard as he regarded Don Esteban's
self-assurance. "Please, sit down, Don Esteban. I am sure
it will not be long before you get all that is coming to
you."

After Dev had seen to both of the messages, he left the
ship. He could not go back to Angelique at the moment.
He sat in deep, dark thought in a local tavern. The battle
within him was like the gathering of dark thunder clouds.
He must continue with his plans. Someone must pay for
the terrible nightmare he had gone through. But if it all
worked out as he had it arranged, within four days, Angel
would be gone forever from his life. Fight the idea as he

ould, his mind would not accept it.

He ordered another drink, then another and another, nd his thoughts grew stormier. Soon, all things blended to one image—Angel. Angel who lay soft and vulnerble in his bed. Angel, whose body drove him to madness; ngel, who possessed him now and would until the day e died. He staggered from the tavern and made his way ack to the ship and down to his cabin. He unlocked the oor and went inside.

Angelique sat on his bunk, wrapped only in the blanket rom his bed. She stood. If Dev was angry, if he was etermined to hurt her, if he wanted to take revenge on er, she destroyed it with the soft words she spoke. "You ave been gone many hours. In that time I have thought f the things that you have said to me. I do not know what s true and what is false for I have no memory beyond six onths ago. You say I am your wife. For some reason I elieve what you say is true, for if my mind does not, my ody remembers you well. Can you not talk to me? Tell ne of what it is thát has made you hate me so? There is no vay for me to know what happened between us if you do ot tell me. Can you not find it in your heart to try to let ne make amends?"

Dev's head was in confusion, both from the words he vas hearing and the vision that stood before him. She eld the blanket loosely about her. It did more to reveal han conceal her loveliness. He reached out and put one and around her slender neck. Angel stood very still. She ad lost her fear of him. She could see an anguished pain n his eyes as his hold loosened and slid to the back of her ead, drawing her to him. Just before their lips touched, e whispered her name softly. "Angel."

Something deep inside her stirred and wakened.

393

At last, the words that Suantee had put in his min[d]
reached him. He would tell her. He would show her wh[at]
had been done to him, but before he did, he had to satisf[y]
the burning desire for her that threatened to wash ever[y]
other conscious thought from his mind. He cupped he[r]
chin, in his hand, lifting her face so that he could rea[d]
those large innocent purple eyes.

"Look at me, Angel. Somewhere in your mind yo[u]
remember me, don't you?"

She nodded, and whispered a soft, "Yes."

"When we made love before, you could feel, just as [I]
did, that you belonged to me couldn't you?"

Again a softly whispered, "Yes."

They stood in the half darkened room and looked a[t]
each other across an ocean of time. Angel took the on[e]
step that separated them. She placed both hands on hi[s]
chest and looked up into his searching gaze. Slowly, he[r]
hands slid up and drew his head down to hers.

Their parted lips met, then blended together. With [a]
low moan, Dev gathered her into his arms. Her soft roun[d]
breasts pressed against his chest, and his hands slid dow[n]
the curve of her back to her hips and held her tightl[y]
against him.

Without a word, Angel helped him remove his clothe[s.]
Then she stood again and pressed the soft round warmt[h]
of her body against his. He lifted her in his arms, holdin[g]
her against him as his lips traced a heated path down he[r]
slender throat.

He lay back on the bed, drawing her with him. She la[y]
atop him, the cloud of silver hair surrounded them a[s]
their lips clung together. His hands searched eagerly fo[r]
the touch that made her sigh with pleasure. A hunge[r]
burnt deep within them that had been untouched for to[o]

ong. She moaned with desire when his lips traced a fiery
ath over her breasts and stomach, to her thighs and the
enter of her need. He tasted deeply the honeyed taste of
er, she writhed in ecstasy and desired more. She was
whirled away on a sea of passion as he joined his body to
ers and lifted them to completion.

She lay against him and her hands gently touched him.
Her sigh of contentment made everything perfection.
There was quietness, and all that could be heard was the
oft lapping of water and the creak of the ship's timbers.

Angel's voice came to him gently. "Now, now we have
onded our faith. Now you believe me, and I, you. Now
will you tell me all that has happened?"

He was silent for a moment, then began to speak. She
emained quiet as the whole story was told to her from
he first day of their meeting. She cried that she could not
emember their past.

"Oh, Dev, will I remember?"

"You will," he smiled. "Have faith."

"Yes, yes I will."

She lay her head against his chest, and after a few
noments she slept. But Dev could not. A worried frown
urrowed his brow. There was still the fate of Don
Esteban. And Miguel Montalban.

Chapter 31

When Andy had discovered that Dev slipped awa
during the night, he set sail for Spain immediately. H
refused to listen to any argument from Polly abou
coming along, and was very surprised that she seemed t
give up so easily.

"All right," she had sighed at the end of their shor
argument, "but don't be away any longer than you hav
to."

"Not only will I promise you that, I also promise not t
look at any pretty girls along the way."

"I'll see to that," she muttered as she twined her arm
about his neck. He regretted that they were on the dock
to say good-bye.

"Hold on to that until you see me again," she sai
when their kiss came to a reluctant end.

"You can be a heartless little wench, can't you?"

He watched the seductive sway of her hips as sh
walked away, and laughed to himself as he turned back t
his work. He wouldn't want her any other way.

His ship eased from its slip a few hours later. By th
time the sun set, they were well at sea.

He left Briggs at the wheel at midnight and went to hi
cabin for some much needed sleep. The cabin was quiet
lit only by one lantern which hung over his desk. H
poured himself a drink and sat behind the desk to mak
an entry into the ship's log. When that was accom

lished, he rose, stripped off his clothes, and cast them carelessly across his sea trunk. Then he blew out the lantern and lay on his bunk. The slow rolling motion of the ship, combined with his fatigue, eased him into a lethargic half slumber.

It was in the wee hours of the morning. The cabin was dark with only a few rays of moonlight stealing through the shadows. Andy stirred uncomfortably in his sleep. He tugged at the covers which seemed to be wrapped too tightly about him. Suddenly, he came completely awake. It was not the blanket that constricted him, but a slender leg thrown carelessly across his stomach, a soft arm about his waist, and a silken-haired head against his shoulder.

For an instant, he was furious, but Polly slept so soundly, so deeply, so far away from his shock and anger at finding her here, that he could only laugh. At the sound of his laughter, she stirred to wakefulness, blinked her eyes, and grinned up at him.

"You little wench," he whispered softly, and pulled her close to him. "I should have known I had not tamed you yet!" He pulled her under him and captured her lips with his. Polly could tell from the warmth of the hands she was decidedly welcome.

It was only afterward, when they lay contentedly together, that he asked her how she had got aboard.

"Can I trust you not to lose your temper?" she replied.

"Polly!" he said threateningly.

"All right. All right. Briggs helped me. He's a soft-hearted man and a romantic, and," she added hastily, "he always has your better welfare at heart." She looked up at him, and although he could not see her face clearly in the dark, he knew she had become serious.

"Andy," she said softly, "please don't be angry with Briggs. Or with me. I want to be with you. I'm still afraid that the only miracle in my life will disappear. I couldn' bear it."

He remained silent for a few minutes, surprised at her fear, and a bit angry at himself for not having seen i before.

"I was just wondering, Polly," he said after they had lain silently for a long time.

"What?"

"I know a captain can marry people at sea. But I'm wondering if he can marry himself."

Polly threw her arms about him. "Just to know you want me is enough. We can get married when we're home. First, we must help our friends. What would a wedding celebration be without all our friends there?"

He agreed with a grin. "You are right. Besides, the bed is too warm for interruptions like wedding plans now."

She laughed as he pulled her back into his arms.

Early the next morning—Polly still lay asleep on his bunk—Andy heard a light rap on his door. "Briggs, with breakfast," he thought with a malicious grin. Then he sobered his face, fixed it with a deep scowl and said harshly, "Come in, Briggs."

The door cracked open and Briggs peered around it. He quickly took in the scene, including Andy's dark look. Instead of coming in as usual, Briggs smiled sheepishly. "If you're ready for breakfast, Andy, I'll tell the cook's boy to bring it right along."

"Don't you think you ought to make that for two?"

"Two? Yes, Sir."

Andy's scowl grew even darker. "I gave Polly orders to

stay home, Briggs. I hadn't counted on a traitor among my men."

Briggs gulped. "She . . . she said . . ."

"Never mind, Briggs, I can imagine what she said, and I already know your soft heart. How about breakfast?"

"Yes, Sir," Briggs said and hastily turned to leave.

"And, Briggs," Andy said with a slow smile.

"Yes, Sir?"

"Thanks."

Briggs' eyes snapped up to Andy's and saw the laughter there. "You're quite welcome," he laughed and closed the door behind him. Andy could hear his off-tune whistling dying away outside.

The closing door wakened Polly. She sat up in bed quickly, and the blanket fell away from her.

"Better dress, my love. Briggs will be back soon with our breakfast, and seeing you like that is a privilege I reserve for myself."

By the time Briggs returned with the cook's boy, they were both seated at the table awaiting the two steaming trays that were carried in.

Polly smiled her thanks to Briggs, who, to Andy's astonishment, blushed furiously. He backed away, refusing to meet Andy's eyes.

"I don't believe it," he chuckled. "I hope you never decide to lead a mutiny on my ship. I've a feeling I'd lose my crew."

"Don't plan on leaving me anywhere again, or I might just do that," she answered.

"What are our plans, Andy? Where are we bound?" she asked when they had finished their meal.

"We're going to Alicante and wait for a message

from Suantee."

"And what do you think Dev is going to do?"

"Without doubt, he will find Esteban and Miguel."

"And Angel?" she said quietly.

"Angel, too," he replied.

"Dev, how long are we staying here?" Angel asked, turning from the ship's window as he entered the cabin.

He was silent, fighting down his new misery.

"I have a few things to take care of here, Angel. It should only take a week or so, then we'll go home."

She looked up at him. "Is your business so very important?"

"To me, it is."

"Well, if it's so important to you, we'll stay. But, can't we inform my father I'm here?"

"I have already sent him a message, Angel," Dev replied in a deadened voice. "I have a house not too far from here. He should be there to meet us in a few days. If you are not too tired, we'll go there now."

She agreed to go, still curious about his secrecy.

Dev took her arm and escorted her to a waiting carriage. They rolled along slowly through the night, and Angel again was puzzled by Dev's silence and his faraway look. They arrived several hours later, and Dev helped her down from the carriage by lifting her in his arms and carrying her to the door. He knocked. Angel was stunned by the immense size of the man who opened it.

"Suantee," Dev said as he put Angel to her feet, and closed the door behind him, "have we had a guest arrive?"

"Don Esteban. He is in the library, waiting for what he

400

believes is a gift he is about to receive from a man who has been bent to his will."

"Let him wait. Take Angel upstairs and make her comfortable. Put her in my room," he added.

Suantee led Angel up the steps. He smiled to himself at the first sign that his hypnotic suggestion had been a success. The girl seemed contented, even happy. He would have liked to question her, but there was no time for that now.

"You are a close friend of Dev's?" Angel asked.

He nodded.

"He seems so suddenly to be . . . .different. Can you tell me, Suantee, anything about our past?"

Suantee smiled down at her, and she was surprised at the warmth that emanated from his eyes. His voice was soothing as he said. "Do not worry, child. I shall see to Dev. Tonight should put an end to all the difficulties. Rest assured, little one, I shall keep a close eye on him while you sleep."

She was strangely calmed by his words. Then, obedient to his hinted suggestion, she lay on the bed and fell into a deep, untroubled sleep.

Suantee went back down the stairs to find Dev waiting for him. "What has your progress been?"

"I have sent a message to Miguel."

"And?"

"Do not worry, Suantee. He'll be here by tomorrow. I will wager that he travels without stopping until he does. As far as Don Esteban is concerned, go and tell him that he must be patient and wait, then let him stew in his own thoughts. By tomorrow night, we will bring them all together and let them know what the real situation is."

"Dev, are you sure you want to continue with what you're doing? Your woman seems to be willing to go with you. Is that not what your true goal has been? What more do you want? Sometimes, it's better to let the evil thoughts die in their own misery."

"And let them both walk away from what they've done? No, Suantee."

"You could be the loser," Suantee said quietly.

"Leave it be, Suantee. If you want Don Esteban, you must wait until I am finished with him. If you do not want Don Esteban, then you can walk away now."

Suantee sighed resignedly. "I will stay with you, my friend." He sighed and turned away, grateful now that he had sent a message to Andy.

Don Esteban paced the floor in impatience.

Dev sat in silence and nursed a glass of brandy.

Suantee watched and waited.

Angel slept.

Andy also paced and waited. He was standing on the deck watching the dock in morose silence when the lone man separated himself from the shadows and walked toward the *Hawk*. It was the messanger he waited for. He moved to the gangplank and met him at the top, then took the message and ripped it open quickly. He turned to thank the man, only to find that he had faded away into the night.

Quickly, he scanned the letter, then sent one of the men to find him a carriage. He went below and wakened Polly, who dressed quickly. In less than an hour, they were on the road, traveling at a breakneck speed.

Another carriage, coming from a different direction,

but traveling at an equal speed, was headed toward the same destination.

Lotta sat erect in the carriage, in her hand she held the small, leather-bound book. She hoped that the truth inside it would free Miguel and change everything that had happened.

It was Miguel's knock that stopped Dev's pacing. He watched as a silent Suantee walked to the door and opened it. Miguel came inside the room and looked across at Dev who stood leaning against the fireplace, his arms folded across his chest and his lips curled in a satanic smile, his eyes cold and hard.

"You, of course, are Devon Carlisle." Miguel said. "Where is my daughter?"

"Safely aboard my ship in a harbor away from here. Out of your reach."

"Damn you. I want her. You said I would see her if I came. I am here. I want my daughter."

Dev laughed and pushed himself away from the fireplace, then walked slowly across the room. He stood face to face with Angel's father. Now was the time for all his injuries to be repaid. He was about to speak when the sounds of another carriage coming to a halt reached them. He turned with a puzzled frown to look at Suantee, whose face remained impassive as he walked to the door and opened it to admit Andy and Polly. Dev glared at them, then motioned them to remain silent.

"Suantee, go to my study and bring our other guest here," he said.

Miguel watched with questioning eyes as Suantee disappeared down a narrow hall. Soon footsteps sounded, and with startled gasps, Miguel Montalban and Don

Esteban Ortega faced each other again.

It was Don Esteban who regained his composure first. He turned to Dev and asked, "What is your price, both for her and for her father?"

"Damn you!" Miguel almost shouted. "Did you bring me here for this? I am here for my daughter. How much do you want, Carlisle?"

Dev chuckled maliciously. Suantee glanced sharply at him, then smiled; he finally saw the plan Dev had in mind.

Dev cursed Montalban under his breath. He ignored Andy and Polly's incredulous stares as he passed them and strode to Miguel. "You," he said coldly, "do not have enough power or wealth to buy your daughter back. The time has come for you to pay with other means."

"Dev . . ." Andy began.

"Stay out of this, Andy."

"I wish I could," Andy said angrily. "But he's not worth this and neither is Don Esteban. Take Angel and let's go home. Forget them both and let *them* kill each other if they want."

Dev smiled grimly and turned to Suantee. "Did you two plan this together? You're not my keeper, Suantee. Neither are you, Andy. These devils deserve anything they get." He turned back to both Miguel and Esteban. "You both, for a reason I do not know, are determined to kill each other. I am going to see that you finally have the opportunity to do so without damaging the lives of other people as you both seem inclined to do. In the patio out back, you will face each other with whatever weapons you choose."

"Don't be ridiculous. I've no intention of doing so only to be eliminated by you should I win," Miguel said stonily.

"Nor will I," Don Esteban added. "If I kill him, what have I to gain?"

"Neither of you seem anxious to face your opponent in an honest duel," Dev said. "Now I will tell you why you will. Upstairs, safely locked away is Angelique Montalban. For you, Miguel, she is the prize. If you win, she is yours. If you lose," he shrugged, "she goes to the winner."

Miguel's face became a mask of rage. "You do not know what you are doing. You cannot give her to him. There is more at stake here than you know. You cannot do this!"

"Oh, can't I?" Dev laughed. "Who is going to stop me? I have the key to the room in my pocket. I intend to see that the winner of your duel is the one who unlocks that door."

Suantee interrupted. He turned to Miguel. "You say there is more at stake here than we know. Why do you not tell us what that is? Perhaps it would temper my friend's justice somewhat."

Miguel's face hardened. "My daughter belongs to me. By birth, by law, by any rule under God." He looked at Dev. "She chose once to stay with me in spite of you, and she will do so again."

Dev stiffened. "You lie," he said coldly. "Your lies deprived her of a mother. Your lies deprived her of her life. Now your lies try to rob her of her husband and her happiness."

Miguel said softly, "If I fight for her, will you give

405

Angel a chance to come with me?"

Suantee, Andy and Polly waited for Dev's answer.

"Yes. If you win, Angel can choose."

"And I?" questioned Esteban arrogantly. "If I win, the girl comes with me."

"I repeat," Dev said smoothly, "the winner of your little duel will be the one who unlocks that door."

Suantee wanted to laugh, for he knew who would be the winner.

"Bastard!" Miguel snarled at Don Esteban.

"Shall we go outside, gentlemen?" Dev said.

On the stone patio, Miguel and Esteban faced each other with drawn swords, tips touching the ground. Suantee stood apart from the others and watched the two antagonists. A sudden feeling rippled over him. Would these two men fight to the death? He looked more closely, and suddenly, the answer to the puzzle fell into place. He was about to speak when another voice called from the lighted doorway. "They cannot kill each other! The truth must be told!"

All of them whirled at the sound of the stranger's voice.

"Lotta!" Miguel said in surprise.

"Yes, Miguel," she replied, her voice gentle with pity. "I do not know all you gentlemen, but I beg you to let me speak. Which of you is Devon Carlisle?"

"I am."

For the first time, Miguel saw the book she held in her hand, and his face became white. "Don't, Lotta, don't."

"Don't," she said bitterly. "Don't tell them, Miguel, that you never deserved their help from the beginning? Don't tell them that you and Esteban are the same kind of selfish greedy monster that would sacrifice one young girl's life to achieve your goals? I hate what you've done, Miguel," she said softly, her eyes filled with tears, "and yet I shall always love you. Love you enough to put an end to all this." She turned to Dev. "Bring Angel down. After she hears what I have to say, she will go with you. Leave her father to live with his own guilt."

"And leave Esteban to me," Suantee finished softly.

Chapter 32

There was not a sound from any of them as they looked at Lotta in shock. Then Suantee left the patio quietly and walked up the stairs. When he returned, he was accompanied by Angel, who ran to her father and threw herself into his arms. Miguel closed his eyes and held her close, knowing deep in his heart that soon he would be releasing her forever.

"Do you want to tell them the story, Miguel?" Lotta said softly. "Or do you want me to read it?"

Miguel looked down into his daughter's questioning eyes. "I shall tell it," he replied softly. "Angelique, will you keep this in mind? I did not know you until six months ago. By that time, it was too late to change anything. I learned to truly love in that six months. I thank you now for what you have given me. Will you try to find it in your heart to forgive me?"

Angel nodded, her eyes filled with fear and compassion. With a deep sigh, Miguel turned and walked a few steps away from them all.

"The whole story begins so many years ago. Yes, Esteban and I are half brothers. We share the same mother. My mother's first marriage was to a beast of a man named Phillipe Ortega. The marriage was a prearranged thing to unite two families, and my mother had nothing to say about it. From this marriage came Esteban, a son in the likeness of the father. When

Phillipe died, his family had enough influence at court to take Esteban away from my mother. She was broken-hearted. It was several years later that she met and married my father. In the eyes of the Ortegas it was a terrible thing for my mother to do, she should have lived out her life grieving for their son.

"My father was an intelligent and ambitious man. He was also a man who had the charm and ability to attract the right people. He rose quickly amid the political intrigue of King Ferdinand's court, but in the process he made great enemies of those who envied his abilities, his charm, and most of all, his effort to serve his king well.

"Of course, it was the Ortega family that opposed him most. They wanted, for some twisted reason, to gain revenge on my mother. There were two opposing factions at the time. One was headed by DeVarga, and the other by the D'Santiago family. The D'Santiagos were the wielders of the most influence at court, but the DeVarga faction was backed by the strong arm of the Inquisition. There was continual intrigue and battle for position and power.

"If DeVarga's tie with the church had been one of love and respect for the church, if it had been respect and love for God, everything would have been different. But it was not. It was to gain the use of another tool, a tool so powerful and so full of dread that it brought terror to the strongest heart.

"Into all this darkness came one ray of light. But the sun of her coming fell on both Esteban and me . . . Anna D'Santiago. She came one day from her schooling and was officially presented at court. There is no way for me to tell you just how beautiful she was."

He turned to face Angelique. "You look so very much

like her," he said gently. "Your beautiful silver hair is exactly like your mother's—and the lovely purple eyes she had that captured the hearts of so many. Both Esteban and I were captivated . . . irretrievably lost. There is no need to tell you that Esteban and I were more than enemies. I wonder how it would have been if we had been allowed to know each other when we were young? How it would have been if Esteban had not been trained to hatred. We might really have been brothers. Instead, a battle began that has ended here. With the D'Santiago wealth and family ties and power, Esteban and DeVarga would almost have owned Spain. The competition began subtly of course. Then it grew into a flame that consumed . . . so many people. I began to hate. It is an ugly thing this hatred, but when I tell you that Esteban and DeVarga were such vile creatures, when I tell you of all the deaths they were responsible for in the name of God, you will see why my hatred blossomed into something that obsessed me day and night.

"When the D'Santiagos began to lean in my direction, Esteban and DeVarga knew that the power and wealth they sought was slipping away from them. It was then that they forged some papers, hired some so called witnesses and brought the charge of heresy against the D'Santiagos. Again there is no way to tell you of the horrors of the torturous questioning during a heresy trial. The D'Santiagos could not stand the torture. They died. I knew then that Anna would be completely in their power." Miguel's voice cracked with hatred and suppressed anger. "I could not let them touch her!" he said, his voice rising with his anger. "I could not let them have the wealth and the power they wanted so easily."

A soft sound came from Angel, and Miguel turned his pain-filled eyes to her.

"No, Angelique, don't believe that it was the only reason. I loved your mother! I truly loved her!" His voice hesitated for a moment, then he continued. "It was then that my political party fell, and Esteban began to realize that he had it in his power to destroy me. He planned on having Anna. We ran. When Anna died, I let Robert think he had talked me into a way of protecting you." His voice stumbled. "In truth, I wanted to be able to use you and what would be your inherited wealth one day to fight Esteban. I had to keep him away from you until you were of age, so . . . so I had you locked away in a convent. I felt pleased that I could play my little game of frustrating Esteban until you were old enough to reclaim your wealth. Then . . . then I would use it to destroy him.

"I did not take three things into consideration. The attack on the island by the pirates, Robert's loyalty, or your husband. He ruined my plans by marrying you, and I wanted him out of the way. When Esteban sent a message that he was a prisoner . . . I wanted him to die, and the best thing was for Esteban to kill him." His voice faded into silence.

"And you would have raised your daughter in hatred as you were raised," Lotta finished. "Poor Miguel. In your greed, you have lost everything worthwhile."

Miguel turned and looked at his daughter and could see the pain in her tear-filled eyes.

"No, Angelique, do not look so. Do not you see what I can give you? We can be the most powerful family in pain. You and I, child, like it was meant from the start. I can offer you the world."

Angelique looked up into Dev's eyes. He had been watching while Miguel told his story. He spoke quietly "He's right, Angel. He *can* give you all that. I can give you only my love and perhaps the remembrance of something very beautiful we had and almost lost. The choice is yours."

"Angelique, come with me," her father said.

"Oh, Father," Angel said softly. She went to him and kissed him, and he looked over her head at Dev, then his heart froze at her words. "I am sorry, Father. I love you and I pity you for all you've suffered, but I will go with Dev. Someday, perhaps you can join us when all the bitterness is gone."

"Angel, think about what you are casting aside so wrecklessly!"

"Wealth, Father? Position? I feel sorry for you, Father, and if the day ever comes that love means more to you than your wealth and position, then, you will be welcome into our lives." She turned to Dev. "May I speak for you, husband?" she whispered.

Dev extended a hand to her, and she went to his arms.

Lotta felt pity for the agony Miguel was suffering and she knew, despite what she had done, she would remain at his side to help him through his dark journey back to his daughter's side.

Suantee turned to Dev. "Put your vengeance behind you. Take the great gift your woman offers. Is it done . . . is it enough?"

Dev smiled, for the first time in a long time, the friendly open smile of long ago. "Yes, Suantee. It is enough."

"Not for me!" came the cold voice of Don Esteban

412

Suantee turned slowly and looked into Esteban's eyes. Dev began to move forward, but Suantee put out an arm to stop him. "You, my friend, belong to me. This day was destined to come when I could fight you on even ground without my people dying for it."

Suantee's voice was soft and melodic as he gazed intently into Esteban's eyes. "You will come to the island with me. My people have a special punishment for you for all they have suffered at your hands."

With a cry of rage, Esteban attacked Suantee with upraised sword. Suantee stood still, his hands at his side, but his eyes leveled on Esteban. Suddenly, inches from Suantee, Esteban hesitated. He stopped and stood motionless as Suantee's voice continued in a slow even tone. "Put down your sword, Esteban Ortega. From this moment, you hear only my voice. You will come with me and gather the reward you have so diligently earned." He continued to talk, and Dev's eyes narrowed as he watched Suantee enthrall Esteban. Then he remembered the chess game and the hours afterward he seemed to have forgotten.

Suantee turned to Dev again. "Take your woman and leave. I shall tend to this one. He will never bother you again. I will be leaving with him, but," he grinned, "I shall return one day to see your firstborn son."

Dev smiled, then looked again at Don Esteban's frozen, sightless state. "Suantee, I remember a chess game once that I played with a friend. Somehow the end of the game was lost to me. Is there anything you can tell me about it?"

Suantee smiled. "You needed help to temper your justice, my friend."

They shook hands, then Suantee left, taking Don Esteban with him.

Dev turned to Angel. "Let me take you home."

He slid his arm about her waist, and she walked out with him, followed by Andy and Polly. A broken Miguel stayed behind in the shadows with the only one left in his life. Lotta.

Epilogue

Polly and Andy were married. After the wedding, Dev prepared the small sailboat for a trip.

Angel did not question him. She had found a great peace of mind with him, and the people he called their family—the fussy Mattie and the watchful Cap.

He helped her into the boat and raised the sail. Soon, they were skimming over the top of the sun-kissed water. She had been sitting relaxed watching the scenery, when Dev began easing the boat toward the shore. She turned and looked toward the shore he was heading for. Something reached out from the past toward her. She had been here before! The feeling was so strong that she could not pull her eyes away.

They walked silently toward the cottage that sat nestled on the edge of the trees.

Angel touched the door. "I've been here with you," she whispered. A veil of clouds seemed to be fading in front of her eyes. "There are two rooms inside. A large room with a fireplace, and a bedroom with a large oak bed . . . swimming. You taught me to swim here! to fish! To . . . to love. Oh, Dev!"

She cried as, suddenly, things began to grow clearer and clearer in her mind. He smiled when he saw the happiness in her tear-filled eyes. She began to laugh and cry at the same time as she threw open the door.

"I remember! Oh, my darling, I remember. We spent

our honeymoon here. No wonder it is the only thing that would bring my memory back. Can we stay for a while?"

"I have brought our things. We're here to stay for a month." He caught her against him and held her close, then kissed her hungrily. He laughed as she pushed the door shut behind them and nestled against him and the glow of his love reached into her soul. This would be forever. She was happy. She was home!